STORIES OF TREES, WOODS, AND THE FOREST

EDITED BY FIONA STAFFORD

EVERYMAN'S POCKET CLASSICS
Alfred A. Knopf New York London Toronto

THIS IS A BORZOI BOOK
PUBLISHED BY ALFRED A. KNOPF

This selection by Fiona Stafford first published in
Everyman's Library 2021
Copyright © 2021 by Everyman's Library

A list of acknowledgments to copyright owners appears at
the back of this volume.
Second printing (US)

www.randomhouse.com/everymans
www.everymanslibrary.co.uk

ISBN 978-0-593-32018-1 (US)
978-1-84159-631-0 (UK)

Library of Congress Control Number: 2021939411

A CIP catalogue reference for this book is available from the
British Library

Typography by Peter B. Willberg

Typeset in the UK by Input Data Services Ltd, Isle Abbotts, Somerset

Printed and bound in Germany by GGP Media GmbH, Pössneck

EVERYMAN,

I WILL GO WITH THEE,

AND BE THY GUIDE,

IN THY MOST NEED

TO GO BY THY SIDE

STORIES OF TREES, WOODS, AND THE FOREST

Contents

7

PREFACE

If, on an early morning in October half-way across a dewy field, a line of trees becomes visible against the light blue sky, what would your impulse be? Perhaps it would depend on whether the wet trodden path through the grass winds away to a distant gate in a close-cut hedge, keeping well clear of the wood, or heads instead towards the scrubby elder, the brambles, field maple and blackthorn, before leading deep into the taller oaks and ashes beyond. If there were two paths, or none, the choice would be clear: on across the open fields or into the woods?

Fields have trees of their own – thinning willows winding along a slow, sedge-edged river, rich brown sycamores towering above a drystone wall, a golden oak spreading over the corner of scarlet-spotted hedges. Sometimes they run beside an old orchard of mossed cottage trees or a Rectory garden dark with Scots pines and yews. A village pond might be ringed with hazel and alder, a scrap of grass where three lanes converge, covered with spiky shells and glossy nuts dropped from a huge horse chestnut. And if autumn walks lead through city streets, the peeling trunks of plane trees are rising from piles of broad, yellow, chamois-leather leaves. Park gates open between clumps of damp euonymus and privet, overlooked by tall hollies, whose upper leaves are glossy and smooth. Along a river banked with warehouses and converted mills, bare buddleia gleam with wet webs under copper sycamores catching the dawn light.

The way into the woods is different. A few steps from open space to arboreal intimacy prompt a momentary pause to taste the difference in the air. Sodden leaves muffle the sound of footsteps, allowing the stillness to fill with the clear call of birds. A slight stir among high branches signals a squirrel moving swiftly in his own element. A tiny brown shape darting from dense ivy to a nearby tangle of brambles is probably a wren. Although it's hard to tell quite what's there, everything seems strangely clarified and pulsing with unseen life.

When the woods are light and open, whether weeks or years ago or in months to come when bare twigs soften again and their light green leaves flap into spring, the damp, dank smells will be overcome by fresh flowers and wild garlic. Quiet or full of noises at any time of year, woods are natural trysting or picnic spots, places to work, play or bury treasure and truths. Solid trunks and branches are easiest to grasp, though filled with holes, nests, hidden lives and running away into ramifications. The overstorey may be flushed with light and colour, but there's undergrowth thick with twisting stems and strands, too dense to follow or fully understand. These are places to hide, places where you might be caught unawares, havens and horrors, where you can't quite see the wood for the trees and there's no one to tell you what comes next. Even on your own, you know you're not alone. There are voices in the woods. Birds and beetles, wood-cutters, witches, wolves and wisemen, secret lovers, spectral horsemen, amateur actors, ardent adventurers, predators and protectors, persecutors and plant-hunters, demons, dragons, dim figures from dreams.

Single trees, standing out in the open under rain and sunlight, can't gang up in quite the same way. Rooted in one special spot, their distinctive forms offer different company, other kinds of imaginative fare. These garden guardians and living giants reach into the past, stirring memories and hopes by still being there. The rarest and most commonplace alike can foster love, laughter, sorrow, fear. The gnarled old bark of a familiar tree can comfort or torment the lonely and lost. Its felling can be more intensely felt than the disappearance of a distant wood.

The stories that follow feature single trees, clumps, copses, woods and vast forests. They're gathered from a great swathe of time: from classical mythology and folk tradition to twenty-first-century conceptions of futures currently taking seed. Within the leaves of this book, the old oaks, ancient woodlands, dark forests and warm groves of Europe flourish beside the great tropical trees of India and New Zealand, the wooded valleys and swamps of America and the African savannah. There are individual trees so real you can feel the bark through the pages and still smell the wood after the trunk's turned into logs. There are trees that glow bright in memory, turn dark in nightmare, pale in the aftermath and green in the words of skilful storytellers. One tree sprouts from a man's head, others have been women in their time. Some trees have done with story-telling and live silently in the tales of those whose memories they haunt. Many have dropped seeds into the fertile minds of other writers, whose stories are to be found here too. All have the power to take root in readers' imaginations.

The natural continuity of woodlands not only nurtures traditional stories, but also provides the conditions for surprising departures from the expected course of events. What seems familiar is suddenly, troublingly, terrifyingly, or delightfully, strange. In some of the stories, trees seem little more than a passing detail, but they have a tendency to grow between the lines and take the final word. In others, they are

13

central from the start, silently – or occasionally eloquently – commanding attention.

As trees often outlive their human observers, they prompt images of childhood and old age, memories of the past and meditations on the future. Trees exactly coeval with individuals have a special capacity to stir deep feelings in those whose births they were originally planted to celebrate. Arboreal veterans, on the other hand, offer access to worlds beyond the normal grasp of those who currently pass beneath their capacious canopies. Seeds and saplings in these tales promise, but cannot guarantee, a green future, since their growth will depend on the human beings they dwarf.

The life of a tree, so intertwined with the life of humankind, at once counterpart and counterbalance, offers vital connections and contrasts to earlier selves and selves to come. When the Irish poet Louis MacNeice reflected on 'Woods', he found his own experience very different from his parents'. While his father 'had hardly in his life walked in a wood', MacNeice knew from an early age that woods were 'a kingdom free of time and sky', filled with knights, nymphs, birds and ghosts. Trees created a world which drew him, man and boy, and on which his imagination drew. Though commonplace enough, woods remained excitingly other, a mystery, while 'the recurring shock' of their 'dark coolness' seemed like a 'foreign voice'. The stories within this collection bring woods and trees from across the globe into the living room, the tube, the train, the plane, the hotel. However familiar, however small-scale some of the tales may seem at first, each is a mystery, a green and giving world. Perhaps you can take them outside to read under a tree.

Fiona Stafford

JOHN LORNE CAMPBELL

WHY EVERYONE SHOULD
BE ABLE TO TELL A STORY

ONCE THERE WAS an Uistman who was travelling home, at the time when the passage wasn't as easy as it is today. In those days travellers used to come by the Isle of Skye, crossing the sea from Dunvegan to Lochmaddy. This man had been away working at the harvest on the mainland. He was walking through Skye on his way home, and at nightfall he came to a house, and thought he would stay there till morning, as he had a long way to go. He went in, and I'm sure he was made welcome by the man of the house, who asked him if he had any tales or stories. The Uistman replied that he had never known any.

'It's very strange you can't tell a story,' said his host. 'I'm sure you've heard plenty.'

'I can't remember one,' said the Uistman.

His host himself was telling stories all night, to pass the night, until it was time to go to bed. When they went to bed, the Uistman was given the closet inside the front door to sleep in. What was there hanging in the closet but the carcass of a sheep! The Uistman hadn't been long in bed when he heard the door being opened, and two men came in and took away the sheep.

The Uistman said to himself that it would be very unfortunate for him to let those fellows take the sheep away, for the people of the house would think that he had taken it himself. He went after the thieves, and he had gone some way after them when one of them noticed him, and said to

17

the other: 'Look at that fellow coming after us to betray us; let's go back and catch him and do away with him.'

They turned back, and the Uistman made off as fast as he could to try to get back to the house. But they got between him and the house. The Uistman kept going, until he heard the sound of a big river; then he made for the river. In his panic he went into the river, and the stream took him away. He was likely to be drowned. But he got ahold of a branch of a tree that was growing on the bank of the river, and clung on to it. He was too frightened to move; he heard the two men going back and forth along the banks of the river, throwing stones wherever the trees cast their shade; and the stones were going past him.

He remained there until dawn. It was a frosty night, and when he tried to get out of the river, he couldn't do it. He tried to shout, but he couldn't shout either. At last he managed to utter one shout, and made a leap; and he woke up, and found himself on the floor beside the bed, holding on to the bedclothes with both hands. In the morning when they were at breakfast, his host said:

'Well, I'm sure that wherever you are tonight, you'll have a story to tell, though you hadn't one last night.'

That's what happened to the man who couldn't tell a story; everyone should be able to tell a tale or a story to help pass the night!

OVID

ORPHEUS' AUDIENCE
OF TREES

From

METAMORPHOSES
(BOOK X)

Translated by Mary M. Innes

ON THE TOP of a certain hill was a level stretch of open ground, covered with green turf. There was no shelter from the sun, but when the divinely-born poet seated himself there and struck his melodious strings, shady trees moved to the spot. The oak tree of Chaonia and poplars, Phaethon's sisters, crowded round, along with Jupiter's great oak, with its lofty branches, and soft lime trees and beeches, and the virgin laurel, brittle hazels, and ash trees, that are used for spear shafts, smooth firs and the holm oak, bowed down with acorns, the genial sycamore, and the variegated maple, willows that grow by the rivers and the water-loving lotus, evergreen box, slender tamarisks, myrtles double-hued, and viburnum with its dark blue berries. There was ivy too, trailing its tendrils, and leafy vines, vine-clad elms and mountain ash, pitchpine and wild stawberry, laden with rosy fruit, waving palms, the victor's prize, and the pine, its leaves gathered up into a shaggy crest, the favourite tree of Cybele, the mother of the gods: for her priest Attis exchanged his human shape for this, and hardened into its trunk.

With the rest of the throng came the cypress, shaped like the cones that mark the turning point on the race-course: though now a tree, it was once a boy, dearly loved by the god who strings both lyre and bow.

This is the story. There was once a magnificent stag, sacred to the nymphs who live in the fields of Carthaea, whose branching antlers cast deep shade over its head.

These antlers gleamed with gold and a necklace of precious stones, encircling the animal's silky neck, hung down over its shoulders. On its forehead swayed a silver charm, kept in place by fine leather straps, which it had worn since it was born, and pearls glistened in either ear, close by its hollow temples. This stag was quite without fear and, its natural timidity forgotten, used to visit people's houses and hold out its neck, even to strangers, to be stroked. But the person who was most attached to it was Cyparissus, the handsomest of the Cean boys. He used to lead it to fresh grazing, or to the waters of some crystal spring, and wove wreaths of different kinds of flowers to hang upon its horns. Sometimes he sat on its back, like a horseman on his horse, and gleefully guided the animal's soft mouth this way and that, by means of scarlet reins.

One summer day, at noon, when the curving arms of the shore-loving Crab were being scorched by the heat of the sun, the stag was tired, and lay down to rest on the grassy ground, finding coolness in the shade of the trees. There Cyparissus unwittingly pierced it with his keen javelin. When he saw his friend cruelly wounded and dying, the boy resolved to die himself. Phoebus said all he could to comfort him, chiding him and telling him that his grief should be moderate, in proportion to its cause. Still the boy groaned and begged, as a last gift from the gods, that he should be allowed to go on mourning for ever. Now, as his blood drained away, by reason of his endless weeping, his limbs began to change to a greenish hue, and the hair which lately curled over his snowy brow bristled and stiffened, pointing upwards in a graceful crest towards the starry sky. Sadly the god Apollo sighed: 'I shall mourn for you,' he said, 'while you yourself will mourn for others, and be the constant companion of those in distress.'

Such was the grove which Orpheus had drawn round him, and now he sat in the midst of a gathering of wild creatures, and a host of birds. He tested the chords of his lyre, striking them with his thumb, till his ear was satisfied that the notes they played, though different, were all in tune. Then he began to sing . . .

ALEXANDER McCALL SMITH

HEAD TREE

A MAN WHO had never done any wrong to anybody else had a great misfortune happen to him. His wife noticed that a tree was beginning to grow out of his head. This was not painful to the man, but it made him feel awkward when there were other people about. They would point at him and say that this was a very strange thing to happen. Some people walked some miles to see this man sitting outside his hut with a tree growing out of his head.

At last the man decided that it was time to do something about the tree. He asked his wife if she would chop it down, but she warned him that this could be dangerous.

'If this tree is growing out of your head,' she said, 'then you might bleed to death if I chop it down.'

The man agreed that this was a danger. So instead of chopping the tree down he went to see a certain woman who was well known in that part for being a woman who could use charms to solve difficult problems. This woman lived in a hut some distance away and so the man had to bear the stares of all the people as he walked to her place.

The charm woman looked at the man and said that she had never seen this sort of thing before, but that her mother had told her that things like this could happen and had given her instructions as to how to deal with it.

'You must have done something bad to have this happen to you,' she said.

'I have not done anything bad,' said the man hotly. 'I have always behaved well.'

'In that case,' said the charm woman, 'you must have been planning to do something bad. If this were not so, then why would a tree grow out of your head?'

The man had no answer for this, and so the charm woman took a special herb out of her bag and gave it to him.

'You must eat this every day for a week,' she said. 'At the end of the week the tree will go. You must also pay me two cows, for this is a very expensive herb and it is not easy to stop trees growing out of people's heads.'

The man promised that he would give the woman her cows once the tree had gone. Then he returned to his home and took the first part of the herb. At the end of the week, when he had taken the last part of the herb, the tree fell off his head. The man's wife chopped it up and they used the wood for their cooking fire. The man was very relieved, and he was now able to walk about without people pointing at him and clicking their tongues in amazement.

'You must give that woman her cows,' his wife said. 'She has cured you well.'

'I shall not,' said the man. 'She is just an old witch with a sharp tongue. There is no reason to give her anything.'

The charm woman heard that the tree had fallen off the man's head and she sent a young boy to tell him to send her two cows. The man listened to the message which the boy brought, but all he did was beat the boy with a stick and send him home.

The next day, when the man was sitting in front of his hut drinking his beer, his wife came to him and looked at the top of his head.

'Another tree seems to be growing,' she said. 'This time it looks very big.'

The man's heart filled with despair. He could not face the thought of having a tree on his head again; and so he went back to the charm woman's house.

'I have come for more medicine,' he said. 'And I have brought those two cows I promised you.'

The charm woman looked at him and shook her head.

'You are a wicked man who does not keep his promises,' she said. 'If you want me to cure you again and to stop that tree forever, you will have to pay me four cows.'

The man stamped his feet on the ground, but he knew that she was the only woman who could stop a tree from growing out of his head. Reluctantly he brought four cows and left them in front of her house. She gave him the herb and told him that he should always keep his promises, even if he thought that he had made a promise to a weak old woman. The man said nothing, but he knew that what she said was quite right.

WASHINGTON IRVING

THE LEGEND OF
SLEEPY HOLLOW

> A pleasing land of drowsy head it was,
>   Of dreams that wave before the half-shut eye;
> And of gay castles in the clouds that pass,
>   For ever flushing round a summer sky.
>
> CASTLE OF INDOLENCE

IN THE BOSOM of one of those spacious coves which indent the eastern shore of the Hudson, at that broad expansion of the river denominated by the ancient Dutch navigators the Tappan Zee, and where they always prudently shortened sail, and implored the protection of St Nicholas when they crossed, there lies a small market-town or rural port, which by some is called Greensburgh, but which is more generally and properly known by the name of Tarry Town. This name was given, we are told, in former days, by the good housewives of the adjacent country, from the inveterate propensity of their husbands to linger about the village tavern on market days. Be that as it may, I do not vouch for the fact, but merely advert to it, for the sake of being precise and authentic. Not far from this village, perhaps about two miles, there is a little valley, or rather lap of land, among high hills, which is one of the quietest places in the whole world. A small brook glides through it, with just murmur enough to lull one to repose; and the occasional whistle of a quail, or tapping of a woodpecker, is almost the only sound that ever breaks in upon the uniform tranquillity.

I recollect that, when a stripling, my first exploit in squirrel-shooting was in a grove of tall walnut-trees that shades one side of the valley. I had wandered into it at noon time, when all nature is peculiarly quiet, and was startled by the roar of my own gun, as it broke the Sabbath stillness around, and was prolonged and reverberated by the angry echoes. If ever I should wish for a retreat, whither I might steal from the world and its distractions, and dream quietly away the remnant of a troubled life, I know of none more promising than this little valley.

From the listless repose of the place, and the peculiar character of its inhabitants, who are descendants from the original Dutch settlers, this sequestered glen has long been known by the name of SLEEPY HOLLOW, and its rustic lads are called the Sleepy Hollow Boys throughout all the neighboring country. A drowsy, dreamy influence seems to hang over the land, and to pervade the very atmosphere. Some say that the place was bewitched by a high German doctor, during the early days of the settlement; others, that an old Indian chief, the prophet or wizard of his tribe, held his pow-wows there before the country was discovered by Master Hendrick Hudson. Certain it is, the place still continues under the sway of some witching power, that holds a spell over the minds of the good people, causing them to walk in a continual reverie. They are given to all kinds of marvellous beliefs; are subject to trances and visions; and frequently see strange sights, and hear music and voices in the air. The whole neighborhood abounds with local tales, haunted spots, and twilight superstitions; stars shoot and meteors glare oftener across the valley than in any other part of the country, and the nightmare, with her whole nine fold, seems to make it the favorite scene of her gambols.

The dominant spirit, however, that haunts this enchanted

34

region, and seems to be commander-in-chief of all the powers of the air, is the apparition of a figure on horseback without a head. It is said by some to be the ghost of a Hessian trooper, whose head had been carried away by a cannon-ball, in some nameless battle during the revolutionary war; and who is ever and anon seen by the country folk hurrying along in the gloom of night, as if on the wings of the wind. His haunts are not confined to the valley, but extend at times to the adjacent roads, and especially to the vicinity of a church at no great distance. Indeed, certain of the most authentic historians of those parts, who have been careful in collecting and collating the floating facts concerning this spectre, allege that the body of the trooper, having been buried in the church-yard, the ghost rides forth to the scene of battle in nightly quest of his head; and that the rushing speed with which he sometimes passes along the Hollow, like a midnight blast, is owing to his being belated, and in a hurry to get back to the church-yard before daybreak.

Such is the general purport of this legendary superstition, which has furnished materials for many a wild story in that region of shadows; and the spectre is known, at all the country firesides, by the name of the Headless Horseman of Sleepy Hollow.

It is remarkable that the visionary propensity I have mentioned is not confined to the native inhabitants of the valley, but is unconsciously imbibed by every one who resides there for a time. However wide awake they may have been before they entered that sleepy region, they are sure, in a little time, to inhale the witching influence of the air, and begin to grow imaginative – to dream dreams, and see apparitions.

I mention this peaceful spot with all possible laud; for it is in such little retired Dutch valleys, found here and there embosomed in the great State of New York, that population,

manners, and customs, remain fixed; while the great tor-
rent of migration and improvement, which is making such
incessant changes in other parts of this restless country,
sweeps by them unobserved. They are like those little nooks
of still water which border a rapid stream; where we may
see the straw and bubble riding quietly at anchor, or slowly
revolving in their mimic harbor, undisturbed by the rush of
the passing current. Though many years have elapsed since
I trod the drowsy shades of Sleepy Hollow, yet I question
whether I should not still find the same trees and the same
families vegetating in its sheltered bosom.

In this by-place of nature, there abode, in a remote
period of American history, that is to say, some thirty years
since, a worthy wight of the name of Ichabod Crane; who
sojourned, or, as he expressed it, 'tarried', in Sleepy Hollow,
for the purpose of instructing the children of the vicinity.
He was a native of Connecticut; a State which supplies the
Union with pioneers for the mind as well as for the forest,
and sends forth yearly its legions of frontier woodsmen
and country schoolmasters. The cognomen of Crane was
not inapplicable to his person. He was tall, but exceedingly
lank, with narrow shoulders, long arms and legs, hands that
dangled a mile out of his sleeves, feet that might have served
for shovels, and his whole frame most loosely hung together.
His head was small, and flat at top, with huge ears, large
green glassy eyes, and a long snipe nose, so that it looked like
a weather-cock, perched upon his spindle neck, to tell which
way the wind blew. To see him striding along the profile of a
hill on a windy day, with his clothes bagging and fluttering
about him, one might have mistaken him for the genius
of famine descending upon the earth, or some scarecrow
eloped from a cornfield.

His school-house was a low building of one large room,

rudely constructed of logs; the windows partly glazed, and partly patched with leaves of old copy-books. It was most ingeniously secured at vacant hours, by a withe twisted in the handle of the door, and stakes set against the window shutters; so that, though a thief might get in with perfect ease, he would find some embarrassment in getting out; an idea most probably borrowed by the architect, Yost Van Houton, from the mystery of an eel-pot. The school-house stood in a rather lonely but pleasant situation just at the foot of a woody hill, with a brook running close by, and a formidable birch tree growing at one end of it. From hence the low murmur of his pupils' voices, conning over their lessons, might be heard in a drowsy summer's day, like the hum of a bee-hive; interrupted now and then by the authoritative voice of the master, in the tone of menace or command; or, peradventure, by the appalling sound of the birch, as he urged some tardy loiterer along the flowery path of knowledge. Truth to say, he was a conscientious man, and ever bore in mind the golden maxim, 'Spare the rod and spoil the child.' – Ichabod Crane's scholars certainly were not spoiled.

I would not have it imagined, however, that he was one of those cruel potentates of the school, who joy in the smart of their subjects; on the contrary, he administered justice with discrimination rather than severity; taking the burthen off the backs of the weak, and laying it on those of the strong. Your mere puny stripling, that winced at the least flourish of the rod, was passed by with indulgence; but the claims of justice were satisfied by inflicting a double portion on some little, tough, wrong-headed, broad-skirted Dutch urchin, who sulked and swelled and grew dogged and sullen beneath the birch. All this he called 'doing his duty by their parents'; and he never inflicted a chastisement without following it by the assurance, so consolatory to the smarting urchin, that 'he would remember it, and thank him for it the longest day he had to live'.

When school hours were over, he was even the companion and playmate of the larger boys; and on holiday afternoons would convoy some of the smaller ones home, who happened to have pretty sisters, or good housewives for mothers, noted for the comforts of the cupboard. Indeed it behoved him to keep on good terms with his pupils. The revenue arising from his school was small, and would have been scarcely sufficient to furnish him with daily bread, for he was a huge feeder, and though lank, had the dilating powers of an anaconda; but to help out his maintenance, he was, according to country custom in those parts, boarded and lodged at the houses of the farmers, whose children he instructed. With these he lived successively a week at a time; thus going the rounds of the neighborhood, with all his worldly effects tied up in a cotton handkerchief.

That all this might not be too onerous on the purses of his rustic patrons, who are apt to consider the costs of schooling a grievous burden, and schoolmasters as mere drones, he had various ways of rendering himself both useful and agreeable. He assisted the farmers occasionally in the lighter labors of their farms; helped to make hay; mended the fences; took the horses to water; drove the cows from pasture; and cut wood for the winter fire. He laid aside, too, all the dominant dignity and absolute sway with which he lorded it in his little empire, the school, and became wonderfully gentle and ingratiating. He found favor in the eyes of the mothers, by petting the children, particularly the youngest; and like the lion bold, which whilom so magnanimously the lamb did hold, he would sit with a child on one knee, and rock a cradle with his foot for whole hours together.

In addition to his other vocations, he was the singing-master of the neighborhood, and picked up many bright shillings by instructing the young folks in psalmody. It was a matter of no little vanity to him, on Sundays, to take his station in front of the church gallery, with a band of chosen singers; where, in his own mind, he completely carried away the palm from the parson. Certain it is, his voice resounded far above all the rest of the congregation; and there are peculiar quavers still to be heard in that church, and which may even be heard half a mile off, quite to the opposite side of the mill-pond, on a still Sunday morning, which are said to be legitimately descended from the nose of Ichabod Crane. Thus, by divers little makeshifts in that ingenious way which is commonly denominated 'by hook and by crook', the worthy pedagogue got on tolerably enough, and was thought, by all who understood nothing of the labor of headwork, to have a wonderfully easy life of it.

The schoolmaster is generally a man of some importance in the female circle of a rural neighborhood; being considered a kind of idle gentlemanlike personage, of vastly superior taste and accomplishments to the rough country swains, and, indeed, inferior in learning only to the parson. His appearance, therefore, is apt to occasion some little stir at the tea-table of a farmhouse, and the addition of a supernumerary dish of cakes or sweetmeats, or, peradventure, the parade of a silver tea-pot. Our man of letters, therefore, was peculiarly happy in the smiles of all the country damsels. How he would figure among them in the church-yard, between services on Sundays! gathering grapes for them from the wild vines that overrun the surrounding trees; reciting for their amusement all the epitaphs on the tombstones; or sauntering, with a whole bevy of them, along the banks of the adjacent mill-pond; while the more bashful country bumpkins hung sheepishly back, envying his superior elegance and address.

From his half itinerant life, also, he was a kind of travelling gazette, carrying the whole budget of local gossip from house to house; so that his appearance was always greeted with satisfaction. He was, moreover, esteemed by the women as a man of great erudition, for he had read several books quite through, and was a perfect master of Cotton Mather's history of New England Witchcraft, in which, by the way, he most firmly and potently believed.

He was, in fact, an odd mixture of small shrewdness and simple credulity. His appetite for the marvellous, and his powers of digesting it, were equally extraordinary; and both had been increased by his residence in this spellbound region. No tale was too gross or monstrous for his capacious swallow. It was often his delight, after his school was dismissed in the afternoon, to stretch himself on the rich bed of clover, bordering the little brook that whimpered by his school-house, and there con over old Mather's direful tales, until the gathering dusk of the evening made the printed page a mere mist before his eyes. Then, as he wended his way, by swamp and stream and awful woodland, to the farmhouse where he happened to be quartered, every sound of nature, at that witching hour, fluttered his excited imagination: the moan of the whip-poor-will from the hill-side; the boding cry of the tree-toad, that harbinger of storm; the dreary hooting of the screech-owl, or the sudden rustling in the thicket of birds frightened from their roost. The fire-flies, too, which sparkled most vividly in the darkest places, now and then startled him, as one of uncommon brightness would stream across his path; and if, by chance, a huge blockhead of a beetle came winging his blundering flight against him, the poor varlet was ready to give up the ghost, with the idea that he was struck with a witch's token. His only resource on such occasions, either to drown thought, or drive away evil spirits, was to sing psalm tunes; – and the good people of Sleepy Hollow, as they sat by their doors of an evening, were often filled with awe, at hearing his nasal melody, 'in linked sweetness long drawn out', floating from the distant hill, or along the dusky road.

Another of his sources of fearful pleasure was, to pass long winter evenings with the old Dutch wives, as they sat spinning by the fire, with a row of apples roasting and spluttering along the hearth, and listen to their marvellous tales of ghosts and goblins, and haunted fields, and haunted brooks, and haunted bridges, and haunted houses, and particularly of the headless horseman, or galloping Hessian of the Hollow, as they sometimes called him. He would delight them equally by his anecdotes of witchcraft, and of the direful omens and portentous sights and sounds in the air, which prevailed in the earlier times of Connecticut; and would frighten them wofully with speculations upon comets and shooting stars; and with the alarming fact that the world did absolutely turn round, and that they were half the time topsy-turvy!

But if there was a pleasure in all this, while snugly cuddling in the chimney corner of a chamber that was all of a ruddy glow from the crackling wood fire, and where, of course, no spectre dared to show his face, it was dearly purchased by the terrors of his subsequent walk homewards. What fearful shapes and shadows beset his path amidst the dim and ghastly glare of a snowy night! – With what wistful look did he eye every trembling ray of light streaming across the waste fields from some distant window! – How often was he appalled by some shrub covered with snow, which, like a sheeted spectre, beset his very path! – How often did he shrink with curdling awe at the sound of his own steps on the frosty crust beneath his feet; and dread to look over his shoulder, lest he should behold some uncouth being tramping close behind him! – and how often was he thrown into complete dismay by some rushing blast, howling among the trees, in the idea that it was the Galloping Hessian on one of his nightly scourings!

All these, however, were mere terrors of the night, phantoms of the mind that walk in darkness; and though he had seen many spectres in his time, and been more than once beset by Satan in divers shapes, in his lonely perambulations, yet daylight put an end to all these evils; and he would have passed a pleasant life of it, in despite of the devil and all his works, if his path had not been crossed by a being that causes more perplexity to mortal man than ghosts, goblins, and the whole race of witches put together, and that was – a woman.

Among the musical disciples who assembled, one evening in each week, to receive his instructions in psalmody, was Katrina Van Tassel, the daughter and only child of a substantial Dutch farmer. She was a blooming lass of fresh eighteen; plump as a partridge; ripe and melting and rosy cheeked as one of her father's peaches, and universally famed, not merely for her beauty, but her vast expectations. She was withal a little of a coquette, as might be perceived even in her dress, which was a mixture of ancient and modern fashions, as most suited to set off her charms. She wore the ornaments of pure yellow gold, which her great-great-grandmother had brought over from Saardam, the tempting stomacher of the olden time; and withal a provokingly short petticoat, to display the prettiest foot and ankle in the country round.

Ichabod Crane had a soft and foolish heart towards the sex; and it is not to be wondered at, that so tempting a morsel soon found favor in his eyes; more especially after he had visited her in her paternal mansion. Old Baltus Van Tassel was a perfect picture of a thriving, contented, liberal-hearted farmer. He seldom, it is true, sent either his eyes or his thoughts beyond the boundaries of his own farm; but within those every thing was snug, happy, and well-conditioned. He was satisfied with his wealth, but not proud of it; and piqued himself upon the hearty abundance, rather than the style in which he lived. His stronghold was situated on the banks of the Hudson, in one of those green, sheltered, fertile nooks, in which the Dutch farmers are so fond of nestling. A great elm-tree spread its broad branches over it; at the foot of which bubbled up a spring of the softest and sweetest water, in a little well, formed of a barrel; and then stole sparkling away through the grass, to a neighboring brook, that bubbled along among alders and dwarf willows. Hard by the farmhouse was a vast barn, that might have served for a church; every window and crevice of which seemed bursting forth with the treasures of the farm; the flail was busily resounding within it from morning to night; swallows and martins skimmed twittering about the eaves; and rows of pigeons, some with one eye turned up, as if watching the weather, some with their heads under their wings, or buried in their bosoms, and others swelling, and cooing, and bowing about their dames, were enjoying the sunshine on the roof. Sleek unwieldy porkers were grunting in the repose and abundance of their pens; whence sallied forth, now and then, troops of sucking pigs, as if to snuff the air. A stately squadron of snowy geese were riding in an adjoining pond, convoying whole fleets of ducks; regiments of turkeys were gobbling through the farmyard, and guinea fowls fretting about it, like ill-tempered housewives, with their peevish discontented cry. Before the barn door strutted the gallant cock, that pattern of a husband, a warrior, and a fine gentleman, clapping his burnished wings, and crowing in the pride and gladness of his heart – sometimes tearing up the earth with his feet, and then generously calling his ever-hungry family of wives and children to enjoy the rich morsel which he had discovered.

The pedagogue's mouth watered, as he looked upon this sumptuous promise of luxurious winter fare. In his devouring mind's eye, he pictured to himself every roasting-pig running about with a pudding in his belly, and an apple in his mouth; the pigeons were snugly put to bed in a comfortable pie, and tucked in with a coverlet of crust; the geese were swimming in their own gravy; and the ducks pairing cosily in dishes, like snug married couples, with a decent competency of onion sauce. In the porkers he saw carved out the future sleek side of bacon, and juicy relishing ham; not a turkey but he beheld daintily trussed up, with its gizzard under its wing, and, peradventure, a necklace of savory sausages; and even bright chanticleer himself lay sprawling on his back, in a side-dish, with uplifted claws, as if craving that quarter which his chivalrous spirit disdained to ask while living.

As the enraptured Ichabod fancied all this, and as he rolled his great green eyes over the fat meadow-lands, the rich fields of wheat, of rye, of buckwheat, and Indian corn, and the orchards burthened with ruddy fruit, which surrounded the warm tenement of Van Tassel, his heart yearned after the damsel who was to inherit these domains, and his imagination expanded with the idea, how they might be readily turned into cash, and the money invested in immense tracts of wild land, and shingle palaces in the wilderness. Nay, his busy fancy already realized his hopes, and presented to him the blooming Katrina, with a whole family of children, mounted on the top of a wagon loaded with household trumpery, with pots and kettles dangling beneath; and he beheld himself bestriding a pacing mare,

44

with a colt at her heels, setting out for Kentucky, Tennessee, or the Lord knows where.

When he entered the house the conquest of his heart was complete. It was one of those spacious farmhouses, with high-ridged, but lowly-sloping roofs, built in the style handed down from the first Dutch settlers; the low projecting eaves forming a piazza along the front, capable of being closed up in bad weather. Under this were hung flails, harness, various utensils of husbandry, and nets for fishing in the neighboring river. Benches were built along the sides for summer use; and a great spinning-wheel at one end, and a churn at the other, showed the various uses to which this important porch might be devoted. From this piazza the wondering Ichabod entered the hall, which formed the centre of the mansion and the place of usual residence. Here, rows of resplendent pewter, ranged on a long dresser, dazzled his eyes. In one corner stood a huge bag of wool ready to be spun; in another a quantity of linsey-woolsey just from the loom; ears of Indian corn, and strings of dried apples and peaches, hung in gay festoons along the walls, mingled with the gaud of red peppers; and a door left ajar gave him a peep into the best parlor, where the claw-footed chairs, and dark mahogany tables, shone like mirrors; and irons, with their accompanying shovel and tongs, glistened from their covert of asparagus tops; mock-oranges and conch-shells decorated the mantelpiece; strings of various colored birds' eggs were suspended above it: a great ostrich egg was hung from the centre of the room, and a corner cupboard, knowingly left open, displayed immense treasures of old silver and well-mended china.

From the moment Ichabod laid his eyes upon these regions of delight, the peace of his mind was at an end, and his only study was how to gain the affections of the peerless daughter of Van Tassel. In this enterprise, however, he had more real difficulties than generally fell to the lot of a knight-errant of yore, who seldom had any thing but giants, enchanters, fiery dragons, and such like easily-conquered adversaries, to contend with; and had to make his way merely through gates of iron and brass, and walls of adamant, to the castle keep, where the lady of his heart was confined; all which he achieved as easily as a man would carve his way to the centre of a Christmas pie; and then the lady gave him her hand as a matter of course. Ichabod, on the contrary, had to win his way to the heart of a country coquette, beset with a labyrinth of whims and caprices, which were for ever presenting new difficulties and impediments; and he had to encounter a host of fearful adversaries of real flesh and blood, the numerous rustic admirers, who beset every portal to her heart; keeping a watchful and angry eye upon each other, but ready to fly out in the common cause against any new competitor.

Among these the most formidable was a burly, roaring, roystering blade, of the name of Abraham, or, according to the Dutch abbreviation, Brom Van Brunt, the hero of the country round, which rang with his feats of strength and hardihood. He was broad-shouldered and double-jointed, with short curly black hair, and a bluff, but not unpleasant countenance, having a mingled air of fun and arrogance. From his Herculean frame and great powers of limb, he had received the nickname of BROM BONES, by which he was universally known. He was famed for great knowledge and skill in horsemanship, being as dexterous on horseback as a Tartar.

He was foremost at all races and cock-fights; and, with the ascendency which bodily strength acquires in rustic life, was the umpire in all disputes, setting his hat on one side, and giving his decisions with an air and tone admitting of no gainsay or appeal. He was always ready for either a fight or a frolic; but had more mischief than ill-will in his composition; and, with all his overbearing roughness, there was a strong dash of waggish good humor at bottom. He had three or four boon companions, who regarded him as their model, and at the head of whom he scoured the country, attending every scene of feud or merriment for miles round. In cold weather he was distinguished by a fur cap, surmounted with a flaunting fox's tail; and when the folks at a country gathering descried this well-known crest at a distance, whisking about among a squad of hard riders, they always stood by for a squall. Sometimes his crew would be heard dashing along past the farmhouses at midnight, with whoop and halloo, like a troop of Don Cossacks; and the old dames, startled out of their sleep, would listen for a moment till the hurry-scurry had clattered by, and then exclaim, 'Ay, there goes Brom Bones and his gang!' The neighbors looked upon him with a mixture of awe, admiration, and good will; and when any madcap prank, or rustic brawl, occurred in the vicinity, always shook their heads, and warranted Brom Bones was at the bottom of it.

This rantipole hero had for some time singled out the blooming Katrina for the object of his uncouth gallantries, and though his amorous toyings were something like the gentle caresses and endearments of a bear, yet it was whispered that she did not altogether discourage his hopes. Certain it is, his advances were signals for rival candidates to retire, who felt no inclination to cross a lion in his amours; insomuch, that when his horse was seen tied to Van Tassel's paling, on a Sunday night, a sure sign that his master was courting, or, as it is termed 'sparking', within, all other suitors passed by in despair, and carried the war into other quarters.

Such was the formidable rival with whom Ichabod Crane had to contend, and, considering all things, a stouter man than he would have shrunk from the competition, and a wiser man would have despaired. He had, however, a happy mixture of pliability and perseverance in his nature; he was in form and spirit like a supple-jack – yielding, but tough; though he bent, he never broke; and though he bowed beneath the slightest pressure, yet, the moment it was away – jerk! he was as erect, and carried his head as high as ever.

To have taken the field openly against his rival would have been madness; for he was not a man to be thwarted in his amours, any more than that stormy lover, Achilles. Ichabod, therefore, made his advances in a quiet and gently-insinuating manner. Under cover of his character of singing-master, he made frequent visits at the farmhouse; not that he had any thing to apprehend from the meddlesome interference of parents, which is so often a stumbling-block in the path of lovers. Balt Van Tassel was an easy indulgent soul; he loved his daughter better even than his pipe, and, like a reasonable man and an excellent father, let her have her way in every thing. His notable little wife, too, had enough to do to attend to her housekeeping and manage her poultry; for, as she sagely observed, ducks and geese are foolish things, and must be looked after, but girls can take care of themselves. Thus while the busy dame bustled about the house, or plied her spinning-wheel at one end of the piazza, honest Balt would sit smoking his evening pipe at the other, watching the achievements of a little wooden warrior, who, armed with a sword in each hand, was most valiantly fighting the wind on the pinnacle of the barn. In the mean time, Ichabod would carry on his suit with the daughter by the side of the spring under the great elm, or sauntering along in the twilight, that hour so favorable to the lover's eloquence.

I profess not to know how women's hearts are wooed and won. To me they have always been matters of riddle and admiration. Some seem to have but one vulnerable point, or door of access; while others have a thousand avenues, and may be captured in a thousand different ways. It is a great triumph of skill to gain the former, but a still greater proof of generalship to maintain possession of the latter, for the man must battle for his fortress at every door and window. He who wins a thousand common hearts is therefore entitled to some renown; but he who keeps undisputed sway over the heart of a coquette, is indeed a hero. Certain it is, this was not the case with the redoubtable Brom Bones; and from the moment Ichabod Crane made his advances, the interests of the former evidently declined; his horse was no longer seen tied at the palings on Sunday nights, and a deadly feud gradually arose between him and the preceptor of Sleepy Hollow.

Brom, who had a degree of rough chivalry in his nature, would fain have carried matters to open warfare, and have settled their pretensions to the lady, according to the mode of those most concise and simple reasoners, the knights-errant of yore – by single combat; but Ichabod was too conscious of the superior might of his adversary to enter the lists against him: he had overheard a boast of Bones, that he would 'double the schoolmaster up, and lay him on a shelf of his own school-house'; and he was too wary to give him an opportunity. There was something extremely provoking in this obstinately pacific system; it left Brom no alternative but to draw upon the funds of rustic waggery in his disposition, and to play off boorish practical jokes upon his rival. Ichabod became the object of whimsical persecution to Bones, and his gang of rough riders. They harried his hitherto peaceful domains; smoked out his singing school, by stopping up the chimney; broke into the school-house at night, in spite of its formidable fastenings of withe and window stakes, and turned every thing topsy-turvy: so that the poor schoolmaster began to think all the witches in the country held their meetings there. But what was still more annoying, Brom took all opportunities of turning him into ridicule in presence of his mistress, and had a scoundrel dog whom he taught to whine in the most ludicrous manner, and introduced as a rival of Ichabod's to instruct her in psalmody.

In this way matters went on for some time, without producing any material effect on the relative situation of the contending powers. On a fine autumnal afternoon, Ichabod, in pensive mood, sat enthroned on the lofty stool whence he usually watched all the concerns of his little literary realm. In his hand he swayed a ferule, that sceptre of despotic power; the birch of justice reposed on three nails, behind the throne, a constant terror to evil doers; while on the desk before him might be seen sundry contraband articles and prohibited weapons, detected upon the persons of idle urchins; such as half-munched apples, popguns, whirligigs, fly-cages, and whole legions of rampant little paper gamecocks. Apparently there had been some appalling act of justice recently inflicted, for his scholars were all busily intent upon their books, or slyly whispering behind them with one eye kept upon the master; and a kind of buzzing stillness reigned throughout the school-room. It was suddenly interrupted by the appearance of a man, in tow-cloth jacket and trowsers, a round-crowned fragment of a hat, like the cap of Mercury, and mounted on the back of a ragged, wild, half-broken colt, which he managed with a rope by way of halter. He came clattering up to the school door with an invitation to Ichabod to attend a merry-making or 'quilting frolic', to be held that evening at Mynheer Van Tassel's; and having delivered his message with an air of great importance and an effort at fine language, he dashed over the brook, and was seen scampering away up the hollow, full of the importance and hurry of his mission.

All was now bustle and hubbub in the late quiet school-room. The scholars were hurried through their lessons, without stopping at trifles; those who were nimble skipped over half with impunity, and those who were tardy, had a smart application now and then in the rear, to quicken their speed, or help them over a tall word. Books were flung aside without being put away on the shelves, inkstands were over-turned, benches thrown down, and the whole school was turned loose an hour before the usual time, bursting forth like a legion of young imps, yelping and racketing about the green, in joy at their early emancipation.

The gallant Ichabod now spent at least an extra half hour at his toilet, brushing and furbishing up his best, and indeed only suit of rusty black, and arranging his looks by a bit of broken looking-glass, that hung up in the school-house. That he might make his appearance before his mistress in the true style of a cavalier, he borrowed a horse from the farmer with whom he was domiciliated, a choleric old Dutchman, of the name of Hans Van Ripper, and, thus gallantly mount-ed, issued forth, like a knight-errant in quest of adventures. But it is meet I should, in the true spirit of romantic story, give some account of the looks and equipments of my hero and his steed. The animal he bestrode was a broken-down plough-horse, that had outlived almost every thing but his viciousness. He was gaunt and shagged, with a ewe neck and a head like a hammer; his rusty mane and tail were tangled and knotted with burrs; one eye had lost its pupil, and was glaring and spectral; but the other had the gleam of a genuine devil in it. Still he must have had fire and mettle in his day, if we may judge from the name he bore of Gunpowder. He had, in fact, been a favorite steed of his master's, the choleric Van Ripper, who was a furious rider, and had infused, very probably, some of his own spirit into the animal; for, old and broken-down as he looked, there was more of the lurking devil in him than in any young filly in the country.

Ichabod was a suitable figure for such a steed. He rode with short stirrups, which brought his knees nearly up to the pommel of the saddle; his sharp elbows stuck out like grasshoppers'; he carried his whip perpendicularly in his hand, like a sceptre, and, as his horse jogged on, the motion of his arms was not unlike the flapping of a pair of wings. A small wool hat rested on the top of his nose, for so his scanty strip of forehead might be called; and the skirts of his black coat fluttered out almost to the horse's tail. Such was the appearance of Ichabod and his steed, as they shambled out of the gate of Hans Van Ripper, and it was altogether such an apparition as is seldom to be met with in broad daylight.

It was, as I have said, a fine autumnal day, the sky was clear and serene, and nature wore that rich and golden livery which we always associate with the idea of abundance. The forests had put on their sober brown and yellow, while some trees of the tenderer kind had been nipped by the frosts into brilliant dyes of orange, purple, and scarlet. Streaming files of wild ducks began to make their appearance high in the air; the bark of the squirrel might be heard from the groves of beech and hickory nuts, and the pensive whistle of the quail at intervals from the neighboring stubble-field.

The small birds were taking their farewell banquets. In the fulness of their revelry, they fluttered, chirping and fro-licking, from bush to bush, and tree to tree, capricious from the very profusion and variety around them. There was the honest cock-robin, the favorite game of stripling sportsmen, with its loud querulous note; and the twittering blackbirds flying in sable clouds; and the golden-winged woodpecker, with his crimson crest, his broad black gorget, and splendid plumage; and the cedar bird, with its red-tipt wings and yellow-tipt tail, and its little monteiro cap of feathers; and the blue-jay, that noisy coxcomb, in his gay light-blue coat and white underclothes; screaming and chattering, nodding and bobbing and bowing, and pretending to be on good terms with every songster of the grove.

As Ichabod jogged slowly on his way, his eye, ever open to every symptom of culinary abundance, ranged with delight over the treasures of jolly autumn. On all sides he beheld vast store of apples; some hanging in oppressive opulence on the trees; some gathered into baskets and barrels for the market; others heaped up in rich piles for the cider-press. Farther on he beheld great fields of Indian corn, with its golden ears peeping from their leafy coverts, and holding out the promise of cakes and hasty pudding; and the yellow pumpkins lying beneath them, turning up their fair round bellies to the sun, and giving ample prospects of the most luxurious of pies; and anon he passed the fragrant buckwheat fields, breathing the odor of the beehive, and as he beheld them, soft anticipations stole over his mind of dainty slapjacks, well buttered, and garnished with honey or treacle, by the delicate little dimpled hand of Katrina Van Tassel.

Thus feeding his mind with many sweet thoughts and 'sugared suppositions', he journeyed along the sides of a range of hills which look out upon some of the goodliest scenes of the mighty Hudson. The sun gradually wheeled his broad disk down into the west. The wide bosom of the Tappan Zee lay motionless and glassy, excepting that here and there a gentle undulation waved and prolonged the blue shadow of the distant mountain. A few amber clouds floated in the sky, without a breath of air to move them. The horizon was of a fine golden tint, changing gradually into a pure apple green, and from that into the deep blue of the mid-heaven. A slanting ray lingered on the woody crests of the precipices that overhung some parts of the river, giving greater depth to the dark-gray and purple of their rocky sides. A sloop was loitering in the distance, dropping slowly down with the tide, her sail hanging uselessly against the mast; and as the reflection of the sky gleamed along the still water, it seemed as if the vessel was suspended in the air.

It was toward evening that Ichabod arrived at the castle of the Heer Van Tassel, which he found thronged with the pride and flower of the adjacent country. Old farmers, a spare leathern-faced race, in homespun coats and breeches, blue stockings, huge shoes, and magnificent pewter buckles. Their brisk withered little dames, in close crimped caps, long-waisted short-gowns, home-spun petticoats, with scissors and pincushions, and gay calico pockets hanging on the outside. Buxom lasses, almost as antiquated as their mothers, excepting where a straw hat, a fine ribbon, or per-haps a white frock, gave symptoms of city innovation. The sons, in short square-skirted coats with rows of stupendous brass buttons, and their hair generally queued in the fashion of the times, especially if they could procure an eel-skin for the purpose, it being esteemed, throughout the country, as a potent nourisher and strengthener of the hair.

Brom Bones, however, was the hero of the scene, having come to the gathering on his favorite steed Daredevil, a creature, like himself, full of mettle and mischief, and which no one but himself could manage. He was, in fact, noted for preferring vicious animals, given to all kinds of tricks, which kept the rider in constant risk of his neck, for he held a tractable well-broken horse as unworthy of a lad of spirit.

Fain would I pause to dwell upon the world of charms that burst upon the enraptured gaze of my hero, as he entered the state parlor of Van Tassel's mansion. Not those of the bevy of buxom lasses, with their luxurious display of red and white; but the ample charms of a genuine Dutch country tea-table, in the sumptuous time of autumn. Such heaped-up platters of cakes of various and almost indescribable kinds, known only to experienced Dutch housewives! There was the doughty dough-nut, the tenderer oly koek, and the crisp and crumbling cruller; sweet cakes and short cakes, ginger cakes and honey cakes, and the whole family of cakes. And then there were apple pies and peach pies and pumpkin pies; besides slices of ham and smoked beef; and moreover delectable dishes of preserved plums, and peaches, and pears, and quinces; not to mention broiled shad and roasted chickens; together with bowls of milk and cream, all mingled higgledy-piggledly, pretty much as I have enumerated them, with the motherly tea-pot sending up its clouds of vapor from the midst – Heaven bless the mark! I want breath and time to discuss this banquet as it deserves, and am too eager to get on with my story. Happily, Ichabod Crane was not in so great a hurry as his historian, but did ample justice to every dainty.

He was a kind and thankful creature, whose heart dilated in proportion as his skin was filled with good cheer; and whose spirits rose with eating as some men's do with drink. He could not help, too, rolling his large eyes round him as he ate, and chuckling with the possibility that he might one day be lord of all this scene of almost unimaginable luxury and splendor. Then, he thought, how soon he'd turn his back upon the old school-house; snap his fingers in the face of

Hans Van Ripper, and every other niggardly patron, and kick any itinerant pedagogue out of doors that should dare to call him comrade!

Old Baltus Van Tassel moved about among his guests with a face dilated with content and good humor, round and jolly as the harvest moon. His hospitable attentions were brief, but expressive, being confined to a shake of the hand, a slap on the shoulder, a loud laugh, and a pressing invitation to 'fall to, and help themselves'.

And now the sound of the music from the common room, or hall, summoned to the dance. The musician was an old gray-headed man, who had been the itinerant orchestra of the neighborhood for more than half a century. His instrument was as old and battered as himself. The greater part of the time he scraped on two or three strings, accompanying every movement of the bow with a motion of the head; bowing almost to the ground, and stamping with his foot whenever a fresh couple were to start.

Ichabod prided himself upon his dancing as much as upon his vocal powers. Not a limb, not a fibre about him was idle; and to have seen his loosely hung frame in full motion, and clattering about the room, you would have thought Saint Vitus himself, that blessed patron of the dance, was figuring before you in person. He was the admiration of all and sundry, who, having gathered, of all ages and sizes, from the farm and the neighborhood, stood forming a pyramid of shining faces at every door and window, gazing with delight at the scene, and grinning from ear to ear. How could the flogger of urchins be otherwise than animated and joyous? the lady of his heart was his partner in the dance, and smiling graciously in reply to all his amorous oglings; while Brom Bones, sorely smitten with love and jealousy, sat brooding by himself in one corner.

When the dance was at an end, Ichabod was attracted to a knot of the sager folks, who, with old Van Tassel, sat smoking at one end of the piazza, gossiping over former times, and drawing out long stories about the war.

This neighborhood, at the time of which I am speaking, was one of those highly-favored places which abound with chronicle and great men. The British and American line had run near it during the war; it had, therefore, been the scene of marauding, and infested with refugees, cowboys, and all kinds of border chivalry. Just sufficient time had elapsed to enable each story-teller to dress up his tale with a little becoming fiction, and, in the indistinctness of his recollection, to make himself the hero of every exploit.

There was the story of Doffue Martling, a large blue-bearded Dutchman, who had nearly taken a British frigate with an old iron nine-pounder from a mud breastwork, only that his gun burst at the sixth discharge. And there was an old gentleman who shall be nameless, being too rich a mynheer to be lightly mentioned, who, in the battle of White-plains, being an excellent master of defence, parried a musket ball with a small sword, insomuch that he absolutely felt it whiz round the blade, and glance off at the hilt: in proof of which, he was ready at any time to show the sword, with the hilt a little bent. There were several more that had been equally great in the field, not one of whom but was persuaded that he had a considerable hand in bringing the war to a happy termination.

But all these were nothing to the tales of ghosts and apparitions that succeeded. The neighborhood is rich in legendary treasures of the kind. Local tales and superstitions thrive best in these sheltered long-settled retreats; but are trampled under foot by the shifting throng that forms the populations of most of our country places. Besides, there is no encouragement for ghosts in most of our villages, for, they have scarcely had time to finish their first nap, and turn themselves in their graves, before their surviving friends have travelled away from the neighborhood; so that when they turn out at night to walk their rounds, they have no acquaintance left to call upon. This is perhaps the reason why we so seldom hear of ghosts except in our long-established Dutch communities.

The immediate cause, however, of the prevalence of supernatural stories in these parts, was doubtless owing to the vicinity of Sleepy Hollow. There was a contagion in the very air that blew from that haunted region; it breathed forth an atmosphere of dreams and fancies infecting all the land. Several of the Sleepy Hollow people were present at Van Tassel's, and, as usual, were doling out their wild and wonderful legends. Many dismal tales were told about funeral trains, and mourning cries and wailing heard and seen about the great tree where the unfortunate Major André was taken, and which stood in the neighborhood. Some mention was made also of the woman in white, that haunted the dark glen at Raven Rock, and was often heard to shriek on winter nights before a storm, having perished there in the snow. The chief part of the stories, however, turned upon the favorite spectre of Sleepy Hollow, the headless horseman, who had been heard several times of late, patrolling the country; and, it was said, tethered his horse nightly among the graves in the church-yard.

The sequestered situation of this church seems always to have made it a favorite haunt of troubled spirits. It stands on a knoll, surrounded by locust-trees and lofty elms, from among which its decent whitewashed walls shine modestly forth, like Christian purity beaming through the shades of retirement. A gentle slope descends from it to a silver sheet of water, bordered by high trees, between which, peeps may be caught at the blue hills of the Hudson. To look upon its grass-grown yard, where the sunbeams seem to sleep so quietly, one would think that there at least the dead might rest in peace. On one side of the church extends a wide woody dell, along which raves a large brook among broken rocks and trunks of fallen trees. Over a deep black part of the stream, not far from the church, was formerly thrown a wooden bridge; the road that led to it, and the bridge itself, were thickly shaded by overhanging trees, which cast a gloom about it, even in the daytime; but occasioned a fearful darkness at night. This was one of the favorite haunts of the headless horseman; and the place where he was most frequently encountered. The tale was told of old Brouwer, a most heretical disbeliever in ghosts, how he met the horseman returning from his foray into Sleepy Hollow, and was obliged to get up behind him; how they galloped over bush and brake, over hill and swamp, until they reached the bridge; when the horseman suddenly turned into a skeleton, threw old Brouwer into the brook, and sprang away over the tree-tops with a clap of thunder.

This story was immediately matched by a thrice mar-vellous adventure of Brom Bones, who made light of the galloping Hessian as an arrant jockey. He affirmed that, on returning one night from the neighboring village of Sing Sing, he had been overtaken by this midnight trooper; that he had offered to race with him for a bowl of punch, and should have won it too, for Daredevil beat the goblin horse all hollow, but, just as they came to the church bridge, the Hessian bolted, and vanished in a flash of fire.

All these tales, told in that drowsy undertone with which men talk in the dark, the countenances of the listeners only now and then receiving a casual gleam from the glare of a pipe, sank deep in the mind of Ichabod. He repaid them in kind with large extracts from his invaluable author, Cotton Mather, and added many marvellous events that had taken place in his native State of Connecticut, and fearful sights which he had seen in his nightly walks about Sleepy Hollow.

The revel now gradually broke up. The old farmers gathered together their families in their wagons, and were heard for some time rattling along the hollow roads, and over the distant hills. Some of the damsels mounted on pillions behind their favorite swains, and their light-hearted laughter, mingling with the clatter of hoofs, echoed along the silent woodlands, sounding fainter and fainter until they gradually died away – and the late scene of noise and frolic was all silent and deserted. Ichabod only lingered behind, according to the custom of country lovers, to have a tête-à-tête with the heiress, fully convinced that he was now on the high road to success. What passed at this interview I will not pretend to say, for in fact I do not know. Something, however, I fear me, must have gone wrong, for he certainly sallied forth, after no very great interval, with an air quite desolate and chop-fallen. – Oh these women! these women! Could that girl have been playing off any of her coquettish tricks? – Was her encouragement of the poor pedagogue all a mere sham to secure her conquest of his rival? – Heaven only knows, not I! – Let it suffice to say, Ichabod stole forth with the air of one who had been sacking a hen-roost, rather than a fair lady's heart. Without looking to the right or left to notice the scene of rural wealth, on which he had so often gloated, he went straight to the stable, and with several hearty cuffs and kicks, roused his steed most uncourteously from the comfortable quarters in which he was soundly sleeping, dreaming of mountains of corn and oats, and whole valleys of timothy and clover.

It was the very witching time of night that Ichabod, heavy-hearted and crest-fallen, pursued his travel homewards, along the sides of the lofty hills which rise above Tarry Town, and which he had traversed so cheerily in the afternoon. The hour was dismal as himself. Far below him, the Tappan Zee spread its dusky and indistinct waste of waters, with here and there the tall mast of a sloop, riding quietly at anchor under the land. In the dead hush of midnight, he could even hear the barking of the watch dog from the opposite shore of the Hudson; but it was so vague and faint as only to give an idea of his distance from this faithful companion of man. Now and then, too, the long-drawn crowing of a cock, accidentally awakened, would sound far, far off from some farmhouse away among the hills – but it was like a dreaming sound in his ear. No signs of life occurred near him, but occasionally the melancholy chirp of a cricket, or perhaps the guttural twang of a bull-frog, from a neighboring marsh, as if sleeping uncomfortably, and turning suddenly in his bed.

All the stories of ghosts and goblins that he had heard in the afternoon, now came crowding upon his recollection. The night grew darker and darker; the stars seemed to sink deeper in the sky, and driving clouds occasionally hid them from his sight. He had never felt so lonely and dismal. He was, moreover, approaching the very place where many of the scenes of the ghost stories had been laid. In the centre of the road stood an enormous tulip-tree, which towered like a giant above all the other trees of the neighborhood, and formed a kind of landmark. Its limbs were gnarled, and fantastic, large enough to form trunks for ordinary trees, twisting down almost to the earth, and rising again into the air.

It was connected with the tragical story of the unfortunate

André, who had been taken prisoner hard by; and was universally known by the name of Major André's tree. The common people regarded it with a mixture of respect and superstition, partly out of sympathy for the fate of its ill-starred namesake, and partly from the tales of strange sights and doleful lamentations told concerning it.

As Ichabod approached this fearful tree, he began to whistle: he thought his whistle was answered – it was but a blast sweeping sharply through the dry branches. As he approached a little nearer, he thought he saw something white, hanging in the midst of the tree – he paused and ceased whistling; but on looking more narrowly, perceived that it was a place where the tree had been scathed by lightning, and the white wood laid bare. Suddenly he heard a groan – his teeth chattered and his knees smote against the saddle: it was but the rubbing of one huge bough upon another, as they were swayed about by the breeze. He passed the tree in safety, but new perils lay before him.

About two hundred yards from the tree a small brook crossed the road, and ran into a marshy and thickly-wooded glen, known by the name of Wiley's swamp. A few rough logs, laid side by side, served for a bridge over this stream. On that side of the road where the brook entered the wood, a group of oaks and chestnuts, matted thick with wild grape-vines, threw a cavernous gloom over it. To pass this bridge was the severest trial. It was at this identical spot that the unfortunate André was captured, and under the covert of those chestnuts and vines were the sturdy yeomen concealed who surprised him. This has ever since been considered a haunted stream, and fearful are the feelings of the schoolboy who has to pass it alone after dark.

As he approached the stream his heart began to thump; he summoned up, however, all his resolution, gave his horse half a score of kicks in the ribs, and attempted to dash briskly across the bridge; but instead of starting forward, the perverse old animal made a lateral movement, and ran broadside against the fence. Ichabod, whose fears increased with the delay, jerked the reins on the other side, and kicked lustily with the contrary foot: it was all in vain; his steed started, it is true, but it was only to plunge to the opposite side of the road into a thicket of brambles and alder bushes. The schoolmaster now bestowed both whip and heel upon the starveling ribs of old Gunpowder, who dashed forward, snuffling and snorting, but came to a stand just by the bridge, with a suddenness that had nearly sent his rider sprawling over his head. Just at this moment a plashy tramp by the side of the bridge caught the sensitive ear of Ichabod. In the dark shadow of the grove, on the margin of the brook, he beheld something huge, misshapen, black and towering. It stirred not, but seemed gathered up in the gloom, like some gigantic monster ready to spring upon the traveller.

The hair of the affrighted pedagogue rose upon his head with terror. What was to be done? To turn and fly was now too late; and besides, what chance was there of escaping ghost or goblin, if such it was, which could ride upon the wings of the wind? Summoning up, therefore, a show of courage, he demanded in stammering accents – 'Who are you?' He received no reply. He repeated his demand in a still more agitated voice. Still there was no answer. Once more he cudgelled the sides of the inflexible Gunpowder, and, shutting his eyes, broke forth with involuntary fervor into a psalm tune. Just then the shadowy object of alarm put itself in motion, and, with a scramble and a bound, stood at once in the middle of the road. Though the night was dark and dismal, yet the form of the unknown might now in some degree be ascertained. He appeared to be a horseman of large dimensions, and mounted on a black horse of powerful frame. He made no offer of molestation or sociability, but kept aloof on one side of the road, jogging along on the blind side of old Gunpowder, who had now got over his fright and waywardness.

Ichabod, who had no relish for this strange midnight companion, and bethought himself of the adventure of Brom Bones with the Galloping Hessian, now quickened his steed, in hopes of leaving him behind. The stranger, however, quickened his horse to an equal pace. Ichabod pulled up, and fell into a walk, thinking to lag behind – the other did the same. His heart began to sink within him; he endeavored to resume his psalm tune, but his parched tongue clove to the roof of his mouth, and he could not utter a stave. There was something in the moody and dogged silence of this pertinacious companion, that was mysterious and appalling. It was soon fearfully accounted for. On mounting a rising ground, which brought the figure of his fellow-traveller in relief against the sky, gigantic in height, and muffled in a cloak, Ichabod was horror-struck, on perceiving that he was headless! – but his horror was still more increased, on observing that the head, which should have rested on his shoulders, was carried before him on the pommel of the saddle; his terror rose to desperation; he rained a shower of kicks and blows upon Gunpowder; hoping, by a sudden movement, to give his companion the slip – but the spectre started full jump with him. Away then they dashed, through thick and thin; stones flying, and sparks flashing at every bound. Ichabod's flimsy garments fluttered in the air, as he stretched his long lanky body away over his horse's head, in the eagerness of his flight.

They had now reached the road which turns off to Sleepy Hollow; but Gunpowder, who seemed possessed with a demon, instead of keeping up it, made an opposite turn, and plunged headlong down hill to the left. This road leads through a sandy hollow, shaded by trees for about a quarter of a mile, where it crosses the bridge famous in goblin story, and just beyond swells the green knoll on which stands the whitewashed church.

As yet the panic of the steed had given his unskilful rider an apparent advantage in the chase; but just as he had got half way through the hollow, the girths of the saddle gave way, and he felt it slipping from under him. He seized it by the pommel, and endeavored to hold it firm, but in vain; and had just time to save himself by clasping old Gunpowder round the neck, when the saddle fell to the earth, and he heard it trampled under foot by his pursuer. For a moment the terror of Hans Van Ripper's wrath passed across his mind – for it was his Sunday saddle; but this was no time for petty fears; the goblin was hard on his haunches; and (unskilful rider that he was!) he had much ado to maintain his seat; sometimes slipping on one side, sometimes on another, and sometimes jolted on the high ridge of his horse's backbone, with a violence that he verily feared would cleave him asunder.

An opening in the trees now cheered him with the hopes that the church bridge was at hand. The wavering reflection of a silver star in the bosom of the brook told him that he was not mistaken. He saw the walls of the church dimly glaring under the trees beyond. He recollected the place where Brom Bones's ghostly competitor had disappeared. 'If I can but reach that bridge,' thought Ichabod, 'I am safe.' Just then he heard the black steed panting and blowing close behind him; he even fancied that he felt his hot breath. Another convulsive kick in the ribs, and old Gunpowder sprang upon the bridge; he thundered over the resounding planks; he gained the opposite side; and now Ichabod cast a look behind to see if his pursuer should vanish, according to rule, in a flash of fire and brimstone. Just then he saw the goblin rising in his stirrups, and in the very act of hurling his head at him. Ichabod endeavored to dodge the horrible missile, but too late. It encountered his cranium with a tremendous crash – he was tumbled headlong into the dust, and Gunpowder, the black steed, and the goblin rider, passed by like a whirlwind.

The next morning the old horse was found without his saddle, and with the bridle under his feet, soberly cropping the grass at his master's gate. Ichabod did not make his appearance at breakfast – dinner-hour came, but no Ichabod. The boys assembled at the school-house, and strolled idly about the banks of the brook; but no schoolmaster. Hans Van Ripper now began to feel some uneasiness about the fate of poor Ichabod, and his saddle. An inquiry was set on foot, and after diligent investigation they came upon his traces. In one part of the road leading to the church was found the saddle trampled in the dirt; the tracks of horses' hoofs deeply dented in the road, and evidently at furious speed, were traced to the bridge, beyond which, on the bank of a broad part of the brook, where the water ran deep and black, was found the hat of the unfortunate Ichabod, and close beside it a shattered pumpkin.

The brook was searched, but the body of the schoolmaster was not to be discovered. Hans Van Ripper, as executor of his estate, examined the bundle which contained all his worldly effects. They consisted of two shirts and a half; two stocks for the neck; a pair or two of worsted stockings; an old pair of corduroy small-clothes; a rusty razor; a book of psalm tunes, full of dogs' ears; and a broken pitchpipe. As to the books and furniture of the school-house, they belonged to the community, excepting Cotton Mather's History of Witchcraft, a New England Almanac, and a book of dreams and fortune-telling; in which last was a sheet of foolscap much scribbled and blotted in several fruitless attempts to make a copy of verses in honor of the heiress of Van Tassel. These magic books and the poetic scrawls were forthwith consigned to the flames by Hans Van Ripper; who from that time forward determined to send his children no more to school; observing, that he never knew any good come of this same reading and writing. Whatever money the school-master possessed, and he had received his quarter's pay but a day or two before, he must have had about his person at the time of his disappearance.

The mysterious event caused much speculation at the church on the following Sunday. Knots of gazers and gossips were collected in the church-yard, at the bridge, and at the spot where the hat and pumpkin had been found. The stories of Brouwer, of Bones, and a whole budget of others, were called to mind; and when they had diligently considered them all, and compared them with the symptoms of the present case, they shook their heads, and came to the conclusion that Ichabod had been carried off by the galloping Hessian. As he was a bachelor, and in nobody's debt, nobody troubled his head any more about him. The school was removed to a different quarter of the hollow, and another pedagogue reigned in his stead.

It is true, an old farmer, who had been down to New York on a visit several years after, and from whom this account of the ghostly adventure was received, brought home the intelligence that Ichabod Crane was still alive; that he had left the neighborhood, partly through fear of the goblin and Hans Van Ripper, and partly in mortification at having been suddenly dismissed by the heiress; that he had changed his quarters to a distant part of the country; had kept school and studied law at the same time, had been admitted to the bar, turned politician, electioneered, written for the newspapers, and finally had been made a justice of the Ten Pound Court. Brom Bones too, who shortly after his rival's disappearance conducted the blooming Katrina in triumph to the altar, was observed to look exceedingly knowing whenever the story of Ichabod was related, and always burst into a hearty laugh at the mention of the pumpkin; which led some to suspect that he knew more about the matter than he chose to tell.

The old country wives, however, who are the best judges of these matters, maintain to this day that Ichabod was spirited away by supernatural means; and it is a favorite story often told about the neighborhood round the winter evening fire. The bridge became more than ever an object of superstitious awe, and that may be the reason why the road has been altered of late years, so as to approach the church by the border of the mill-pond. The school-house being deserted, soon fell to decay, and was reported to be haunted by the ghost of the unfortunate pedagogue; and the plough-boy, loitering homeward of a still summer evening, has often fancied his voice at a distance, chanting a melancholy psalm tune among the tranquil solitudes of Sleepy Hollow.

DAPHNE DU MAURIER

THE APPLE TREE

IT WAS THREE months after she died that he first noticed the apple tree. He had known of its existence, of course, with the others, standing upon the lawn in front of the house, sloping upwards to the field beyond. Never before, though, had he been aware of this particular tree looking in any way different from its fellows, except that it was the third one on the left, a little apart from the rest and leaning more closely to the terrace.

It was a fine clear morning in early spring, and he was shaving by the open window. As he leant out to sniff the air, the lather on his face, the razor in his hand, his eye fell upon the apple tree. It was a trick of light, perhaps, something to do with the sun coming up over the woods, that happened to catch the tree at this particular moment; but the likeness was unmistakable.

He put his razor down on the window-ledge and stared. The tree was scraggy and of a depressing thinness, possessing none of the gnarled solidity of its companions. Its few branches, growing high up on the trunk like narrow shoulders on a tall body, spread themselves in martyred resignation, as though chilled by the fresh morning air. The roll of wire circling the tree, and reaching to about halfway up the trunk from the base, looked like a grey tweed skirt covering lean limbs; while the topmost branch, sticking up into the air above the ones below, yet sagging slightly, could have been a drooping head poked forward in an attitude of weariness.

71

How often he had seen Midge stand like this, dejected. No matter where it was, whether in the garden, or in the house, or even shopping in the town, she would take upon herself this same stooping posture, suggesting that life treated her hardly, that she had been singled out from her fellows to carry some impossible burden, but in spite of it would endure to the end without complaint. 'Midge, you look worn out, for heaven's sake sit down and take a rest!' But the words would be received with the inevitable shrug of the shoulder, the inevitable sigh, 'Someone has got to keep things going,' and straightening herself she would embark upon the dreary routine of unnecessary tasks she forced herself to do, day in, day out, through the interminable changeless years.

He went on staring at the apple tree. That martyred bent position, the stooping top, the weary branches, the few withered leaves that had not blown away with the wind and rain of the past winter and now shivered in the spring breeze like wispy hair; all of it protested soundlessly to the owner of the garden looking upon it, 'I am like this because of you, because of your neglect.'

He turned away from the window and went on shaving. It would not do to let his imagination run away with him and start building fancies in his mind just when he was settling at long last to freedom. He bathed and dressed and went down to breakfast. Egg and bacon were waiting for him on the hot-plate, and he carried the dish to the single place laid for him at the dining-table. *The Times*, folded smooth and new, was ready for him to read. When Midge was alive he had handed it to her first, from long custom, and when she gave it back to him after breakfast, to take with him to the study, the pages were always in the wrong order and folded crookedly, so that part of the pleasure of reading it was spoilt. The news, too, would be stale to him after she had read the worst of it aloud, which was a morning habit she used to take upon herself, always adding some derogatory remark of her own about what she read. The birth of a daughter to mutual friends would bring a click of the tongue, a little jerk of the head, 'Poor things, another girl,' or if a son, 'A boy can't be much fun to educate these days.' He used to think it psychological, because they themselves were childless, that she should so grudge the entry of new life into the world; but as time passed it became thus with all bright or joyous things, as though there was some fundamental blight upon good cheer.

'It says here that more people went on holiday this year than ever before. Let's hope they enjoyed themselves, that's all.' But no hope lay in her words, only disparagement. Then, having finished breakfast, she would push back her chair and sigh and say, 'Oh well . . .', leaving the sentence unfinished; but the sigh, the shrug of the shoulders, the slope of her long, thin back as she stooped to clear the dishes from the serving-table – thus sparing work for the daily maid – was all part of her long-term reproach, directed at him, that had marred their existence over a span of years.

Silent, punctilious, he would open the door for her to pass through to the kitchen quarters, and she would labour past him, stooping under the weight of the laden tray that there was no need for her to carry, and presently, through the half-open door, he would hear the swish of the running water from the pantry tap. He would return to his chair and sit down again, the crumpled *Times*, a smear of marmalade upon it, lying against the toast-rack; and once again, with monotonous insistence, the question hammered at his mind, 'What have I done?'

It was not as though she nagged. Nagging wives, like mothers-in-law, were chestnut jokes for music-halls. He could not remember Midge ever losing her temper or quarrelling. It was just that the undercurrent of reproach, mingled with suffering nobly borne, spoilt the atmosphere of his home and drove him to a sense of furtiveness and guilt.

Perhaps it would be raining and he, seeking sanctuary within his study, electric fire aglow, his after-breakfast pipe filling the small room with smoke, would settle down before his desk in a pretence of writing letters, but in reality to hide, to feel the snug security of four safe walls that were his alone. Then the door would open and Midge, struggling into a raincoat, her wide-brimmed felt hat pulled low over her brow, would pause and wrinkle her nose in distaste.

'Phew! What a fug.'

He said nothing, but moved slightly in his chair, covering with his arm the novel he had chosen from a shelf in idleness.

'Aren't you going into the town?' she asked him.

'I had not thought of doing so.'

'Oh! Oh, well, it doesn't matter.' She turned away again towards the door.

'Why, is there anything you want done?'

'It's only the fish for lunch. They don't deliver on Wednesdays. Still, I can go myself if you are busy. I only thought . . .'

She was out of the room without finishing her sentence.

'It's all right, Midge,' he called, 'I'll get the car and go and fetch it presently. No sense in getting wet.'

Thinking she had not heard he went out into the hall. She was standing by the open front door, the mizzling rain driving in upon her. She had a long flat basket over her arm and was drawing on a pair of gardening gloves.

'I'm bound to get wet in any case,' she said, 'so it doesn't make much odds. Look at those flowers, they all need staking. I'll go for the fish when I've finished seeing to them.'

Argument was useless. She had made up her mind. He

74

shut the front door after her and sat down again in the study. Somehow the room no longer felt so snug, and a little later, raising his head to the window, he saw her hurry past, her raincoat not buttoned properly and flapping, little drips of water forming on the brim of her hat and the garden basket filled with limp michaelmas daisies already dead. His conscience pricking him, he bent down and turned out one bar of the electric fire.

Or yet again it would be spring, it would be summer. Strolling out hatless into the garden, his hands in his pockets, with no other purpose in his mind but to feel the sun upon his back and stare out upon the woods and fields and the slow winding river, he would hear, from the bedrooms above, the high-pitched whine of the Hoover slow down suddenly, gasp, and die. Midge called down to him as he stood there on the terrace.

'Were you going to do anything?' she said.

He was not. It was the smell of spring, of early summer, that had driven him out into the garden. It was the delicious knowledge that being retired now, no longer working in the City, time was a thing of no account, he could waste it as he pleased.

'No,' he said, 'not on such a lovely day. Why?'

'Oh, never mind,' she answered, 'it's only that the wretched drain under the kitchen window has gone wrong again. Completely plugged up and choked. No one ever sees to it, that's why. I'll have a go at it myself this afternoon.'

Her face vanished from the window. Once more there was a gasp, a rising groan of sound, and the Hoover warmed to its task again. What foolishness that such an interruption could damp the brightness of the day. Not the demand, nor the task itself – clearing a drain was in its own way a schoolboy piece of folly, playing with mud – but that wan face of hers looking out upon the sunlit terrace, the hand that went up wearily to push back a strand of falling hair, and the inevitable sigh before she turned from the window, the unspoken, 'I wish I had the time to stand and do nothing in the sun. Oh, well . . .'

He had ventured to ask once why so much cleaning of the house was necessary. Why there must be the incessant turning out of rooms. Why chairs must be lifted to stand upon other chairs, rugs rolled up and ornaments huddled together on a sheet of newspaper. And why, in particular, the sides of the upstairs corridor, on which no one ever trod, must be polished laboriously by hand, Midge and the daily woman taking it in turns to crawl upon their knees the whole endless length of it, like slaves of bygone days.

Midge stared at him, not understanding.

'You'd be the first to complain,' she said, 'if the house was like a pigsty. You like your comforts.'

So they lived in different worlds, their minds not meeting. Had it been always so? He did not remember. They had been married nearly twenty-five years and were two people who, from force of habit, lived under the same roof.

When he had been in business, it seemed different. He had not noticed it so much. He came home to eat, to sleep, and to go up by train again in the morning. But when he retired he became aware of her forcibly, and day by day his sense of her resentment, of her disapproval, grew stronger.

Finally, in that last year before she died, he felt himself engulfed in it, so that he was led into every sort of petty deception to get away from her, making a pretence of going up to London to have his hair cut, to see the dentist, to lunch with an old business friend; and in reality he would be sitting by his club window, anonymous, at peace.

It was mercifully swift, the illness that took her from

him. Influenza, followed by pneumonia, and she was dead within a week. He hardly knew how it happened, except that as usual she was overtired and caught a cold, and would not stay in bed. One evening, coming home by the late train from London, having sneaked into a cinema during the afternoon, finding release amongst the crowd of warm friendly people enjoying themselves – for it was a bitter December day – he found her bent over the furnace in the cellar, poking and thrusting at the lumps of coke.

She looked up at him, white with fatigue, her face drawn.

'Why, Midge, what on earth are you doing?' he said.

'It's the furnace,' she said, 'we've had trouble with it all day, it won't stay alight. We shall have to get the men to see it tomorrow. I really cannot manage this sort of thing myself.'

There was a streak of coal dust on her cheek. She let the stubby poker fall on the cellar floor. She began to cough, and as she did so winced with pain.

'You ought to be in bed,' he said, 'I never heard of such nonsense. What the dickens does it matter about the furnace?'

'I thought you would be home early,' she said, 'and then you might have known how to deal with it. It's been bitter all day, I can't think what you found to do with yourself in London.'

She climbed the cellar stairs slowly, her back bent, and when she reached the top she stood shivering and half closed her eyes.

'If you don't mind terribly,' she said, 'I'll get your supper right away, to have it done with. I don't want anything myself.'

'To hell with my supper,' he said, 'I can forage for myself. You go up to bed. I'll bring you a hot drink.'

'I tell you, I don't want anything,' she said. 'I can fill my

77

hot-water bottle myself. I only ask one thing of you. And that is to remember to turn out the lights everywhere, before you come up.' She turned into the hall, her shoulders sagging.

'Surely a glass of hot milk?' he began uncertainly, starting to take off his overcoat; and as he did so the torn half of the ten-and-sixpenny seat at the cinema fell from his pocket on to the floor. She saw it. She said nothing. She coughed again and began to drag herself upstairs.

The next morning her temperature was a hundred and three. The doctor came and said she had pneumonia. She asked if she might go to a private ward in the cottage hospital, because having a nurse in the house would make too much work. This was on the Tuesday morning. She went there right away, and they told him on the Friday evening that she was not likely to live through the night. He stood inside the room, after they told him, looking down at her in the high impersonal hospital bed, and his heart was wrung with pity, because surely they had given her too many pillows, she was propped too high, there could be no rest for her that way. He had brought some flowers, but there seemed no purpose now in giving them to the nurse to arrange, because Midge was too ill to look at them. In a sort of delicacy he put them on a table beside the screen, when the nurse was bending down to her.

'Is there anything she needs?' he said. 'I mean, I can easily . . .' He did not finish the sentence, he left it in the air, hoping the nurse would understand his intention, that he was ready to go off in the car, drive somewhere, fetch what was required.

The nurse shook her head. 'We will telephone you,' she said, 'if there is any change.'

What possible change could there be, he wondered, as he found himself outside the hospital? The white pinched face upon the pillows would not alter now, it belonged to no one.

Midge died in the early hours of Saturday morning.

He was not a religious man, he had no profound belief in immortality, but when the funeral was over, and Midge was buried, it distressed him to think of her poor lonely body lying in that brand-new coffin with the brass handles: it seemed such a churlish thing to permit. Death should be different. It should be like bidding farewell to someone at a station before a long journey, but without the strain. There was something of indecency in this haste to bury underground the thing that but for ill-chance would be a living breathing person. In his distress he fancied he could hear Midge saying with a sigh, 'Oh, well . . .' as they lowered the coffin into the open grave.

He hoped with fervour that after all there might be a future in some unseen Paradise and that poor Midge, unaware of what they were doing to her mortal remains, walked somewhere in green fields. But who with, he wondered? Her parents had died in India many years ago; she would not have much in common with them now if they met her at the gates of Heaven. He had a sudden picture of her waiting her turn in a queue, rather far back, as was always her fate in queues, with that large shopping bag of woven straw which she took everywhere, and on her face that patient martyred look. As she passed through the turnstile into Paradise she looked at him, reproachfully.

These pictures, of the coffin and the queue, remained with him for about a week, fading a little day by day. Then he forgot her. Freedom was his, and the sunny empty house, the bright crisp winter. The routine he followed belonged to him alone. He never thought of Midge until the morning he looked out upon the apple tree.

Later that day he was taking a stroll round the garden, and

he found himself drawn to the tree through curiosity. It had been stupid fancy after all. There was nothing singular about it. An apple tree like any other apple tree. He remembered then that it had always been a poorer tree than its fellows, was in fact more than half dead, and at one time there had been talk of chopping it down, but the talk came to nothing. Well, it would be something for him to do over the weekend. Axing a tree was healthy exercise, and apple wood smelt good. It would be a treat to have it burning on the fire.

Unfortunately wet weather set in for nearly a week after that day, and he was unable to accomplish the task he had set himself. No sense in pottering out of doors this weather, and getting a chill into the bargain. He still noticed the tree from his bedroom window. It began to irritate him, humped there, straggling and thin, under the rain. The weather was not cold, and the rain that fell upon the garden was soft and gentle. None of the other trees wore this aspect of dejection. There was one young tree – only planted a few years back, he recalled quite well – growing to the right of the old one and standing straight and firm, the lithe young branches lifted to the sky, positively looking as if it enjoyed the rain. He peered through the window at it, and smiled. Now why the devil should he suddenly remember that incident, years back, during the war, with the girl who came to work on the land for a few months at the neighbouring farm? He did not suppose he had thought of her in months. Besides, there was nothing to it. At weekends he had helped them at the farm himself – war work of a sort – and she was always there, cheerful and pretty and smiling; she had dark curling hair, crisp and boyish, and a skin like a very young apple.

He looked forward to seeing her, Saturdays and Sundays; it was an antidote to the inevitable news bulletins put on throughout the day by Midge, and to ceaseless war talk. He liked looking at the child – she was scarcely more than that, nineteen or so – in her slim breeches and gay shirts; and when she smiled it was as though she embraced the world.

He never knew how it happened, and it was such a little thing; but one afternoon he was in the shed doing something to the tractor, bending over the engine, and she was beside him, close to his shoulder, and they were laughing together; and he turned round, to take a bit of waste to clean a plug, and suddenly she was in his arms and he was kissing her. It was a happy thing, spontaneous and free, and the girl so warm and jolly, with her fresh young mouth. Then they went on with the work of the tractor, but united now, in a kind of intimacy that brought gaiety to them both, and peace as well. When it was time for the girl to go and feed the pigs he followed her from the shed, his hand on her shoulder, a careless gesture that meant nothing really, a half caress; and as they came out into the yard he saw Midge standing there, staring at them.

'I've got to go in to a Red Cross meeting,' she said. 'I can't get the car to start. I called you. You didn't seem to hear.'

Her face was frozen. She was looking at the girl. At once guilt covered him. The girl said good evening cheerfully to Midge, and crossed the yard to the pigs.

He went with Midge to the car and managed to start it with the handle. Midge thanked him, her voice without expression. He found himself unable to meet her eyes. This, then, was adultery. This was sin. This was the second page in a Sunday newspaper – 'Husband Intimate with Land Girl in Shed. Wife Witnesses Act.' His hands were shaking when he got back to the house and he had to pour himself a drink. Nothing was ever said. Midge never mentioned the matter. Some craven instinct kept him from the farm the next weekend, and then he heard that the girl's mother had been taken ill and she had been called back home.

He never saw her again. Why, he wondered, should he remember her suddenly, on such a day, watching the rain falling on the apple trees? He must certainly make a point of cutting down the old dead tree, if only for the sake of bringing more sunshine to the little sturdy one; it hadn't a fair chance, growing there so close to the other.

On Friday afternoon he went round to the vegetable garden to find Willis, the jobbing gardener, who came three days a week, to pay him his wages. He wanted, too, to look in the toolshed and see if the axe and saw were in good condition. Willis kept everything neat and tidy there – this was Midge's training – and the axe and saw were hanging in their accustomed place upon the wall.

He paid Willis his money, and was turning away when the man suddenly said to him, 'Funny thing, sir, isn't it, about the old apple tree?'

The remark was so unexpected that it came as a shock. He felt himself change colour.

'Apple tree? What apple tree?' he said.

'Why, the one at the far end, near the terrace,' answered Willis. 'Been barren as long as I've worked here, and that's some years now. Never an apple from her, nor as much as a sprig of blossom. We were going to chop her up that cold winter, if you remember, and we never did. Well, she's taken on a new lease now. Haven't you noticed?' The gardener watched him smiling, a knowing look in his eye.

What did the fellow mean? It was not possible that he had been struck also by that fantastic freak resemblance – no, it was out of the question, indecent, blasphemous; besides, he had put it out of his own mind now, he had not thought of it again.

'I've noticed nothing,' he said, on the defensive.

Willis laughed. 'Come round to the terrace, sir,' he said, 'I'll show you.'

They went together to the sloping lawn, and when they came to the apple tree Willis put his hand up and pulled down a branch within reach. It creaked a little as he did so, as though stiff and unyielding, and Willis brushed away some of the dry lichen and revealed the spiky twigs. 'Look there, sir,' he said, 'she's growing buds. Look at them, feel them for yourself. There's life here yet, and plenty of it. Never known such a thing before. See this branch too.' He released the first, and leant up to reach another.

Willis was right. There were buds in plenty, but so small and brown that it seemed to him they scarcely deserved the name, they were more like blemishes upon the twig, dusty and dry. He put his hands in his pockets. He felt a queer distaste to touch them.

'I don't think they'll amount to much,' he said.

'I don't know, sir,' said Willis, 'I've got hopes. She's stood the winter, and if we get no more bad frosts there's no knowing what we'll see. It would be some joke to watch the old tree blossom. She'll bear fruit yet.' He patted the trunk with his open hand, in a gesture at once familiar and affectionate.

The owner of the apple tree turned away. For some reason he felt irritated with Willis. Anyone would think the damned tree lived. And now his plan to axe the tree, over the weekend, would come to nothing.

'It's taking the light from the young tree,' he said. 'Surely it would be more to the point if we did away with this one, and gave the little one more room?'

He moved across to the young tree and touched a limb. No lichen here. The branches smooth. Buds upon every twig, curling tight. He let go the branch and it sprang away from him, resilient.

'Do away with her, sir,' said Willis, 'while there's still life in her? Oh no, sir, I wouldn't do that. She's doing no harm to the young tree. I'd give the old tree one more chance. If she doesn't bear fruit, we'll have her down next winter.'

'All right, Willis,' he said, and walked swiftly away. Somehow he did not want to discuss the matter any more.

That night, when he went to bed, he opened the window wide as usual and drew back the curtains; he could not bear to wake up in the morning and find the room close. It was full moon, and the light shone down upon the terrace and the lawn above it, ghostly pale and still. No wind blew. A hush upon the place. He leant out, loving the silence. The moon shone full upon the little apple tree, the young one. There was a radiance about it in this light that gave it a fairy-tale quality. Small and lithe and slim, the young tree might have been a dancer, her arms upheld, poised ready on her toes for flight. Such a careless, happy grace about it. Brave young tree. Away to the left stood the other one, half of it in shadow still. Even the moonlight could not give it beauty. What in heaven's name was the matter with the thing that it had to stand there, humped and stooping, instead of looking upwards to the light? It marred the still quiet night, it spoilt the setting. He had been a fool to give way to Willis and agree to spare the tree. Those ridiculous buds would never blossom, and even if they did . . .

His thoughts wandered, and for the second time that week he found himself remembering the land-girl and her joyous smile. He wondered what had happened to her. Married probably, with a young family. Made some chap happy, no doubt. Oh, well . . . He smiled. Was he going to make use of that expression now? Poor Midge! Then he caught his breath and stood quite still, his hand upon the curtain. The apple tree, the one on the left, was no longer in shadow. The moon shone upon the withered branches, and they looked like skeleton's arms raised in supplication. Frozen arms, stiff and numb with pain. There was no wind, and the other trees were motionless; but there, in those topmost branches, something shivered and stirred, a breeze that came from nowhere and died away again. Suddenly a branch fell from the apple tree to the ground below. It was the near branch, with the small dark buds upon it, which he would not touch. No rustle, no breath of movement came from the other trees. He went on staring at the branch as it lay there on the grass, under the moon. It stretched across the shadow of the young tree close to it, pointing as though in accusation.

For the first time in his life that he could remember he drew the curtains over the window to shut out the light of the moon.

Willis was supposed to keep to the vegetable garden. He had never shown his face much round the front when Midge was alive. That was because Midge attended to the flowers. She even used to mow the grass, pushing the wretched machine up and down the slope, her back bent low over the handles.

It had been one of the tasks she set herself, like keeping the bedrooms swept and polished. Now Midge was no longer there to attend to the front garden and to tell him where he should work, Willis was always coming through to the front. The gardener liked the change. It made him feel responsible.

'I can't understand how that branch came to fall, sir,' he said on the Monday.

'What branch?'

85

'Why, the branch on the apple tree. The one we were looking at before I left.'

'It was rotten, I suppose. I told you the tree was dead.'

'Nothing rotten about it, sir. Why, look at it. Broke clean off.'

Once again the owner was obliged to follow his man up the slope above the terrace. Willis picked up the branch. The lichen upon it was wet, bedraggled looking, like matted hair.

'You didn't come again to test the branch, over the weekend, and loosen it in some fashion, did you, sir?' asked the gardener.

'I most certainly did not,' replied the owner, irritated. 'As a matter of fact I heard the branch fall, during the night. I was opening the bedroom window at the time.'

'Funny. It was a still night too.'

'These things often happen to old trees. Why you bother about this one I can't imagine. Anyone would think . . .'

He broke off; he did not know how to finish the sentence.

'Anyone would think that the tree was valuable,' he said.

The gardener shook his head. 'It's not the value,' he said. 'I don't reckon for a moment that this tree is worth any money at all. It's just that after all this time, when we thought her dead, she's alive and kicking, as you might say. Freak of nature, I call it. We'll hope no other branches fall before she blossoms.'

Later, when the owner set off for his afternoon walk, he saw the man cutting away the grass below the tree and placing new wire around the base of the trunk. It was quite ridiculous. He did not pay the fellow a fat wage to tinker about with a half-dead tree. He ought to be in the kitchen garden, growing vegetables. It was too much effort, though, to argue with him.

He returned home about half past five. Tea was a discarded

meal since Midge had died, and he was looking forward to his armchair by the fire, his pipe, his whisky-and-soda, and silence.

The fire had not long been lit and the chimney was smoking. There was a queer, rather sickly smell about the living-room. He threw open the windows and went upstairs to change his heavy shoes. When he came down again the smoke still clung about the room and the smell was as strong as ever. Impossible to name it. Sweetish, strange. He called to the woman out in the kitchen.

'There's a funny smell in the house,' he said. 'What is it?'

The woman came out into the hall from the back.

'What sort of a smell, sir?' she said, on the defensive.

'It's in the living-room,' he said. 'The room was full of smoke just now. Have you been burning something?'

Her face cleared. 'It must be the logs,' she said. 'Willis cut them up specially, sir, he said you would like them.'

'What logs are those?'

'He said it was apple wood, sir, from a branch he had sawed up. Apple wood burns well, I've always heard. Some people fancy it very much. I don't notice any smell myself, but I've got a slight cold.'

Together they looked at the fire. Willis had cut the logs small. The woman, thinking to please him, had piled several on top of one another, to make a good fire to last. There was no great blaze. The smoke that came from them was thin and poor. Greenish in colour. Was it possible she did not notice that sickly rancid smell?

'The logs are wet,' he said abruptly. 'Willis should have known better. Look at them. Quite useless on my fire.'

The woman's face took on a set, rather sulky expression. 'I'm very sorry,' she said. 'I didn't notice anything wrong with them when I came to light the fire. They seemed to start

87

well. I've always understood apple wood was very good for burning, and Willis said the same. He told me to be sure and see that you had these on the fire this evening, he had made a special job of cutting them for you. I thought you knew about it and had given orders.'

'Oh, all right,' he answered, abruptly. 'I dare say they'll burn in time. It's not your fault.'

He turned his back on her and poked at the fire, trying to separate the logs. While she remained in the house there was nothing he could do. To remove the damp smouldering logs and throw them somewhere round the back, and then light the fire afresh with dry sticks would arouse comment. He would have to go through the kitchen to the back passage where the kindling wood was kept, and she would stare at him, and come forward and say, 'Let me do it, sir. Has the fire gone out then?' No, he must wait until after supper, when she had cleared away and washed up and gone off for the night. Meanwhile, he would endure the smell of the apple wood as best he could.

He poured out his drink, lit his pipe and stared at the fire. It gave out no heat at all, and with the central heating off in the house the living-room struck chill. Now and again a thin wisp of the greenish smoke puffed from the logs, and with it seemed to come that sweet sickly smell, unlike any sort of wood smoke that he knew. That interfering fool of a gardener . . . Why saw up the logs? He must have known they were damp. Riddled with damp. He leant forward, staring more closely. Was it damp, though, that oozed there in a thin trickle from the pale logs? No, it was sap, unpleasant, slimy.

He seized the poker, and in a fit of irritation thrust it between the logs, trying to stir them to flame, to change that green smoke into a normal blaze. The effort was useless. The logs would not burn. And all the while the trickle of sap ran on to the grate and the sweet smell filled the room, turning his stomach. He took his glass and his book and went and turned on the electric fire in the study and sat in there instead.

It was idiotic. It reminded him of the old days, how he would make a pretence of writing letters, and go and sit in the study because of Midge in the living-room. She had a habit of yawning in the evenings, when her day's work was done; a habit of which she was quite unconscious. She would settle herself on the sofa with her knitting, the click-click of the needles going fast and furious; and suddenly they would start, those shattering yawns, rising from the depths of her, a prolonged 'Ah . . . Ah . . . Hi-Oh!' followed by the inevitable sigh. Then there would be silence except for the knitting needles, but as he sat behind his book, waiting, he knew that within a few minutes another yawn would come, another sigh.

A hopeless sort of anger used to stir within him, a longing to throw down his book and say, 'Look, if you are so tired, wouldn't it be better if you went to bed?'

Instead, he controlled himself, and after a little while, when he could bear it no longer, he would get up and leave the living-room, and take refuge in the study. Now he was doing the same thing, all over again, because of the apple logs. Because of the damned sickly smell of the smouldering wood.

He went on sitting in his chair by the desk, waiting for supper. It was nearly nine o'clock before the daily woman had cleared up, turned down his bed and gone for the night.

He returned to the living-room, which he had not entered since leaving it earlier in the evening. The fire was out. It had made some effort to burn, because the logs were thinner than they had been before, and had sunk low into the basket grate. The ash was meagre, yet the sickly smell clung to the dying embers. He went out into the kitchen and found an empty scuttle and brought it back into the living-room. Then he lifted the logs into it, and the ashes too. There must have been some damp residue in the scuttle, or the logs were still not dry, because as they settled there they seemed to turn darker than before, with a kind of scum upon them. He carried the scuttle down to the cellar, opened the door of the central heating furnace, and threw the lot inside.

He remembered then, too late, that the central heating had been given up now for two or three weeks, owing to the spring weather, and that unless he relit it now the logs would remain there, untouched, until the following winter. He found paper, matches, and a can of paraffin, and setting the whole alight closed the door of the furnace, and listened to the roar of flames. That would settle it. He waited a moment and then went up the steps, back to the kitchen passage, to lay and relight the fire in the living-room. The business took time, he had to find kindling and coal, but with patience he got the new fire started, and finally settled himself down in his arm-chair before it.

He had been reading perhaps for twenty minutes before he became aware of the banging door. He put down his book and listened. Nothing at first. Then, yes, there it was again. A rattle, a slam of an unfastened door in the kitchen quarters. He got up and went along to shut it. It was the door at the top of the cellar stairs. He could have sworn he had fastened it. The catch must have worked loose in some way. He switched on the light at the head of the stairs, and bent to examine the catch. There seemed nothing wrong with it. He was about to close the door firmly when he noticed the smell again. The sweet sickly smell of smouldering apple wood. It was creeping up from the cellar, finding its way to the passage above.

Suddenly, for no reason, he was seized with a kind of fear, a feeling of panic almost. What if the smell filled the whole house through the night, came up from the kitchen quarters to the floor above, and while he slept found its way into his bedroom, choking him, stifling him, so that he could not breathe? The thought was ridiculous, insane – and yet . . .

Once more he forced himself to descend the steps into the cellar. No sound came from the furnace, no roar of flames. Wisps of smoke, thin and green, oozed their way from the fastened furnace door; it was this that he had noticed from the passage above.

He went to the furnace and threw open the door. The paper had all burnt away, and the few shavings with them. But the logs, the apple logs, had not burnt at all. They lay there as they had done when he threw them in, one charred limb above another, black and huddled, like the bones of someone darkened and dead by fire. Nausea rose in him. He thrust his handkerchief into his mouth, choking. Then, scarcely knowing what he did, he ran up the steps to find the empty scuttle, and with a shovel and tongs tried to pitch the logs back into it, scraping for them through the narrow door of the furnace. He was retching in his belly all the while. At last the scuttle was filled, and he carried it up the steps and through the kitchen to the back door.

He opened the door. Tonight there was no moon and it was raining. Turning up the collar of his coat he peered about him in the darkness, wondering where he should throw the logs. Too wet and dark to stagger all the way to the kitchen garden and chuck them on the rubbish heap, but in the field behind the garage the grass was thick and long and they might lie there hidden. He crunched his way over the gravel drive, and coming to the fence beside the field threw his burden on to the concealing grass. There they could rot and perish, grow sodden with rain, and in the end become part of the mouldy earth; he did not care. The responsibility was his no longer. They were out of his house, and it did not matter what became of them.

He returned to the house, and this time made sure the cellar door was fast. The air was clear again, the smell had gone.

He went back to the living-room to warm himself before the fire, but his hands and feet, wet with the rain, and his stomach, still queasy from the pungent smoke, combined together to chill his whole person, and he sat there, shuddering.

He slept badly when he went to bed that night, and awoke in the morning feeling out of sorts. He had a headache, and an ill-tasting tongue. He stayed indoors. His liver was thoroughly upset. To relieve his feelings he spoke sharply to the daily woman.

'I've caught a bad chill,' he said to her, 'trying to get warm last night. So much for apple wood. The smell of it has affected my inside as well. You can tell Willis, when he comes tomorrow.'

She looked at him in disbelief.

'I'm sure I'm very sorry,' she said. 'I told my sister about the wood last night, when I got home, and that you had not fancied it. She said it was most unusual. Apple wood is considered quite a luxury to burn, and burns well, what's more.'

'This lot didn't, that's all I know,' he said to her, 'and I never want to see any more of it. As for the smell . . . I can taste it still, it's completely turned me up.'

Her mouth tightened. 'I'm sorry,' she said. And then, as

92

she left the dining-room, her eye fell on the empty whisky bottle on the sideboard. She hesitated a moment, then put it on her tray.

'You've finished with this, sir?' she said.

Of course he had finished with it. It was obvious. The bottle was empty. He realized the implication, though. She wanted to suggest that the idea of apple-wood smoke upsetting him was all my eye, he had done himself too well. Damned impertinence.

'Yes,' he said, 'you can bring another in its place.'

That would teach her to mind her own business.

He was quite sick for several days, queasy and giddy, and finally rang up the doctor to come and have a look at him. The story of the apple wood sounded nonsense, when he told it, and the doctor, after examining him, appeared unimpressed.

'Just a chill on the liver,' he said, 'damp feet, and possibly something you've eaten combined. I hardly think wood smoke has much to do with it. You ought to take more exercise, if you're inclined to have a liver. Play golf. I don't know how I should keep fit without my weekend golf.' He laughed, packing up his bag. 'I'll make you up some medicine,' he said, 'and once this rain has cleared off I should get out and into the air. It's mild enough, and all we want now is a bit of sunshine to bring everything on. Your garden is farther ahead than mine. Your fruit trees are ready to blossom.' And then, before leaving the room, he added, 'You mustn't forget, you had a bad shock a few months ago. It takes time to get over these things. You're still missing your wife, you know. Best thing is to get out and about and see people. Well, take care of yourself.'

His patient dressed and went downstairs. The fellow meant well, of course, but his visit had been a waste of time.

'You're still missing your wife, you know.' How little the doctor understood. Poor Midge . . . At least he himself had the honesty to admit that he did not miss her at all, that now she was gone he could breathe, he was free, and that apart from the upset liver he had not felt so well for years.

During the few days he had spent in bed the daily woman had taken the opportunity to spring-clean the living-room. An unnecessary piece of work, but he supposed it was part of the legacy Midge had left behind her. The room looked scrubbed and straight and much too tidy. His own personal litter cleared, books and papers neatly stacked. It was an infernal nuisance, really, having anyone to do for him at all. It would not take much for him to sack her and fend for himself as best he could. Only the bother, the tie of cooking and washing up, prevented him. The ideal life, of course, was that led by a man out East, or in the South Seas, who took a native wife. No problem there. Silence, good service, perfect waiting, excellent cooking, no need for conversation; and then, if you wanted something more than that, there she was, young, warm, a companion for the dark hours. No criticism ever, the obedience of an animal to its master, and the light-hearted laughter of a child. Yes, they had wisdom all right, those fellows who broke away from convention. Good luck to them.

He strolled over to the window and looked out up the sloping lawn. The rain was stopping and tomorrow it would be fine; he would be able to get out, as the doctor had suggested. The man was right, too, about the fruit trees. The little one near the steps was in flower already, and a blackbird had perched himself on one of the branches, which swayed slightly under his weight.

The rain-drops glistened and the opening buds were very curled and pink, but when the sun broke through tomorrow they would turn white and soft against the blue of the sky. He must find his old camera, and put a film in it, and photograph the little tree. The others would be in flower, too, during the week. As for the old one, there on the left, it looked as dead as ever; or else the so-called buds were so brown they did not show up from this distance. Perhaps the shedding of the branch had been its finish. And a good job too.

He turned away from the window and set about rearranging the room to his taste, spreading his things about. He liked pottering, opening drawers, taking things out and putting them back again. There was a red pencil in one of the side tables that must have slipped down behind a pile of books and been found during the turn-out. He sharpened it, gave it a sleek fine point. He found a new film in another drawer, and kept it out to put in his camera in the morning. There were a number of papers and old photographs in the drawer, heaped in a jumble, and snapshots too, dozens of them. Midge used to look after these things at one time and put them in albums; then during the war she must have lost interest, or had too many other things to do.

All this junk could really be cleared away. It would have made a fine fire the other night, and might have got even the apple logs to burn. There was little sense in keeping any of it. This appalling photo of Midge, for instance, taken heaven knows how many years ago, not long after their marriage, judging from the style of it. Did she really wear her hair that way? That fluffy mop, much too thick and bushy for her face, which was long and narrow even then. The low neck, pointing to a V, and the dangling earrings, and the smile, too eager, making her mouth seem larger than it was. In the left-hand corner she had written 'To my own darling Buzz, from his loving Midge'. He had completely forgotten his old nickname. It had been dropped years back, and he seemed to remember he had never cared for it: he had found it ridiculous and embarrassing and had chided her for using it in front of people.

He tore the photograph in half and threw it on the fire. He watched it curl up upon itself and burn, and the last to go was that vivid smile. My own darling Buzz . . . Suddenly he remembered the evening dress in the photograph. It was green, not her colour ever, turning her sallow; and she had bought it for some special occasion, some big dinner party with friends who were celebrating their wedding anniversary. The idea of the dinner had been to invite all those friends and neighbours who had been married roughly around the same time, which was the reason Midge and he had gone.

There was a lot of champagne, and one or two speeches, and much conviviality, laughter, and joking – some of the joking rather broad – and he remembered that when the evening was over, and they were climbing into the car to drive away, his host, with a gust of laughter, said, 'Try paying your addresses in a top hat, old boy, they say it never fails!' He had been aware of Midge beside him, in that green evening frock, sitting very straight and still, and on her face that same smile which she had worn in the photograph just destroyed, eager yet uncertain, doubtful of the meaning of the words that her host, slightly intoxicated, had let fall upon the evening air, yet wishing to seem advanced, anxious to please, and more than either of these things desperately anxious to attract.

When he had put the car away in the garage and gone into the house he had found her waiting there, in the living-room, for no reason at all. Her coat was thrown off to show the evening dress, and the smile, rather uncertain, was on her face.

He yawned, and settling himself down in a chair picked up a book. She waited a little while, then slowly took up her coat and went upstairs. It must have been shortly afterwards that she had that photograph taken. 'My own darling Buzz, from his loving Midge.' He threw a great handful of dry sticks on to the fire. They crackled and split and turned the photograph to ashes. No damp green logs tonight . . .

It was fine and warm the following day. The sun shone, and the birds sang. He had a sudden impulse to go to London. It was a day for sauntering along Bond Street, watching the passing crowds. A day for calling in at his tailors, for having a hair-cut, for eating a dozen oysters at his favourite bar. The chill had left him. The pleasant hours stretched before him. He might even look in at a matinée.

The day passed without incident, peaceful, untiring, just as he had planned, making a change from day-by-day country routine. He drove home about seven o'clock, looking forward to his drink and to his dinner. It was so warm he did not need his overcoat, not even now, with the sun gone down. He waved a hand to the farmer, who happened to be passing the gate as he turned into the drive.

'Lovely day,' he shouted.

The man nodded, smiled. 'Can do with plenty of these from now on,' he shouted back. Decent fellow. They had always been very matey since those war days, when he had driven the tractor.

He put away the car and had a drink, and while waiting for supper took a stroll around the garden. What a difference those hours of sunshine had made to everything. Several daffodils were out, narcissi too, and the green hedgerows fresh and sprouting. As for the apple trees, the buds had burst, and they were all of them in flower. He went to his little favourite and touched the blossom. It felt soft to his

97

hand and he gently shook a bough. It was firm, well-set, and would not fall. The scent was scarcely perceptible as yet, but in a day or two, with a little more sun, perhaps a shower or two, it would come from the open flower and softly fill the air, never pungent, never strong, a modest scent. A scent which you would have to find for yourself, as the bees did. Once found it stayed with you, it lingered always, alluring, comforting, and sweet. He patted the little tree, and went down the steps into the house.

Next morning, at breakfast, there came a knock on the dining-room window, and the daily woman said that Willis was outside and wanted to have a word with him. He asked Willis to step in.

The gardener looked aggrieved. Was it trouble, then?

'I'm sorry to bother you, sir,' he said, 'but I had a few words with Mr Jackson this morning. He's been complaining.'

Jackson was the farmer, who owned the neighbouring fields.

'What's he complaining about?'

'Says I've been throwing wood over the fence into his field, and the young foal out there, with the mare, tripped over it and went lame. I've never thrown wood over the fence in my life, sir. Quite nasty he was, sir. Spoke of the value of the foal, and it might spoil his chances to sell it.'

'I hope you told him, then, it wasn't true.'

'I did, sir. But the point is someone has been throwing wood over the fence. He showed me the very spot. Just behind the garage. I went with Mr Jackson, and there they were. Logs had been tipped there, sir. I thought it best to come to you about it before I spoke in the kitchen, otherwise you know how it is, there would be unpleasantness.'

He felt the gardener's eye upon him. No way out, of course. And it was Willis's fault in the first place.

'No need to say anything in the kitchen, Willis,' he said. 'I threw the logs there myself. You brought them into the house, without my asking you to do so, with the result that they put out my fire, filled the room with smoke, and ruined an evening. I chucked them over the fence in a devil of a temper, and if they have damaged Jackson's foal you can apologize for me, and tell him I'll pay him compensation. All I ask is that you don't bring any more logs like those into the house again.'

'No sir, I understood they had not been a success. I didn't think, though, that you would go so far as to throw them out.'

'Well, I did. And there's an end to it.'

'Yes, sir.' He made as if to go, but before he left the dining-room he paused and said, 'I can't understand about the logs not burning, all the same. I took a small piece back to the wife, and it burnt lovely in our kitchen, bright as anything.'

'It did not burn here.'

'Anyway, the old tree is making up for one spoilt branch, sir. Have you seen her this morning?'

'No.'

'It's yesterday's sun that has done it, sir, and the warm night. Quite a treat she is, with all the blossom. You should go out and take a look at her directly.'

Willis left the room, and he continued his breakfast.

Presently he went out on to the terrace. At first he did not go up on to the lawn; he made a pretence of seeing to other things, of getting the heavy garden seat out, now that the weather was set fair. And then, fetching a pair of clippers, he did a bit of pruning to the few roses, under the windows. Yet, finally, something drew him to the tree.

It was just as Willis said. Whether it was the sun, the warmth, the mild still night, he could not tell; but the small brown buds had unfolded themselves, had ripened into flower, and now spread themselves above his head into a fantastic cloud of white, moist blossom. It grew thickest at the top of the tree, the flowers so clustered together that they looked like wad upon wad of soggy cotton wool, and all of it, from the topmost branches to those nearer to the ground, had this same pallid colour of sickly white.

It did not resemble a tree at all; it might have been a flapping tent, left out in the rain by campers who had gone away, or else a mop, a giant mop, whose streaky surface had been caught somehow by the sun, and so turned bleached. The blossom was too thick, too great a burden for the long thin trunk, and the moisture clinging to it made it heavier still. Already, as if the effort had been too much, the lower flowers, those nearest the ground, were turning brown; yet there had been no rain.

Well, there it was. Willis had been proved right. The tree had blossomed. But instead of blossoming to life, to beauty, it had somehow, deep in nature, gone awry and turned a freak. A freak which did not know its texture or its shape, but thought to please. Almost as though it said, self-conscious, with a smirk, 'Look. All this is for you.'

Suddenly he heard a step behind him. It was Willis.

'Fine sight, sir, isn't it?'

'Sorry, I don't admire it. The blossom is far too thick.'

The gardener stared at him and said nothing. It struck him that Willis must think him very difficult, very hard, and possibly eccentric. He would go and discuss him in the kitchen with the daily woman.

He forced himself to smile at Willis.

'Look here,' he said, 'I don't mean to damp you. But all this blossom doesn't interest me. I prefer it small and light and colourful, like the little tree. But you take some of it back home, to your wife. Cut as much of it as you like, I don't mind at all. I'd like you to have it.'

He waved his arm, generously. He wanted Willis to go now, and fetch a ladder, and carry the stuff away.

The man shook his head. He looked quite shocked.

'No, thank you, sir, I wouldn't dream of it. It would spoil the tree. I want to wait for the fruit. That's what I'm banking on, the fruit.'

There was no more to be said.

'All right, Willis. Don't bother, then.'

He went back to the terrace. But when he sat down there in the sun, looking up the sloping lawn, he could not see the little tree at all, standing modest and demure above the steps, her soft flowers lifting to the sky. She was dwarfed and hidden by the freak, with its great cloud of sagging petals, already wilting, dingy white, on to the grass beneath. And whichever way he turned his chair, this way or that upon the terrace, it seemed to him that he could not escape the tree, that it stood there above him, reproachful, anxious, desirous of the admiration that he could not give.

That summer he took a longer holiday than he had done for many years – a bare ten days with his old mother in Norfolk, instead of the customary month that he had been used to spend with Midge, and the rest of August and the whole of September in Switzerland and Italy.

He took his car, and so was free to motor from place to place as the mood inclined. He cared little for sight-seeing or excursions, and was not much of a climber. What he liked most was to come upon a little town in the cool of the evening, pick out a small but comfortable hotel, and then stay there, if it pleased him, for two or three days at a time, doing nothing, mooching.

He liked sitting about in the sun all morning, at some café or restaurant, with a glass of wine in front of him, watching the people; so many gay young creatures seemed to travel nowadays. He enjoyed the chatter of conversation around him, as long as he did not have to join in; and now and again a smile would come his way, a word or two of greeting from some guest in the same hotel, but nothing to commit him, merely a sense of being in the swim, of being a man of leisure on his own, abroad.

The difficulty in the old days, on holiday anywhere with Midge, would be her habit of striking up acquaintance with people, some other couple who struck her as looking 'nice' or, as she put it, 'our sort'. It would start with conversation over coffee, and then pass on to mutual planning of shared days, car drives in foursomes – he could not bear it, the holiday would be ruined.

Now, thank heaven, there was no need for this. He did what he liked, in his own time. There was no Midge to say, 'Well, shall we be moving?' when he was still sitting contentedly over his wine, no Midge to plan a visit to some old church that did not interest him.

He put on weight during his holiday, and he did not mind. There was no one to suggest a good long walk to keep fit after the rich food, thus spoiling the pleasant somnolence that comes with coffee and dessert; no one to glance, surprised, at the sudden wearing of a jaunty shirt, a flamboyant tie.

Strolling through the little towns and villages, hatless, smoking a cigar, receiving smiles from the jolly young folk around him, he felt himself a dog. This was the life, no worries, no cares. No 'We have to be back on the fifteenth because of that committee meeting at the hospital'; no 'We can't possibly leave the house shut up for longer than a fortnight, something might happen'. Instead, the bright lights of a little country fair, in a village whose name he did not even bother to find out; the tinkle of music, boys and girls laughing, and he himself, after a bottle of the local wine, bowing to a young thing with a gay handkerchief round her head and sweeping her off to dance under the hot tent. No matter if her steps did not harmonize with his – it was years since he had danced – this was the thing, this was it. He released her when the music stopped, and off she ran, giggling, back to her young friends, laughing at him no doubt. What of it? He had had his fun.

He left Italy when the weather turned, at the end of September, and was back home the first week in October. No problem to it. A telegram to the daily woman, with the probable date of arrival, and that was all. Even a brief holiday with Midge and the return meant complications. Written instructions about groceries, milk, and bread; airing of beds, lighting of fires, reminders about the delivery of the morning papers. The whole business turned into a chore.

He turned into the drive on a mellow October evening and there was smoke coming from the chimneys, the front door open, and his pleasant home awaiting him. No rushing through to the back regions to learn of possible plumbing disasters, breakages, water shortages, food difficulties; the daily woman knew better than to bother him with these. Merely, 'Good evening, sir. I hope you had a good holiday. Supper at the usual time?' And then silence. He could have his drink, light his pipe, and relax; the small pile of letters did not matter. No feverish tearing of them open, and then the start of the telephoning, the hearing of those endless one-sided conversations between women friends. 'Well? How are things? Really? My dear . . . And what did you say to that? . . . She did? . . . I can't possibly on Wednesday . . .'

He stretched himself contentedly, stiff after his drive, and gazed comfortably around the cheerful, empty living-room. He was hungry, after his journey up from Dover, and the chop seemed rather meagre after foreign fare. But there it was, it wouldn't hurt him to return to plainer food. A sardine on toast followed the chop, and then he looked about him for dessert.

There was a plate of apples on the sideboard. He fetched them and put them down in front of him on the dining-room table. Poor-looking things. Small and wizened, dullish brown in colour. He bit into one, but as soon as the taste of it was on his tongue he spat it out. The thing was rotten. He tried another. It was just the same. He looked more closely at the pile of apples. The skins were leathery and rough and hard; you would expect the insides to be sour. On the contrary they were pulpy soft, and the cores were yellow. Filthy-tasting things. A stray piece stuck to his tooth and he pulled it out. Stringy, beastly . . .

He rang the bell, and the woman came through from the kitchen.

'Have we any other dessert?' he said.

'I am afraid not, sir. I remembered how fond you were of apples, and Willis brought in these from the garden. He said they were especially good, and just ripe for eating.'

'Well, he's quite wrong. They're uneatable.'

'I'm very sorry, sir. I wouldn't have put them through had I known. There's a lot more outside, too. Willis brought in a great basketful.'

'All the same sort?'

'Yes, sir. The small brown ones. No other kind, at all.'

'Never mind, it can't be helped. I'll look for myself in the morning.'

He got up from the table and went through to the living-room. He had a glass of port to take away the taste of the apples, but it seemed to make no difference, not even a biscuit with it. The pulpy rotten tang clung to his tongue and the roof of his mouth, and in the end he was obliged to go up to the bathroom and clean his teeth. The maddening thing was that he could have done with a good clean apple, after that rather indifferent supper: something with a smooth clear skin, the inside not too sweet, a little sharp in flavour. He knew the kind. Good biting texture. You had to pick them, of course, at just the right moment.

He dreamt that night he was back again in Italy, dancing under the tent in the little cobbled square. He woke with the tinkling music in his ear, but he could not recall the face of the peasant girl or remember the feel of her, tripping against his feet. He tried to recapture the memory, lying awake, over his morning tea, but it eluded him.

He got up out of bed and went over to the window, to glance at the weather. Fine enough, with a slight nip in the air.

Then he saw the tree. The sight of it came as a shock, it was so unexpected. Now he realized at once where the apples had come from the night before. The tree was laden, bowed down, under her burden of fruit. They clustered, small and brown, on every branch, diminishing in size as they reached the top, so that those on the high boughs, not grown yet to full size, looked like nuts. They weighed heavy on the tree, and because of this it seemed bent and twisted out of shape, the lower branches nearly sweeping the ground; and on the grass, at the foot of the tree, were more and yet more apples, windfalls, the first-grown, pushed off by their clamouring brothers and sisters. The ground was covered with them, many split open and rotting where the wasps had been. Never in his life had he seen a tree so laden with fruit. It was a miracle that it had not fallen under the weight.

He went out before breakfast – curiosity was too great – and stood beside the tree, staring at it. There was no mistake about it, these were the same apples that had been put in the dining-room last night. Hardly bigger than tangerines, and many of them smaller than that, they grew so close together on the branches that to pick one you would be forced to pick a dozen.

There was something monstrous in the sight, something distasteful; yet it was pitiful too that the months had brought this agony upon the tree, for agony it was, there could be no other word for it. The tree was tortured by fruit, groaning under the weight of it, and the frightful part about it was that not one of the fruit was eatable. Every apple was rotten through and through. He trod them underfoot, the windfalls on the grass, there was no escaping them; and in a moment they were mush and slime, clinging about his heels – he had to clean the mess off with wisps of grass.

It would have been far better if the tree had died, stark and bare, before this ever happened. What use was it to him or anyone, this load of rotting fruit, littering up the place, fouling the ground? And the tree itself humped, as it were, in pain, and yet he could almost swear triumphant, gloating.

Just as in spring, when the mass of fluffy blossom, col-ourless and sodden, dragged the reluctant eye away from the other trees, so it did now. Impossible to avoid seeing the tree, with its burden of fruit. Every window in the front part of the house looked out upon it. And he knew how it would be. The fruit would cling there until it was picked, staying upon the branches through October and November, and it never would be picked, because nobody could eat it. He could see himself being bothered with the tree throughout the autumn. Whenever he came out on to the terrace there it would be, sagging and loathsome.

It was extraordinary the dislike he had taken to the tree. It was a perpetual reminder of the fact that he . . . well, he was blessed if he knew what . . . a perpetual reminder of all the things he most detested, and always had, he could not put a name to them. He decided then and there that Willis should pick the fruit and take it away, sell it, get rid of it, anything, as long as he did not have to eat it, and as long as he was not forced to watch the tree drooping there, day after day, throughout the autumn.

He turned his back upon it and was relieved to see that none of the other trees had so degraded themselves to excess. They carried a fair crop, nothing out of the way, and as he might have known the young tree, to the right of the old one, made a brave little show on its own, with a light load of medium-sized, rosy-looking apples, not too dark in colour, but freshly reddened where the sun had ripened them. He would pick one now, and take it in, to eat with breakfast. He made his choice, and the apple fell at the first touch into his hand. It looked so good that he bit into it with appetite. That was it, juicy, sweet-smelling, sharp, the dew upon it still. He did not look back at the old tree. He went indoors, hungry, to breakfast.

It took the gardener nearly a week to strip the tree, and it was plain he did it under protest.

'I don't care what you do with them,' said his employer. 'You can sell them and keep the money, or you can take them home and feed them to your pigs. I can't stand the sight of them, and that's all there is to it. Find a long ladder, and start on the job right away.'

It seemed to him that Willis, from sheer obstinacy, spun out the time. He would watch the man from the windows act as though in slow motion. First the placing of the ladder. Then the laborious climb, and the descent to steady it again.

After that the performance of plucking off the fruit, dropping them, one by one, into the basket. Day after day it was the same. Willis was always there on the sloping lawn with his ladder, under the tree, the branches creaking and groaning, and beneath him on the grass baskets, pails, basins, any receptacle that would hold the apples.

At last the job was finished. The ladder was removed, the baskets and pails also, and the tree was stripped bare. He looked out at it, the evening of that day, in satisfaction. No more rotting fruit to offend his eye. Every single apple gone.

Yet the tree, instead of seeming lighter from the loss of its burden, looked, if it were possible, more dejected than ever. The branches still sagged, and the leaves, withering now to the cold autumnal evening, folded upon themselves and shivered. 'Is this my reward?' it seemed to say. 'After all I've done for you?'

As the light faded, the shadow of the tree cast a blight upon the dank night. Winter would soon come. And the short, dull days.

He had never cared much for the fall of the year. In the old days, when he went up to London every day to the office, it had meant that early start by train, on a nippy morning. And then, before three o'clock in the afternoon, the clerks were turning on the lights, and as often as not there would be fog in the air, murky and dismal, and a slow chugging journey home, daily bread-ers like himself sitting five abreast in a carriage, some of them with colds in their heads. Then the long evening followed, with Midge opposite him before the living-room fire, and he listening, or feigning to listen, to the account of her days and the things that had gone wrong.

If she had not shouldered any actual household disaster, she would pick upon some current event to cast a gloom.

'I see fares are going up again, what about your season ticket?', or 'This business in South Africa looks nasty, quite a long bit about it on the six o'clock news', or yet again 'Three more cases of polio over at the isolation hospital. I don't know, I'm sure, what the medical world thinks it's doing . . .'

Now, at least, he was spared the role of listener, but the memory of those long evenings was with him still, and when the lights were lit and the curtains were drawn he would be reminded of the click-click of the needles, the aimless chatter, and the 'Heigh-ho' of the yawns. He began to drop in, sometimes before supper, sometimes afterwards, at the Green Man, the old public house a quarter of a mile away on the main road. Nobody bothered him there. He would sit in a corner, having said good evening to genial Mrs Hill, the proprietress, and then, with a cigarette and a whisky-and-soda, watch the local inhabitants stroll in to have a pint, to throw a dart, to gossip.

In a sense it made a continuation of his summer holiday. It bore resemblance, admittedly slight, to the care-free atmosphere of the cafés and the restaurants; and there was a kind of warmth about the bright smoke-filled bar, crowded with working men who did not bother him, which he found pleasant, comforting. These visits cut into the length of the dark winter evenings, making them more tolerable.

A cold in the head, caught in mid-December, put a stop to this for more than a week. He was obliged to keep to the house. And it was odd, he thought to himself, how much he missed the Green Man, and how sick to death he became of sitting about in the living-room or in the study, with nothing to do but read or listen to the wireless. The cold and the boredom made him morose and irritable, and the enforced inactivity turned his liver sluggish. He needed exercise. Whatever the weather, he decided towards the end of yet another cold grim day, he would go out tomorrow. The sky had been heavy from mid-afternoon and threatened snow, but no matter, he could not stand the house for a further twenty-four hours without a break.

The final edge to his irritation came with the fruit tart at supper. He was in that final stage of a bad cold when the taste is not yet fully returned, appetite is poor, but there is a certain emptiness within that needs ministration of a particular kind. A bird might have done it. Half a partridge, toasted to perfection, followed by a cheese soufflé. As well ask for the moon. The daily woman, not gifted with imagination, produced plaice, of all fish the most tasteless, the most dry. When she had borne the remains of this away – he had left most of it upon his plate – she returned with a tart, and because hunger was far from being satisfied he helped himself to it liberally.

One taste was enough. Choking, spluttering, he spat out the contents of his spoon upon the plate. He got up and rang the bell.

The woman appeared, a query on her face, at the unexpected summons.

'What the devil is this stuff?'

'Jam tart, sir.'

'What sort of jam?'

'Apple jam, sir. Made from my own bottling.'

He threw down his napkin on the table.

'I guessed as much. You've been using some of those apples that I complained to you about months ago. I told you and Willis quite distinctly that I would not have any of those apples in the house.'

The woman's face became tight and drawn.

'You said, sir, not to cook the apples, or to bring them in for dessert. You said nothing about not making jam.

I thought they would taste all right as jam. And I made some myself, to try. It was perfectly all right. So I made several bottles of jam from the apples Willis gave me. We always made jam here, madam and myself.'

'Well, I'm sorry for your trouble, but I can't eat it. Those apples disagreed with me in the autumn, and whether they are made into jam or whatever you like they will do so again. Take the tart away, and don't let me see it, or the jam, again. I'll have some coffee in the living-room.'

He went out of the room, trembling. It was fantastic that such a small incident should make him feel so angry. God! What fools people were. She knew, Willis knew, that he disliked the apples, loathed the taste and smell of them, but in their cheese-paring way they decided that it would save money if he was given home-made jam, jam made from the apples he particularly detested.

He swallowed down a stiff whisky and lit a cigarette.

In a moment or two she appeared with the coffee. She did not retire immediately on putting down the tray.

'Could I have a word with you, sir?'

'What is it?'

'I think it would be for the best if I gave in my notice.'

Now this, on top of the other. What a day, what an evening.

'What reason? Because I can't eat apple-tart?'

'It's not just that, sir. Somehow I feel things are very different from what they were. I have meant to speak several times.'

'I don't give much trouble, do I?'

'No, sir. Only in the old days, when madam was alive, I felt my work was appreciated. Now it's as though it didn't matter one way or the other. Nothing's ever said, and although I try to do my best I can't be sure. I think I'd be happier if I went

III

where there was a lady again who took notice of what I did.'

'You are the best judge of that, of course. I'm sorry if you haven't liked it here lately.'

'You were away so much too, sir, this summer. When madam was alive it was never for more than a fortnight. Everything seems so changed. I don't know where I am, or Willis either.'

'So Willis is fed up too?'

'That's not for me to say, of course. I know he was upset about the apples, but that's some time ago. Perhaps he'll be speaking to you himself.'

'Perhaps he will. I had no idea I was causing so much concern to you both. All right, that's quite enough. Goodnight.'

She went out of the room. He stared moodily about him. Good riddance to them both, if that was how they felt. Things aren't the same. Everything so changed. Damned nonsense. As for Willis being upset about the apples, what infernal impudence. Hadn't he a right to do what he liked with his own tree? To hell with his cold and with the weather. He couldn't bear sitting about in front of the fire thinking about Willis and the cook. He would go down to the Green Man and forget the whole thing.

He put on his overcoat and muffler and his old cap and walked briskly down the road, and in twenty minutes he was sitting in his usual corner in the Green Man, with Mrs Hill pouring out his whisky and expressing her delight to see him back. One or two of the habitués smiled at him, asked after his health.

'Had a cold, sir? Same everywhere. Everyone's got one.'

'That's right.'

'Well, it's the time of year, isn't it?'

'Got to expect it. It's when it's on the chest it's nasty.'

'No worse than being stuffed up, like, in the head.'

'That's right. One's as bad as the other. Nothing to it.'

Likeable fellows. Friendly. Not harping at one, not bothering.

'Another whisky, please.'

'There you are, sir. Do you good. Keep out the cold.'

Mrs Hill beamed behind the bar. Large, comfortable old soul. Through a haze of smoke he heard the chatter, the deep laughter, the click of the darts, the jocular roar at a bull's eye.

'. . . and if it comes on to snow, I don't know how we shall manage,' Mrs Hill was saying, 'them being so late delivering the coal. If we had a load of logs it would help us out, but what do you think they're asking? Two pounds a load. I mean to say . . .'

He leant forward and his voice sounded far away, even to himself.

'I'll let you have some logs,' he said.

Mrs Hill turned round. She had not been talking to him. 'Excuse me?' she said.

'I'll let you have some logs,' he repeated. 'Got an old tree, up at home, needed sawing down for months. Do it for you tomorrow.'

He nodded, smiling.

'Oh no, sir. I couldn't think of putting you to the trouble. The coal will turn up, never fear.'

'No trouble at all. A pleasure. Like to do it for you, the exercise, you know, do me good. Putting on weight. You count on me.'

He got down from his seat and reached, rather carefully, for his coat.

'It's apple wood,' he said. 'Do you mind apple wood?'

'Why no,' she answered, 'any wood will do. But can you spare it, sir?'

He nodded, mysteriously. It was a bargain, it was a secret.

113

'I'll bring it down to you in my trailer tomorrow night,' he said.

'Careful, sir,' she said, 'mind the step . . .'

He walked home, through the cold crisp night, smiling to himself. He did not remember undressing or getting into bed, but when he woke the next morning the first thought that came to his mind was the promise he had made about the tree.

It was not one of Willis's days, he realized with satisfaction. There would be no interfering with his plan. The sky was heavy and snow had fallen in the night. More to come. But as yet nothing to worry about, nothing to hamper him.

He went through to the kitchen garden, after breakfast, to the tool shed. He took down the saw, the wedges, and the axe. He might need all of them. He ran his thumb along the edges. They would do. As he shouldered his tools and walked back to the front garden he laughed to himself, thinking that he must resemble an executioner of old days, setting forth to behead some wretched victim in the Tower.

He laid his tools down beneath the apple tree. It would be an act of mercy, really. Never had he seen anything so wretched, so utterly woebegone, as the apple tree. There couldn't be any life left in it. Not a leaf remained. Twisted, ugly, bent, it ruined the appearance of the lawn. Once it was out of the way the whole setting of the garden would change.

A snow-flake fell on to his hand, then another. He glanced down past the terrace to the dining-room window. He could see the woman laying his lunch. He went down the steps and into the house. 'Look,' he said, 'if you like to leave my lunch ready in the oven, I think I'll fend for myself today. I may be busy, and I don't want to be pinned down for time. Also it's going to snow. You had better go off early today and get

114

home, in case it becomes really bad. I can manage perfectly well. And I prefer it.'

Perhaps she thought his decision came through offence at her giving notice the night before. Whatever she thought, he did not mind. He wanted to be alone. He wanted no face peering from the window.

She went off at about twelve-thirty, and as soon as she had gone he went to the oven and got his lunch. He meant to get it over, so that he could give up the whole short afternoon to the felling of the tree.

No more snow had fallen, apart from a few flakes that did not lie. He took off his coat, rolled up his sleeves, and seized the saw. With his left hand he ripped away the wire at the base of the tree. Then he placed the saw about a foot from the bottom and began to work it, backwards, forwards.

For the first dozen strokes all went smoothly. The saw bit into the wood, the teeth took hold. Then after a few moments the saw began to bind. He had been afraid of that.

He tried to work it free, but the opening that he had made was not yet large enough, and the tree gripped upon the saw and held it fast. He drove in the first wedge, with no result. He drove in the second, and the opening gaped a little wider, but still not wide enough to release the saw.

He pulled and tugged at the saw, to no avail. He began to lose his temper. He took up his axe and started hacking at the tree, pieces of the trunk flying outwards, scattering on the grass.

That was more like it. That was the answer.

Up and down went the heavy axe, splitting and tearing at the tree. Off came the peeling bark, the great white strips of under-wood, raw and stringy. Hack at it, blast at it, gouge at the tough tissue, throw the axe away, claw at the rubbery flesh with the bare hands. Not far enough yet, go on, go on.

There goes the saw, the wedge, released. Now up with the axe again. Down there, heavy, where the stringy threads cling so steadfast. Now she's groaning, now she's splitting, now she's rocking and swaying, hanging there upon one bleeding strip. Boot her, then. That's it, kick her, kick her again, one final blow, she's over, she's falling . . . she's down . . . damn her, blast her . . . she's down, splitting the air with sound, and all her branches spread about her on the ground.

He stood back, wiping the sweat from his forehead, from his chin. The wreckage surrounded him on either side, and below him, at his feet, gaped the torn, white, jagged stump of the axed tree.

It began snowing.

His first task, after felling the apple tree, was to hack off the branches and the smaller boughs, and so to grade the wood in stacks, which made it easier to drag away.

The small stuff, bundled and roped, would do for kindling; Mrs Hill would no doubt be glad of that as well. He brought the car, with the trailer attached, to the garden gate, hard by the terrace. This chopping up of the branches was simple work; much of it could be done with a hook. The fatigue came with bending and tying the bundles, and then heaving them down past the terrace and through the gate up on to the trailer. The thicker branches he disposed of with the axe, then split them into three or four lengths, which he could also rope and drag, one by one, to the trailer.

He was fighting all the while against time. The light, what there was of it, would be gone by half past four, and the snow went on falling. The ground was already covered, and when he paused for a moment in his work, and wiped the sweat away from his face, the thin frozen flakes fell upon his lips and made their way, insidious and soft, down his collar to his neck and body. If he lifted his eyes to the sky he was blinded at once. The flakes came thicker, faster, swirling about his head, and it was as though the heaven had turned itself into a canopy of snow, ever descending, coming nearer, closer, stifling the earth. The snow fell upon the torn boughs and the hacked branches, hampering his work. If he rested but an instant to draw breath and renew his strength, it seemed to throw a protective cover, soft and white, over the pile of wood.

He could not wear gloves. If he did so he had no grip upon his hook or his axe, nor could he tie the rope and drag the branches. His fingers were numb with cold, soon they would be too stiff to bend. He had a pain now, under the heart, from the strain of dragging the stuff on to the trailer; and the work never seemed to lessen. Whenever he returned to the fallen tree the pile of wood would appear as high as ever, long boughs, short boughs, a heap of kindling there, nearly covered with the snow, which he had forgotten: all must be roped and fastened and carried or pulled away.

It was after half past four, and almost dark, when he had disposed of all the branches, and nothing now remained but to drag the trunk, already hacked into three lengths, over the terrace to the waiting trailer.

He was very nearly at the point of exhaustion. Only his will to be rid of the tree kept him to the task. His breath came slowly, painfully, and all the while the snow fell into his mouth and into his eyes and he could barely see.

He took his rope and slid it under the cold slippery trunk, knotting it fiercely. How hard and unyielding was the naked wood, and the bark was rough, hurting his numb hands.

'That's the end of you,' he muttered, 'that's your finish.'

Staggering to his feet he bore the weight of the heavy trunk over his shoulder, and began to drag it slowly down over the slope to the terrace and to the garden gate. It followed him, bump . . . bump . . . down the steps of the terrace. Heavy and lifeless, the last bare limbs of the apple tree dragged in his wake through the wet snow.

It was over. His task was done. He stood panting, one hand upon the trailer. Now nothing more remained but to take the stuff down to the Green Man before the snow made the drive impossible. He had chains for the car, he had thought of that already.

He went into the house to change the clothes that were clinging to him and to have a drink. Never mind about his fire, never mind about drawing curtains, seeing what there might be for supper, all the chores the daily woman usually did – that would come later. He must have his drink and get the wood away.

His mind was numb and weary, like his hands and his whole body. For a moment he thought of leaving the job until the following day, flopping down into the arm-chair, and closing his eyes. No, it would not do. Tomorrow there would be more snow, tomorrow the drive would be two or three feet deep. He knew the signs. And there would be the trailer, stuck outside the garden gate, with the pile of wood inside it, frozen white. He must make the effort and do the job tonight.

He finished his drink, changed, and went out to start the car. It was still snowing, but now that darkness had fallen a colder, cleaner feeling had come into the air, and it was freezing. The dizzy, swirling flakes came more slowly now, with precision.

The engine started and he began to drive downhill, the trailer in tow. He drove slowly, and very carefully, because of the heavy load. And it was an added strain, after the hard work of the afternoon, peering through the falling snow, wiping the windscreen. Never had the lights of the Green Man shone more cheerfully as he pulled up into the little yard.

He blinked as he stood within the doorway, smiling to himself.

'Well, I've brought your wood,' he said.

Mrs Hill stared at him from behind the bar, one or two fellows turned and looked at him, and a hush fell upon the dart-players.

'You never . . .' began Mrs Hill, but he jerked his head at the door and laughed at her.

'Go and see,' he said, 'but don't ask me to unload it tonight.'

He moved to his favourite corner, chuckling to himself, and there they all were, exclaiming and talking and laughing by the door, and he was quite a hero, the fellows crowding round with questions, and Mrs Hill pouring out his whisky and thanking him and laughing and shaking her head. 'You'll drink on the house tonight,' she said.

'Not a bit of it,' he said, 'this is my party. Rounds one and two to me. Come on, you chaps.'

It was festive, warm, jolly, and good luck to them all, he kept saying, good luck to Mrs Hill, and to himself, and to the whole world. When was Christmas? Next week, the week after? Well, here's to it, and a merry Christmas. Never mind the snow, never mind the weather. For the first time he was one of them, not isolated in his corner. For the first time he drank with them, he laughed with them, he even threw a dart with them, and there they all were in that warm stuffy smoke-filled bar, and he felt they liked him, he belonged, he was no longer 'the gentleman' from the house up the road.

The hours passed, and some of them went home, and

others took their place, and he was still sitting there, hazy, comfortable, the warmth and the smoke blending together. Nothing of what he heard or saw made very much sense but somehow it did not seem to matter, for there was jolly, fat, easy-going Mrs Hill to minister to his needs, her face glowing at him over the bar.

Another face swung into his view, that of one of the labourers from the farm, with whom, in the old war days, he had shared the driving of the tractor. He leant forward, touching the fellow on the shoulder.

'What happened to the little girl?' he said.

The man lowered his tankard. 'Beg pardon, sir?' he said.

'You remember. The little land-girl. She used to milk the cows, feed the pigs, up at the farm. Pretty girl, dark curly hair, always smiling.'

Mrs Hill turned round from serving another customer.

'Does the gentleman mean May, I wonder?' she asked.

'Yes, that's it, that was the name, young May,' he said.

'Why, didn't you ever hear about it, sir?' said Mrs Hill, filling up his glass. 'We were all very much shocked at the time, everyone was talking of it, weren't they, Fred?'

'That's right, Mrs Hill.'

The man wiped his mouth with the back of his hand.

'Killed,' he said, 'thrown from the back of some chap's motorbike. Going to be married very shortly. About four years ago, now. Dreadful thing, eh? Nice kid too.'

'We all sent a wreath, from just around,' said Mrs Hill. 'Her mother wrote back, very touched, and sent a cutting from the local paper, didn't she, Fred? Quite a big funeral they had, ever so many floral tributes. Poor May. We were all fond of May.'

'That's right,' said Fred.

'And fancy you never hearing about it, sir!' said Mrs Hill.

'No,' he said, 'no, nobody ever told me. I'm sorry about it. Very sorry.'

He stared in front of him at his half-filled glass.

The conversation went on around him but he was no longer part of the company. He was on his own again, silent, in his corner. Dead. That poor, pretty girl was dead. Thrown off a motorbike. Been dead for three or four years. Some careless, bloody fellow, taking a corner too fast, the girl behind him, clinging on to his belt, laughing probably in his ear, and then crash . . . finish. No more curling hair, blowing about her face, no more laughter.

May, that was the name; he remembered clearly now. He could see her smiling over her shoulder, when they called to her. 'Coming,' she sang out, and put a clattering pail down in the yard and went off, whistling, with big clumping boots. He had put his arm about her and kissed her for one brief, fleeting moment. May, the land-girl, with the laughing eyes.

'Going, sir?' said Mrs Hill.

'Yes. Yes, I think I'll be going now.'

He stumbled to the entrance and opened the door. It had frozen hard during the past hour and it was no longer snowing. The heavy pall had gone from the sky and the stars shone.

'Want a hand with the car, sir?' said someone.

'No, thank you,' he said, 'I can manage.'

He unhitched the trailer and let it fall. Some of the wood lurched forward heavily. That would do tomorrow. Tomorrow, if he felt like it, he would come down again and help to unload the wood. Not tonight. He had done enough. Now he was really tired; now he was spent.

It took him some time to start the car, and before he was halfway up the side-road leading to his house he realized that he had made a mistake to bring it at all. The snow was heavy all about him, and the track he had made earlier in the evening was now covered. The car lurched and slithered, and suddenly the right wheel dipped and the whole body plunged sideways. He had got into a drift.

He climbed out and looked about him. The car was deep in the drift, impossible to move without two or three men to help him, and even then, if he went for assistance, what hope was there of trying to continue further, with the snow just as thick ahead? Better leave it. Try again in the morning, when he was fresh. No sense in hanging about now, spending half the night pushing and shoving at the car, all to no purpose. No harm would come to it, here on the side-road; nobody else would be coming this way tonight.

He started walking up the road towards his own drive. It was bad luck that he had got the car into the drift. In the centre of the road the going was not bad and the snow did not come above his ankles. He thrust his hands deep in the pockets of his overcoat and ploughed on, up the hill, the countryside a great white waste on either side of him.

He remembered that he had sent the daily woman home at midday and that the house would strike cheerless and cold on his return. The fire would have gone out, and in all probability the furnace too. The windows, uncurtained, would stare bleakly down at him, letting in the night. Supper to get into the bargain. Well, it was his own fault. No one to blame but himself. This was the moment when there should be someone waiting, someone to come running through from the living-room to the hall, opening the front-door, flooding the hall with light. 'Are you all right, darling? I was getting anxious.'

He paused for breath at the top of the hill and saw his home, shrouded by trees, at the end of the short drive. It looked dark and forbidding, without a light in any window.

There was more friendliness in the open, under the bright stars, standing on the crisp white snow, than in the sombre house.

He had left the side-gate open, and he went through that way to the terrace, shutting the gate behind him. What a hush had fallen upon the garden – there was no sound at all. It was as though some spirit had come and put a spell upon the place, leaving it white and still.

He walked softly over the snow towards the apple trees.

Now the young one stood alone, above the steps, dwarfed no longer; and with her branches spread, glistening white, she belonged to the spirit world, a world of fantasy and ghosts. He wanted to stand beside the little tree and touch the branches, to make certain she was still alive, that the snow had not harmed her, so that in the spring she would blossom once again.

She was almost within his reach when he stumbled and fell, his foot twisted underneath him, caught in some obstacle hidden by the snow. He tried to move his foot but it was jammed, and he knew suddenly, by the sharpness of the pain biting his ankle, that what had trapped him was the jagged split stump of the old apple tree he had felled that afternoon.

He leant forward on his elbows, in an attempt to drag himself along the ground, but such was his position, in falling, that his leg was bent backwards, away from his foot, and every effort that he made only succeeded in imprisoning the foot still more firmly in the grip of the trunk. He felt for the ground, under the snow, but where he felt his hands touched the small broken twigs from the apple tree that had scattered there, when the tree fell, and then were covered by the falling snow. He shouted for help, knowing in his heart no one could hear.

'Let me go,' he shouted, 'let me go,' as though the thing

that held him there in its mercy had the power to release him, and as he shouted tears of frustration and of fear ran down his face. He would have to lie there all night, held fast in the clutch of the old apple tree. There was no hope, no escape, until they came to find him in the morning, and supposing it was then too late, that when they came he was dead, lying stiffly in the frozen snow?

Once more he struggled to release his foot, swearing and sobbing as he did so. It was no use. He could not move. Exhausted, he laid his head upon his arms, and wept. He sank deeper, ever deeper into the snow, and when a stray piece of brushwood, cold and wet, touched his lips, it was like a hand, hesitant and timid feeling its way towards him in the darkness.

SYLVIA TOWNSEND WARNER

HAPPINESS

'THE BATHROOM'S THE awkwardest feature,' said Mr Naylor, of Elwes & Sons, house agents, 'being situated on the ground floor. People don't like ground-floor bathrooms. You might say, they just won't hear of them.'

'No, I suppose not. Yet . . .' Lavinia Benton broke off.

'I know what you were going to say, Mrs Benton. You were going to say, Why not convert the dressing room upstairs, leaving the bathroom for what one might call a playroom, or a children's lounge, or a study, if there happened to be no family. Once we'd got the bath out, it could be called ideal for that, being so inordinately large for a bathroom. But then the pipes would have to be carried upstairs. Think of the plumbing, Mrs Benton! Prohibitive! No buyer would contemplate it, not for this class of residence – it isn't as if this were one of those old oak jobs. And I understand you don't want to let the estate in for any extra expense. So there we are, I'm afraid. Back where we started from!'

Mr Naylor had, in fact, scotched a snake that wasn't there. Lavinia's 'Yet' had been provoked by the reflection that an increasingly large acreage of southern England was occupied between 7.30 and 8.30 a.m. by people resignedly bathing on ground level. Not so resignedly, either, since there are always buyers for bungalows. Both Mr Petherick, of Petherick, Petherick & Sampson, and Mr Cox, of Ransom & Titters, had already explained that Aller Lodge, the late Miss Esther Jeudwine's brick-built, two-storey residence in sound repair, would have been easy enough to sell if only it had been a bungalow. All a matter of social psychology, thought Lavinia who, as a columnist on superior Women's Pages, was accustomed to making something out of not much; a mass apprehension of being surprised with no clothes on, which if not primitive, since primitive man had other and more pressing things to be surprised by, must certainly go a long way back, being later reinforced by class distinction – the wealthy are draped, the poor go bare – and Christianity's insistence on modesty; for though a fakir can be venerable in a light handful of marigolds, an archdeacon can scarcely leave off his gaiters. In short, the discomposure of being surprised with no clothes on is, like the pleasurability of possessing a virgin, one of the things long taken for granted – and really even more of an *idée reçue*, being subscribed to by both sexes alike. Yet here was this mass apprehension, fortified by tradition, smoothed by acceptance, part of the British way of life, suddenly ceasing to function when brought into bungalows, where the hazards that might justify it – housebreakers, mad dogs, cars out of control, voyeurs, private detectives, almost anything, in fact, except the atom bomb – would be much more on the cards. But one must remember that bathrooms being so recent an introduction, public opinion could not have made up its mind about them yet, and was bound to be rather hypothetical.

Lavinia became aware that Mr Naylor was observing her with sympathy, but at the same time giving little coughs. Of course. The poor man wanted to go.

'Well, goodbye, Mr Naylor. And thank you for being so helpful. I'm afraid it's a bad lookout, but I'm sure you'll do your best.'

'I'll do my best,' he said, and his voice, being more sincere than hers, sounded less sanguine.

She was almost sorry to see him go, he was so much the nicest of them, and the only one to show the slightest comprehension of the fix she was in. Nothing could have been more straightforward than Cousin Esther's will. Her legacies were proportionate to her estate and left a proper margin for expenses. A short list of remembrance gifts – and she had kept it up to date – was pinned to the will itself. She wished for a funeral service without hymns. She willed her house and personal property, other than the items specified in the attached list, to be sold and the proceeds to form a trust fund for the education of her great-great-nieces, Emily and Jemima Jeudwine, any residue to be divided between them when they reached the age of twenty-one (they were twins); and she appointed Hugh Dickenson Jeudwine and Lavinia Benton as her executors. Unfortunately, Hugh had died of his injuries a few hours after the car crash in which his great-aunt had been killed, and the house which was to provide the mainstay of the trust for Hugh's three-year-old daughters was proving unsellable.

During the four months of her executorship Lavinia's snatched visits to Aller Lodge, at first so nostalgic and so executive, had become heartless and vacant. The two servants, a married couple named Mullins, had received their legacies and gone off to let lodgings in Felixstowe; the cat, Dollop, had gone with them. The gifts had been dispatched; the best of the furniture, china and books had gone to the auction rooms in the county town, the silver, the Dutch flower paintings and the collection of clocks to Sotheby's. Remarking that this was no era for fish kettles (thereby providing Lavinia with the germ of half a column about the effects of broadcasting in Mandarin English to English listeners who with their native genius for phrase-making would seize on some devitalised term like 'era' and burnish it into a new arrestingness), the local second-hand dealer had removed several miscellaneous vanloads. What remained was just enough to emphasise that the house needed considerable repair and total redecoration.

Being so empty, it seemed brimful of the noise of the traffic speeding past its ironwork railings and the laurel hedge that protected the long narrow garden. 'All those laurels, too,' Mr Petherick had commented. 'Who's going to keep up laurels nowadays? Laurels are O-U-T Out!'

Yet on Lavinia's visits to Cousin Esther she had never noticed the noise of traffic. During the day, they had so much to say to each other; and Lavinia's bedroom was at the back, looking straight into the pear tree.

'Well, child, here we are, all ready for a nice long talk. Sit down, dear. Have you brought any parlour work?'

'My petit point.'

'Let me look at it. H'm. Not too bad, not too bad. Is this the same panel you brought last time? Oh, well, no doubt you've got other things to do in London. Now tell me the latest nonsense.'

'Red flannel nightdresses, with long sleeves, high necks and crochet lace edgings.'

'We had featherstitching. Far more practical, and didn't rag out in the wash.' If Lavinia had cited starched ruffs, ankle-length pantalettes or tiffany aprons as being the latest nonsenses it would turn out that Cousin Esther had worn them, with improvements. 'Will you have a cigar?'

'Not till after dinner, thank you.'

The cigars had begun when Lavinia decided to leave her husband and earn her own living, and they were Cousin Esther's idea. 'You aren't shocked, are you, at my taking a job?' Lavinia had asked. Since childhood, Cousin Esther's approval had been her fortress. And Cousin Esther had said,

'Shocked, dear? Why should I be? Now you can give up those trivial little cigarettes and smoke cigars. I've always liked George Sand. Charming woman, and so capable. But keep to cigars, duckie; you aren't made for de Mussets.'

Now there was only the noise of traffic, for Cousin Esther was in her grave, and the Boulle clock and the clock that played *Partant pour la Syrie* were ticking at Sotheby's; and the house – the only house where Lavinia smoked cigars – was for sale and no one would buy it.

A section of the noise stopped at the gate. The doorbell rang. A possible buyer? But it was Mr Naylor back again, back with something in his jaws: his expression plainly said so.

'Mrs Benton, I've had an idea. I was thinking about those laurels as I drove along, what a job it would be to keep them trimmed. "Another handicap" I said to myself. Handicap! Why, it's the main feature, though I didn't realise it until one of our own "FOR SALE" boards caught my eye, just outside Beck St Mary's. "AMPLE FRONTAGE". Ample frontage! If ever there was ample frontage, we've got it here. So I turned straight round and came back. And here I am.'

'In time for a cup of tea,' she said. 'I'm just making myself one. Do sit down. I won't be a moment.'

She knew and she did not know. What she unequivocally knew was that unless she kept a firm hand on herself, she was going to be silly.

When she carried in the tray, the French windows had been opened and Mr Naylor was walking up the garden, looking pleased as Adam. He came in, rubbing his hands, flowing with kindheartedness.

'Yes, Mrs Benton, it's perfect; couldn't be better. You can forget about that bathroom now. All we've got to do is to apply for a building permit. And you'll get it, never fear. All this end of Long Monkton is scheduled for development, now that we're getting the bypass. Yes, you'll soon be out of your troubles. I've been pacing it. There's ample room for two.'

'Two?' she said, holding on to the teapot.

'Two bungalows,' said Mr Naylor, as though he were promising oranges to a child – to a Victorian child in a pinafore, to whom oranges meant oranges. Two bungalows. Two families bathing in confidence in Cousin Esther's garden.

'Two bungalows?'

'With garages. Up as soon as winking,' said Mr Naylor. 'And double the money you were hoping to get for the place as it is.'

Double the money. And if not double the thankfulness of Hugh's widow – who whatever she might be about to receive would retain a bleak unthankfulness – a possible ten-per-cent abatement in her conviction that because poor Hughie wasn't there to stand up for his children Lavinia would sell the house to the first comer who offered sixpence for it.

'Which I'm not likely to get, you think?'

'To be honest with you, which would always be my wish, not in a month of Sundays.'

A flimsy hope brushed her.

'Unfortunately, I don't think I could afford to build.'

'Build? Heaven forbid! Why, they'd ruin you. No, no, what you've got to do is to sell as building land. Once you've got the permit through, it'll sell before we can say "knife".'

Two rather tipsy butterflies that had been feasting in the buddleia chased each other in through the French window and chased each other out again. Mr Naylor and me saying 'knife', she thought.

'Two bungalows,' she repeated.

'Or it might be three,' said Mr Naylor, wooing her with

three oranges, since only a couple appeared to have fallen rather flat with this lady. 'Yes, that's quite a possibility. For the right sort of buyer, someone with enterprise and enough labour, would think nothing of demolishing the house and putting the third bungalow here, where we are sitting. He could use a lot of the bricks; the lead on the roof alone would be worth a fortune. You could ask according, and get it.'

'But the pear tree!'

'True, that's an item. These old trees, their roots get everywhere. But half an hour with a bulldozer – you'd be surprised. Isn't that the front door?'

The lady dotted with mink carried an order to view from Ransom & Titters. 'Sweet old place, isn't it?' she remarked. 'Georgian all over. I never tire of Georgian. It's got so much character.'

'I'm afraid this is Victorian.'

'Oh! Then why does it look so Georgian? I suppose it was an imitation.'

She was so plainly no buyer that Lavinia did not even feel the adulterous embarrassment of being interrupted while drinking tea with one house agent by the client of another. Mr Naylor was not embarrassed, either. Combining tact with business, he returned to the garden and paced it more scrupulously. The dotted lady was scrupulous, too. Before she left, she had gone into every room, opened every closet, asked every question, saying in the tone of one worn out by bestowing benefits, 'Really? Quite quaint!'

Mr Naylor said chivalrously that with ladies of that kind it was hard to tell. Something might come of her.

'Horrible woman!' said Lavinia. By contrast, Mr Naylor seemed such a bosom friend that she allowed her voice to express some of the dejection she felt. If he felt that dejection was a poor response to the happy issue he had opened before her, he did not show it. He remembered something he must be getting along to, thanked her for the tea, said he would leave her to think it over. In the morning, all she would have to do would be to give him a tinkle. He would bring the application forms and see to the rest.

Still fending it off, she went through the house, opening doors and windows. The lady who adored Georgian had a Georgian insensibility to stinks, and her perfume resounded like a cornet. There was the bedroom, the defrauded bedroom in which Cousin Esther had not died. Everything had gone wrong at the last; the house had been robbed of its due.

'I might as well say Done,' she said to herself, at last. 'Say Done, and say Goodbye.'

Goodbye is a thing best said out-of-doors. She went out, and walked up and down the long flower border, being careful not to glance towards the house, to which the opened windows gave a curious air of animation, of a party being held. She looked at the flowers; she noticed the strong growth of late summer weeds. The jobbing gardener she had hired to give the place a tidy-up was not thorough like Mullins. Never mind, never mind! The flowers did not seem to mind, either; the zinnias, the hollyhocks, the velvety dahlias looked exceptionally sumptuous and thriving. One must admit that flowers prefer the company of weeds to the company of a weeder. Their loyalty is to the vegetable kingdom; they are delighted to get away from the fostering, censuring, interfering guardianship of man. All at once, a dahlia shed its petals. She realised that for the last ten minutes she had not been looking at the flowers; she had not even been conscious of them, she had been exploiting them, spinning a true observation into another whimsical paragraph. Never mind, never mind! Come to that, Mullins would have sent them to the flower show. No wonder they felt more at home with their weeds.

Slowly, with hanging head, she walked across the lawn towards the pear tree. It was an old tree. It was said to have been there before Aller Lodge was built; it was already tall and thick-limbed when Cousin Esther arrived, and none could name it. Its fruit, a dark obsidian green, smooth-rinded, narrow, almost cylindrical, ripened very late and kept throughout the winter. Being so old, the pear tree was also rather fitful and cranky. In the spring of last year it had bloomed so abundantly, so triumphantly, that Cousin Esther had telegraphed to her to come and see it. This year, so Mullins reported when she came for the funeral, there had been a very poor show of bloom and no bees. She laid her hand on its rough bark. 'I have sold you,' she said. At the sound of her words, tears of shame started painfully from her eyes. Shaking her head to free her cheeks of them, she looked up and saw something white. It was a cluster of pear blossoms, newly, perfectly unfolded.

It was startling – she need not let it be more. It was the whim of an old tree, and in fact she had seen other such blossomings in other Augusts. To hear a cuckoo would have been much more remarkable. The blossoms' extreme white-ness enforced the sudden presence of dusk. She must go in and shut those windows before dewfall. She sat down on the plank bench that encircled the trunk of the tree. Suppose she bought the house? She could not afford to; she didn't really want to. Suppose she bought the house? Not from senti-ment, not from piety, not from resentment of bungalows, but for her own pleasure. She would keep her old bedroom, of course, smelling the pear blossom in the early morning, sharing bees with it, hearing a pear fall, and another pear fall, as she lay under the eiderdown on the first frosty night, and thinking how, first thing in the morning, she would go down and hunt for them in the long grass. After a time – there need be no hurry about it – Cousin Esther's bedroom would become her spare room, and Emily and Jemima, who by then would be old enough to go visiting without their mother, would sleep there, feeling grand in a grown-up bed, as she had felt, and supported by a night light, as she had been. The traffic would not disturb them – besides, by then the bypass would have taken most of it away; the laurel hedge would be a boundary again. She would repaint the white seat. At night she would go round, locking up the house, turning the familiar, heavy, infallible keys, and afterwards she would lie in the ground-floor bathroom, hearing the owls hooting, and looking at the map of Europe, which fortunately even the reluctant fish-kettle remover had refused to take away. If she bought the house, she would buy other things, too. She would buy an inkpot, a penholder, a packet of steel nibs – and never touch her typewriter again. There should be no more clever slavery. To be on the safe side, she would not even keep a diary, and 'LAVINIA BENTON' would vanish from the printed page until it made its curt farewell appearance in the deaths column. Till then, she would be Mrs Benton, an ageing English lady with a winter hat and a summer hat, who sometimes went to church, who sometimes smoked a cigar after dinner, who sat reading by candlelight because it is more restful for the eyes, or for some such decorous reason. The candlelight would be known because its glow would be seen through the gap in the curtains; no one would know the exquisite pleasure she would find in the smell of sweet wax, lingering on into the next morning. No one would know, since she would not speak of it.

As though her moderate intention of churchgoing had encouraged the church clock, it now chimed a quarter.

Looking at her watch, she found it was too dark to read its face. Car lights were stabbing through the laurel hedge. Gently, she got up; gently, she laid her lips to the rough bark of the tree, and kissed it a gentle farewell. It had put out its cluster of blossom – a pure statement of spring, since nothing would come of it. It had given her an hour of happiness.

JANE AUSTEN

A TALE

A GENTLEMAN WHOSE family name I shall conceal, bought a small Cottage in Pembrokeshire about two Years ago. This daring Action was suggested to him by his elder Brother who promised to furnish two rooms & a Closet for him, provided he would take a small house near the Borders of an extensive Forest, and about three Miles from the Sea. Wilhelminus gladly accepted the Offer and continued for some time searching after such a retreat when he was one morning agreably releived from his Suspence by reading this advertisement in a Newspaper.

To be Lett

A Neat Cottage on the borders of an extensive forest & about three Miles from the Sea. It is ready furnished except two rooms & a Closet.

The delighted Wilhelminus posted away immediately to his brother, and shewed him the advertisement. Robertus congratulated him & sent him in his Carriage to take possession of the Cottage. After travelling for three days & six Nights without Stopping, they arrived at the Forest & following a track which led by it's side down a steep Hill over which ten Rivulets meandered, they reached the Cottage in half an hour. Wilhelminus alighted, and after knocking for some time without receiving any answer or hearing any one stir within, he opened the door which was fastened only by a wooden latch & entered a small room, which he immediately perceived to be one of the two that were unfurnished – From thence he proceeded into a Closet equally bare. A pair of Stairs that went out of it led him into a room above, no less destitute, & these apartments he found composed the whole of the House. He was by no means displeased with this discovery, as he had the comfort of reflecting that he should not be obliged to lay out any thing on furniture himself –. He returned immediately to his Brother, who took him next day to every Shop in Town, & bought what ever was requisite to furnish the two rooms & the Closet. In a few days every thing was completed, and Wilhelminus returned to take possession of the Cottage. Robertus accompanied him, with his Lady and amiable Cecelia & her two lovely Sisters Arabella and Marina to whom Wilhelminus was tenderly attached, and a large number of Attendants – An ordinary Genius might probably have been embarrassed in endeavouring to accomodate so large a party, but Wilhelminus with admirable presence of mind gave order for the immediate erection of two noble Tents in an open Spot in the Forest adjoining to the house. Their Construction was both simple & elegant – A couple of old blankets, each supported by four sticks, gave a striking proof of that taste for Architecture & that happy ease in overcoming difficulties which were some of Wilhelminus's most striking Virtues.

YURI OLYESHA

LOVE

Translated by Anthony Wolfe

SHUVALOV WAS WAITING for Lelia in the park. It was warm, midday. A lizard crept on a stone. He thought: a lizard on a stone is quite defenceless; you can see it at once. 'Mimicry,' he thought. And the thought of mimicry made him think about chameleons.

'Good morning,' said Shuvalov. But not one single chameleon appeared.

The lizard crept away.

Shuvalov was angry. He left the bench and walked quickly along the path. He was bitterly angry. He had a sudden impulse to attack someone, anyone. He stood quite still and shouted at the top of his voice:

'Oh, to hell with it all! Why should I be thinking of mimicry and chameleons. Really, they are quite useless – these thoughts.'

He crossed the grass and sat down on the stump of a tree. Insects flew all round him. The grass rustled gently. The architectural flight of the birds, of the gnats, of the winged beetles seemed curiously unreal; but he discerned the shapes they made in their flight, arches, bridges, towers, terraces – a whole city quickly changing, every second altering its shape.

'They are beginning to have power over me,' he thought. 'The sphere of my vision is becoming choked by them. I am becoming an eclectic. What is this which has power over me? I am beginning to see things which don't exist.'

Lelia did not come. He remained longer than he had

intended in the garden. He went for a stroll. He became convinced of the existence of many different species of insects. A small insect climbed a blade of grass. He seized it and placed it in the palm of his hand. Suddenly its little stomach glittered brilliantly. He was still angry.

'Hell! In another half-hour I shall become a naturalist!'

The blades of grass were of many kinds; leaves, stems; he saw grasses jointed like bamboo-canes. And he was surprised at the variety of colours on the flower called the 'Grassy Shroud,' and many colours of the soil seemed entirely unexpected.

'I don't want to be a naturalist,' he cried out. There was a note of an anguish in his voice. 'There is no need for me to make these fortuitous observations.'

But Lelia did not come. Already he had made some statistical deductions and drawn up a list of classifications. Already he was in a position to affirm that the majority of the trees in the park had broad leaves shaped like trefoils. He recognised the vibrations of the insects. And his vision, contrary to his desires, was filled with a number of things which had no interest for him.

But Lelia did not come. He sighed for her; he was angry. Instead of Lelia an unknown stranger appeared, a stranger in a black hat. He sat opposite Shuvalov on the green grass. His head hung down a little. On each of his knees lay a white hand. He was young, silent. Later it appeared that this singular young man was suffering from colour-blindness. They began to talk.

'I envy you,' said the young man. 'People say the leaves are green. But I have never seen a green leaf. On the other hand, I have occasionally seen blue pears.'

'You can't eat blue,' thought Shuvalov. 'If you had blue pears, you would be starving in no time.'

'But I do eat blue pears,' said the man who was colour-blind, sorrowfully.

Shuvalov shuddered.

'Tell me,' he said. 'Have you noticed, when birds fly all round you, you get an impression of a town, of imaginary lines.'

'No, I haven't noticed it,' said the man who was colour-blind.

'You mean – you see everything just as other people see it?'

'Everything, except a few colours,' he replied, turning his pale face in the direction of Shuvalov. 'Are you in love?' he asked a moment later.

'Yes,' said Shuvalov truthfully.

'Some of the colours, of course, seem a little confused. But otherwise I see everything just as other people see it,' said the man who was colour-blind, happily. Thereupon he made a patronising gesture at Shuvalov.

'But blue pears! That's – terrible!' said Shuvalov. He was smiling.

In the distance Lelia could be seen coming towards them. Shuvalov jumped up. The man who was colour-blind raised his hat and began to move away.

'Do you play the violin?' asked Shuvalov. He was relentless.

'You can see that I don't exist. It's quite obvious,' he replied.

Shuvalov cried out in a loud voice:

'But you look exactly like a violinist!'

The man who was colour-blind was still speaking as he moved away and Shuvalov thought he heard him saying: 'You're taking a dangerous course—'

Lelia was walking quickly. He moved towards her, made a few steps towards her. The boughs, which were covered with leaves shaped like trefoils, stirred gently in the wind.

147

Shuvalov stood in the middle of the pathway. The branches roared. She walked on, receiving an ovation from the leaves. The man who was colour-blind was thinking as he moved away to the right: 'There's windy weather coming.' He looked up at the leaves. A leaf, like all the other leaves, was stirring in the wind. He saw the blue tree swinging from side to side. Shuvalov saw a green tree; and all the time he was making preposterous theories about them. He thought: 'The trees are greeting her and she is receiving an ovation.' The man who was colour-blind was making a mistake, but Shuvalov was making a still greater mistake.

'I see what is not,' said Shuvalov.

Lelia came up to him. In one hand she held a small bag filled with apricots. The other was outstretched towards him. The whole world made a violent *volte-face*.

'Why are you making such a face?' she asked.

'I must be blind,' he replied.

Lelia took an apricot out of the bag, broke it across its tiny rump and threw the stone away. The stone fell on the grass. He watched it, fascinated. He watched it and saw that the stone which had fallen there was now a tree, a thin glittering sapling, a miraculous umbrella. Then Shuvalov turned to Lelia.

'This is absurd. I am beginning to think in images. For me the laws of nature have ceased to exist. Here, in five years' time, there will be an apricot-tree. Of course, it is quite possible, quite possible. It is something quite according to the laws of nature. But in defiance of all natural laws, I have seen the tree five years before its appointed time. Absurd! I am becoming an idealist.'

'It's because you're in love,' she replied, bleeding with apricot juice.

She sat up on the pillows, waiting for him. The bed had

been moved into a corner. Over their heads golden haloes glowed. He went up to her and she embraced him. She was so young, so light, that when she was undressed, wearing only her dressing-gown, it seemed absurd to think that she could be naked. Their first embrace was tempestuous. The childhood locket leapt from her breast and caught in her hair: like a golden almond. Shuvalov bent his head towards her slowly, while she sank down into the pillows, as though she was dying.

The lamp was burning.

'I'll blow it out,' she said.

Shuvalov lay under the wall. The corner of the room drew near. Shuvalov traced the pattern of the wall-paper with his fingers. He thought: 'That part of the pattern of the wall-paper, that part of the wall under which he was sleeping, led a double existence – by day no one would notice it, it was too ordinary, a number of haloes; but at night it led an altogether different existence, one which one could know only five minutes before falling asleep. If you watched closely, you would see the pattern suddenly growing, becoming more detailed, continually changing.' On the verge of falling asleep, when he was almost living among sensations which came from his childhood, he refused to cry out against the changes taking place among familiar shapes bound together according to definite laws; and there was all the more reason for his refusal because these movements stirred him to the quick and instead of the old curls and flourishes, he saw live goats and kitchen-maids.

'And there's the key of your violin,' said Lelia, throwing her arms round him.

'And there's the chameleon,' he whispered as he fell asleep.

He woke up early in the morning. Too early. He woke up and looked from side to side and screamed. A powerful note

of music issued from his throat. After that night the transformation which had taken place in the world when first
they had come to know each other became complete. He
awoke into a new world. The brillant morning-light filled
the room. He saw the window-sill and on the window-sill he
saw a flowerpot filled with many coloured flowers. Lelia was
still asleep, her back turned towards him. She lay curled up,
her back arched, and through her skin he could pick out the
lines of her spine, the thin bamboo-cane. 'A fishing-rod,' he
thought. 'Or a bamboo-cane.' In this new world everything
moved him deeply and everything was absurd. Voices flew
through the open window. Men in the street below remarked
on the bowl of flowers which stood in her window.

He got up, dressed, with difficulty held himself to the
earth. Gravitation no longer had any existence for him.
He did not yet understand the laws of this new world and
therefore he behaved carefully, cautiously, afraid that the
least careless movement on his part would precipitate a clap
of thunder. He felt that it was dangerous even to think, even
to touch anything. Had he developed during the night the
faculty of being able to materialise his dreams? He had every
reason to imagine that he had. For example, buttons fastened
themselves. For example, the moment he decided to moisten
his hairbrush – he wanted to plaster his hair – he heard the
sound of water dripping. He looked round. Against the wall,
where the sun was shining, a bundle of Lelia's clothes were
burning like a fire-balloon.

'Here I am!' said the voice of the tap out of the pile of
clothes.

Under the pile of clothes he found the sink and the tap.
A piece of pink soap lay quite close to them. Then Shuvalov
began to be afraid of thinking of anything terrible. 'Into
the room came a tiger.' He was prepared to fight against

this desire of his: but all he could do was to turn away from his thought. Once, in a terrible fear, he looked towards the door. Something did materialise, but his thought was not complete enough and the materialisation was only approximate, not at all perfect. Through the window flew a wasp, stippled, bloodthirsty.

'Lelia! The tiger!' he screamed.

Lelia woke up. The wasp hung suspended over a plate. It was droning like a gyroscope. Lelia jumped out of bed: the wasp flew at her. She brushed it aside and soon both the wasp and the trinket were flying all round her. Shuvalov killed the trinket with the palm of his hand. Then they started to massacre the wasp. Lelia covered it with her straw hat.

Shuvalov left her. They bade farewell to each other in a draught which seemed curiously real and loud-voiced for the world they were living in. The draught opened a door downstairs. It sang like a washerwoman. It wrapped itself round the flowers in the window-sill, lifted Lelia's straw hat, let free the wasp, hurled it among the lettuce. It made her hair stand on end. It whistled.

It lifted her dressing-gown above her head.

They said farewell to each other and Shuvalov rushed down the stairs so happily that he could not feel the stairs and even when he reached the door he did not notice the doorstep and even when he reached the porch he did not feel the steps leading down into the road. And it was there, in the roadway, that he discovered that it was not a mirage and that it was all so real that his legs were hanging suspended in the air and he was flying.

'To fly on the wings of love,' they were saying, as he passed an open window.

He shot up while his shirt revolved like a crinoline, a fever on his lips, flying in the air, snapping his fingers at everyone.

At two o'clock he went to the park. Tired out with joy and love for Lelia he fell asleep on a green bench. He slept; and sweat from the sun seethed from his face. He slept; and his collarbone protruded from his unbuttoned shirt.

Slowly, along the road, his hands behind his back, as demure as a Roman Catholic priest, wearing clothes which at once suggested a *soutane*, in a black hat and powerful blue spectacles, stooping, his head perched high above his body, came the stranger.

He came to the bench and sat opposite Shuvalov.

'I am Isaac Newton,' said the stranger as he removed his hat. Through his spectacles the world seemed blue, photographical.

'Good morning,' said Shuvalov.

The venerable scientist sat straight up, alert, on pins and needles. He listened intently, his ears jerked, one of the fingers of his left hand waved in the air, accurately following the music of an invisible choir which was ready to burst into song at a sign from his fingers. Everything in nature seemed to be holding its breath. Stealthily, Shuvalov hid himself behind the bench. Once the gravel under his heels screamed out aloud. The famous scientist was listening to the deep silence of nature. Far in the distance above a cluster of green, like an eclipse of the sun, a star appeared. It grew cold.

'Over there!' shouted Newton. 'Can you hear it?'

Without looking towards him, Newton stretched out his hand and drew Shuvalov towards him, raising his body and pulling him away from his hiding-place. They moved across the grass. As Newton's huge boots tripped gently across the grass, they left a white trace. In front of them, often looking over its shoulder, ran a lizard. They passed through a thicket while swan's down and ladybirds decorated the iron rim of his spectacles. A clearing opened to their gaze. Shuvalov recognised the sapling he had seen the day before.

'An apricot-tree?' he asked.

'No,' replied the scientist in a tone of exasperation. 'An apple-tree.'

The pattern of the tree, the close-cropped outline of the branches, light and fragile like a fire-balloon, stood there with a sparse covering of leaves. Nothing stirred, everywhere there was silence.

'Well,' said the scientist, bending his body backwards. Through bending back too much, his voice rose to a shout. He held an apple in his hands. 'What do you think it means?' he asked.

It was obvious that he did not often bend his back like that. Stiffening his body, he shook himself several times, easing his spine, the old bamboo-cane of his spine. An apple which he held in three fingers remained perfectly still.

'What does it all mean?' he asked. The sound of his words mingled with a sigh. 'Why did the apple fall down? Tell me that.'

Like William Tell Shuvalov regarded the apple.

He murmured: 'The laws of gravitation.'

After a short pause the venerable scientist turned to him again:

'Young man, they tell me you made a flight to-day.' His eyebrows flew up above his glasses.

'You're a young Marxist, aren't you, and to-day you made a flight?'

A ladybird crept from his finger on to the apple. His eyes narrowed. In his eyes the ladybird was a dazzling blue. He made a wry face. The ladybird jumped off the highest point of the apple and flew away, spreading wings which she had drawn from some place behind her body, just as a man draws his handkerchief from the swallow-tail of his morning coat.

'So you went for a flight to-day?'

Shuvalov was silent.

'Swine!' said Isaac Newton.

Shuvalov woke up.

'You swine!' said Lelia who was standing near. 'You little swine! What do you mean by going to sleep while you are waiting for me?'

She flicked the ladybird off his forehead, smiling gently as she thought that the belly of the insect was like iron.

'Hell!' he shouted. 'I hate you! Once I thought of it as a ladybird and I knew nothing else about it, except that it was a ladybird. I might even have come to the conclusion that its name was somehow anti-religious. Since the day we first met, something has happened to my eyes. I see blue pears and fly-agaric the colour of a ladybird.'

She wanted to embrace him.

'Leave me alone! Leave me alone!' he shouted. 'I'm tired of you! I'm ashamed!'

And still crying out, he ran away: he was like a stag. Laughing and with wild leaps he ran, trying to escape from his own shadow, his eyes squinting. When he was out of breath he stopped short. Lelia vanished. He decided to forget everything. The world which he had lost had to be restored again.

'Good-bye,' he whispered. 'We shall never see each other again.'

He sat down at last on a slope, on a tuft of earth; from there he could see far in the distance, a wide view studded with little country villas. He sat on the tip of a prism, his legs dangling down the sides. Below him spun the sunshade of an ice-cream merchant and all the trappings of the ice-cream merchant at that moment seemed to suggest an African village.

'I am living in Paradise,' said the young Marxist softly.

'Are you really a Marxist?' said the voice at his side.

It was the young man in the black hat, his friend, the man who was colour-blind. He sat quite close to Shuvalov.

'Yes – I am a Marxist,' said Shuvalov.

'Then you can't possibly live in Paradise,' said the man.

He was playing with a twig. Shuvalov sighed.

'What am I to do? The world has turned into a Paradise,' he sighed.

The man who was colour-blind whistled. He was scratching his ear with the twig.

'Do you know,' Shuvalov continued, whimpering. 'Do you know what I have been doing? Well, to-day I flew.'

Obliquely, like the lines of a postmark, a kite appeared in the sky.

'Do you want me to show you. I'll fly over there if you like.' (He pointed with his hand).

'Thank you, no. I have no intention of watching you reduced to infamy.'

'Yes it *is* terrible,' said Shuvalov in a soft voice. 'I know exactly how terrible it is.' Then he continued: 'You know how much I envy you?'

'No.'

'I can easily tell you. Your world, except for a few colours, is correctly defined. But you never live in Paradise. The world does not escape from *you*. Everything is in its accustomed place. And what about me? You think I am just a healthy materialist. But sometimes my eyes see suddenly illegal, unscientific deformations in things.'

'Terrible,' said the man who was colour-blind. 'But then, it is because you are in love.'

With unexpected warmth Shuvalov seized the stranger by the hand.

'Listen,' he shouted. 'Yes, that's true. I agree with you! Give me your rainbow-coloured world and take away from me my love.'

The man who was colour-blind slipped down the slope.

'I'm sorry,' he said. 'I'm in a terrible hurry. Good-bye. Live in Paradise.'

He moved with difficulty down the slope. As he fell, his legs wide apart, he lost his resemblance to men and assumed a resemblance to a man's reflection in water. At last he reached level ground. He moved away, joyful. He threw the twig away and blew a kiss to Shuvalov. Then he shouted: 'My kind regards to Paradise!'

But Lelia was asleep. An hour after he had met the man who was colour-blind Shuvalov went in search for her, into the depths, into the heart of the park. He was not a naturalist and he could no longer distinguish among the things which surrounded him, hazel-nut, hawthorn, elderberry, eglantine. On all sides branches, shrubbery, pressed upon him and he walked like a tramp, weighed down and dispirited as he sought to make a pathway through the timid interlacing of the branches – and they became still more entangled towards the centre. He brought a basket with him, and filled it with leaves, petals, thorns, berries, birds.

Lelia lay on her back in her red dressing-gown, her breast uncovered. She was asleep. He heard the gentle crackling of the film in her nose. He lay by her side.

Then he placed his head on her breast and with his fingers felt the calico of the cloth and his head lay on her clammy breast and he saw the nipple, rose-tinted, with soft wrinkles, like the wrinkles on the scum over milk. He heard neither the rustle of her dress nor her groans nor the sound of her movements.

The man who was colour-blind leapt from the shrubbery on to the transom. But he fell down again.

'Listen,' said the man who was colour-blind.

Shuvalov lifted his head from her sweet face.

'Don't come near me, you little fool!' said Shuvalov.

'Listen, Shuvalov. Oh, I agree with you now. Take away from me my rainbow-coloured world and give me your love instead!'

'Go and eat blue pears,' said Shuvalov.

D. H. LAWRENCE

THE SHADES OF SPRING

I

IT WAS A MILE nearer through the wood. Mechanically, Syson turned up by the forge and lifted the field-gate. The blacksmith and his mate stood still, watching the trespasser. But Syson looked too much a gentleman to be accosted. They let him go in silence across the small field to the wood.

There was not the least difference between this morning and those of the bright springs, six or eight years back. White and sandy-gold fowls still scratched round the gate, littering the earth and the field with feathers and scratched-up rubbish. Between the two thick holly bushes in the wood-hedge was the hidden gap, whose fence one climbed to get into the wood; the bars were scored just the same by the keeper's boots. He was back in the eternal.

Syson was extraordinarily glad. Like an uneasy spirit he had returned to the country of his past, and he found it waiting for him, unaltered. The hazel still spread glad little hands downwards, the bluebells here were still wan and few, among the lush grass and in shade of the bushes.

The path through the wood, on the very brow of a slope, ran winding easily for a time. All around were twiggy oaks, just issuing their gold, and floor spaces diapered with woodruff, with patches of dog-mercury and tufts of hyacinth. Two fallen trees still lay across the track. Syson jolted down a steep, rough slope, and came again upon the open land, this time looking north as through a great window in the wood. He stayed to gaze over the level fields of the hill-top, at the village which strewed the bare upland as if it had tumbled off the passing waggons of industry, and been forsaken. There was a stiff, modern, grey little church, and blocks and rows of red dwellings lying at random; at the back, the twinkling headstocks of the pit, and the looming pit-hill. All was naked and out-of-doors, not a tree! It was quite unaltered.

Syson turned, satisfied, to follow the path that sheered downhill into the wood. He was curiously elated, feeling himself back in an enduring vision. He started. A keeper was standing a few yards in front, barring the way.

'Where might you be going this road, sir?' asked the man. The tone of his question had a challenging twang. Syson looked at the fellow with an impersonal, observant gaze. It was a young man of four or five and twenty, ruddy and well favoured. His dark blue eyes now stared aggressively at the intruder. His black moustache, very thick, was cropped short over a small, rather soft mouth. In every other respect the fellow was manly and good-looking. He stood just above middle height; the strong forward thrust of his chest, and the perfect ease of his erect, self-sufficient body, gave one the feeling that he was taut with animal life, like the thick jet of a fountain balanced in itself. He stood with the butt of his gun on the ground, looking uncertainly and questioningly at Syson. The dark, restless eyes of the trespasser, examining the man and penetrating into him without heeding his office, troubled the keeper and made him flush.

'Where is Naylor? Have you got his job?' Syson asked.

'You're not from the House, are you?' inquired the keeper. It could not be, since everyone was away.

'No, I'm not from the House,' the other replied. It seemed to amuse him.

'Then might I ask where you were making for?' said the keeper, nettled.

'Where I am making for?' Syson repeated. 'I am going to Willey-Water Farm.'

'This isn't the road.'

'I think so. Down this path, past the well, and out by the white gate.'

'But that's not the public road.'

'I suppose not. I used to come so often, in Naylor's time, I had forgotten. Where is he, by the way?'

'Crippled with rheumatism,' the keeper answered reluctantly.

'Is he?' Syson exclaimed in pain.

'And who might you be?' asked the keeper, with a new intonation.

'John Adderley Syson; I used to live in Cordy Lane.'

'Used to court Hilda Millership?'

Syson's eyes opened with a pained smile. He nodded. There was an awkward silence.

'And you – who are you?' asked Syson.

'Arthur Pilbeam – Naylor's my uncle,' said the other.

'You live here in Nuttall?'

'I'm lodgin' at my uncle's – at Naylor's.'

'I see!'

'Did you say you was goin' down to Willey-Water?' asked the keeper.

'Yes.'

There was a pause of some moments, before the keeper blurted: '*I'm* courtin' Hilda Millership.'

The young fellow looked at the intruder with a stubborn defiance, almost pathetic. Syson opened new eyes.

'Are you?' he said, astonished. The keeper flushed dark.

'She and me are keeping company,' he said.

'I didn't know!' said Syson. The other man waited uncomfortably.

'What, is the thing settled?' asked the intruder.

'How, settled?' retorted the other sulkily.

'Are you going to get married soon, and all that?'

The keeper stared in silence for some moments, impotent.

'I suppose so,' he said, full of resentment.

'Ah!' Syson watched closely.

'I'm married myself,' he added, after a time.

'You are?' said the other incredulously.

Syson laughed in his brilliant, unhappy way.

'This last fifteen months,' he said.

The keeper gazed at him with wide, wondering eyes, apparently thinking back, and trying to make things out.

'Why, didn't you know?' asked Syson.

'No, I didn't,' said the other sulkily.

There was silence for a moment.

'Ah well!' said Syson, 'I will go on. I suppose I may.' The keeper stood in silent opposition. The two men hesitated in the open, grassy space, set around with small sheaves of sturdy bluebells; a little open platform on the brow of the hill. Syson took a few indecisive steps forward, then stopped.

'I say, how beautiful!' he cried.

He had come in full view of the downslope. The wide path ran from his feet like a river, and it was full of bluebells, save for a green winding thread down the centre, where the keeper walked. Like a stream the path opened into azure shallows at the levels, and there were pools of bluebells, with still the green thread winding through, like a thin current of ice-water through blue lakes. And from under the twig-purple of the bushes swam the shadowed blue, as if the flowers lay in flood water over the woodland.

'Ah, isn't it lovely!' Syson exclaimed; this was his past, the country he had abandoned, and it hurt him to see it so beautiful. Woodpigeons cooed overhead, and the air was full of the brightness of birds singing.

'If you're married, what do you keep writing to her for, and sending her poetry books and things?' asked the keeper. Syson stared at him, taken aback and humiliated. Then he began to smile.

'Well,' he said, 'I did not know about you . . .'

Again the keeper flushed darkly.

'But if you are married –' he charged.

'I am,' answered the other cynically.

Then, looking down the blue, beautiful path, Syson felt his own humiliation. 'What right *have* I to hang on to her?' he thought, bitterly self-contemptuous.

'She knows I'm married and all that,' he said.

'But you keep sending her books,' challenged the keeper.

Syson, silenced, looked at the other man quizzically, half pitying. Then he turned.

'Good day,' he said, and was gone. Now, everything irritated him: the two sallows, one all gold and perfume and murmur, one silver-green and bristly, reminded him, that here he had taught her about pollination. What a fool he was! What god-forsaken folly it all was!

'Ah well,' he said to himself; 'the poor devil seems to have a grudge against me. I'll do my best for him.' He grinned to himself, in a very bad temper.

II

The farm was less than a hundred yards from the wood's edge. The wall of trees formed the fourth side to the open quadrangle. The house faced the wood. With tangled emotions, Syson noted the plum blossom falling on the profuse, coloured primroses, which he himself had brought here and set. How they had increased! There were thick tufts of scarlet, and pink, and pale purple primroses under the plum trees. He saw somebody glance at him through the kitchen window, heard men's voices.

The door opened suddenly: very womanly she had grown! He felt himself going pale.

'You? – Addy!' she exclaimed, and stood motionless.

'Who?' called the farmer's voice. Men's low voices answered. Those low voices, curious and almost jeering, roused the tormented spirit in the visitor. Smiling brilliantly at her, he waited.

'Myself – why not?' he said.

The flush burned very deep on her cheek and throat.

'We are just finishing dinner,' she said.

'Then I will stay outside.' He made a motion to show that he would sit on the red earthenware pipkin that stood near the door among the daffodils, and contained the drinking water.

'Oh no, come in,' she said hurriedly. He followed her. In the doorway, he glanced swiftly over the family, and bowed. Everyone was confused. The farmer, his wife, and the four sons sat at the coarsely laid dinner-table, the men with arms bare to the elbows.

'I am sorry I come at lunch-time,' said Syson.

'Hello, Addy!' said the farmer, assuming the old form of address, but his tone cold. 'How are you?'

And he shook hands.

'Shall you have a bit?' he invited the young visitor, but taking for granted the offer would be refused. He assumed that Syson was become too refined to eat so roughly. The young man winced at the imputation.

'Have you had any dinner?' asked the daughter.

'No,' replied Syson. 'It is too early. I shall be back at half-past one.'

'You call it lunch, don't you?' asked the eldest son, almost ironical. He had once been an intimate friend of this young man.

'We'll give Addy something when we've finished,' said the mother, an invalid, deprecating.

'No – don't trouble. I don't want to give you any trouble,' said Syson.

'You could allus live on fresh air an' scenery,' laughed the youngest son, a lad of nineteen.

Syson went round the buildings, and into the orchard at the back of the house, where daffodils all along the hedgerow swung like yellow, ruffled birds on their perches. He loved the place extraordinarily, the hills ranging round, with bear-skin woods covering their giant shoulders, and small red farms like brooches clasping their garments; the blue streak of water in the valley, the bareness of the home pasture, the sound of myriad-threaded bird-singing, which went mostly unheard. To his last day, he would dream of this place, when he felt the sun on his face, or saw the small handfuls of snow between the winter twigs, or smelt the coming of spring.

Hilda was very womanly. In her presence he felt constrained. She was twenty-nine, as he was, but she seemed to him much older. He felt foolish, almost unreal, beside her. She was so static. As he was fingering some shed plum blossom on a low bough, she came to the back door to shake the table-cloth. Fowls raced from the stackyard, birds rustled from the trees. Her dark hair was gathered up in a coil like a crown on her head. She was very straight, distant in her bearing. As she folded the cloth, she looked away over the hills.

Presently Syson returned indoors. She had prepared eggs and curd cheese, stewed gooseberries and cream.

'Since you will dine to-night,' she said, 'I have only given you a light lunch.'

'It is awfully nice,' he said. 'You keep a real idyllic atmosphere – your belt of straw and ivy buds.'

Still they hurt each other.

He was uneasy before her. Her brief, sure speech, her distant bearing, were unfamiliar to him. He admired again her grey-black eyebrows, and her lashes. Their eyes met. He saw, in the beautiful grey and black of her glance, tears and a strange light, and at the back of all, calm acceptance of herself, and triumph over him.

He felt himself shrinking. With an effort he kept up the ironic manner.

She sent him into the parlour while she washed the dishes. The long low room was refurnished from the Abbey sale, with chairs upholstered in claret-coloured rep, many years old, and an oval table of polished walnut, and another piano, handsome, though still antique. In spite of the strangeness, he was pleased. Opening a high cupboard let into the thickness of the wall, he found it full of his books, his old lesson-books, and volumes of verse he had sent her, English and German. The daffodils in the white window-bottoms shone across the room, he could almost feel their rays. The old glamour caught him again. His youthful water-colours on the wall no longer made him grin; he remembered how fervently he had tried to paint for her, twelve years before.

She entered, wiping a dish, and he saw again the bright, kernel-white beauty of her arms.

'You are quite splendid here,' he said, and their eyes met.

'Do you like it?' she asked. It was the old, low, husky tone of intimacy. He felt a quick change beginning in his blood.

It was the old, delicious sublimation, the thinning, almost the vaporizing of himself, as if his spirit were to be liberated.

'Aye,' he nodded, smiling at her like a boy again. She bowed her head.

'This was the countess's chair,' she said in low tones. 'I found her scissors down here between the padding.'

'Did you? Where are they?'

Quickly, with a lilt in her movement, she fetched her work-basket, and together they examined the long-shanked old scissors.

'What a ballad of dead ladies!' he said, laughing, as he fitted his fingers into the round loops of the countess's scissors.

'I knew you could use them,' she said, with certainty. He looked at his fingers, and at the scissors. She meant his fingers were fine enough for the small-looped scissors.

'That is something to be said for me,' he laughed, putting the scissors aside. She turned to the window. He noticed the fine, fair down on her cheek and her upper lip, and her soft, white neck, like the throat of a nettle flower, and her forearms, bright as newly blanched kernels. He was looking at her with new eyes, and she was a different person to him. He did not know her. But he could regard her objectively now.

'Shall we go out awhile?' she asked.

'Yes!' he answered. But the predominant emotion, that troubled the excitement and perplexity of his heart, was fear, fear of that which he saw. There was about her the same manner, the same intonation in her voice, now as then, but she was not what he had known her to be. He knew quite well what she had been for him. And gradually he was realizing that she was something quite other, and always had been.

She put no covering on her head, merely took off her

apron, saying, 'We will go by the larches.' As they passed the old orchard, she called him in to show him a blue-tit's nest in one of the apple trees, and a sycock's in the hedge. He rather wondered at her surety, at a certain hardness like arrogance hidden under her humility.

'Look at the apple buds,' she said, and he then perceived myriads of little scarlet balls among the drooping boughs. Watching his face, her eyes went hard. She saw the scales were fallen from him, and at last he was going to see her as she was. It was the thing she had most dreaded in the past, and most needed, for her soul's sake. Now he was going to see her as she was. He would not love her, and he would know he never could have loved her. The old illusion gone, they were strangers, crude and entire. But he would give her her due – she would have her due from him.

She was brilliant as he had not known her. She showed him nests: a jenny wren's in a low bush.

'See this jinty's!' she exclaimed.

He was surprised to hear her use the local name. She reached carefully through the thorns, and put her fingers in the nest's round door.

'Five!' she said. 'Tiny little things.'

She showed him nests of robins, and chaffinches, and linnets, and buntings; of a wagtail beside the water.

'And if we go down, nearer the lake, I will show you a kingfisher's . . .'

'Among the young fir trees,' she said, 'there's a throstle's or a blackie's on nearly every bough, every ledge. The first day, when I had seen them all, I felt as if I mustn't go in the wood. It seemed a city of birds: and in the morning, hearing them all, I thought of the noisy early markets. I was afraid to go in my own wood.'

She was using the language they had both of them

invented. Now it was all her own. He had done with it. She did not mind his silence, but was always dominant, letting him see her wood. As they came along a marshy path where forget-me-nots were opening in a rich blue drift: 'We know all the birds, but there are many flowers we can't find out,' she said. It was half an appeal to him, who had known the names of things.

She looked dreamily across to the open fields that slept in the sun.

'I have a lover as well, you know,' she said, with assurance, yet dropping again almost into the intimate tone.

This woke in him the spirit to fight her.

'I think I met him. He is good-looking – also in Arcady.'

Without answering, she turned into a dark path that led up-hill, where the trees and undergrowth were very thick.

'They did well,' she said at length, 'to have various altars to various gods, in old days.'

'Ah yes!' he agreed. 'To whom is the new one?'

'There are no old ones,' she said. 'I was always looking for this.'

'And whose is it?' he asked.

'I don't know,' she said, looking full at him.

'I'm very glad, for your sake,' he said, 'that you are satisfied.'

'Aye – but the man doesn't matter so much,' she said. There was a pause.

'No!' he exclaimed, astonished, yet recognizing her as her real self.

'It is one's self that matters,' she said. 'Whether one is being one's own self and serving one's own God.'

There was silence, during which he pondered. The path was almost flowerless, gloomy. At the side, his heels sank into soft clay.

171

'I,' she said, very slowly, 'I was married the same night as you.'

He looked at her.

'Not legally, of course,' she replied. 'But – actually.'

'To the keeper?' he said, not knowing what else to say.

She turned to him.

'You thought I could not?' she said. But the flush was deep in her cheek and throat, for all her assurance.

Still he would not say anything.

'You see' – she was making an effort to explain – '*I* had to understand also.'

'And what does it amount to, this *understanding*?' he asked.

'A very great deal – does it not to you?' she replied. 'One is free.'

'And you are not disappointed?'

'Far from it!' Her tone was deep and sincere.

'You love him?'

'Yes, I love him.'

'Good!' he said.

This silenced her for a while.

'Here, among his things, I love him,' she said.

His conceit would not let him be silent.

'It needs this setting?' he asked.

'It does,' she cried. 'You were always making me to be not myself.'

He laughed shortly.

'But is it a matter of surroundings?' he said. He had considered her all spirit.

'I am like a plant,' she replied. 'I can only grow in my own soil.'

They came to a place where the undergrowth shrank away, leaving a bare, brown space, pillared with the brick-red and purplish trunks of pine trees. On the fringe, hung the sombre green of elder trees, with flat flowers in bud, and below were bright, unfurling pennons of fern. In the midst of the bare space stood a keeper's log hut. Pheasant-coops were lying about, some occupied by a clucking hen, some empty.

Hilda walked over the brown pine-needles to the hut, took a key from among the eaves, and opened the door. It was a bare wooden place with a carpenter's bench and form, carpenter's tools, an axe, snares, straps, some skins pegged down, everything in order. Hilda closed the door. Syson examined the weird flat coats of wild animals, that were pegged down to be cured. She turned some knotch in the side wall, and disclosed a second, small apartment.

'How romantic!' said Syson.

'Yes. He is very curious – he has some of a wild animal's cunning – in a nice sense – and he is inventive, and thought-ful – but not beyond a certain point.'

She pulled back a dark green curtain. The apartment was occupied almost entirely by a large couch of heather and bracken, on which was spread an ample rabbit-skin rug. On the floor were patchwork rugs of cat-skin, and a red calf-skin, while hanging from the wall were other furs. Hilda took down one, which she put on. It was a cloak of rabbit-skin and of white fur, with a hood, apparently of the skins of stoats. She laughed at Syson from out of this barbaric mantle, saying:

'What do you think of it?'

'Ah –! I congratulate you on your man,' he replied.

'And look!' she said.

In a little jar on a shelf were some sprays, frail and white, of the first honeysuckle.

'They will scent the place at night,' she said.

He looked round curiously.

'Where does he come short, then?' he asked. She gazed at him for a few moments. Then, turning aside:

'The stars aren't the same with him,' she said. 'You could make them flash and quiver, and the forget-me-nots come up at me like phosphorescence. You could make things *wonderful*. I have found it out – it is true. But I have them all for myself, now.'

He laughed, saying:

'After all, stars and forget-me-nots are only luxuries. You ought to make poetry.'

'Aye,' she assented. 'But I have them all now.'

Again he laughed bitterly at her.

She turned swiftly. He was leaning against the small window of the tiny, obscure room, and was watching her, who stood in the doorway, still cloaked in her mantle. His cap was removed, so she saw his face and head distinctly in the dim room. His black, straight, glossy hair was brushed clean back from his brow. His black eyes were watching her, and his face, that was clear and cream, and perfectly smooth, was flickering.

'We are very different,' she said bitterly.

Again he laughed.

'I see you disapprove of me,' he said.

'I disapprove of what you have become,' she said.

'You think we might' – he glanced at the hut – 'have been like this – you and I?'

She shook her head.

'You! no; never! You plucked a thing and looked at it till

174

you had found out all you wanted to know about it, then you threw it away,' she said.

'Did I?' he asked. 'And could your way never have been my way? I suppose not.'

'Why should it?' she said. 'I am a separate being.'

'But surely two people sometimes go the same way,' he said.

'You took me away from myself,' she said.

He knew he had mistaken her, had taken her for something she was not. That was his fault, not hers.

'And did you always know?' he asked.

'No – you never let me know. You bullied me. I couldn't help myself. I was glad when you left me, really.'

'I know you were,' he said. But his face went paler, almost deathly luminous.

'Yet,' he said, 'it was you who sent me the way I have gone.'

'I!' she exclaimed, in pride.

'You *would* have me take the Grammar School scholarship – and you would have me foster poor little Botell's fervent attachment to me, till he couldn't live without me – and because Botell was rich and influential. You triumphed in the wine-merchant's offer to send me to Cambridge, to befriend his only child. You wanted me to rise in the world. And all the time you were sending me away from you – every new success of mine put a separation between us, and more for you than for me. You never wanted to come with me: you wanted just to send me to see what it was like. I believe you even wanted me to marry a lady. You wanted to triumph over society in me.'

'And I am responsible,' she said, with sarcasm.

'I distinguished myself to satisfy you,' he replied.

'Ah!' she cried, 'you always wanted change, change, like a child.'

'Very well! And I am a success, and I know it, and I do some good work. But – I thought you were different. What right have you to a man?'

'What do you want?' she said, looking at him with wide, fearful eyes.

He looked back at her, his eyes pointed, like weapons.

'Why, nothing,' he laughed shortly.

There was a rattling at the outer latch, and the keeper entered. The woman glanced round, but remained standing, fur-cloaked, in the inner doorway. Syson did not move.

The other man entered, saw, and turned away without speaking. The two also were silent.

Pilbeam attended to his skins.

'I must go,' said Syson.

'Yes,' she replied.

'Then I give you "To our vast and varying fortunes." ' He lifted his hand in pledge.

' "To our vast and varying fortunes," ' she answered gravely, and speaking in cold tones.

'Arthur!' she said.

The keeper pretended not to hear. Syson, watching keenly, began to smile. The woman drew herself up.

'Arthur!' she said again, with a curious upward inflection, which warned the two men that her soul was trembling on a dangerous crisis.

The keeper slowly put down his tool and came to her.

'Yes,' he said.

'I wanted to introduce you,' she said, trembling.

'I've met him a'ready,' said the keeper.

'Have you? It is Addy, Mr Syson, whom you know about. – This is Arthur, Mr Pilbeam,' she added, turning to Syson.

The latter held out his hand to the keeper, and they shook hands in silence.

'I'm glad to have met you,' said Syson. 'We drop our correspondence, Hilda?'

'Why need we?' she asked.

The two men stood at a loss.

'*Is* there no need?' said Syson.

Still she was silent.

'It is as you will,' she said.

They went all three together down the gloomy path.

' "Qu'il était bleu, le ciel, et grand l'espoir," ' quoted Syson, not knowing what to say.

'What do you mean?' she said. 'Besides, *we* can't walk in *our* wild oats – we never sowed any.'

Syson looked at her. He was startled to see his young love, his nun, his Botticelli angel, so revealed. It was he who had been the fool. He and she were more separate than any two strangers could be. She only wanted to keep up a correspondence with him – and he, of course, wanted it kept up, so that he could write to her, like Dante to some Beatrice who had never existed save in the man's own brain.

At the bottom of the path she left him. He went along with the keeper, towards the open, towards the gate that closed on the wood. The two men walked almost like friends. They did not broach the subject of their thoughts.

Instead of going straight to the high-road gate, Syson went along the wood's edge, where the brook spread out in a little bog, and under the alder trees, among the reeds, great yellow stools and bosses of marigolds shone. Threads of brown water trickled by, touched with gold from the flowers. Suddenly there was a blue flash in the air, as a kingfisher passed.

Syson was extraordinarily moved. He climbed the bank to the gorse bushes, whose sparks of blossom had not yet gathered into a flame. Lying on the dry brown turf, he discovered sprigs of tiny purple milkwort and pink spots of lousewort. What a wonderful world it was – marvellous, for ever new. He felt as if it were underground, like the fields of monotone hell, notwithstanding. Inside his breast was a pain like a wound. He remembered the poem of William Morris, where in the Chapel of Lyonesse a knight lay wounded, with the truncheon of a spear deep in his breast, lying always as dead, yet did not die, while day after day the coloured sunlight dipped from the painted window across the chancel, and passed away. He knew now it never had been true, that which was between him and her, not for a moment. The truth had stood apart all the time.

Syson turned over. The air was full of the sound of larks, as if the sunshine above were condensing and falling in a shower. Amid this bright sound, voices sounded small and distinct.

'But if he's married, an' quite willing to drop it off, what has ter against it?' said the man's voice.

'I don't want to talk about it now. I want to be alone.'

Syson looked through the bushes. Hilda was standing in the wood, near the gate. The man was in the field, loitering by the hedge, and playing with the bees as they settled on the white bramble flowers.

There was silence for a while, in which Syson imagined her will among the brightness of the larks. Suddenly the keeper exclaimed 'Ah!' and swore. He was gripping at the sleeve of his coat, near the shoulder. Then he pulled off his jacket, threw it on the ground, and absorbedly rolled up his shirt sleeve right to the shoulder.

'Ah!' he said vindictively, as he picked out the bee and

flung it away. He twisted his fine, bright arm, peering awkwardly over his shoulder.

'What is it?' asked Hilda.

'A bee – crawled up my sleeve,' he answered.

'Come here to me,' she said.

The keeper went to her, like a sulky boy. She took his arm in her hands.

'Here it is – and the sting left in – poor bee!'

She picked out the sting, put her mouth to his arm, and sucked away the drop of poison. As she looked at the red mark her mouth had made, and at his arm, she said, laughing:

'That is the reddest kiss you will ever have.'

When Syson next looked up, at the sound of voices, he saw in the shadow the keeper with his mouth on the throat of his beloved, whose head was thrown back, and whose hair had fallen, so that one rough rope of dark brown hair hung across his bare arm.

'No,' the woman answered. 'I am not upset because he's gone. You won't understand . . .'

Syson could not distinguish what the man said. Hilda replied, clear and distinct:

'You know I love you. He has gone quite out of my life – don't trouble about him . . .' He kissed her, murmuring. She laughed hollowly.

'Yes,' she said, indulgent. 'We will be married, we will be married. But not just yet.' He spoke to her again. Syson heard nothing for a time. Then she said:

'You must go home, now, dear – you will get no sleep.'

Again was heard the murmur of the keeper's voice, troubled by fear and passion.

'But why should we be married at once?' she said. 'What more would you have, by being married? It is most beautiful as it is.'

At last he pulled on his coat and departed. She stood at the gate, not watching him, but looking over the sunny country.

When at last she had gone, Syson also departed, going back to town.

STELLA GIBBONS

From

COLD COMFORT FARM

SHE WAS FREQUENTLY cheered by letters from her friends in London. Mrs Smiling was now in Egypt, but she wrote often. When abroad in hot climates she wore a great many white dresses, said very little, and all the men in the hotel fell in love with her. Charles also wrote in reply to Flora's little notes. Her short, informative sentences on two sides of deep blue note-paper brought details in return from Charles about the weather in Hertfordshire and messages from his mother. What little else he wrote about, Flora seemed to find mightily satisfying. She looked forward to his letters. She also heard from Julia, who collected books about gangsters, from Claud Hart-Harris, and from all her set in general. So, though exiled, she was not lonely.

Occasionally, while taking her daily walk on the Downs, she saw Elfine: a light, rangy shape which had the plastic contours of a choir-boy etched by Botticelli, drawn against the thin cold sky of spring. Elfine never came near her, and this annoyed Flora. She wanted to get hold of Elfine, and to give her some tactful advice about Dick Hawk-Monitor.

Adam had confided to Flora his fears about Elfine. She did not think he had done it consciously. He was milking at the time, and she was watching him, and he was talking half to himself.

'She's ay a-speerin' at the windows of Hautcouture Hall' (he pronounced it 'Howchiker', in the local manner) 'to get

183

a sight of that young chuck-stubbard, Mus' Richard,' he had said.

Something earthly, something dark and rooty as the barran that thrust its tenacious way through the yeasty soil had crept into the old man's voice with the words. He was moved. Old tides lapped his loins.

'Is that the young squire?' asked Flora, casually. She wanted to get to the bottom of this business without seeming inquisitive.

'Aye – blast un fer a capsy, set-up yearling of a womaniser.' The reply came clotted with rage, but behind the rage were traces of some other and more obscure emotion; a bright-eyed grubbing in the lore of farmyard and bin, a hint of the casual lusts of chicken-house and duck-pond, a racy, yeasty, posty-toasty interest in the sordid drama of man's eternal blind attack and woman's inevitable yielding and loss.

Flora had experienced some distaste, but her wish to tidy up Cold Comfort had compelled her to pursue her inquiries.

She asked when the young people were to be married, knowing full well what the answer would be. Adam gave a loud and unaccustomed sound which she had with some difficulty interpreted as a mirthless laugh.

'When apples grow on the sukebind ye may see lust buy hissen a wedding garment,' he had replied meaningly.

Flora nodded, more gloomily than she felt. She thought that Adam took too black a view of the case. Probably, Richard Hawk-Monitor was only mildly attracted by Elfine, and the thought of behaving as Adam feared had never occurred to him. Even if it had, it would have been instantly dismissed.

Flora knew her hunting gentry. They were what the Americans, bless them! call dumb. They hated fuss. Poetry (Flora was pretty sure Elfine wrote poetry) bored them. They preferred the society of persons who spoke once in twenty minutes. They liked dogs to be well trained and girls to be well turned out and frosts to be of short duration. It was most unlikely that Richard was planning a Lyceum betrayal of Elfine. But it was even less likely that he wanted to marry her. The eccentricity of her dress, behaviour, and hairdressing would put him off automatically. Like most other ideas, the idea would simply not have entered his head.

'So, unless I do something about it,' thought Flora, 'she will simply be left on my hands. And heaven knows nobody will want to marry her while she looks like that and wears those frocks. Unless, of course, I fix her up with Mr Mybug.'

But Mr Mybug was, temporarily at least, in love with Flora herself, so that was another obstacle. And was it quite fair to fling Elfine, all unprepared, to those Bloomsbury-cum-Charlotte-Street lions which exchanged their husbands and wives every other week-end in the most broad-minded fashion? They always made Flora think of the description of the wild boars painted on the vases in Dickens's story – 'each wild boar having his leg elevated in the air at a painful angle to show his perfect freedom and gaiety'. And it must be so discouraging for them to find each new love exactly resembling the old one: just like trying balloon after balloon at a bad party and finding they all had holes in and would not blow up properly.

No. Elfine must not be thrown into Charlotte Street. She must be civilised, and then she must marry Richard.

So Flora continued to look out for Elfine when she went out for walks on the Downs.

* * *

It was a fresh, pleasant morning and she felt the more disposed to enjoy her walk because Mr Mybug (she could not learn to think of him as Meyerburg) was not with her.

For the last three mornings he had been with her, but this morning she had said that he really ought to do some work. Flora did not see why, but one excuse was as good as another to get rid of him.

It cannot be said that Flora really enjoyed taking walks with Mr Mybug. To begin with, he was not really interested in anything but sex. This was understandable, if deplorable. After all, many of our best minds have had the same weakness. The trouble about Mr Mybug was that ordinary subjects, which are not usually associated with sex even by our best minds, did suggest sex to Mr Mybug, and he pointed them out and made comparisons and asked Flora what she thought about it all. Flora found it difficult to reply because she was not interested. She was therefore obliged merely to be polite, and Mr Mybug mistook her lack of enthusiasm and thought it was due to inhibitions. He remarked how curious it was that most Englishwomen (most young Englishwomen, that was, Englishwomen of about nineteen to twenty-four) were inhibited. Cold, that was what young Englishwomen from nineteen to twenty-four were.

They used sometimes to walk through a pleasant wood of young birch trees which were just beginning to come into bud. The stems reminded Mr Mybug of phallic symbols and the buds made Mr Mybug think of nipples and virgins. Mr Mybug pointed out to Flora that he and she were walking on seeds which were germinating in the womb of the earth. He said it made him feel as if he were trampling on the body of a great brown woman. He felt as if he were a partner in some mighty rite of gestation.

Flora used sometimes to ask him the name of a tree, but he never knew.

Yet there were few occasions when he was not reminded of a pair of large breasts by the distant hills. Then, he would

186

stand looking at the woods upon the horizon. He would wrinkle up his eyes and breathe deeply through his nostrils and say that the view reminded him of one of Poussin's lovely things. Or he would pause and peer in a pool and say it was like a painting by Manet.

And, to be fair to Mr Mybug, it must be admitted he was sometimes interested by the social problems of the day. Only yesterday, while he and Flora were walking through an alley of rhododendrons on an estate which was open to the public, he had discussed a case of arrest in Hyde Park. The rhododendrons made him think of Hyde Park. He said that it was impossible to sit down for five minutes in Hyde Park after seven in the evening without being either accosted or arrested.

There were many homosexuals to be seen in Hyde Park. Prostitutes, too. God! those rhododendron buds had a phallic, urgent look!

Sooner or later we should have to tackle the problem of homosexuality. We should have to tackle the problem of Lesbians and old maids.

God! that little pool down there in the hollow was shaped just like somebody's navel! He would like to drag off his clothes and leap into it. There was another problem. . . . We should have to tackle that, too. In no other country but England was there so much pruriency about nakedness. If we all went about naked, sexual desire would automatically disappear. Had Flora ever been to a party where everybody took off all their clothes? Mr Mybug had. Once a whole lot of us bathed in the river with nothing on and afterwards little Harriet Belmont sat naked in the grass and played to us on her flute. It was delicious; so gay and simple and natural. And Billie Polswett danced a Hawaiian love-dance, making all the gestures that are usually omitted in the stage version.

Her husband had danced too. It had been lovely; so warm and natural and *real*, somehow.

So, taking it all round, Flora was pleased to have her walk in solitude.

She passed a girl riding on a pony and two young men walking with knapsacks and sticks, but no one else. She went down into a valley, filled with bushes of hazel and gorse, and made her way towards a little house built of grey stones, its roof painted turquoise green, which stood on the other side of the Down. It was a shepherd's hut; she could see the stone hut close to it in which ewes were kept at lambing-time and a shallow trough from which they drank.

If Mr Mybug had been there, he would have said that the ewes were paying the female thing's tribute to the Life Force. He said a woman's success could only be estimated by the success of her sexual life, and Flora supposed he would say the same thing about a ewe.

Oh, she *was* so glad he wasn't there!

She went skipping round the corner of the little sheep-house and saw Elfine, sitting on a turf and sunning herself.

Both cousins were startled. But Flora was quite pleased. She wanted a chance to talk to Elfine.

Elfine jumped to her feet and stood poised; she had something of the brittle grace of a yearling foal. A dryad's smile played on the curious sullen purity of her mouth, and her eyes were unawake and unfriendly. Flora thought, 'What a dreadful way of doing one's hair; surely it must be a mistake.'

'You're Flora – I'm Elfine,' said the other girl simply. Her voice had a breathless, broken quality that suggested the fluty sexless timbre of a choir-boy's notes (only choir-boys are seldom sexless, as many a harassed vicaress knows to her cost).

'No prizes offered,' thought Flora, rather rudely. But she said politely: 'Yes. Isn't it a delicious morning. Have you been far?'

'Yes . . . No . . . Away over there . . .' The vague gesture of her outflung arm sketched, in some curious fashion, illimitable horizons. Judith's gestures had the same barrierless quality; there was not a vase left anywhere in the farm.

'I feel stifled in the house,' Elfine went on, shyly and abruptly. 'I hate houses.'

'Indeed?' said Flora.

She observed Elfine draw a deep breath, and knew that she was about to get well away on a good long description of herself and her habits, as these shy dryads always did if you gave them half a chance. So she sat down on another turf in the sun and composed herself to listen, looking up at the tall Elfine.

'Do you like poetry?' asked Elfine, suddenly. A pure flood of colour ran up under her skin. Her hands, burnt and bone-modelled as a boy's, were clenched.

'Some of it,' responded Flora, cautiously.

'I adore it,' said Elfine, simply. 'It says all the things I can't say for myself . . . somehow . . . It means . . . oh, I don't know. Just everything, somehow. It's *enough*. Do you ever feel that?'

Flora replied that she had, occasionally, felt something of the sort, but her reply was limited by the fact that she was not quite sure exactly what Elfine meant.

'I write poetry,' said Elfine. (So I was right! thought Flora.) 'I'll show you some . . . if you promise not to laugh. I can't bear my children being laughed at . . . I call my poems my children.'

Flora felt that she could promise this with safety.

'And love, too,' muttered Elfine, her voice breaking and

changing shyly like the Finnish ice under the first lusty rays and wooing winds of the Finnish spring. 'Love and poetry go together, somehow . . . out here on the hills, when I'm alone with my dreams . . . oh, I can't tell you how I feel. I've been chasing a squirrel all the morning.'

Flora said severely:

'Elfine, are you engaged?'

Her cousin stood perfectly still. Slowly the colour receded from her face. Her head dropped. She muttered: 'There's someone . . . We don't want to spoil things by having anything definite and binding . . . it's horrible . . . to bind anyone down.'

'Nonsense. It is a very good idea,' said Flora, austerely, 'and it is a good thing for you to be bound down, too. Now, what do you suppose will happen to you if you don't marry this Someone?'

Elfine's face brightened. 'Oh . . . but I've got it all planned out,' she said, eagerly. 'I shall get a job in an arts and crafts shop in Horsham and do barbola work in my spare time. I shall be all right . . . and later on I can go to Italy and perhaps learn to be a little like St Francis of Assisi . . .'

'It is quite unnecessary for a young woman to resemble St Francis of Assisi,' said Flora coldly; 'and in your case it would be downright suicidal. A large girl like you *must* wear clothes that *fit*; and, Elfine, *whatever* you do, always wear court shoes. Remember – c-o-u-r-t. You are so handsome that you can wear the most conventional clothes and look very well in them; but do, for heaven's sake, avoid orange linen jumpers and hand-wrought jewellery. Oh, and shawls in the evening.'

She paused. She saw by Elfine's expression that she had been progressing too quickly. Elfine looked puzzled and extremely wretched. Flora was penitent. She had taken a fancy to the ridiculous chit. She said in a very friendly tone, drawing her cousin down to sit beside her:

'Now, what is it? Tell me. Do you hate being at home?'

'Yes . . . but I'm not often there,' whispered Elfine. 'No . . . it's Urk.'

Urk . . . That was the foxy-looking little man who was always staring at Flora's ankles or else spitting into the well.

'What about Urk?' she demanded.

'He . . . they . . . I think he wants to marry me,' stammered Elfine. 'I think Grandmother means me to marry him when I am eighteen. He . . . he . . . climbs the apple-tree outside my window and tries to watch me going to . . . to bed. I had to hang up three face-towels over the window, and then he poked them down with a fishing-rod and laughed and shook his fist at me . . . I don't know what to do.'

Flora was justly indignant, but concealed her nasty temper. It was at this moment that she resolved to adopt Elfine and rescue her in the teeth of all the Starkadders of Cold Comfort.

'And does Someone know this?' she asked.

'Well . . . I told him.'

'What did he say?'

'Oh . . . he said, "Rotten luck, old girl".'

'It's Dick Hawk-Monitor, isn't it?'

'Oh . . . how did you know? Oh . . . I suppose everybody knows by now. It's beastly.'

'Things are certainly in rather a mess, but I do not think we need go so far as to say they are beastly,' said Flora, more calmly. 'Now, you must forgive my asking you these questions, Elfine, but has the young Hawk-Monitor actually *asked* you to marry him?'

'Well . . . he said he thought it would be a good idea if we did.'

'Bad . . . bad . . .' muttered Flora, shaking her head. 'Forgive me, but does he seem to love you?'

'He . . . he does when I'm there, Flora, but I don't somehow think he thinks much about me when I'm not there.'

'And I suppose you care enough for him, my dear, to wish to become his wife?'

Elfine after some hesitation admitted that she had sometimes been selfish enough to wish that she had Dick all to herself. It appeared that there was a dangerous cousin named Pamela, who often came down from London for week-ends. Dick thought she was great fun.

Flora's expression did not change when she heard this piece of news, but her spirits sank. It would be difficult enough to win Dick for Elfine as it was; it would be a thousandfold more difficult with a rival in the field.

But her spirit was of that rare brand which becomes cold and pleased at the prospect of a battle, and her dismay did not last.

Elfine was saying:

'. . . And then there's this dance. Of course, I hate dancing unless it's in the woods with the wind-flowers and the birds, but I did rather want to go to this one, because, you see, it's Dick's twenty-first birthday party and . . . somehow . . . I think it would be rather fun.'

'Amusing or diverting . . . not "rather fun",' corrected Flora, kindly. 'Have you been invited?'

'Oh, no . . . You see, Grandmother does not allow the Starkadders to accept invitations, unless it is to funerals or the churching of women. So now no one sends us invitations. Dick did say he wished that I was coming, but I think he was only being kind. I don't think he really thought for a minute that I should be able to.'

'I suppose it would be of no use asking your grandmother

for permission to go? In dealing with old and tyrannical persons it is wise to do the correct thing whenever one can; they are then less likely to suspect when one does something incorrect.'

'Oh, I am sure she would never let me go. She quarrelled with Mr Hawk-Monitor nearly thirty years ago and she hates Dick's mother. She would be mad with rage if she thought that I even knew Dick. Besides, she thinks dancing is wicked.'

'An interesting survival of medieval superstition,' commented Flora. 'Now listen, Elfine. I think it would be an excellent move if you went to this dance. I will try and see if I can manage it. I shall go, too, and keep an eye on you. It may be a little difficult to secure invitations for us, but I will do my best. And when we have got our invitations, I will take you up to Town with me and we will buy you a frock.'

'Oh, Flora!'

Flora was pleased to see that the wild-bird-cum-dryad atmosphere which hung over Elfine like a pestilential vapour was wearing thin. She was talking quite naturally. If this was the good effect of a little ordinary feminine gossip and a little interest in her poor childish affairs, the effect of a well-cut dress and a brushed and burnished head of hair might be miraculous. Flora could have rubbed her hands with glee.

'When is this dance?' she asked. 'Will many people be asked?'

'It's on the twenty-first of April, just a month from tomorrow. Oh, yes, it will be very big; they are holding it in the Assembly Rooms at Godmere, and all the county will be asked, because, you see, it is Dick's twenty-first birthday.'

'All the better,' thought Flora. 'It will be easier to work an invitation.' She had so many friends in London; surely there must be among them someone who knew these Hawk-Monitors? And Claud Hart-Harris could come down to partner her, because he waltzed so well, and who could be an escort for Elfine?

'Does Seth dance?' she asked.

'I don't know. I hate him,' replied Elfine, simply.

'I cannot say that I like him much myself,' confessed Flora, 'but if he dances, I think it would be as well if he came with us. You must have a partner, you know. Or perhaps you could ask some other man?'

But Elfine, being a dryad, naturally knew no other men; and the only man Flora could think of who would be sure to be available for April 21st was Mr Mybug. She had only to ask *him*, she knew, and he would come bounding along to partner Elfine. It was dreadful to have no choice but Seth or Mr Mybug, but Sussex was like that.

'Well, we can arrange these details later,' she said. 'What I must do now is to find out if anyone in London among my friends know these Hawk-Monitors. I will ask Claud; he knows positive herds of people who live in country houses. I will write to him this afternoon.'

She was well disposed enough towards Elfine, but she really did not wish to spend with her the rest of an exquisite morning. So she rose to her feet and with a pleasant smile (having promised her cousin to let her know how matters were progressing) she went on her way.

RODERICK FINLAYSON

THE TOTARA TREE

PEOPLE CAME RUNNING from all directions wanting to know what all the fuss was about. 'Oho! it's crazy old Taranga perching like a crow in her tree because the Pakeha boss wants his men to cut it down,' Panapa explained, enjoying the joke hugely.

'What you say, cut it down? Cut the totara down?' echoed Uncle Tuna, anger and amazement wrinkling yet more his old wrinkled face. 'Cut Taranga down first!' he exclaimed. 'Everyone knows that totara is Taranga's birth tree.'

Uncle Tuna was so old he claimed to remember the day Taranga's father had planted the young tree when the child was born. Nearly one hundred years ago, Uncle Tuna said. But many people doubted that he was quite as old as that. He always boasted so.

'Well, it looked like they'll have to cut down both Taranga *and* her tree,' chuckled Panapa to the disgust of Uncle Tuna, who disapproved of joking about matters of tapu.

'Can't the Pakeha bear the sight of one single tree without reaching for his axe?' Uncle Tuna demanded angrily. 'However, this tree is tapu,' he added with an air of finality, 'so let the Pakeha go cut down his own weeds.' Uncle Tuna hated the Pakeha.

'Ae, why do they want to cut down Taranga's tree?' a puzzled woman asked.

'It's the wires,' Panapa explained loftily. 'The tree's right in the way of the new power wires they're taking up the valley.

Ten thousand volts, ehoa! That's power, I tell you! A touch of that to her tail would soon make old Taranga spring out of her tree, ehoa,' Panapa added with impish delight and a sly dig in the ribs for old Uncle Tuna. The old man simply spat his contempt and stumped away.

'Oho!' gurgled Panapa, 'now just look at the big Pakeha boss down below dancing and cursing at mad old Taranga up the tree; and she doesn't know a single word and cares nothing at all!'

And indeed Taranga just sat up there smoking her pipe of evil-smelling torori. Now she turned her head away and spat slowly and deliberately on the ground. Then she fixed her old half-closed eyes on the horizon again. Aue! how those red-faced Pakehas down below there jabbered and shouted! Well, no matter.

Meanwhile a big crowd had collected near the shanty where Taranga lived with her grandson, in front of which grew Taranga's totara tree right on the narrow road that divided the struggling little hillside settlement from the river. Men lounged against old sheds and hung over sagging fences; women squatted in open doorways or strolled along the road with babies in shawls on their backs. The bolder children even came right up and made marks in the dust on the Inspector's big car with their grubby little fingers. The driver had to say to them: 'Hey, there, you! Keep away from the car.' And they hung their heads and pouted their lips and looked shyly at him with great sombre eyes.

But a minute later the kiddies were jigging with delight behind the Inspector's back. How splendid to see such a show – all the big Pakehas from town turned out to fight mad old Taranga perching in a tree! But she was a witch all right – like her father the tohunga. Maybe she'd just flap her black shawl like wings and give a cackle and turn into a bird and fly away. Or maybe she'd curse the Pakehas, and they'd all wither up like dry sticks before their eyes! Uncle Tuna said she could do even worse than that. However, the older children didn't believe that old witch stuff.

Now as long as the old woman sat unconcernedly smoking up the tree, and the Pakehas down below argued and appealed to her as unsuccessfully as appealing to Fate, the crowd thoroughly enjoyed the joke. But when the Inspector at last lost his temper and shouted to his men to pull the old woman down by force, the humour of the gathering changed. The women in the doorways shouted shrilly. One of them said, 'Go away, Pakeha, and bully city folk! We Maoris don't yet insult trees or old women!' The men on the fences began grumbling sullenly, and the younger fellows started to lounge over toward the Pakehas. Taranga's grandson, Taikehu, who had been chopping wood, had a big axe in his hand. Taranga may be mad but after all it was her birth tree. You couldn't just come along and cut down a tree like that. Ae, you could laugh your fill at the old woman perched among the branches like an old black crow, but it wasn't for a Pakeha to come talking about pulling her down and destroying her tree. That smart man had better look out.

The Inspector evidently thought so too. He made a sign to dismiss the linesmen who were waiting with ladders and axes and ropes and saws to cut the tree down. Then he got into his big car, tight-lipped with rage. 'Hey, look out there, you kids!' the driver shouted. And away went the Pakehas amid a stench of burnt benzine, leaving Taranga so far victorious.

'They'll be back tomorrow with the police all right and drag old Taranga down by a leg,' said Panapa gloatingly. 'She'll have no chance with the police. But by korry! I'll laugh to see the first policeman to sample her claws.'

'Oho, they'll be back with soljers,' chanted the kiddies in

great excitement. 'They'll come with machine guns and go r-r-r-r-r- at old Taranga, but she'll just swallow the bullets!'

'Shut up, you kids,' Panapa commanded.

But somehow the excitement of the besieging of Taranga in her tree had spread like wildfire through the usually sleepy little settlement. The young bloods talked about preparing a hot welcome for the Pakehas tomorrow. Uncle Tuna encouraged them. A pretty state of affairs, he said, if a tapu tree could be desecrated by mere busybodies. The young men of his day knew better how to deal with such affairs. He remembered well how he himself had once tomahawked a Pakeha who broke the tapu of a burial ground. If people had listened to him long ago all the Pakehas would have been put in their place, under the deep sea – shark food! said Uncle Tuna ferociously. But the people were weary of Uncle Tuna's many exploits, and they didn't stop to listen. Even the youngsters nowadays merely remarked: 'Oh yeah,' when the old man harangued them.

Yet already the men were dancing half-humorous hakas around the totara tree. A fat woman with rolling eyes and a long tongue encouraged them. Everyone roared with laughter when she tripped in her long red skirts and fell bouncingly in the road. It was taken for granted now that they would make a night of it. Work was forgotten, and everyone gathered about Taranga's place. Taranga still waited quietly in the tree.

Panapa disappeared as night drew near but he soon returned with a barrel of home-brew on a sledge to enliven the occasion. That soon warmed things up, and the fun became fast and more furious. They gathered dry scrub and made bonfires to light the scene. They told Taranga not to leave her look-out, and they sent up baskets of food and drink to her; but she wouldn't touch bite nor sup. She alone of all the crowd was now calm and dignified. The men were dancing mad hakas armed with axes, knives and old taiahas. Someone kept firing a shot-gun till the cartridges gave out. Panapa's barrel of home-brew was getting low too, and Panapa just sat there propped against it and laughed and laughed; men and women alike boasted what they'd do with the Pakehas tomorrow. Old Uncle Tuna was disgusted with the whole business though. That was no way to fight the Pakeha, he said; that was the Pakeha's own ruination. He stood up by the meeting-house and harangued the mob, but no one listened to him.

The children were screeching with delight and racing around the bonfires like demons. They were throwing fire-sticks about here, there, and everywhere. So it's no wonder the scrub caught fire, and Taikehu's house beside the tree was ablaze before anybody noticed it. Heaven help us, but there was confusion then! Taikehu rushed in to try to save his best clothes. But he only got out with his old overcoat and a broken gramophone before the flames roared up through the roof. Some men started beating out the scrub with their axes and sticks. Others ran to the river for water. Uncle Tuna capered about urging the men to save the totara tree from the flames. Fancy wasting his breath preaching against the Pakeha, he cried. Trust this senseless generation of Maoris to work their own destruction, he sneered.

It seemed poor old Taranga was forgotten for the moment. Till a woman yelled at Taikehu, 'What you doing there with your old rags, you fool? Look alive and get the old woman out of the tree.' Then she ran to the tree and called, 'Eh there, Taranga, don't be mad. Come down quick, old mother!'

But Taranga made no move.

Between the woman and Taikehu and some others, they

got Taranga down. She looked to be still lost in meditation. But she was quite dead.

'Aue! she must have been dead a *long* time – she's quite cold and stiff,' Taikehu exclaimed. 'So it couldn't be the fright of the fire that killed her.'

'Fright?' jeered Uncle Tuna. 'I tell you, pothead, a woman who loaded rifles for me under the cannon shells of the Pakeha isn't likely to die in fright at a rubbish fire.' He cast a despising glance at the smoking ruins of Taikehu's shanty. 'No! but I tell you what she died of,' Uncle Tuna exclaimed. 'Taranga was just sick to death of you and your Pakeha ways. Sick to death!' The old man spat on the ground and turned his back on Taikehu and Panapa and their companions.

Meanwhile the wind had changed, and the men had beaten out the scrub fire, and the totara tree was saved. The fire and the old woman's strange death and Uncle Tuna's harsh words had sobered everybody by now, and the mood of the gathering changed from its former frenzy to melancholy and a kind of superstitious awe. Already some women had started to wail at the meeting-house where Taranga has been carried. Arrangements would have to be made for the tangi.

'Come here, Taikehu,' Uncle Tuna commanded. 'I have to show you where you must bury Taranga.'

Well, the Inspector had the grace to keep away while the tangi was on. Or rather Sergeant O'Connor, the chief of the local people and a good friend of Taranga's people, advised the Inspector not to meddle till it was over. 'A tangi or a wake, sure it's just as sad and holy,' he said. 'Now I advise you, don't interfere till they've finished.'

But when the Inspector did go to the settlement afterwards – well! Panapa gloatingly told the story in the pub in town later. 'O boy,' he said: 'you should have heard what plurry Mr. Inspector called Sergeant O'Connor when he found out they'd buried the old woman right under the roots of the plurry tree! I think O'Connor like the joke though. When the Inspector finish cursing, O'Connor say to him, "Sure the situation's still unchanged then. Taranga's still in her tree." '

Well, the power lines were delayed more than ever and in time this strange state of affairs was even mentioned in the Houses of Parliament, and the Maori members declared the Maoris' utter refusal to permit the desecration of burial places, and the Pakeha members all applauded these fine orations. So the Power Board was brought to the pass at last of having to build a special concrete foundation for the poles in the river bed so that the wires could be carried clear of Taranga's tree.

'Oho!' Panapa chuckles, telling the story to strangers who stop to look at the tomb beneath the totara on the roadside. 'Taranga dead protects her tree much better than Taranga alive. Py korry she cost the Pakeha thousands *and* thousands of pounds I guess!'

EUDORA WELTY

A STILL MOMENT

LORENZO DOW RODE the Old Natchez Trace at top speed upon a race horse, and the cry of the itinerant Man of God, 'I must have souls! And souls I must have!' rang in his own windy ears. He rode as if never to stop, toward his night's appointment.

It was the hour of sunset. All the souls that he had saved and all those he had not took dusky shapes in the mist that hung between the high banks, and seemed by their great number and density to block his way, and showed no signs of melting or changing back into mist, so that he feared his passage was to be difficult forever. The poor souls that were not saved were darker and more pitiful than those that were, and still there was not any of the radiance he would have hoped to see in such a congregation.

'Light up, in God's name!' he called, in the pain of his disappointment.

Then a whole swarm of fireflies instantly flickered all around him, up and down, back and forth, first one golden light and then another, flashing without any of the weariness that had held back the souls. These were the signs sent from God that he had not seen the accumulated radiance of saved souls because he was not able, and that his eyes were more able to see the fireflies of the Lord than His blessed souls.

'Lord, give me the strength to see the angels when I am in Paradise,' he said. 'Do not let my eyes remain in this failing proportion to my loving heart always.'

He gasped and held on. It was that day's complexity of horse-trading that had left him in the end with a Spanish race horse for which he was bound to send money in November from Georgia. Riding faster on the beast and still faster until he felt as if he were flying he sent thoughts of love with matching speed to his wife Peggy in Massachusetts. He found it effortless to love at a distance. He could look at the flowering trees and love Peggy in fullness, just as he could see his visions and love God. And Peggy, to whom he had not spoken until he could speak fateful words ('Would she accept of such an object as him?'), Peggy, the bride, with whom he had spent a few hours of time, showing of herself a small round handwriting, declared all in one letter, her first, that she felt the same as he, and that the fear was never of separation, but only of death.

Lorenzo well knew that it was Death that opened underfoot, that rippled by at night, that was the silence the birds did their singing in. He was close to death, closer than any animal or bird. On the back of one horse after another, winding them all, he was always riding toward it or away from it, and the Lord sent him directions with protection in His mind.

Just then he rode into a thicket of Indians taking aim with their new guns. One stepped out and took the horse by the bridle, it stopped at a touch, and the rest made a closing circle. The guns pointed.

'Incline!' The inner voice spoke sternly and with its customary lightning-quickness.

Lorenzo inclined all the way forward and put his head to the horse's silky mane, his body to its body, until a bullet meant for him would endanger the horse and make his death of no value. Prone he rode out through the circle of Indians, his obedience to the voice leaving him almost fearless, almost careless with joy.

But as he straightened and pressed ahead, care caught up with him again. Turning half-beast and half-divine, dividing himself like a heathen Centaur, he had escaped his death once more. But was it to be always by some metamorphosis of himself that he escaped, some humiliation of his faith, some admission to strength and argumentation and not frailty? Each time when he acted so it was at the command of an instinct that he took at once as the word of an angel, until too late, when he knew it was the word of the Devil. He had roared like a tiger at Indians, he had submerged himself in water blowing the savage bubbles of the alligator, and they skirted him by. He had prostrated himself to appear dead, and deceived bears. But all the time God would have protected him in His own way, less hurried, more divine.

Even now he saw a serpent crossing the Trace, giving out knowing glances.

He cried, 'I know you now!,' and the serpent gave him one look out of which all the fire had been taken, and went away in two darts into the tangle.

He rode on, all expectation, and the voices in the throats of the wild beasts went, almost without his noticing when, into words. 'Praise God,' they said. 'Deliver us from one another.' Birds especially sang of divine love which was the one ceaseless protection. 'Peace, in peace,' were their words so many times when they spoke from the briars, in a courteous sort of inflection, and he turned his countenance toward all perched creatures with a benevolence striving to match their own.

He rode on past the little intersecting trails, letting himself be guided by voices and by lights. It was battlesounds he heard most, sending him on, but sometimes ocean sounds, that long beat of waves that would make his heart pound and retreat as heavily as they, and he despaired again in his failure in Ireland when he took a voyage and persuaded with the Catholics with his back against the door, and then ran away to their cries of 'Mind the white hat!' But when he heard singing it was not the militant and sharp sound of Wesley's hymns, but a soft, tireless and tender air that had no beginning and no end, and the softness of distance, and he had pleaded with the Lord to find out if all this meant that it was wicked, but no answer had come.

Soon night would descend, and a camp-meeting ground ahead would fill with its sinners like the sky with its stars. How he hungered for them! He looked in prescience with a longing of love over the throng that waited while the flames of the torches threw change, change, change over their faces. How could he bring them enough, if it were not divine love and sufficient warning of all that could threaten them? He rode on faster. He was a filler of appointments, and he filled more and more, until his journeys up and down creation were nothing but a shuttle, driving back and forth upon the rich expanse of his vision. He was homeless by his own choice, he must be everywhere at some time, and somewhere soon. There hastening in the wilderness on his flying horse he gave the night's torch-lit crowd a premature benediction, he could not wait. He spread his arms out, one at a time for safety, and he wished, when they would all be gathered in by his tin horn blasts and the inspired words would go out over their heads, to brood above the entire and passionate life of the wide world, to become its rightful part.

He peered ahead. 'Inhabitants of Time! The wilderness is your souls on earth!' he shouted ahead into the treetops. 'Look about you, if you would view the conditions of your spirit, put here by the good Lord to show you and afright you. These wild places and these trails of awesome loneliness lie nowhere, nowhere, but in your heart.'

* * *

A dark man, who was James Murrell the outlaw, rode his horse out of a cane brake and began going along beside Lorenzo without looking at him. He had the alternately proud and aggrieved look of a man believing himself to be an instrument in the hands of a power, and when he was young he said at once to strangers that he was being used by Evil, or sometimes he stopped a traveler by shouting, 'Stop! I'm the Devil!' He rode along now talking and drawing out his talk, by some deep control of the voice gradually slowing the speed of Lorenzo's horse down until both the horses were softly trotting. He would have wondered that nothing he said was heard, not knowing that Lorenzo listened only to voices of whose heavenly origin he was more certain.

Murrell riding along with his victim-to-be, Murrell riding, was Murrell talking. He told away at his long tales, with always a distance and a long length of time flowing through them, and all centered about a silent man. In each the silent man would have done a piece of evil, a robbery or a murder, in a place of long ago, and it was all made for the revelation in the end that the silent man was Murrell himself, and the long story had happened yesterday, and the place *here* – the Natchez Trace. It would only take one dawning look for the victim to see that all of this was another story and he himself had listened his way into it, and that he too was about to recede in time (to where the dread was forgotten) for some listener and to live for a listener in the long ago. Destroy the present! – that must have been the first thing that was whispered in Murrell's heart – the living moment and the man that lives in it must die before you can go on. It was his habit to bring the journey – which might even take days – to a close with a kind of ceremony. Turning his face at last into the face of the victim, for he had never

211

seen him before now, he would tower up with the sudden height of a man no longer the tale teller but the speechless protagonist, silent at last, one degree nearer the hero. Then he would murder the man.

But it would always start over. This man going forward was going backward with talk. He saw nothing, observed no world at all. The two ends of his journey pulled at him always and held him in a nowhere, half asleep, smiling and witty, dangling his predicament. He was a murderer whose final stroke was over-long postponed, who had to bring himself through the greatest tedium to act, as if the whole wilderness, where he was born, were his impediment. But behind him and before him he kept in sight a victim, he saw a man fixed and stayed at the point of death – no matter how the man's eyes denied it, a victim, hands spreading to reach as if for the first time for life. Contempt! That is what Murrell gave that man.

Lorenzo might have understood, if he had not been in haste, that Murrell in laying hold of a man meant to solve his mystery of being. It was as if other men, all but himself, would lighten their hold on the secret, upon assault, and let it fly free at death. In his violence he was only treating of enigma. The violence shook his own body first, like a force gathering, and now he turned in the saddle.

Lorenzo's despair had to be kindled as well as his ecstasy, and could not come without that kindling. Before the awe-filled moment when the faces were turned up under the flares, as though an angel hand tipped their chins, he had no way of telling whether he would enter the sermon by sorrow or by joy. But at this moment the face of Murrell was turned toward him, turning at last, all solitary, in its full, and Lorenzo would have seized the man at once by his black coat and shaken him like prey for a lost soul, so instantly was he certain that the false fire was in his heart instead of the true fire. But Murrell, quick when he was quick, had put his own hand out, a restraining hand, and laid it on the wavelike flesh of the Spanish race horse, which quivered and shuddered at the touch.

They had come to a great live-oak tree at the edge of a low marshland. The burning sun hung low, like a head lowered on folded arms, and over the long reaches of violet trees the evening seemed still with thought. Lorenzo knew the place from having seen it among many in dreams, and he stopped readily and willingly. He drew rein, and Murrell drew rein, he dismounted and Murrell dismounted, he took a step, and Murrell was there too; and Lorenzo was not surprised at the closeness, how Murrell in his long dark coat and over it his dark face darkening still, stood beside him like a brother seeking light.

But in that moment instead of two men coming to stop by the great forked tree, there were three.

From far away, a student, Audubon, had been approaching lightly on the wilderness floor, disturbing nothing in his lightness. The long day of beauty had led him this certain distance. A flock of purple finches that he tried for the first moment to count went over his head. He made a spelling of the soft *pet* of the ivory-billed woodpecker. He told himself always: remember.

Coming upon the Trace, he looked at the high cedars, azure and still as distant smoke overhead, with their silver roots trailing down on either side like the veins of deepness in this place, and he noted some fact to his memory – this earth that wears but will not crumble or slide or turn to dust, they say it exists in one other spot in the world, Egypt – and then forgot it. He walked quietly. All life used this Trace, and

213

he liked to see the animals move along it in direct, oblivious journeys, for they had begun it and made it, the buffalo and deer and the small running creatures before man ever knew where he wanted to go, and birds flew a great mirrored course above. Walking beneath them Audubon remembered how in the cities he had seen these very birds in his imagination, calling them up whenever he wished, even in the hard and glittering outer parlors where if an artist were humble enough to wait, some idle hand held up promised money. He walked lightly and he went as carefully as he had started at two that morning, crayon and paper, a gun, and a small bottle of spirits disposed about his body. (*Note: 'The mocking birds so gentle that they would scarcely move out of the way.'*) He looked with care; great abundance had ceased to startle him, and he could see things one by one. In Natchez they had told him of many strange and marvelous birds that were to be found here. Their descriptions had been exact, complete, and wildly varying, and he took them for inventions and believed that like all the worldly things that came out of Natchez, they would be disposed of and shamed by any man's excursion into the reality of Nature.

In the valley he appeared under the tree, a sure man, very sure and tender, as if the touch of all the earth rubbed upon him and the stains of the flowery swamp had made him so.

Lorenzo welcomed him and turned fond eyes upon him. To transmute a man into an angel was the hope that drove him all over the world and never let him flinch from a meeting or withhold good-byes for long. This hope insistently divided his life into only two parts, journey and rest. There could be no night and day and love and despair and longing and satisfaction to make partitions in the single ecstasy of this alternation. All things were speech.

'God created the world,' said Lorenzo, 'and it exists to give testimony. Life is the tongue: speak.'

But instead of speech there happened a moment of deepest silence.

Audubon said nothing because he had gone without speaking a word for days. He did not regard his thoughts for the birds and animals as susceptible, in their first change, to words. His long playing on the flute was not in its origin a talking to himself. Rather than speak to order or describe, he would always draw a deer with a stroke across it to communicate his need of venison to an Indian. He had only found words when he discovered that there is much otherwise lost that can be noted down each item in its own day, and he wrote often now in a journal, not wanting anything to be lost the way it had been, all the past, and he would write about a day, 'Only sorry that the Sun Sets.'

Murrell, his cheated hand hiding the gun, could only continue to smile at Lorenzo, but he remembered in malice that he had disguised himself once as an Evangelist, and his final words to this victim would have been, 'One of my disguises was what you are.'

Then in Murrell Audubon he saw what he thought of as 'acquired sorrow' – that cumbrousness and darkness from which the naked Indian, coming just as he was made from God's hand, was so lightly free. He noted the eyes – the dark kind that loved to look through chinks, and saw neither closeness nor distance, light nor shade, wonder nor familiarity. They were narrowed to contract the heart, narrowed to make an averting plan. Audubon knew the finest-drawn tendons of the body and the working of their power, for he had touched them, and he supposed then that in man the enlargement of the eye to see started a motion in the hands to make or do, and that the narrowing of the eye stopped the hand and contracted the heart. Now Murrell's eyes followed an ant on a blade of grass, up the blade and down, many times in the single moment. Audubon had examined the Cave-In Rock where one robber had lived his hiding life, and the air in the cave was the cavelike air that enclosed this man, the same odor, flinty and dark. O secret life, he thought – is it true that the secret is withdrawn from the true disclosure, that man is a cave man, and that the openness I see, the ways through forests, the rivers brimming light, the wide arches where the birds fly, are dreams of freedom? If my origin is withheld from me, is my end to be unknown too? Is the radiance I see closed into an interval between two darks, or can it not illuminate them both and discover at last, though it cannot be spoken, what was thought hidden and lost?

In that quiet moment a solitary snowy heron flew down not far away and began to feed beside the marsh water.

At the single streak of flight, the ears of the race horse lifted, and the eyes of both horses filled with the soft lights of sunset, which in the next instant were reflected in the eyes of the men too as they all looked into the west toward the heron, and all eyes seemed infused with a sort of wildness.

Lorenzo gave the bird a triumphant look, such as a man may bestow upon his own vision, and thought, Nearness is near, lighted in a marshland, feeding at sunset. Praise God, His love has come visible.

Murrell, in suspicion pursuing all glances, blinking into a haze, saw only whiteness ensconced in darkness, as if it were a little luminous shell that drew in and held the eyesight. When he shaded his eyes, the brand 'H.T.' on his thumb thrust itself into his own vision, and he looked at the bird with the whole plan of the Mystic Rebellion darting from him as if in rays of the bright reflected light, and he stood looking proudly, leader as he was bound to become of the slaves, the brigands and outcasts of the entire Natchez country, with plans, dates, maps burning like a brand into his brain, and he saw himself proudly in a moment of prophecy going down rank after rank of successively bowing slaves to unroll and flaunt an awesome great picture of the Devil colored on a banner.

Audubon's eyes embraced the object in the distance and he could see it as carefully as if he held it in his hand. It was a snowy heron alone out of its flock. He watched it steadily, in his care noting the exact inevitable things. When it feeds it muddies the water with its foot. . . . It was as if each detail about the heron happened slowly in time, and only once. He felt again the old stab of wonder – what structure of life bridged the reptile's scale and the heron's feather? That knowledge too had been lost. He watched without moving. The bird was defenseless in the world except for the intensity of its life, and he wondered, how can heat of blood and speed of heart defend it? Then he thought, as always as if it were new and unbelievable, it has nothing in space or time to prevent its flight. And he waited, knowing that some birds will wait for a sense of their presence to travel to men before they will fly away from them.

Fixed in its pure white profile it stood in the precipitous moment, a plumicorn on its head, its breeding dress extended in rays, eating steadily the little water creatures. There was a little space between each man and the others, where they stood overwhelmed. No one could say the three had ever met, or that this moment of intersection had ever come in their lives, or its promise had been fulfilled. But before them the white heron rested in the grasses with the evening all around it, lighter and more serene than the evening, flight closed in its body, the circuit of its beauty closed, a bird seen

217

and a bird still, its motion calm as if it were offered: Take my flight. . . .

What each of them had wanted was simply *all*. To save all souls, to destroy all men, to see and to record all life that filled this world – all, all – but now a single frail yearning seemed to go out of the three of them for a moment and to stretch toward this one snowy, shy bird in the marshes. It was as if three whirlwinds had drawn together at some center, to find there feeding in peace a snowy heron. Its own slow spiral of flight could take it away in its own time, but for a little it held them still, it laid quiet over them, and they stood for a moment unburdened. . . .

Murrell wore no mask, for his face was that, a face that was aware while he was somnolent, a face that watched for him, and listened for him, alert and nearly brutal, the guard of a planner. He was quick without that he might be slow within, he staved off time, he wandered and plotted, and yet his whole desire mounted in him toward the end (was this the end – the sight of a bird feeding at dusk?), toward the instant of confession. His incessant deeds were thick in his heart now, and flinging himself to the ground he thought wearily, when all these trees are cut down, and the Trace lost, then my Conspiracy that is yet to spread itself will be disclosed, and all the stone-loaded bodies of murdered men will be pulled up, and all everywhere will know poor Murrell. His look pressed upon Lorenzo, who stared upward, and Audubon, who was taking out his gun, and his eyes squinted up to them in pleading, as if to say, 'How soon may I speak, and how soon will you pity me?' Then he looked back to the bird, and he thought if it would look at him a dread penetration would fill and gratify his heart.

Audubon in each act of life was aware of the mysterious origin he half-concealed and half-sought for. People along the way asked him in their kindness or their rudeness if it were true, that he was born a prince, and was the Lost Dauphin, and some said it was his secret, and some said that that was what he wished to find out before he died. But if it was his identity that he wished to discover, or if it was what a man had to seize beyond that, the way for him was by endless examination, by the care for every bird that flew in his path and every serpent that shone underfoot. Not one was enough; he looked deeper and deeper, on and on, as if for a particular beast or some legendary bird. Some men's eyes persisted in looking outward when they opened to look inward, and to their delight, there outflung was the astonishing world under the sky. When a man at last brought himself to face some mirror surface he still saw the world looking back at him, and if he continued to look, to look closer and closer, what then? The gaze that looks outward must be trained without rest, to be indomitable. It must see as slowly as Murrell's ant in the grass, as exhaustively as Lorenzo's angel of God, and then, Audubon dreamed, with his mind going to his pointed brush, it must see like this, and he tightened his hand on the trigger of the gun and pulled it, and his eyes went closed. In memory the heron was all its solitude, its total beauty. All its whiteness could be seen from all sides at once, its pure feathers were as if counted and known and their array one upon the other would never be lost. But it was not from that memory that he could paint.

His opening eyes met Lorenzo's, close and flashing, and it was on seeing horror deep in them, like fires in abysses, that he recognized it for the first time. He had never seen horror in its purity and clarity until now, in bright blue eyes. He went and picked up the bird. He had thought it to be a female, just as one sees the moon as female; and so it was. He put it in his bag, and started away. But Lorenzo had already gone on, leaning a-tilt on the horse which went slowly.

Murrell was left behind, but he was proud of the dispersal, as if he had done it, as if he had always known that three men in simply being together and doing a thing can, by their obstinacy, take the pride out of one another. Each must go away alone, each send the others away alone. He himself had purposely kept to the wildest country in the world, and would have sought it out, the loneliest road. He looked about with satisfaction, and hid. Travelers were forever innocent, he believed: that was his faith. He lay in wait; his faith was in innocence and his knowledge was of ruin; and had these things been shaken? Now, what could possibly be outside his grasp? Churning all about him like a cloud about the sun was the great folding descent of his thought. Plans of deeds made his thoughts, and they rolled and mingled about his ears as if he heard a dark voice that rose up to overcome the wilderness voice, or was one with it. The night would soon come; and he had gone through the day.

Audubon, splattered and wet, turned back into the wilderness with the heron warm under his hand, his head still light in a kind of trance. It was undeniable, on some Sunday mornings, when he turned over and over his drawings they seemed beautiful to him, through what was dramatic in the conflict of life, or what was exact. What he would draw, and what he had seen, became for a moment one to him then. Yet soon enough, and it seemed to come in that same moment, like Lorenzo's horror and the gun's firing, he knew that even the sight of the heron which surely he alone had appreciated, had not been all his belonging, and that never could any vision, even any simple sight, belong to him or to any man. He knew that the best he could make would be, after it was apart from his hand, a dead thing and not a

220

live thing, never the essence, only a sum of parts; and that it would always meet with a stranger's sight, and never be one with the beauty in any other man's head in the world. As he had seen the bird most purely at its moment of death, in some fatal way, in his care for looking outward, he saw his long labor most revealingly at the point where it met its limit. Still carefully, for he was trained to see well in the dark, he walked on into the deeper woods, noting all sights, all sounds, and was gentler than they as he went.

In the woods that echoed yet in his ears, Lorenzo riding slowly looked back. The hair rose on his head and his hands began to shake with cold, and suddenly it seemed to him that God Himself, just now, thought of the Idea of Separateness. For surely He had never thought of it before, when the little white heron was flying down to feed. He could understand God's giving Separateness first and then giving Love to follow and heal in its wonder; but God had reversed this, and given Love first and then Separateness, as though it did not matter to Him which came first. Perhaps it was that God never counted the moments of Time; Lorenzo did that, among his tasks of love. Time did not occur to God. Therefore – did He even know of it? How to explain Time and Separateness back to God, Who had never thought of them, Who could let the whole world come to grief in a scattering moment?

Lorenzo brought his cold hands together in a clasp and stared through the distance at the place where the bird had been as if he saw it still; as if nothing could really take away what had happened to him, the beautiful little vision of the feeding bird. Its beauty had been greater than he could account for. The sweat of rapture poured down from his forehead, and then he shouted into the marshes.

'Tempter!'

He whirled forward in the saddle and began to hurry the horse to its high speed. His camp ground was far away still, though even now they must be lighting the torches and gathering in the multitudes, so that at the appointed time he would duly appear in their midst, to deliver his address on the subject of 'In that day when all hearts shall be disclosed.'

Then the sun dropped below the trees, and the new moon, slender and white, hung shyly in the west.

OVID

THE TRANSFORMATION
OF DAPHNE

From

METAMORPHOSES
(BOOK I)

Translated by Mary M. Innes

AS SOON AS Phoebus saw Daphne, he fell in love with her, and wanted to marry her. His own prophetic powers deceived him and he hoped to achieve his desire. As the light stubble blazes up in a harvested field, or as the hedge is set alight, if a traveller chance to kindle a fire too close, or leaves one smouldering when he goes off at daybreak, so the god was all on fire, his whole heart was aflame, and he nourished his fruitless love on hope. He eyed her hair as it hung carelessly about her neck, and sighed: 'What if it were properly arranged!' He looked at her eyes, sparkling bright as stars, he looked at her lips, and wanted to do more than look at them. He praised her fingers, her hands and arms, bare almost to the shoulder. Her hidden charms he imagined lovelier still.

But Daphne ran off, swifter than the wind's breath, and did not stop to hear his words, though he called her back: 'I implore you, nymph, daughter of Peneus, do not run away! Though I pursue you, I am no enemy. Stay, sweet nymph! You flee as the lamb flees the wolf, or the deer the lion, as doves on fluttering wings fly from an eagle, as all creatures flee their natural foes! But it is love that drives me to follow you. Alas, how I fear lest you trip and fall, lest briars scratch your innocent legs, and I be the cause of your hurting yourself. These are rough places through which you are running – go less swiftly, I beg of you, slow your flight, and I in turn shall pursue less swiftly!

'Yet stay to inquire whose heart you have charmed. I am

no peasant, living in a mountain hut, nor am I a shepherd or boorish herdsman who tends his flocks and cattle in these regions. Silly girl, you do not know from whom you are fleeing: indeed, you do not, or else you would not flee. I am lord of Delphi, Claros, and Tenedos, and of the realms of Patara too. I am the son of Jupiter. By my skill, the past, the present, and the future are revealed; thanks to me, the lyre strings thrill with music. My arrow is sure, though there is one surer still, which has wounded my carefree heart. The art of medicine is my invention, and men the world over give me the name of healer. All the properties of herbs are known to me: but alas, there are no herbs to cure love, and the skill which helps others cannot help its master.'

He would have said more, but the frightened maiden fled from him, leaving him with his words unfinished; even then, she was graceful to see, as the wind bared her limbs and its gusts stirred her garments, blowing them out behind her. Her hair streamed in the light breeze, and her beauty was enhanced by her flight. But the youthful god could not endure to waste his time on further blandishments and, as love itself prompted, sped swiftly after her. Even so, when a Gallic hound spies a hare in some open meadow he tries by his swiftness to secure his prey, while the hare, by her swiftness, seeks safety: the dog, seeming just about to fasten on his quarry, hopes at every moment that he has her, and grazes her hind quarters with outstretched muzzle, but the hare, uncertain whether she has not already been caught, snatches herself out of his very jaws, and escapes the teeth which almost touch her.

Thus the god and the nymph sped on, one made swift by hope and one by fear; but he who pursued was swifter, for he was assisted by love's wings. He gave the fleeing maiden no respite, but followed close on her heels, and his breath touched the locks that lay scattered on her neck, till Daphne's strength was spent, and she grew pale and weary with the effort of her swift flight. Then she saw the waters of the Peneus: 'O father,' she cried, 'help me! If you rivers really have divine powers, work some transformation, and destroy this beauty which makes me please all too well!' Her prayer was scarcely ended when a deep languor took hold on her limbs, her soft breast was enclosed in thin bark, her hair grew into leaves, her arms into branches, and her feet that were lately so swift were held fast by sluggish roots, while her face became the treetop. Nothing of her was left, except her shining loveliness.

Even as a tree, Phoebus loved her. He placed his hand against the trunk, and felt her heart still beating under the new bark. Embracing the branches as if they were limbs he kissed the wood: but, even as a tree, she shrank from his kisses. Then the god said: 'Since you cannot be my bride, surely you will at least be my tree. My hair, my lyre, my quivers will always display the laurel. You will accompany the generals of Rome, when the Capitol beholds their long triumphal processions, when joyful voices raise the song of victory. You will stand by Augustus' gateposts too, faithfully guarding his doors, and keeping watch from either side over the wreath of oak leaves that will hang there. Further, as my head is ever young, my tresses never shorn, so do you also, at all times, wear the crowning glory of never-fading foliage.' Paean, the healer, had done: the laurel tree inclined her newmade branches, and seemed to nod her leafy top, as if it were a head, in consent.

MICHAEL McLAVERTY

THE ROAD TO THE SHORE

'TIS GOING TO be a lovely day, thanks be to God,' sighed Sister Paul to herself, as she rubbed her wrinkled hands together and looked out at the thrushes hopping across the lawn. 'And it was a lovely day last year and the year before,' she mused, and in her mind saw the fresh face of the sea where, in an hour or two, she and the rest of the community would be enjoying their annual trip to the shore. 'And God knows it may be my last trip,' she said resignedly, and gazed abstractedly at a butterfly that was purring its wings against the sunny pane. She opened the window and watched the butterfly swing out into the sweet air, zigzagging down to a cushion of flowers that bordered the lawn. 'Isn't it well Sister Clare wasn't here,' she said to herself, 'for she'd be pestering the very soul out of me with her questions about butterflies and birds and flowers and the fall of dew?' She gave her girdle of beads a slight rattle. Wasn't it lovely to think of the pleasure that little butterfly would have when it found the free air under its wings again and its little feet pressing on the soft petals of the flowers and not on the hard pane? She always maintained it was better to enjoy Nature without searching and probing and chattering about the what and the where and the wherefore. But Sister Clare! – what she got out of it all, goodness only knew, for she'd give nobody a minute's peace – not a moment's peace would she give to a saint, living or dead. 'How long would that butterfly live in the air of a classroom?' she'd be asking. 'Do you think it

231

would use up much of the active part of the air – the oxygen part, I mean? . . . What family would that butterfly belong to? . . . You know it's wrong to say that a butterfly lives only a day. . . . When I am teaching my little pupils I always try to be accurate. I don't believe in stuffing their heads with fantastical nonsense however pleasurable it may be. . . .' Sister Paul turned round as if someone had suddenly walked into the room, and she was relieved when she saw nothing only the quiet vacancy of the room, the varnished desks with the sun on them and their reflections on the parquet floor.

She hoped she wouldn't be sitting beside Clare in the car today! She'd have no peace with her – not a bit of peace to look out at the countryside and see what changes had taken place inside twelve months. But Reverend Mother, she knew, would arrange all that – and if it'd be her misfortune to be parked beside Clare she'd have to accept it with resignation; yes, with resignation, and in that case her journey to the sea would be like a pilgrimage.

At that moment a large limousine drove up the gravel path, and as it swung round to the convent door she saw the flowers flow across its polished sides in a blur of colour. She hurried out of the room and down the stairs. In the hall Sister Clare and Sister Benignus were standing beside two baskets and Reverend Mother was staring at the stairs. 'Where were you, Sister Paul?' she said with mild reproof. 'We searched the whole building for you. . . . We're all ready this ages. . . . And Sister Francis has gone to put out the cat. Do you remember last year it had been in all the time we were at the shore and it ate the bacon?' As she spoke a door closed at the end of the corridor and Sister Francis came along, polishing her specs with the corner of her veil. Reverend Mother glanced away from her, that continual polishing of the spectacles irritated her; and then that empty expression on Sister Francis's face when the spectacles were off – vacuous, that's what it was!

'All ready now,' Reverend Mother tried to say without any trace of perturbation. Sister Clare and Sister Benignus lifted two baskets at their feet, Reverend Mother opened the hall-door, and they all glided out into the flat sunlight.

The doors of the car were wide open, the engine purring gently, and a perfume of new leather fingering the air. The chauffeur, a young man, touched his cap and stood deferentially to the side. Reverend Mother surveyed him quickly, noting his clean-bright face and white collar. 'I think there'll be room for us all in the back,' she said.

'There's a seat in the front, Sister,' the young man said, touching his cap again.

'Just put the baskets on it, if you please,' said Reverend Mother. And Sister Clare who, at that moment, was smiling at her own grotesque reflection in the back of the car came forward with her basket, Sister Benignus following. Sister Paul sighed audibly and fingered her girdle of beads.

'Now, Sister Paul, you take one of the corner seats, Sister Clare you sit beside her, and Sister Benignus and Sister Francis on the spring-up seats facing them – they were just made for you, the tiny tots!' And they all laughed, a brittle laugh that emphasised the loveliness of the day.

When they were all seated, Reverend Mother made sure that the hall-door was locked, glanced at the fastened windows, and then stood for a minute watching the gardener who was pushing his lawn-mower with unusual vigour and concentration. He stopped abruptly when her shadow fell across his path. 'And, Jack,' she said, as if continuing a conversation that had been interrupted, 'you'll have that lawn finished today?'

'Yes, Mother,' and he took off his hat and held it in front of his breast. 'To be sure I'll have it finished today. Sure what'd prevent me to finish it, and this the grandest day God sent this many a long month – a wholesome day!'

'And Jack, I noticed some pebbles on the lawn yesterday – white ones.'

'I remarked them myself, Mother. A strange terrier disporting himself in the garden done it.'

'Did it!'

'Yes, Mother, he did it with his two front paws, scratching at the edge of the lawn like it was a rabbit burrow. He done it yesterday, and when I clodded him off the grounds he'd the impertinence to go out a different way than he came in. But I've now his entrances and exits all blocked and barricaded and I'm afraid he'll have to find some other constituency to disport himself. Dogs is a holy terror for bad habits.'

'Be sure and finish it all today,' she said with some impatience. She turned to go away, hesitated, and turned back. 'By the way, Jack, if there are any drips of oil made by the car on the gravel you'll scuffle fresh pebbles over them.'

'I'll do that. But you need have no fear of oil from her engine,' and he glanced over at the limousine. 'She'll be as clean as a Swiss clock. 'Tis them grocery vans that leak – top, tail and middle.'

Crossing to the car, she heard with a feeling of pleasure the surge of the lawn-mower over the grass. Presently the car swung out of the gate on to a tree-lined road at the edge of the town. The nuns relaxed, settled themselves more comfortably in their seats and chatted about the groups on bicycles that were all heading for the shore.

'We will go to the same quiet strip as last year,' said Reverend Mother, and then as she glanced out of the window a villa on top of a hill drew her attention. 'There's a house that has been built since last year,' she said.

'No, no,' said Sister Francis. 'It's more than a year old for I remember seeing it last year,' and she peered at it through her spectacles.

Reverend Mother spoke through the speaking-tube to the driver: 'Is that villa on the hill newly built?' she asked.

He stopped the car. 'A doctor by the name of McGrath built it two years ago,' he said. 'He's married to a daughter of Solicitor O'Kane.'

'Oh, thank you,' said Reverend Mother; and the car proceeded slowly up the long hill above the town.

Sister Francis took off her spectacles, blew her breath on them, and rubbed them with her handkerchief. She took another look at the villa and said with obvious pride: 'A fine site, indeed, I remember last year that they had that little gadget over the door.'

'The architrave,' said Sister Clare importantly.

'Aye,' said Sister Paul, and she looked out at the trees and below them the black river with its strings of froth moving through the valley. How lovely it would be, she thought, to sit on the edge of that river, dabble her parched feet in it and send bubbles out into the race of the current. She had often done that when she was a child, and now that river and its trees, which she only saw once a year, brought her childhood back to her. She sighed and opened the window so as to hear the mumble of the river far below them. The breeze whorled in, and as it lifted their veils they all smiled, invigorated by the fresh loveliness of the air. A bumble bee flew in and crawled up the pane at Reverend Mother's side of the car. She opened the window and assisted the bee towards the opening with the top of her fountain-pen, but the bee clung to the pen and as she tried to shake it free the wind carried it in again. 'Like everything else it hates to leave you,' said Sister Benignus. Reverend Mother smiled and the bee flew

235

up to the roof of the car and then alighted on the window beside Sister Paul. Sister Paul swept the bee to safety with the back of her hand.

'You weren't one bit afraid of it,' said Sister Clare. 'And if it had stung you, you would in a way have been responsible for its death. If it had been a Queen bee – though Queens wouldn't be flying at this time of the year – you would have been responsible for the deaths of potential thousands. A Queen bumble bee lays over two thousand eggs in one season!'

''Tis a great pity we haven't a hen like that,' put in Sister Francis, and they all laughed except Sister Clare. Sister Francis laughed till her eyes watered and, once more, she took off her spectacles. Reverend Mother fidgeted slightly and, in order to control her annoyance, she fixed her gaze on Sister Clare and asked her to continue her interesting account of the life of bumble bees. Sister Paul put her hands in her sleeves and sought distraction in the combings of cloud that streaked the sky.

Reverend Mother pressed her toe on the floor of the car and, instead of listening to Sister Clare, she was glaring unconsciously at Sister Francis who was tapping her spectacles on the palm of her hand and giving an odd laugh.

'Your spectacles are giving you much trouble today,' she broke in, unable any longer to restrain herself. 'Perhaps you would like to sit in the middle. It may provide your poor eyes with some rest.'

'No, thank you,' said Sister Francis, 'I like watching the crowds of cyclists passing on the road. But sometimes the sun glints on their handlebars and blinds me for a moment and makes me feel that a tiny thread or two has congregated on my lenses. It's my imagination of course.'

'Maybe you would care to have a look at *St. Anthony's Annals*,' and Reverend Mother handed her the magazine.

'Thank you, Mother. I'll keep it until we reach the shore, for the doctor told me not to read in moving vehicles.'

The car rolled on slowly and when it reached the top of a hill, where there was a long descent of five miles to the sea, a strange silence came over the nuns, and each became absorbed in her own premeditation on the advancing day. 'Go slowly down the hill,' Reverend Mother ordered the driver.

Boys sailed past them on bicycles, and when some did so with their hands off the handlebars a little cry of amazement would break from Sister Francis and she would discuss with Sister Clare the reckless irresponsibility of boys and the worry they must bring to their parents.

Suddenly at a bend on the hill they all looked at Sister Paul for she was excitedly drawing their attention to a line of young poplars. 'Look, look!' she was saying. 'Look at the way their leaves are dancing and not a flicker out of the other trees. And to think I never noticed them before!'

'I think they are aspens,' said Sister Clare, 'and anyway they are not indigenous to this country.'

'We had four poplars in our garden when I was growing up – black poplars, my father called them,' said Sister Paul, lost in her own memory.

'What family did they belong to? There's *angustifolia*, *laurifolia*, and *balsamifera* and others among the poplar family.'

'I don't know what family they belonged to,' Sister Paul went on quietly. 'I only know they were beautiful – beautiful in very early spring when every tree and twig around them would still be bleak – and there they were bursting into leaf, a brilliant yellow leaf like a flake of sunshine. My father, God be good to his kindly soul, planted four of them when I was young, for there were four in our family, all girls, and one of the trees my father called Kathleen, another Teresa, another

237

Eileen, and lastly my own, Maura. And I remember how he used to stand at the dining-room window gazing out at the young poplars with the frost white and hard around them. "I see a leaf or two coming on Maura," he used to say, and we would all rush to the window and gaze into the garden, each of us fastening her eye on her own tree and then measuring its growth of leaf with the others. And to the one whose tree was first in leaf he used to give a book or a pair of rosary beads. . . . Poor Father,' she sighed, and fumbled in her sleeve for her handkerchief.

'Can you not think of what special name those trees had?' pressed Clare. 'Did their leaves tremble furiously – *tremula, tremuloides?*'

'They didn't quiver very much,' said Sister Paul, her head bowed. 'My father didn't plant aspens, I remember. He told us it was from an aspen that Our Saviour's rood was made, and because their leaves remember the Crucifixion they are always trembling. . . . But our poplars had a lovely warm perfume when they were leafing and that perfume always reminded my father of autumn. Wasn't that strange?' she addressed the whole car, 'a tree coming into leaf and it reminding my poor father of autumn.'

'I know its family now,' said Clare, clapping her hands together. '*Balsamifera* – that's the family it belonged to – it's a native of Northern Italy.'

'And I remember,' said Paul, folding and unfolding her handkerchief on her lap, 'how my poor father had no gum once to wrap up a newspaper that he was posting. It was in winter and he went out to the poplars and dabbed his finger here and there on the sticky buds and smeared it on the edge of the wrapping paper.'

'That was enough to kill the buds,' said Clare. 'The gum, as you call it, is their only protective against frost.'

'It was himself he killed,' said Paul. 'He had gone out from a warm fire in his slippers, out into the bleak air and got his death.'

'And what happened to the poplars?' said Clare. But Sister Paul had turned her head to the window again and was trying to stifle the tears that were rising to her eyes.

'What other trees grew in your neighbourhood?' continued Clare. Sister Paul didn't seem to hear her, but when the question was repeated she turned and said slowly: 'I'm sorry that I don't know their names. But my father, Lord have mercy on him, used to say that a bird could leap from branch to branch for ten miles around without using its wings.'

Sister Clare smiled and Reverend Mother nudged her with her elbow, signing to her to keep quiet; and when she, herself, glanced at Paul she saw the sun shining through the fabric of her veil and a handkerchief held furtively to her eyes.

There was silence now in the sun-filled car while outside cyclists continued to pass them, free-wheeling down the long hill. Presently there was a rustle of paper in the car as Sister Francis drew forth from her deep pocket a bag of soft peppermints, stuck together by the heat. Carefully she peeled the bits of paper off the sweets, and as she held out the bag to Reverend Mother she said: 'Excuse my fingers.' But Reverend Mother shook her head, and Clare and Benignus, seeing that she had refused, felt it would be improper for them to accept. Francis shook the bag towards Paul but since she had her eyes closed, as if in prayer, she neither saw nor heard what was being offered to her. '*In somno pacis,*' said Francis, popping two peppermints into her own mouth and hiding the bag in her wide sleeve. 'A peppermint is soothing and cool on a hot day like this,' she added with apologetic good nature.

A hot smell of peppermint drifted around the car. Reverend Mother lowered her window to its full length, and though the air rushed in in soft folds around her face it was unable to quench the flaming odour. Somehow, for Reverend Mother, the day, that had hardly begun yet, was spoiled by an old nun with foolish habits and by a young nun unwise enough not to know when to stop questioning. Everything was going wrong, and it would not surprise her that before evening clouds of rain would blow in from the sea and blot out completely the soft loveliness of the sunny day. Once more she looked at Paul, and, seeing her head bowed in thought, she knew that there was some aspect of the countryside, some shape in cloud or bush, that brought back to Paul a sweet but sombre childhood. For herself she had no such memories – there was nothing in her own life, she thought, only a mechanical ordering, a following of routine, that may have brought some pleasure into other people's lives but none to her own. However, she'd do her best to make the day pleasant for them; after all, it was only one day in the year and if the eating of peppermints gave Sister Francis some satisfaction it was not right to thwart her.

She smiled sweetly then at Francis, and as Francis offered the sweets once more, and she was stretching forward to take one there was a sudden dunt to the back of the car and a crash of something falling on the road. The car stopped and the nuns looked at one another, their heads bobbing in consternation. They saw the driver raise himself slowly from his seat, walk back the road, and return again with a touch of his cap at the window.

'A slight accident, Sister,' he said, addressing Reverend Mother. 'A cyclist crashed into our back wheel. But it's nothing serious, I think.'

Reverend Mother went out leaving the door open, and

through it there came the free sunlight, the cool air, and the hum of people talking. She was back again in a few minutes with her handkerchief dabbed with blood, and collected other handkerchiefs from the nuns, who followed her out on to the road. Sister Paul stood back and saw amongst the bunch of people a young man reclining on the bank of the road, a hand to his head. 'I can't stand the sight of blood,' she said to herself, her fingers clutching her rosary beads. She beckoned to a lad who was resting on his bicycle: 'Is he badly hurt, lad? He'll not die, will he?'

'Not a bit of him, Sister. He had his coat folded over the handlebars and the sleeve of it caught in the wheel and flung him against the car.'

'Go up, like a decent boy, and have a good look at him again.'

But before the lad had reached the group the chauffeur had assisted the injured man to his feet and was leading him to the car. The handkerchiefs were tied like a turban about his head, his trousers were torn at the knee, and a holy medal was pinned to his braces.

'Put his coat on or he'll catch cold,' Reverend Mother was saying.

'Och, Sister, don't worry about me,' the man was saying. 'Sure it was my own fault. Ye weren't to blame at all. I'll go back again on my own bicycle – I'm fit enough.'

Reverend Mother consulted the chauffeur and whatever advice he gave her the injured man was put into the back of the car. Sister Francis was ordered into the vacant seat beside the driver, the baskets were handed to Paul and Clare, and when the man's bicycle was tied to the carrier they drove off for the hospital in the town.

The young man, sitting between Reverend Mother and Sister Paul, shut his eyes in embarrassment, and when the blood oozed through the pile of handkerchiefs Reverend Mother took the serviettes from the baskets and tied them round his head and under his chin, and all the time the man kept repeating: 'I'm a sore trouble to you, indeed. And sure it was my own fault.' She told him to button his coat or he would catch cold, and when he had done so she noticed a Total Abstinence badge in the lapel.

'A good clean-living man,' she thought, and to think that he was the one to meet with an injury while many an old drunkard could travel the roads of Ireland on a bicycle and arrive home without pain or scratch or cough.

"'Tis a blessing of God you weren't killed,' she said, with a rush of protectiveness, and she reached for the thermos flask from the basket and handed the man a cup of tea.

Now and again Sister Paul would steal a glance at him, but the sight of his pale face and the cup trembling in his hand and rattling on the saucer made her turn to the window where she tried to lose herself in contemplation. But all her previous mood was now scattered from her mind, and she could think of nothing only the greatness of Reverend Mother and the cool way she took command of an incident that would have left the rest of them weak and confused.

'How are you feeling now?' she could hear Reverend Mother asking. 'Would you like another sandwich?'

'No, thank you, Sister; sure I had my good breakfast in me before I left the house. I'm a labouring man and since I'm out of work this past three months my wife told me to go off on the bike and have a swim with myself. I was going to take one of the youngsters on the bar of the bike but my wife wouldn't let me.'

'She had God's grace about her,' said Reverend Mother. 'That should be a lesson to you,' and as she refilled his cup from the thermos flask she thought that if the young man had been killed they, in a way, would have had to provide his widow and children with some help. 'And we were only travelling slowly,' she found herself saying aloud.

'Sure, Sister, no one knows that better than myself. You were keeping well into your own side of the road and when I was ready to sail past you on the hill my coat caught in the front wheel and my head hit the back of your car.'

'S-s-s,' and the nuns drew in their breath with shrinking solicitude.

They drove up to the hospital, and after Reverend Mother had consulted the doctor and was told that the wound was only a slight abrasion and contusion she returned light-heartedly to the car. Sister Clare made no remark when she heard the news but as the wheels of the car rose and fell on the road they seemed to echo what was in her mind: *abrasion and contusion, abrasion and contusion.* 'Abrasion and contusion of what?' she asked herself. 'Surely the doctor wouldn't say "head" – abrasion and contusion of the head?' No, there must be some medical term that Reverend Mother had withheld from them, and as she was about to probe Reverend Mother for the answer the car swung unexpectedly into the convent avenue. 'Oh,' she said with disappointment, and when alighting from the car and seeing Sister Francis give the remains of her sweets to the chauffeur she knew that for her, too, the day was at an end.

They all passed inside except Reverend Mother who stood on the steps at the door noting the quiet silence of the grounds and the heat-shadows flickering above the flower-beds. With a mocking smile she saw the lawn-mower at rest on the uncut lawn and found herself mimicking the gardener: 'I'll have it all finished today, Sister, I'll have it all finished today.' She put a hand to her throbbing head and crossed the gravel path to look for him, and there in the slump of laurel bushes she found him fast asleep, his hat over his face to keep off the flies, and three empty porter bottles beside him. She tiptoed away from him. 'He has had a better day than we have had,' she said to herself, 'so let him sleep it out, for it's the last he'll have at my expense. . . . Oh, drink is a curse,' and she thought of the injury that had befallen the young man with the Abstinence Badge and he as sober as any judge. Then she drew up suddenly as something quick and urgent came into her mind. 'Of course! – he would take the job as gardener, and he unemployed this past three months!' With head erect she sped quickly across the grass and into the convent. Sister Paul was still in the corridor when she saw Reverend Mother lift the phone and ring up the hospital: 'Is he still there? . . . He's all right? . . . That's good. . . . Would you tell him to call to see me sometime this afternoon?' There was a transfigured look on her face as she put down the receiver and strode across to Sister Paul. 'Sister Paul,' she said, 'you may tell the other Sisters that on tomorrow we will set out again for the shore.' Sister Paul smiled and whisked away down the corridor: 'Isn't Reverend Mother great the way she can handle things?' she said to herself. 'And to think that on tomorrow I'll be able to see the poplars again.'

DOROTHY BAKER

SUMMER

A WOMAN STOOD on a river bridge, leaning her arms on sunlit stone. Behind her, in a clearing, a black wooden tea-shed and a notice: TEAS. MINERALS. CIGARETTES. In the clearing, at the edge of the woods, two children gathered blackberries, gravely intent, heads straight with concentration on their slender necks. They picked slowly, without moving, ceremoniously inspecting each fruit before they placed it in the basket. They were little children, dwarfed almost to nothing by wooded hills descending steeply on every side into a narrow valley. For a few moments the woman watched them with detachment. They were not her children. She turned her attention to the river.

She leaned over the bridge and stared at the water. It was warm and golden and restless where everything else was deathly still. The woman had pale hair and a pale face, with large blunt features that shone like wax, as though suffering a melting change from heat of the sun. Her eyes, too, were pale, and she wore a stiff apron with a bib, the sort now only worn by country women. Her anxious, ugly face and homely apron, at humble odds with rich woods, brought a kind of back-door intimacy to the lonely place. A place that should have sheltered none but fairy folk or stolen children, or maybe a prince riding to a castle in the hills.

The castle in the hills had long ceased to expect a fairy prince, or, indeed, a man of any kind. The woman on the bridge knew all about that. A female stronghold, the castle.

247

No man penetrated farther than its grass-green courtyard; tradesmen at that, bringing food to Mrs. Thompson and her three daughters, earthly remnants of a butcher from the north. He'd made a good thing out of the last war. Those days you could make a fortune. There's been a chance for profits – even for profiteering. Butchering. A castle at the end of it for his womenfolk – he hadn't lived long to enjoy it. Time to make a packet – and then good-bye. Still, money hadn't made his daughters marriageable. Three ugly elderly females and a miserly mother, living snug and secure up there. From every window finest views of England, and they stuffed round a fire, seeing only pet dogs on the hearth or their own unlikeable faces. And she working for them, nine till one every morning, before coming to the bridge. Great fat women with rolling r's and clipped e's. Dyed hair. Not folks you respected. They couldn't go out riding in a car any more than other people nowadays.

The woman shifted her elbows for ease on the stone, and looked again to where the children played. She cried with perfunctory suddenness:

'Polly. Sam. Don't go too far in.'

Woods and hills indignantly echoed her words; like a religious meeting profaned by an unbeliever, echo bestirred itself to protest. Polly's blue dress startled back on to green grass, the little boy followed. His voice excited and friendly, he shouted:

'We seen a rabbit. Just here.'

He didn't expect any reply, but he went on shouting:

'We got some blackberries. Big ones.'

The little girl looked silent and smiling towards the bridge. She was too young to shout sentences.

Their guardian didn't seem to hear or see them. She continued to stare at the water. The way it moved, the transparent

248

amber colour it took from yellow boulders, held her there. In spite of its urge to be gone, it was more soothing than the hills that swung narrow paths down to the valley, till your head turned giddy with looping twists of downwardness. To come here six afternoons only to stare at water. Ten years without ever considering it, except as a tourist attraction, or for washing up. Six days and she watching the river till she knew every trick by which it took the boulders, every bough that bent and stroked its surface. Six days and none but wood-cutters going through the valley on their way home. They brought their tea with them. She saw them swinging blue empty cans as they descended the paths, smoking and talking together, and a nod for her as they passed the hut. A silent woman, a nod was all she expected.

Wood-cutters' work didn't depend on people. Trees were there, waiting to be cut down. A shame, the way they felled the lovely things. There'd be none left by the end of the war. To grow like that for patient years, and then laid low in a single afternoon. The same with the business – grown and flourishing – now cut off by war. All the blessed summer you could count the customers on your two hands.

Nobody knew when the war would end. As many opinions about that as there were tongues to utter them. It all depended how hard they were hit, what they believed. Maybe you could trust Old Moore, but he wrapped things up so. Still, her brother swore by him, and he was shrewd enough. She slipped her hand into her apron pocket and took out *Old Moore's Almanac*. Eyes screwed in concentration, she turned pages slowly, looking for the place. According to Old Moore, the war *might* be over next autumn. A year and more to get through, the rent of the hut still going on. Another winter after the war had finished before her trade could look up. Then spring for folks to settle down to peaceful ways again, and by summer maybe, char-à-bancs on the road in search of tea and beauty spots. Not that she really believed things would be as good as before. Sunshine, fine weather, made you sad for times that were gone. She wasn't looking forward all that eagerly. The good days they'd seen. Her three helpers in the rush season, the kettle boiling for dear life, no sooner emptied than filled and on again; plates of ham, cakes, and she ordering it all, as busy as a body could wish. Times she'd felt almost merry. Hard work? Who minded, with money going into your pocket and customers in rows on the benches. It took townsfolk for spending and talking. The more they went on the more they ate and drank to strengthen themselves. They could never finish about the view. They praised it till she puffed with possessive pride in hills and woods and water; wild daffodils in spring and heather purpling the summer. The view had made the trade. She'd never bothered about it much, growing up with it. Not till these last few weeks. And now she watched the river with forlorn affection, grieving over their shared desertion. What was the good of scenery without folks to admire it and take a little refreshment?

Four years, near enough, the war had gone on, and visitors getting fewer and fewer. Scraping the rent together. Daren't let the place go, others would get in first, offering more money for the business she and her brother had built up. Foolish of him to marry. Especially that feeble creature. Till then they'd been well enough together. And now four children in the little cottage. And she going back to cleaning. After tasting independence and being your own master. Dyed hair and ugliness, too fat to stir. Pay somebody else to stir for them. And little enough *pay* at that.

She folded *Old Moore* and pushed it back into her pocket. If it told the truth, things weren't too bad. Hold on for two winters. Thinking of her brother, she looked for the children. She called out with automatic suddenness:

'Polly. Sam. Don't go too far in.'

The children were lost in play and their aunt's words came flatly through the sunshine, no more than call of bird or droning of insect or familiar murmur of water. The woman was too absorbed, too tired and dispirited, to repeat her cry. She struggled with thought like a fly in a web, and freeing herself one way, came back to the snare of the river. Six days and no one to ask a cup of tea. Six days of mellow golden weather, woods at their best, sometimes a buzzard hovering in the still air, sometimes a kingfisher darting. That had been a star turn. In good days.

At last she moved from the bridge. TEAS. MINERALS. CIGARETTES. She read the sign outside the tea-shed with a touch of old pride. Ten shillings to have it painted. Leaving the sun-soaked road she went into the dark shed, into the back room, where she kept her stores. She opened cupboards aimlessly. Rows of empty shelves. Cups hanging on hooks, spoons in a box and a solitary cake made a week ago in case of customers. She might light a fire and put the kettle on. Supposing she were to make tea, the fragrant smell, curling among the trees, might tempt somebody down to her. Would it be inviting bad luck? She hesitated between superstition and wishing. Then she went out and collected sticks, drew them together on the bit of hard earth behind the shed and kindled them.

The fire smoked, crackled, burst into thin flame, scarcely visible in sunshine. She hung the great black kettle on the tripod. She took down dusty cups and saucers and arranged them on the trestle tables. When she had laid out every cup and saucer the place looked busy, as though waiting for a crowd. The sight of so many cups peopled the valley with memories – hoot of horn, stealthy sound of cars on soft earth, singing and shouts of children among trees, lovers holding hands by the river. The fire burned with a sweet wood smell, and while she moved from table to table, with an illusion of old importance the kettle began to sing. She fetched the cake from the cupboard. It would have been nice to have one for each table. She set it on the table nearest the road, warmed the teapot and went back to the bridge.

She looked along the valley road. As far as her sharp eyes could see, there was no one. She returned to the hut and made the tea, then poured herself a cup. It was fresh and comforting and wood-smoke blended with the tea's scented flavour. She sat for a long time, crouched at the table by the road. She might as well call the children and give them a piece of cake – nobody else seemed to want it. She shouted to her nephew and niece, but they did not answer. They had gone too far into the woods.

She looked round the hut at the cups and saucers mutely shining there. It had been a good cup. Nothing now to do but put things back. She wasn't inclined to do that. She walked out of the hut without a backward glance. She had forgotten the children. All her worries yielded to a trance-like pleasure. The tea and the hot sun made her features more meltingly waxen than ever.

She began to walk along the river, towards a bald and conical hill. The woods and heights soared round her, and she a piebald speck in the narrow valley. The woods and hills were unstable, in danger of falling, she alone remained firm. She touched the swelling toadflax growing sturdily, stems thrust first outward, then upward, from the boulders by the river. She smelt the late honeysuckle, tangled high in briars. Every sound, every smell, was sharp and sweet. When she had walked for some time she remembered the hut, as though it were a place far off in time as well as space. She looked back. The place was lost to sight. If she returned there would be cups to put away, children to find, the tea-shed to lock, and the drag back to the village. She never wanted to do these things again. Her brother's house, her brother's children, her brother's wife, and not a sixpence taken.

She intended to go a long way. She pushed her way through difficult places, slopped over marshy ground. But when she had gone round the foot of the bald hill, back into woods again, and it was good to be with trees, she began to feel tired. She sat down by the river, thinking only of sleep. As far as she had come the river was amber, with golden stones and yellow boulders. Willow and mountain ash grew here, darkening the water with splashes of shadow. Little currents and eddies were drawn out from the boulders, wavering into fine black lines, like bars for river music. The longer she looked at the water, the deeper she seemed to sink into herself, as though that self were now seized by the strong arms of the river and pushed into cool and secret places.

In spite of sun, on the bank it was chilly. Trees made earth cold, cold as a tomb. She wanted to escape the coldness of earth, the calculations of seasons and times; she wanted to go away from hills, twisting their paths above her, like screws of anxiety turning in her head. She thought of ways to escape. She knelt at the river edge and bent to see the woman reflected there. Moist features, broad, folded arms, hair straggled and bunned, and the water breaking up furrows of care into delicate movement. Not so ugly after all, not fat and dyed and raddled like some she knew. The river split care, cut it into pieces of watery colour, covered it with a cloth of clear gold. With one hand grasping the grasses at the edge, she leaned far over the water. Her image was already captive there, a promise of surrender. Hills and trees and water whirled in fearful invitation. She knelt rigid and cold on the bank, waiting. Then hope like a patient stream revived, fed her with reckonings of seasons and times, steadied the hills and warmed her to reality. Two more winters. Four already gone through. Hold on – somehow. The summer afternoon divided into duties and anxieties, cups to put back, hut to lock, children to find. Just go on.

But her body was rooted to earth, she was too tired yet to move. Remembering only sleep, warm golden sleep, she stretched out on the broad grasses. Deep and dark and protective, sleep covered her, held her in forgetfulness till stars came out and she woke, thinking of the children.

The children played in the woods. They heard their aunt's sharp cry from time to time, then until sunset nothing. They pretended to be rabbits, the little boy showing his sister how to jump and how to burrow. When he felt tired, he emptied the blackberries on to the turf and counted out ten for his sister and ten for himself and put them in the basket. The rest he left on the grass. When he had done this they went to find their aunt. They stood in the doorway of the hut and saw cups and saucers on every table, ready for a party. And the cake cut in slices. The little boy was puzzled. It was late and he couldn't see his aunt anywhere. She was not in the yard with the kettle; she was not getting water from the river. The sun was red and the woods dark. He stood waiting, not knowing what to do. At last he chose two pieces of cake and gave one of them to his sister. Taking the little girl's hand, he began to walk home, up the steep road through the woods.

JOSEPH ZOBEL

FLOWERS! LOVELY FLOWERS!

Translated by Robert Baldick

NOBODY COULD REMEMBER spring coming so late before. On the first of May the lily of the valley was still not in flower. It was raining and the skies were grey. Everybody was saying that the florists must have made a fortune with their hot-house lily of the valley and that anybody who had found in the woods a few sprigs with two or three little bell-flowers on them must have made thousands and thousands of francs.

As a matter of fact, it was leaves that were being sold everywhere – leaves with, at the very most, a fragile crook studded with a few greenish granules.

That gives some idea how late spring was!

Yet the fact remains that in the forest everything was on the point of bursting out into buds and blossoms; everything was like us, swollen with the longing for spring; and there was no doubt that as soon as the sun broke through, the fine weather would rush on to the scene, all tousled and frisky.

'Because when it's like this, it comes quickly,' the women forecast, on the street corners or in the grocers' shops.

Sure enough, this particular Sunday, the weather was fine. Nobody could have expected it to be such a fine day.

Immediately after lunch the town had spilled out into the forest, where every car which arrived had a great deal of trouble finding a shady spot to park in; just as anybody who had hoped to read or rest by himself could be seen wandering about for a long time. The whole town was there, with its cars, its sweethearts and its newly-married couples; its prams, its crowds of children, and its white-haired inhabitants, always dressed in black, even in warm, sunny weather, whom the Government had just respectfully christened the 'financially underprivileged'; not to mention the Parisians who could be seen everywhere, in whole families – children, parents and grandparents gathered round folding tables, playing cards and arguing while they drank liquids of all colours from plastic bottles.

Others stayed in their cars where the radio poured out the voluble flow of the commentary on some football match at the Parc des Princes.

There were some who were playing ball games, and also a few bald, pot-bellied gentlemen who had already taken off their jackets, feeling younger that way, to run races with their grandsons, to the women's vast amusement.

It was good to be laughing in the sunshine.

There were a great many of those boys in shorts and those young girls in jeans who, with rucksacks on their backs, explored the forest every Sunday and in every season.

For the first time in the year, the ice-cream vendor had reappeared, in a white linen jacket and a white cap, under the canopy of his little car which had been repainted white and bore a sort of pattern of red letters forming a Spanish-sounding name. The children went towards him like lambs to a drinking trough, and for twenty or thirty centimes he handed them ice-cream cornets in one or two colours – pink, yellow, brown – which at a distance you might have taken for bunches of flowers.

This was in the forest, at a spot where the oaks and the beeches had graciously left a big green space for the grass, and the ladies in their bright coloured skirts bent down there to pick dandelions, daisies, or four-leaf clovers.

The road cut through this big green clearing, a road which you couldn't even cross, because the cars drove by in both directions in two uninterrupted lines; so that you stood there as if you were on the banks of a river, watching the waters flowing past, torn into two contrary currents in the middle.

The speed of the cars produced a violent current of air which everybody treated with caution, because it raised the women's skirts or threatened to fill people's eyes with the fine dust which hemmed the edges of the road.

He was the only person who, on the contrary, remained standing at the roadside, and as each car approached, instead of drawing back, he bent a little further forward, raising his arms. The faster the car was moving, the more he insisted on waving at it, even taking a few steps towards it, as if he were trying to hypnotize it; and now and then, in fact, to everybody's astonishment, a car would slow down, like a bird coming to rest, and draw up a little farther on, while he rushed towards it, brandishing the two bunches of white flowers which had produced the miracle.

The day before, he had probably felt the fine weather coming, beyond any shadow of a doubt, and had thought of all the lily of the valley which had not flowered in time for the first of May and about which people had said: 'A week or so from now . . . as soon as the sun comes out. . . .'

Besides, he had been able to see how far advanced it was already: he had watched it opening, wandering through the forest as he did every day, in all weathers, either to pick mushrooms, daffodils, or dandelions, according to the season, or to gather dead wood.

He knew the whole forest.

He had therefore got up early – not that there was anything unusual about that, for he boasted that he never slept – and he had gone off in the direction of Verneuil, which is the lily of the valley district, just as Recloses is the daffodil district. Everybody knows that, but he was almost certain that nobody would get there before him if he went early in the morning; it is a long way.

And there was plenty of lily of the valley, just as he had suspected. There was so much that, without exaggeration, he could have brought along a scythe instead of bending down to gather it sprig by sprig. He did not stop picking it all morning, either squatting on his haunches and moving forward like a child imitating a duck's walk, or else dragging himself along on his knees. His back and shoulders had hurt, and his thighs and calves had ached as if they had been beaten with a stick. That was what had given him a rather jerky, unsteady walk; but Heaven could be his witness that all the time he had been alone in the forest, his tongue had been stuck to his palate for want of a bottle of red wine. Indeed, he had been so thirsty that he had said to himself:

'At the first pub I come to, even if I haven't sold anything yet, I'm going to give the landlady a bunch of lily of the valley in exchange for a glass of wine.'

The landlady would not have lost on the deal.

It was beautiful lily of the valley, sweet-smelling and – he could be proud of this – prettily arranged.

When he had finished gathering it, he had sat down in the grass, in the sunshine, with the lily of the valley heaped up between his legs; the whole heap of little white flowers next to his boots which looked as if they were made of earth, they were so dirty, and his corduroy trousers which shone like old bark. Then he put them together sprig by sprig in one fist cupped to form a flower-holder, a fist carved and covered with a network of black crevices, which he raised to examine the bunch of lily of the valley. This bunch, with each new sprig, grew and took shape in the sunshine, gradually becoming a big white flower which to all intents and purposes he had made himself, and which he surrounded with a collarette of soft green leaves, carefully chosen. Next, after tying it with a strip of fibre which he held between his teeth, he spun it round with a wink before laying it gently on the grass.

It was like a game, like something that was not really serious, at least for a man of his age who could not be expected to waste his time over flowers.

Yet it was work all the same, and it took a whole morning.

'Anyhow, bunches of lily of the valley as good as this ought to sell well at a franc each,' he thought.

And in fact, business had begun quite well. He had chosen this place specially. Farther down, there was a bend, and a little farther up, a hill. Here, the cars could stop easily and drive off again easily.

True, there were some which drove straight at him at top speed, threatening to wipe him out if he didn't jump back in time on to the side of the road; but now and then the sight of the two bunches of lily of the valley which he held out in both hands reduced the frenzied speed of a handsome car which, gently, obediently, came to him like a good dog being offered a piece of sugar.

'Oh, how lovely they are!'

It was the same exclamation every time. And they seemed to think that the price was very reasonable.

'Oh, they're beautiful!' exclaimed the fine ladies, leaning out of the windows of their cars.

And he would add:

'See how good they smell, Madame.'

Then the lady would stay for a moment with her eyelids – mother-of-pearl eyelids fringed with long black lashes – lowered over the bouquet – offering a prayer – which the dirty, bruised old hand was dedicating to her delicate face.

Sometimes the lady refused the flowers he offered her, making him come closer to the car in order to choose for herself, out of the bag which he carried slung over his shoulder, a bunch which struck her as even bigger or better arranged.

Two bunches, three bunches – and sometimes he was allowed to keep the change.

'Thanks, ladies and gents. My lily of the valley will bring you luck.'

Speed would snatch the car away and carry it off in a roar promptly reduced by distance, and just as promptly increased by the arrival of another car.

Then, passing his hand over his bag, like an animal polishing its fur, he would think to himself with a half-smile:

'If it keeps up like this. . . .'

Quickly he would resume his position at the roadside, his arms in the air, bending forward or stepping forward, or else taking a step back whenever he felt the attraction of his bouquets giving way in the face of the blind speed of the car which had appeared. For the fact of the matter was that it was not at all easy to stop one.

But for some time it had become a sport for him, and he had been keeping a note of the points he scored.

The consequence was that he had failed to notice the van which had drawn up some way behind him; a black van looking like a bumble-bee with all the colours of the forest and the roadside caught in its enamel shell, and its long antenna vibrating nervously, tracing dazzling curves in the air.

Two gendarmes had got out of it, wearing blue uniforms, peaked caps, and boots so tight-fitting and shining that anybody might have thought they were brand-new toys straight out of the window of a big department-store.

He had not seen them.

And what if he had?

So that now, all of a sudden, he heard a voice behind him say:

'What the hell are you up to?'

To tell the truth, he wasn't afraid of the police; he had never killed or stolen, as the saying goes.

All the same, he still thought that it was a bad sign when they came on the scene, especially when they spoke to you like that.

He turned round, holding up his bunches of lily of the valley in both hands.

'Me?' he asked.

'Yes, you!' retorted the other gendarme, coming up behind. 'We asked you what the hell you're up to.'

'But, sergeant . . . I wasn't. . . .'

'Have you an identity card on you?'

'But I wasn't doing anything, sergeant. . . .'

His arms had fallen to his sides like two branches struck by lightning and, immediately, the two bunches of flowers seemed to have lost their brilliance.

'I told you to give me your papers,' the gendarme repeated.

Then, after putting the two bunches of lily of the valley back into his bag, he pulled the lapel of his old jacket away from his chest with one hand, and with the other took out of his inside pocket something like a packet of rotten leaves, which he opened and thumbed through with trembling fingers, under the impatient eyes of the two gendarmes.

'Here you are, sergeant.'

The gendarme turned the card over and, pursing his lips, examined it in an effort to decipher some handwriting half-obliterated with grease. The other gendarme came up and read the identity card over his colleague's shoulder, and then took a thick notebook bound in imitation black leather out of his pocket.

'But I wasn't doing anything wrong, officer.'

'Where do you live?'

'Pardon, officer?'

'I asked you where you live.'

'In the village.'

He pointed to Barbigou, which was out of sight but quite close, barely two kilometres away by road, or else at the end of the little lane leading away from the other side of the road.

'At whose house in the village?'

'Well, to tell the truth, officer, it's with the people I work for now and then.'

'And who are you working for just now?'

'Well, the fact is that, for the moment, people aren't taking on much seasonal labour, because of this never-ending winter. But there are quite a few people who've booked me already. As you can imagine, what with the delay we've had, there'll be lots of new potatoes to pick round here.'

The gendarme, who had taken out of a loop on the cover of his notebook a little pencil with a nickel-plated clip, had started writing, and went on writing, occasionally darting a glance at the card his colleague was holding.

'But I haven't done anything wrong, officer.'

And as the gendarme went on writing imperturbably, he asked:

'What the devil have I done wrong? Don't you think you're being a bit hard on me?'

'You haven't any right to sell lily of the valley from the forest,' one of the gendarmes replied in exasperation. 'You know that perfectly well.'

'What do you mean, I haven't any right? The lily of the valley in the forest belongs to everybody.'

The other gendarme, the one who was writing, lifted his pencil and retorted:

'Exactly: it belongs to everybody, but when you pick it and sell it, it's like robbing the public. Don't you understand that?'

He said this without raising his voice, with a cold look.

Already the children and a few adults who were on the same side of the road had come nearer, and it was turning towards them that he repeated, more and more exasperated:

'What have I done wrong?'

'Not to mention the accidents you risked causing with your antics in the roadway,' the gendarme went on.

The policeman handed his card back to him.

'I swear I didn't know it was against the law, officer, seeing that only last week everybody . . .'

'Yes, but selling lily of the valley is allowed only on the first of May. It's no use acting the innocent.'

From the other side of the road, he could be seen gesticulating, bending over as he spoke and thumping his chest in front of the gendarme, who put his notebook back in his pocket as if to say: 'All right, we'll see.'

Everybody was watching, even those who, sitting on the rocks or stretched out on the grass, were putting on a show of indifference.

The mad flood of cars went on flowing past.

All of a sudden, the onlookers saw him distributing his flowers: one to this gentleman, two to that lady, and then another two at the same time to a little boy who promptly ran off with them. Some children rushed towards him, while others dashed away, shouting:

'Mummy! Daddy! Look!'

Those on the other side of the road couldn't manage to

cross because of the speed at which the cars were following one another. There were a good four or five who started off, then drew back, until at last, taking advantage of a lull, they all set off together like a pack of hounds, while a panic-stricken lady screamed:

'Jean-Claude! Jean-Claude! Oh, Heavens above!'

But it was too late.

The bag containing the lily of the valley was empty.

Now the man was cursing and stamping, throwing his cap into the air, picking it up again, and flinging his arms about in all directions as if he would have liked to explode.

The children drew back in amazement, possibly afraid that he might suddenly turn vicious, but a lady went over to him and said:

'It's really very pretty, your lily of the valley. Thank you for the lovely bunch you gave my grand-daughter.'

She showed him the bunch of lily of the valley which, held delicately between her fingers, had become a positive adornment. But he wasn't listening to her.

'Can any of you tell me what crime I was committing?' he shouted.

'Here,' said the lady, 'take this.'

Seeing the coin she was holding out to him, he protested:

'Keep your money, Madame. I'm a tramp, a vagrant as they put it. I've no family, I've no right to eat.'

'Oh,' said the lady, 'don't get so upset!'

'I'm not entitled to the workhouse,' he went on. 'There's only prison for me, you understand?'

Braving his wild gesture, the lady succeeded in slipping the coin into the pocket of his jacket and went off, stroking her nose with the bunch of lily of the valley.

Then, grumbling to himself, he walked along the bank with hesitant, unsteady steps, and finally dropped on to the grass and stayed there, curled up, with his face buried in his hands.

He wasn't crying.

He curled up more and more, and now and then let out a groan, like a wounded animal losing all its blood – or a vagrant, a tramp, shamelessly sleeping off his drink.

But nobody was paying attention to him any more.

The clearing had taken on the appearance of a huge country fair in which the sun-topped trees were playing the trumpets and the bagpipes.

YVONNE VERA

WHY DON'T YOU CARVE
OTHER ANIMALS

HE SITS OUTSIDE the gates of the Africans-Only hospital, making models out of wood. The finished products are on old newspapers on the ground around him. A painter sits to his right, his finished work leaning against the hospital fence behind them. In the dense township, cars screech, crowds flow by, voices rise, and ambulances speed into the emergency unit of the hospital, their flashing orange light giving fair warning to oncoming traffic. Through the elephants he carves, and also the giraffes, with oddly slanting necks, the sculptor brings the jungle to the city. His animals walk on the printed newspaper sheets, but he mourns that they have no life in them. Sometimes in a fit of anger he collects his animals and throws them frenziedly into his cardboard box, desiring not to see their lifeless forms against the chaotic movement of traffic which flows through the hospital gates.

'Do you want that crocodile? It's a good crocodile. Do you want it?' A mother coaxes a little boy who has been crying after his hospital visit. A white bandage is wrapped tight around his right arm. The boy holds his arm with his other hand, aware of the mother's attention, which makes him draw attention to his temporary deformity. She kneels beside him and looks into his eyes, pleading.

'He had an injection. You know how the children fear the needle,' the mother informs the man. She buys the crocodile, and hands it to the boy. The man watches one of his animals go, carried between the little boy's tiny fingers. His

271

animals have no life in them, and the man is tempted to put them back in the box. He wonders if the child will ever see a moving crocodile, surrounded as he is by the barren city, where the only rivers are the tarred roads.

A man in a white coat stands looking at the elephants, and at the man who continues carving. He picks a red elephant, whose tusk is carved along its body, so that it cannot raise it. A red elephant? The stranger is perplexed, and amused, and decides to buy the elephant, though it is poorly carved and cannot lift its tusk. He will place it beside the window in his office, where it can look out at the patients in the queue. Why are there no eyes carved on the elephant? Perhaps the paint has covered them up.

The carver suddenly curses.

'What is wrong?' the painter asks.

'Look at the neck of this giraffe.'

The painter looks at the giraffe, and the two men explode into uneasy laughter. It is not easy to laugh when one sits so close to the sick. The carver wonders if he has not carved some image of himself, or of some afflicted person who stopped and looked at his breathless animals. He looks at the cardboard box beside him, and decides to place it in the shade, away from view.

'Why don't you carve other animals. Like lions and chimpanzees?' the painter asks. 'You are always carving giraffes and your only crocodile has been bought!' The painter has had some influence on the work of the carver, lending him the paints to colour his animals. The red elephant was his idea.

'The elephant has ruled the forest for a long time, he is older than the forest, but the giraffe extends his neck and struts above the trees, as though the forest belonged to him. He eats the topmost leaves, while the elephant spends the day rolling in the mud. Do you not find it interesting? This struggle between the elephant and the giraffe, to eat the topmost leaves in the forest?' The ambulances whiz past, into the emergency unit of the Africans-Only hospital.

The painter thinks briefly, while he puts the final touches on an image of the Victoria Falls which he paints from a memory gathered from newspapers and magazines. He has never seen the Falls. The water must be blue, to give emotion to the picture, he thinks. He has been told that when the water is shown on a map, it has to be blue, and that indeed when there is a lot of it, as in the sea, the water looks like the sky. So he is generous in his depiction, and shocking blue waves cascade unnaturally over the rocky precipice.

'The giraffe walks proudly, majestically, because of the beautiful tapestry that he carries on his back. That is what the struggle is about. Otherwise they are equals, the elephant has his long tusk to reach the leaves and the giraffe has his long neck.'

He inserts two lovers at the corner of the picture, their arms around each other as they stare their love into the blue water. He wants to make the water sing to them. So he paints a bird at the top of the painting, hovering over the falls, its beak open in song. He wishes he had painted a dove, instead of this black bird which looks like a crow.

The carver borrows some paint and puts yellow and black spots on the giraffe with the short neck. He has long accepted that he cannot carve perfect animals, but will not throw them away. Maybe someone, walking out of the Africans-Only hospital, will seek some cheer in his piece. But when he has finished applying the dots, the paint runs down the sides of the animal, and it looks a little like a zebra.

'Why do you never carve a dog or a cat? Something that city people have seen. Even a rat would be good, there are lots of rats in the township!' There is much laughter. The painter realizes that a lot of spray from the falls must be reaching the lovers, so he paints off their heads with a red umbrella. He notices suddenly that something is missing in the picture, so he extends the lovers' free hands, and gives them some yellow ice cream. The picture is now full of life.

'What is the point of carving a dog? Why do you not paint dogs and cats and mice?' The carver has never seen the elephant or the giraffe that he carves so ardently. He picks up a piece of unformed wood.

Will it be a giraffe or an elephant? His carving is also his dreaming.

DAMON GALGUT

SHADOWS

THE TWO OF us are pedalling down the road. The light of the moon makes shadows under the trees, through which we pass, going fast. Robert is a little ahead of me, standing up in his seat. On either side of his bike the dogs are running, Ben and Sheba, I can never tell the difference between them.

It's lovely to be like this; him and me, with the warm air going over us like hands.

'Oh,' I say. 'Oh, oh, oh . . .'

He turns, looking at me over his shoulder. 'What?' he calls.

I shake my head at him. He turns away.

As we ride, I can see the round shape of the moon as it appears between the trees. With the angle of the road it's off to the right, above the line of the slope. The sky around it is pale, as if it's been scrubbed too long. It hurts to look up.

It's that moon we're riding out to see. For two weeks now people have talked about nothing else. 'The eclipse,' they say. 'Are you going to watch the eclipse?' I didn't understand at first, but my father explained it to me. 'The shadow of the earth,' he says, 'thrown across the moon.' It's awesome to think of that, of the size of some shadows. When people ask me after this, I tell them, 'Yes,' I tell them. 'I'm going to watch the eclipse.'

But this is Robert's idea. A week ago he said to me, 'D'you want to go down to the lake on Saturday night? We can watch the eclipse from there.'

'Yes,' I said. 'We can do that.'

So we ride down towards the lake under the moon. On either side the dogs are running, making no sound in the heavy dust, their tongues trailing wetly from the corners of their mouths.

The road is beginning to slope down now as we come near to the lake. The ground on either side becomes higher, so that we're cycling down between two shoulders of land. The forest is on either side, not moving in the quiet air. It gives off a smell: thick and green. I breathe deeply, and my lungs are full of the raw, hairy scent of the jungle.

We're moving quite fast on the downhill, so we don't have to pedal any more. Ahead of me, I see Robert break from the cut in the road and emerge again into the flat path that runs across the floor of the forest. A moment later I do so too, whizzing into the heavy layers of shadows as if they are solid. The momentum is wonderful, full of danger, as if we're close to breaking free of gravity. But it only lasts a moment. Then we're slowing again, dragged back by the even surface of the road and the sand on the wheels.

The turnoff is here. I catch up with Robert and we turn off side by side, pedalling again to keep moving. Ahead of us the surface of the lake is between the trees, stretched out greenly in the dark. The trees thin out, there's a bare strip along the edge of the water.

We stop here. The path we were riding on goes, straight and even, into the water. That's because it used to lead somewhere before they flooded the valley to make the lake. They say that under the water there are houses and gardens, standing empty and silent in the currents below. I think of them and shiver. It's always night down there at the bottom of the lake; the moon never shines.

But we've stopped far from where the path disappears.

We're still side by side, straddling the bikes, looking out. The dogs have also stopped, stock-still, as if they can smell something in the air. There's a faint wind coming in off the water, more of a breeze really. On the far side of the lake we can see the lights of houses. Far off to the right, at the furthest corner of the water, are the lights of my house. I glance towards it and try to imagine them: my father and mother, sitting out on the front veranda, looking across the water to us. But there are no lights where we are.

'There,' says Robert.

He's pointing. I follow his finger and I also see it: the moon, clear of the trees on the other side. It really is huge tonight, as if it's been swollen with water. If you stare at it for long enough you can make out the craters on its surface, faint and blue, like shadows. Its light comes down softly like rain and I see I was wrong – it makes the water silver, not green.

'We've got a view of it,' I say.

But Robert is moving away already. 'Come,' he says. 'Let's make a fire.'

We leave the bikes leaning together against the trunk of a tree and set out to look for firewood. We separate and walk out by ourselves into the forest. But I can still see Robert a little distance away as he wanders around, bending now and then to pick up bits of wood. The dogs are with him. It isn't dense or overgrown down here. The floor of the forest is smooth. Apart from the sound of our feet and the lapping of the lake, it's quiet here.

There isn't much dead wood around. I pick up a few branches, some chunks of log. I carry them down to where the bikes are. Robert has already made one trip here, I see from a small pile of twigs. I don't much feel like this hunting in the dark, so I delay a while, wiping my hands on my pants.

I look out over the water again. I feel so calm and happy as I stand, as if the rest of my life will be made up of evenings like this. I hear Robert's whistling coming down to me out of the dark behind. It's a tune I almost recognise. I start to hum along.

As I do I can see Robert in my mind's eye, the way he must be. When he whistles, small creases appear round his lips. He has a look of severe concentration on his face. The image of him comes often to me in this way, even when I'm alone. Sometimes late at night as I lie trying to sleep, a shadow cast in from outside will move against the wall and then he breaks through me in a pang, quick and deep. We've been friends for years now, since I started high school. It's often as if I have no other friends. *He* has, though. I see him sometimes with other boys from the school, riding past my house in a swirling khaki pack down to the lake. It hurts me when this happens. I don't know what they speak about, whether they talk of things that I could understand. I wonder sometimes if they mention me. I wonder if they mock me when I'm not there and if Robert laughs at me with the rest of them.

He comes down now, carrying a load of wood in his arms. 'Is that all?' he says, looking at what I collected. 'What's the matter with you?'

'Nothing,' I say, and smile.

He drops his wood along with the rest and turns. He's grinning at me: a big skew grin, little bits of bark stuck to his hair and the front of his shirt.

'Do we need any more?'

'No,' he says. 'That should do fine.'

We build a fire. Rather – he builds the fire and I sit against a tree to watch. It always seems to be this way: him doing the work, me watching. But it's a comfortable arrangement, he doesn't mind. I like the way he moves. He's a skinny boy, Robert, his clothes are always slightly loose on him. Now as I watch, my eye is on his hands as they reach for the wood and stack it. His hands are slender and brown. He's brought a wad of newspaper on his bike. He twists rolls of paper into the openings between the logs.

Like me, the dogs are sitting still and watching. They stare at him with quiet attention, obedient and dumb.

He lights the fire. He holds the burning match and I'm looking for a moment at this white-haired boy with flame in his hand. Then he leans and touches it to the paper. Smoke. He shakes out the match.

The fire burns, the flames go up. In a minute or two there's a nice blaze going. We're making our own light to send across the water. I think of my parents on the wooden veranda, looking across to the spark that's started up in the darkness. They point. 'There,' they say. 'That's where they are.' I smile. The fire burns. The flames go up. The heat wraps over my face like a second skin. The dogs get up and move away, back into the dark where they shift restlessly, mewing like kittens.

In a little time the fire burns down to a heap of coals. They glow and pulse, sending up tiny spurts of flame. We only have to throw on a stick now and then. Sitting and staring into the ring of heat, it would be easy to be quiet, but we talk, though our voices are soft.

'We should camp out here sometime,' he says. 'It's so still.'

'Yes,' I say. 'We should do that.'

'It's great to be away,' he says. 'From them.'

He's speaking of his family; his home. He often speaks of them this way. I don't know what he means by this: they all seem nice enough. They live in a huge, two-storeyed house made out of wood, about half an hour's ride from us. They're further up the valley, though, out of sight of the lake. There are five of them: Robert, his parents, his two brothers. I'm alone in my home, I have no brothers. Perhaps it's this that makes their house a beautiful place to me. Perhaps there really is something ugly in it that I haven't seen. Either way, we don't spend much time there. It's to my home that Robert likes to come in the afternoons when school is done. He's familiar to us all. He comes straight up to my room, I know the way he knocks on my door. Bang-bang, thud.

My mother has spoken to me about him. At least twice that I can remember she's sat on my bed, smiling at me and playing with her hands.

'But what's wrong with it?' I say. 'Everyone has friends.'

'But lots,' she says. 'Lots of friends. You do nothing else, you see no one else . . .'

'There's nothing else to do,' I say. 'Other people bore me.'

'There's sport,' she says. 'I've seen them at the school, every afternoon. Why don't you play sport like other boys? You're becoming thinner and thinner.'

It's true. I am. When I look at myself in the mirror I'm surprised at how thin I am. But I'm not unhealthy, my skin is dark, I'm fit. We ride for miles together, Robert and me, along the dust roads that go around the lake.

'It's him,' I say. 'Isn't it? It's him you don't like.'

'No,' she says. 'It isn't that. I like him well enough. It's you, you that's the matter.'

I don't want to upset them, my parents. I want to be a good son to them. But I don't know any way to be fatter than I am, to please them. I do my best.

'I'll try,' I say. 'I'll try to see less of him.'

But it doesn't help. Most afternoons I hear his knock at my door and I'm glad at the sound. We go out on our bikes. This happens at night too, from time to time. As now – when we find ourselves at the edge of the lake, staring at the moon.

'D'you want a smoke?' he says.

I don't answer. But he takes one out of the box anyway, leaning forward to light it in the fire. He puffs. Then he hands it to me. I take a drag, trying to be casual. But I've never felt as easy about it as Robert seems to. The smoke is rough in my throat, it makes my tongue go sour. I don't enjoy it. But for the sake of Robert I allow this exchange to take place, this wordless passing back and forth, this puffing in the dark. I touch his hand as I give it back to him.

'Are you bored?' he asks. 'Why're you so quiet?'

'No,' I say. 'I'm fine.' I think for a while, then ask, 'Are you?'

'No,' he says.

But I wonder if he is. In sudden alarm I think of the places he might rather be, the people he might rather be with. To confirm my fear, he mutters just then:

'Emma Brown –'

'Why are you thinking about Emma Brown?' I say. 'What made you think of her now?'

He's looking at me, surprised. He takes the cigarette out of his mouth. 'I was just wondering,' he says. 'I was just wondering where she is.'

'Why?' I say.

'I just wondered if she was also watching the moon.'

'Oh,' I say, and smile bitterly into the fire. I don't know what's going through his head, but mine is full of thoughts of her: of silly little Emma Brown, just a bit plump, with her brown hair and short white socks. I remember a few times lately that I've seen her talking to Robert; I remember him smiling at her as she came late to class.

'I was just thinking,' he says, and shrugs.

I finish the cigarette. I throw the butt into the fire. We don't talk for a long time after that. I can hear the dogs licking each other, the rasping noise of their tongues. I begin to feel sad. I think of my anger and something in me slides, as if my heart is displaced.

He reaches out a hand and grazes my arm. It's just a brief touch, a tingle of fingers, but it goes into me like a coal. 'Hey,' he says. 'What's the matter?'

'Nothing,' I say. 'Nothing.' I want to say more, but I don't like to lie. Instead I say again, 'Nothing.' I feel stupid.

The fire burns down to a red smear on the ground. Across the water the lights have started to go out. Only a few are left. I look off to the right: the lights in my house are still on. My parents keep watch.

When I look back, Robert is on his feet. His head is thrown back. I don't stand, but I gaze over his shoulder at what he's watching: the white disc of the moon, from which a piece has been broken. While we were talking, the great shadow of the earth has started to cover the moon. If you look hard enough, the dark piece can still be seen, but only in outline, as if it's been sketched with chalk.

We stare for a long time. As we do, the shadow creeps on perceptibly. You can actually see it move.

'Wow,' he says.

Sensing something, one of the dogs throws back its head in imitation of us and begins to howl. The noise goes up, wobbling on the air like smoke.

'Sheba,' says Robert. 'Be quiet.'

We watch the moon as it sinks slowly out of sight. Its light is still coming down, but more faintly than before. On the whole valley, lit weirdly in the strange blue glow, a kind of quiet has fallen. There is nothing to say. I lower my eyes and look out over the water. Robert sits down next to me on his heels, hugging his knees. 'You know,' he says, 'there's times when everything feels . . . feels . . .'

He doesn't finish.

'I know,' I say.

We sit and watch. Time goes by. The trees are behind us, black and big. I look across to my home again and see that the lights have gone out. All along the far shore there is dark. We're alone.

'It's taking a long time,' he says. 'Don't you think?'

'Yes,' I say. 'It is.'

It's hot. The dogs are panting like cattle in the gloom. I feel him along my arm. A warmth. I spring up, away. 'I'm going to swim,' I say, unbuttoning my shirt.

I take off my clothes, and drop them on the sand. The dogs are standing, staring at me. Robert also watches, still crouched on his heels, biting his arm. When I'm naked I turn my back on him and walk into the lake. I stop when the water reaches my knees and stand, arms folded across my chest, hands clinging to my ribs as if they don't belong to me. It isn't cold, but my skin goes tight as if it is. One of the dogs lets out a bark. I walk on, hands at my sides now, while the water gets higher and higher. When it reaches my hips I dive. It covers my head like a blanket. I come up, spluttering. 'It's warm,' I say, 'as blood.'

'Hold on,' he calls. 'I'm –'

As I turn he's already running. I catch a glimpse of his body, long and bright as a blade, before he also dives. When he comes up, next to me, the air is suddenly full of noise: the barking of the dogs as they run along the edge of the lake, the splashing of water, the shouts of our voices. It is our voices I hear, I'm surprised at the sound. I'm laughing. I'm calling out.

'Don't you,' I say, 'don't you *try* –'

We're pushing at each other, and pulling. Water flies. The bottom of the lake is slippery to my feet, I feel stones turn.

I have hold of Robert's shoulder. I have a hand in his hair. I'm trying to push him under, wrenching at him while he does the same to me. He laughs.

Nothing like this has taken place between us before. I feel his skin against me, I feel the shape of his bones as we wrestle and lunge. We're touching each other. Then I slide, the water hits my face. I go under, pulling him with me, and for a moment we're tangled below the surface, leg to leg, neck to neck, furry with bubbles, as if we'll never pull free.

We come up together into quiet. The laughter has been doused. We still clutch to each other, but his fingers are hurting me. We stand, face to face. While we were below, the last sliver of moon has been blotted out. A total dark has fallen on the valley, so that the trees are invisible against the sky. The moon is a faint red outline overhead. I can't see Robert's face, though I can feel his breath against my nose. We gasp for air. The only sound to be heard is the howling of the dogs that drifts in from the shore: an awful noise, bereaved and bestial.

I let go. And he lets go of me. Finger by finger, joint by joint, we release one another till we are standing, separate and safe, apart. I rub my arm where he hurt it.

'Sorry,' he mutters.

'It's okay,' I say. 'It doesn't matter.'

After that we make our way to shore. I wade with heavy steps, as if through sand. By the time I reach the edge and am standing, dripping, beside my clothes, the moon has begun to emerge from shadow and a little light is falling. The dogs stop howling. I don't look up as I dress. I put my clothes on just so, over my wet body. They stick to me like mud.

I wait for him to finish dressing. As he ties his shoelaces I say, not even looking at him, 'What d'you think will happen?'

'What d'you mean?' he says.

'To us,' I say. 'D'you think in ten years from now we're even going to know each other?'

'I don't know what you mean,' he says.

He sounds irritated as he says this, as if I say a lot of things he doesn't understand. Maybe I do. I turn away and start to walk back to the bikes.

'Hey,' he calls. 'What you ... don'tcha want another smoke or somethin' before we go?'

'No,' I say. 'Not me.'

I wait for him at the tree where the bikes are leaning. He takes his time. I watch him scoop water over the coals. They make a hissing noise, like an engine beneath the ground. Then he walks up towards me along the bank, hands in his pockets. The sight of him this way, sulking and slow, rings in me long after we've mounted our bikes and started back up the path.

By the time we rejoin the dust road a little way on, the soreness in me is smaller than it was. One of the dogs runs into his way and he swears. At this I even manage to laugh. I look off and up to the left, at the moon which is becoming rounder by the minute. Its light comes down in soft white flakes, settling on us coldly as we ride.

TOVE JANSSON

THE FOREST

Translated by Silvester Mazzarella

IN THOSE DAYS there was nothing but cow paths through the forest, which was so big that if you went looking for berries you could get lost and not find your way home again for days. We didn't dare go more than a little way in, and even then we would just stand there and listen to the silence for a while before running back. Matti was more scared than I was, but then he wasn't yet six years old. There was a drop-off below the hill, and Mum had given us quite a lecture about that hill before we said goodbye.

Mum worked in town so that we could spend our summer at the cottage, which she had rented through an advertisement. She had also hired Anna to make our meals. Mostly Anna just wanted to be left in peace. 'Go out and play,' she'd say.

Matti followed me everywhere, saying, 'Wait for me!' and 'What'll we play?' but he was way too little to hang out with. What are you supposed to do with a little brother? The days were really long.

Then, one very special day, Mum sent us a parcel and in the parcel was a book that changed everything – it was called *Tarzan of the Apes*.

Of course Matti couldn't read yet, but I would read him bits of it from time to time. Mostly though, I'd take Tarzan with me into a tree. Matti would stand at the bottom and pester me with questions. 'What's happening now? Is Tarzan okay?'

Then Mum sent us *The Beasts of Tarzan* and *The Son of Tarzan*.

Anna said, 'What a nice mum you boys have. It's such a shame you lost your poor papa.'

'He's not lost!' Matti said. 'He's big and strong and he's not afraid of anything, so you watch what you say about him!'

Later Matti announced that he was Tarzan's son.

The summer changed totally, and the biggest change was that we started going into the forest. We discovered that it was a jungle that no one had ever explored, and we ventured in farther and farther to where the trees crowded together in perpetual twilight. We had to learn to tread silently like Tarzan so as not to crack the smallest twig, and we learned to listen a new way. I explained that for the time being we couldn't use the cow paths, because the jungle beasts used them to reach their watering holes. I told Matti we had to be a bit careful with our wild friends, at least for now.

'All right, Tarzan,' said Matti.

I taught him how to tell directions by the sun so we could find our way home, and I explained we must never set out in cloudy weather. My son became braver and more skilful, but he never quite overcame his fear of deadly ants.

Sometimes we lay on our backs in the moss, in some safe place, and gazed up into a mighty world of green. We hardly ever caught a glimpse of the sky, although the forest bore the sky on its roof. And though we could hear the wind moving through the treetops, the air was utterly still. There was never any danger because the jungle concealed and protected us.

One time we came to a stream. Tarzan's son knew the stream was full of piranhas, but he waded across it all the same – very quickly. I was proud of him, perhaps never more so than the time he ventured a little way into deep water, all by himself. I was standing behind a rock holding a safety line but he didn't know that.

I made us bows and arrows but we shot only one or two hyenas – we didn't really count them among our wild friends – and once a boa constrictor. We hit it right in the mouth and it died instantly.

When we came home to eat, Anna asked what we'd been playing and my son told her we were much too old to play. We were exploring the jungle.

'That's nice,' said Anna. 'You go right ahead. But do try not to be late for supper.'

We discovered a new independence and followed only the Law of the Jungle, which can never be questioned and is strict and just. And the jungle opened its arms and accepted us. Each day, we had the heady experience of daring, of stretching our limits to the utmost, of being stronger than we'd dreamed. But we never killed anything smaller than ourselves.

August arrived with its black nights. When the sunset cast its red light between the tree trunks we would run home because we didn't want to see the darkness fall.

Then, when Anna had turned off the lamp and closed the kitchen door, we would lie in bed and listen. Something howled a long way off, then a hooting close to the cottage.

'Tarzan?' Matti whispered. 'Did you hear that?'

'Sleep,' I said. 'Nothing can get in. Trust me, my son.'

But suddenly I knew with a terrible certainty that my wild friends were friends no longer. I caught the rank smell of wild beasts rubbing their hairy bodies against the wall of the cottage . . . It was I who had conjured them, and only I could send them away before it was too late.

'Papa!' Matti cried. 'They're coming in!'

'Don't be silly,' I said. 'It's only some old owls and foxes making a noise; now go to sleep. All that stuff about the jungle was something we made up. It isn't true.'

I said it very loud so they would hear outside.

'Of course it's true,' Matti shrieked. 'You're wrong! They're real!' He worked himself up into a real state.

The next summer Matti wanted us to go into the jungle again. But to be honest, that would just have been leading him on.

URSULA MORAY WILLIAMS

THE OUTLAWS

THE FRENCH SCHOOLS began their holidays early in July.

Robert, on an exchange summer holiday to the Williams family, had to content himself for nearly two weeks with very little company of his own age until David Williams should come home from boarding-school.

Jenny and Sarah Williams were at day school from half-past nine until teatime. It was the only peace that Robert had. When they were at home they dragged him round the stables, hoisted him onto their ponies and made fun of his accent.

'Rob-bair!' they repeated when he pronounced his name. In England they called it Robbut. And not content with saying *his* name wrong they criticized him when he mispronounced theirs.

'Jenni! Sairah!' he could manage, but his tongue betrayed him when he tried to say 'Williams'. 'Vill-ee-ams!' Robert said, but the girls insisted he should pronounce it Willyums. Robert wished he had a surname five syllables long to confound the mocking English accents. Nobody had much difficulty in pronouncing Legros.

The girls were older than he. They were kind in a boisterous and patronizing way, but they beat him at everything they did together: at tennis, at swimming – even at clock golf.

When they were absent Robert followed Mrs Williams comfortably round the house, went shopping with her, took the dog out and watched television. She reminded him of his mother and he was very nearly perfectly happy. But Mrs Williams was under the constant misapprehension that he must be bored in her company. 'Only another week till David comes!' she would tell him as if they were making a tremendous joint effort to keep their chins up until David arrived, and every half hour during the afternoon she looked at the clock and said encouragingly: 'The girls will soon be home!'

The girls put such energy into everything they did that Robert felt sure his father would have approved of them. It was Monsieur Legros who had pounced upon the sentence in Mrs Williams's letter offering tennis and riding at their home. 'Le sport', his father called it rather reverently. He approved of 'le sport'.

In return the Legros offered sailing and 'le water ski' at their summer house to David when he should come back to France with Robert in the middle of August. Robert hated both, but since arriving at the Williamses' he had decided that either was preferable to riding.

Jenny and Sarah put him onto a pony called 'Greenfly' and took him into a paddock where the grass was soft. They put a hard hat on his head that belonged to David, but David had quite a different kind of head. The hat slipped forward onto Robert's nose or shot off backwards and got left behind.

The girls made a little jump from brushwood, and encouraged Greenfly to jump over it. Robert fell off and they put him back in the saddle because they said it was bad for him not to mount again immediately after a fall. It seemed to Robert the best of all possible reasons for staying on the ground, but even after he took a second tumble they persuaded him to get on again. When he fell off a third time they said it was bad for the horse, and let him retire to the railings and watch. Both girls rode very well, and by the trophies hanging round the stables and in the house Robert had a strong suspicion that David did too.

Robert wished now that he had made himself proficient at sailing and water ski-ing last summer when he had had the chance, so that he would have something to excel at when David came back to France with him. For nobody could possibly be so bad at either sport as he was. David was exactly his own age, but his family, his enthusiasm and his British education had almost certainly given him an advantage over Robert when it came to 'le sport'. He almost dreaded David coming to his home.

The girls had joined in the chorus now. 'David will be here on Friday!' they chanted on Monday morning. There was a note of relief in their voices that Robert did not miss, for he knew they were getting tired of having him at their heels. They only offered him one set of tennis now, after tea, and then made excuses or played singles with each other.

On Tuesday morning came a letter from David's school that caused consternation around the breakfast table.

'David,' the school matron wrote, 'has had measles, but not very badly. If you can fetch him by car the doctor says he can travel on Wednesday and the journey won't hurt him.'

David's parents looked so concerned that Robert became anxious.

'David . . . is he *malade?*' he inquired.

'He has *spots!*' Jenny said in the loud clear voice she reserved for explaining things to Robert. She dabbed at her face with her finger. 'Have you had spots?'

Robert shook his head. Childish diseases had passed him by.

'Worse and worse!' said Sarah. She exchanged a look with her sister that Robert might not have noticed if Mrs

299

Williams had not said '*Sarah!*' so reprovingly that he knew Jenny must be getting at him again.

'David won't be able to do anything with Robert, because of giving him measles!' said Sarah, as if her mother had not spoken. 'And David won't be able to do anything at all. He'll miss the cricket match on the twenty-ninth and the garden fête and gymkhana this Saturday. I suppose Jen and I can go to the Pony Club camp as we've both had measles, but you do realize, Mummy, that if Robert gets measles from David he'll be here for most of the holidays?'

'And David won't be able to go back with him to France!' added Jenny.

'Well, never mind about that,' said Mrs Williams, looking embarrassed and pushing the breakfast things about. Jenny and Sarah always behaved as if Robert understood no conversation that was not directed at him loudly and personally. Mrs Williams took the opposite view, that he understood everything, and nothing must be said that could possibly hurt his feelings as a foreigner and a visitor. The truth lay somewhere in between. Robert perfectly understood the situation that had arisen, and was trying to remember the number of days that had separated him from his cousins having measles during the previous summer holidays. He also understood without being told that Jenny and Sarah did not want his visit prolonged by one day if they had to undertake the hospitality. He heartily agreed with them.

'I know!' said Sarah. 'He can go to Grandmère till David is better!'

'Great!' said Jenny. 'He'd enjoy that.'

'I think that is a very good idea!' said Mrs Williams. 'He would have a lovely time with Grandmère!'

'Let's ring her!' Sarah said, 'Shall I do it?'

'*I* will!' said Mrs Williams.

'Who will ring what?' said Mr Williams who had been reading his papers. He was a solicitor, and he hardly ever spoke to Robert, but when he did he was always kind and polite.

'We don't want Robert to be in quarantine and get measles from David!' Mrs Williams said. 'So it might be a good idea for him to go and stay with Grandmère for a few days until David gets over it.'

'And would Robert like that?' Mr Williams said, pronouncing his name in the French way and looking straight at him.

'I think I go home to France!' said Robert decidedly.

'Well now you know what Robert would like!' said Mr Williams, picking up his papers. 'Come on, girls, I'm leaving the house in three minutes and I shan't wait.'

Jenny and Sarah dashed after him, squealing.

'My mother has a very nice home,' Mrs Williams said across the empty breakfast table. 'We call her Grandmère because she loves France so much, but her real name is Lady Swayne. She will love to have you. If you stayed with her just till David isn't infectious any more you can come back here afterwards and go off to France together just as was planned. Don't you think that would really be quite a good idea?'

'Yes, madame!' said Robert, subdued.

'I'll go and telephone Grandmère and see if she can have you from tomorrow, when we fetch David!' Mrs Williams said. 'It would all fit in so well if she could.'

'Yes, madame,' said Robert. He began to clear away the breakfast things. Mrs Williams came back very quickly from the telephone.

'No reply!' she said. 'Grandmère often goes shopping on a Tuesday. I'll ring again directly after lunch.'

During the morning Mrs Williams and Robert made

fifteen pounds of raspberry jam. Robert wrote the labels and sealed the tops. During the whole operation, while Mrs Williams chatted, he was thinking hard. He forgave Mrs Williams for having a situation forced upon her that was not of her making, but he strongly resented being discussed at the breakfast table like a superfluous object, and disposed of as if he had been a parcel to be sent here and there. He felt that his parents ought to have been brought into the discussion. They might not approve of his being sent away into the house of a French-speaking old lady they had never met. They had been particularly anxious that he should not speak any French at all while he was in England. He tried to explain this to Mrs Williams, but it was really too difficult, and too much trouble to fetch a dictionary with his fingers covered with raspberry jam. He slaughtered thirteen wasps and earned Mrs Williams's grateful thanks, for she was frightened of them.

When he had disposed of the wasps he went upstairs and packed his suitcase. He discovered that for the first time since he left Paris he was feeling homesick. He had felt strange, of course, for the first few days, and chilled by Jenny and Sarah's mockery, but they had been kind after their own fashion, and Mrs Williams had been affectionate and very kind indeed. Slowly he had settled in, and now he was to be uprooted and transplanted. He was not even to be allowed to meet David.

And his parents knew nothing about it! He had no doubt that Mrs Williams would telephone his mother when all was settled, but meanwhile he felt as if he had been dropped into a void, as if he belonged to nowhere and nobody. Tears smarted at the back of his eyes accompanied by a band of grief that constricted his throat and broke into a sob that he tried to stifle by burrowing inside his suitcase.

His fingers closed on the familiar shape of his return air ticket. At once his desolation seeped away. He felt like a prisoner who has accidentally discovered the key of his cell.

The Williams family had met him at the airport, only seven miles from their home. In Mr Williams's fast car it had seemed even less. All he had to do was walk to the airport, change his ticket for the evening flight and telephone his father when he arrived. He would then explain to his family that David had measles and he could not stay any longer. They would much rather have him at home he felt sure. Or nearly sure. David could come over later. Madame Legros was not likely to object to that just because Robert had returned a few days early. He packed very rapidly and completely.

For lunch, Mrs Williams cooked him the English sausages that he liked so much, and he realized that he loved her dearly. When she spoke of the things they would do when David had finished having measles and Robert came back again he agreed with her whole-heartedly rather than face the pain of knowing that this was their last meal together.

'Such a hot afternoon!' she said as they cleared the table and washed up. 'I'm afraid we shall have a storm before dark. Are you going to sunbathe? Only two hours and the girls will be back!'

She went away to telephone 'la Grandmère'. Robert went to his bedroom, picked up his suitcase and left the house by the back stairs to catch the five o'clock plane from Hardington to Paris that was charted on his ticket. He wrote 'Thank you very much!' on a piece of paper and left it under his pillow.

It was a hot and sultry afternoon. Since one o'clock the sun had slowly eased itself behind a blanket of haze. Robert hurried through the orchard where caterpillars, suspended on long threads, brushed his face before dropping limply to the ground, all their labours shattered. He skirted the meadow where the girls had made their practice jumps, glad that no ponies came galloping to greet him. They were grazing elsewhere.

The suitcase was heavy, as suitcases invariably are, but Robert disregarded this. He changed it from hand to hand as he strode along, finding it less unbearable than the folded mackintosh clinging with disagreeable moisture to his neck and shoulders already clammy with heat.

The girls had taken him, jogging uncomfortably on a pony, through woods that later joined the Hardington road. From the far side they had pointed out the airfield on the distant horizon, and Robert took this way now, thankful for the shade of the trees and absence of traffic that had passed him on the main road without ceasing. Nobody took the slightest notice of the hesitating hand he raised to beseech a lift. Perhaps people did not hitchhike in England, Robert wondered.

The great woods! The beeches and the oaks! reminding him vaguely of the forests south of Paris, at Barbizon. Trees, he thought, were like kind quiet ladies, like Mrs Williams who was good to him, while the prickly spiky bushes were like Jenny and Sarah. He turned in sudden panic, half expecting to see or hear them galloping up the track on their ponies, but Jenny and Sarah were ending their summer term at school and the woods were empty, except for buzzing insects and a sudden green woodpecker, calling for rain.

He heard the first roll of thunder as a warm raindrop fell on his forehead, and stopped, prudently, to put on his mackintosh. The sky above the trees was very black. Would the plane leave for Paris if there were a thunderstorm? He did not want to hang about the airport waiting. It would be natural for the Williams family to make inquiries when they found him gone, and it would be humiliating to say the least if he were found and apprehended in public. Nothing, he told himself, would now prevent him from boarding the plane, but let it be with dignity and a minimum of fuss.

Sheet lightning lit up the woods. Storms could be unpleasant but Robert had had his baptism of them while climbing in the high mountains with his uncle, a sport that he enjoyed with all his heart and soul. After the fury of the Alps he had little dread of a small British thunderstorm. It was however inconvenient as the rain gathered force and began to seep down the back of his neck. It poured off his suitcase into his shoes. The ends of his trousers were sopping wet. His smart new mackintosh, called showerproof, was not standing up to the deluge that now fell out of the sky, and as the trees were sparse at that point Robert left the track to find shelter where they grew more thickly. Then he smelt woodsmoke.

It was a sweet and comfortable smell. Robert thought in terms of a charcoal burner's hut where he could shelter, but at least he hoped to find a British workman with some kind of roof over his head.

Not quite so solid, but in its way quite as satisfactory was the sight he saw when he thrust his way through the bushes and found a small car.

The car itself was familiar, being a continental model that he saw constantly in and about Paris. Beside it was pitched a small tent. From a nearby tree projected a canvas roof, too restricted to protect the fire underneath it that an elderly lady was energetically trying to keep alive.

She lay almost flat on the ground, blowing so hard at the fire that her eyes were closed and her face bright pink. She must, Robert thought, be a tinker woman, until something about her clothes and the atmosphere of the tiny encampment told him that this was no tinker, but an English 'madame' very busy 'making le camping'.

The fire smouldered, sulked and hissed. The lady blew and hissed back. The rain poured down and she took not the slightest notice of Robert. He longed for the shelter of the tent or of the car, if it were only for five minutes or until the rain stopped, but he did not like to introduce himself.

Finally he remembered passing some bundles of birch cuttings only a short way behind him, and birch wood burned well, as he knew from camping with his uncle. He turned back, and presently stood at the lady's side holding an armful of birch twigs almost dry under his mackintosh. He had prudently left his suitcase sheltering underneath her car.

The lady had paused to wipe her streaming eyes. She stared at him in astonishment.

'Permettez!' Robert said gently, and lowered himself to the ground. He pushed the birch twigs underneath the grumbling wood ends and slowly they began to burn. More twigs, more wood, the sullen little fire sprang into life, and as it burned the old lady hurled a small kettle on top of it with a glee that was almost vindictive.

'Wonderful!' she exclaimed. 'We'll have a cup of tea! Come and keep dry inside the car!'

They rushed for shelter. Robert felt every seam now in his sodden clothing, every inch of his squelching socks. He grabbed his suitcase and dragged it into the car behind him.

'And who may you be?' the lady asked him.

'Please?'

'What is your name?'

Too close, too close to the Williamses to tell his real name, thought Robert. What if the lady was a personal friend who had heard all about him?

'André,' he said. 'André Prevost.'

'Oh!' she said, staring at him. 'You are a French boy?'

'*Oui madame!*' he answered automatically.

'And where are you going?' she asked, looking at the suitcase.

'I go to the airport!' said Robert readily. 'I catch the flight to Paris. Five o'clock,' he added to show her that he had himself completely organized.

'Not on a *Tuesday!*' the lady exclaimed. 'Mondays, Wednesdays and Fridays, but there is no flight to Paris from Hardington on a Tuesday.'

Inside him Robert's heart took a rush downwards to his shoes. Such a thought had never crossed his mind.

'The kettle's boiling!' shrieked the lady. She bolted into the rain, fetched a teapot from the tent, and returned to the car with two mugs, a milk bottle and the steaming brew. 'One moment!' she cried, and bolted back for the sugar.

The tea was almost as welcome as coffee. Robert clasped his damp fingers round the mug and tried to pretend he was not feeling desperate. The lady drank and said nothing. Outside, the rain poured down, but rather more gently now.

'Thank you, madame!' Robert said, preparing to go. Then he remembered he had nowhere to go to.

'Where are you off to?' she asked. 'Back where you came from?'

He shook his head automatically. Anything but that. Such ignominy! Such humiliation! He could almost hear the muffled laughter of Jenny and Sarah behind his back. Though his chin remained rigid tears pricked behind his eyes.

'Are you fond of camping?' the lady asked. He nodded violently.

'Then perhaps you would like to camp here with me until your plane goes tomorrow afternoon?' she said politely.

Above, the sky was inky black and solid, but Robert could have sworn that the sun came out at that moment.

'*Oui madame . . . s'il vous plaît!*' he murmured, as the awful gulf beneath his feet closed, leaving him once more on solid ground.

'You will have to sleep in the car!' she told him, 'and I shall have to get some more food from the village. Will you come with me?'

He hesitated. Twenty-four hours to go, and in any one of them he might be discovered. Better remain hidden deep in the woods.

'I stay here, madame!' he said. 'I make a good fire and . . . and . . .' he indicated the amount of wood that he meant to collect in her absence. The little car bubbled into life and rattled away out of sight.

When the lady returned, carrying a string bag full of groceries, the sun was shining again, turning the wet tree trunks into pillars of gold. The wood looked like a cathedral. Robert had peeled potatoes and changed into dry clothes from his suitcase. His hostess was delighted with him.

'I have sausages!' she told him. 'And peaches and cornflakes and chocolate biscuits and coffee! And Mars bars to eat in bed. Do you like Mars bars?'

The Williamses had not introduced Robert to Mars bars but he said: 'Yes, madame!' with enthusiasm.

'There's only one thing,' the lady said. 'I haven't really got enough blankets for us both. I shall have to go back to my house and get some.'

He stared, not having connected her with a home of her own, but blankets were not so important as supper, and he had just built a splendid fire. As they ate, although she asked no questions, he told her a little bit about his holiday, with friends . . . far from here, he explained, half in French and half in English . . . but there was illness in the family and it was necessary for him to go home early.

'I see,' she said with feeling. 'What a shame!'

Dusk was falling as they washed up the supper plates in a stream muddied by the rain. 'Don't drink that!' she said. 'You can have some wine. I expect you often drink it in France.'

The wine made him so sleepy he would have liked to go to bed, but the dark wet woods seemed so lonely that he chose instead to go with her in her little car to fetch the blankets. They took a track he did not recognize and drove a long way among the trees without meeting any other traffic. Then they travelled a short distance down a main road till they came to a drive gate. The drive wound up a sloping hill to a very beautiful old house. The lady drove round to the back and produced a large key.

'Is this your house?' Robert asked, astonished.

'Yes. There is nobody here. Come in!'

They entered the house by the back door, almost tiptoeing in, Robert thought. It was not yet dark, but deep twilight. The lady switched on no lights as they crossed a hall into a large sitting-room, with comfortable sofa and chairs, beautiful furniture, old pictures and a grand piano.

While the lady plucked cushions and travelling rugs from the sofa and chairs Robert stood peering round the room in the dusk. The first thing he recognized was a large photograph of Jenny and Sarah on their ponies, standing on top of the grand piano. He jumped quite violently at the sight of them. The lady turned round.

'You know . . . these people?' Robert quavered.

'Those are my grandchildren,' the lady said calmly. 'But it is quite all right, Robert, there is nothing to worry about. When I was in the village I telephoned to my daughter and told her you were with me and we were going away for a little holiday together. She thinks we are on tour.' As Robert still stared she added in French: 'I knew you were staying there, my dear, and your initials were on your suitcase. It wasn't difficult to guess who you were. But we all have our independent ideas, you know. *I* like to get away from friends and relations now and again and live my own life exactly as I please. I adore camping!'

'And I do!' said Robert fervently.

'Good. So we will camp. And nobody shall call us silly old lady and silly young boy. We will do as we like. *Bon?*'

'*Très bon!*' said Robert, delighted.

'It has worked out very well!' the Grandmère said. 'They wanted to send you to me and now you have come! And we will let them think that we have gone away so we shall not have lots of horses galloping through our camp every morning . . . eh?' They laughed together. 'And if you want to catch the plane to Paris tomorrow, or on Friday, or the next Monday, it is all the same to me,' the Grandmère concluded. '*Bon?*'

'*Très bon!*' said Robert, entirely happy.

They lived like outlaws until the end of the week. At night they crept back to the house to raid the larder and the frozen cabinet in case anyone mentioned their shopping at the village store. On the Wednesday afternoon when the Grandmère asked if he wanted to catch the Paris plane Robert was quite startled.

'No, thank you, madame, I will go on Friday,' he told her.

They prattled together in French, and to compensate she brought English story books from the house, which they read together in the evenings. She gave him English lessons which Mrs Williams had never had time for, although she had always meant to do so.

The Grandmère taught him more about camping and the

woods than he had ever dreamed of, and took him early in the morning and in the dusk of the evening to fly fish on a small stream behind the woods. During the day he practised the intricate art of casting with a fly rod, using a feather tied to the end of the line that he learned to drop lightly here and there, now on a daisy, now on a wild strawberry plant. The little trout they caught were grilled on the fires Robert made so successfully. They tasted better than anything he had eaten in Paris.

One day when they were gathering toadstools to eat (the Williamses called them all poisonous, but Robert and the Grandmère knew which were the edible kinds) they heard horses' hooves, and flung themselves flat in the bushes just in time, as Jenny and Sarah galloped by. Afterwards they could hardly stop laughing as they crept back to their camp by a roundabout route in case the girls came back again.

The Grandmère brought a folding bed from the house and Robert slept in the open. Never would he forget the dawn choruses ... or the soft darkness that spread itself across his blankets while owls called and recalled each other, and mosquitoes hummed away in discontent, repulsed by the oil of lavender with which the Grandmère drenched his pillow. And just now and then he was awakened by soft rain damping his brow that sent him scampering for the car with his blankets clutched underneath his chin.

'Shall you catch the plane tomorrow?' the Grandmère asked him on Thursday.

'*Non merci, madame!*'

'There is just one thing,' she said, 'I have to open a garden fête on Saturday. They will expect me to be there.'

'That is okay!' he said graciously in English.

'I shall fetch my clothes from the house tonight,' she said. 'We can go to the fête from here, and when I have opened it I'll just vanish. We can't miss the evening rise on the trout stream, can we?'

'*Bien sûr, madame!*' said Robert.

Late that evening they crept into the house and came away with a suitcase packed with the Grandmère's dress, shoes and a triple string of pearls. 'I always open garden fêtes in pearls,' the Grandmère said. 'But I have never cooked sausages in them before!'

As they crept down the back stairs with a torch they heard a car entering the drive from the road.

'Run!' said the Grandmère. 'It's the family coming to see if I have got home. We mustn't be caught. Run!'

They ran, and were down the back drive and into the woods before the visitors had turned the last bend. The little Fiat was parked in some bushes opposite the back gate.

'You didn't lock the back door!' Robert said.

'Oh, they'll bang at the front. They'll never notice!' the Grandmère said. She wore her pearls to cook the sausages and they drank each other's health in Coca-Cola, calling themselves the New Outlaws.

'This is our last evening of liberty,' the Grandmère said on the next night, which was Friday. 'I am going to cook the best meal in the world in case we never come back again. Because once we get back into the ordinary world nothing will ever be quite the same again.'

She was very anxious to know if Robert had a clean shirt to wear at the garden fête, and it was while she was looking through his clothes that she remembered she had left her Fête-Opening-Hat behind her in the house. 'Why does it matter?' said Robert, but the Grandmère said she could not possibly open a garden fête without her proper hat on.

'I will fetch it for you!' Robert offered. He knew the way so well. He knew the house too, quite intimately, and it was not dark, and the Grandmère was very busy preparing the marvellous meal.

'Excellent!' she agreed. 'You don't even need a key.' And she told him where to find the hat. It sounded a very splendid kind of hat.

'Just bring it in your hands!' said Grandmère. 'But mind you wash them in the bathroom first!'

Robert went off through the woods as if the place belonged to him. With one ear cocked for bird song and the other for horses' hoofs he loped though the trees, remembering as if from long ago the weary pilgrimage in the rain that had led to his enchanting adventure. He knew now just where a pheasant was likely to start up, and where the first owl would wake. He jumped with delight when a badger lumbered away through the nettles, and cursed back under his breath when a jay swore at him. Once in the grounds of Grandmère's house he slipped through the sombre laurels at the back, and found the door unlocked as they had left it.

Robert had never been in Grandmère's house alone, but it had become so familiar that he was not afraid. He leapt lightly up the back stairs and down the long corridor to her bedroom. The hat was on the top shelf of her cupboard, Grandmère had said, in a deep blue box with a broken lid. He was to treat it carefully.

Robert did, but he was not tall, and he had to move several other boxes first. These, with the blue box on top, cascaded down on his head, and he had only time to salvage the hat before he heard the back door open and close downstairs, while voices and footsteps became louder and clearer as they mounted the back stairs.

The voices sounded like the voices of people who had every right to be in the house, not outlaws like himself. Who they could be he could not imagine, but he felt he had every reason to hide from them.

In a panic he dashed for the cupboard, but it was stuffed so full of boxes, dresses and bags of oddments that there was not a corner left for him to hide in. He flung himself down to look under the bed, but the weighty old-fashioned springs nearly touched the floor.

The footsteps had mounted the stairs now and were tramping along the corridor. The voices sounded as powerful as foghorns.

Robert leapt for the bed as his last hope of shelter. He dived under the silk coverlet, down under the matching eiderdown to the foot, where he lay as flat as he could spread himself. Somewhere on the way he lost hold of the hat, which sat in all its majesty on the Grandmère's pillow.

The footsteps came nearer. They did not even pause at the bedroom door but came right inside.

'Well I had a good look round last night, Sergeant, when I found the back door unlocked,' one voice said, 'and Police Constable Taylor has stayed round the place all day. We couldn't find nothing wrong.'

'Well look at that, then!' said the second voice grimly. It was a stern, superior voice, and Robert knew they were looking at the fumbled boxes. 'You didn't see *that*, I suppose?'

'Well no, Sergeant, we must have missed this room out!' said the first voice, sounding most guilty and unhappy. 'Funny, I thought we'd been everywhere, I really did, Sergeant!'

'Well, somebody has been having a high old time here,' the Sergeant said. 'Have a look where Mr Williams told you to look. It's the pearls he was worried about. Never locked them up, he said . . . she just used to leave them about in her drawer. Go on . . . top left-hand drawer, in a velvet case . . . that's right, that's the case. . . .'

There was a terrible silence. Terrible, because Robert was scared clean out of his wits. 'Yes, they're gone all right!' said the heavier voice.

The next moment all the breath seemed to be pressed out of Robert's head. It was the police officer being knocked down as it were by a feather. He sat down heavily on the bed on top of Robert.

Robert would have suffered the crushing of a leg or an arm, but to have his head sat on was so like suffocation that he began to flail wildly with his legs and arms, with the result that the police officer sprang up with a yelp, while the Sergeant turned back the bedclothes and hauled Robert out of bed.

There was nothing he could say. Every word of English was scared clean out of him. He could not give his name, nor his address, nor any reason for his being there, and although he knew they were trying to make him say that he had not been the only person inside the house, he could not tell them that either. Because above all else he was not going to betray the Grandmère to anybody, least of all to the police.

'We had better take him down with us to the station,' the Sergeant said. 'Heaven knows how we get hold of his parents. The kid seems dumb. Perhaps one of the policewomen can cope.'

As they took him from the bed Robert made a last snatch at Grandmère's hat, but the police officer snatched it away again. They took him down the back stairs sobbing.

Before they reached the bottom they met someone coming up. It was Mr Williams.

'*Robert!*' Mr Williams exclaimed, and then: 'All right, officer, he's staying with my mother-in-law. He belongs to the house.'

The Sergeant dropped Robert like a hot brick.

315

'The pearls are gone, sir,' he said. 'And the bedroom is all upside down.'

Mr Williams pushed past them, leading Robert very kindly by the arm. He looked round the untidy bedroom in perplexity.

'Who did this?' he asked.

'*Moi*. I did it!' said Robert.

'Why? *Pourquoi?*'

'I was looking for the hat of madame.'

'And for her pearls?' broke in the Sergeant.

'Madame has her pearls *déjà* . . . already.'

'And where is madame now?'

Robert closed his mouth with a snap.

'Where is madame?'

'*Je ne sais pas.*'

'Nonsense!' For the first time Robert saw Mr Williams look angry. He took Robert's arm and shook it.

Robert pulled it away. Made fierce by indignation he dived under Mr Williams's elbow, past the policemen, out of the bedroom door, snatching up the Grandmère's hat from the chair where the Sergeant had carefully placed it.

Down the back stairs Robert ran, and out of the door. Under the laurels he slipped like a rabbit, cutting a long corner off the back drive. He dodged his way down to the road, crossed it, and was into the woods like a young animal that has escaped the hounds. Still he ran, and arrived at last quite breathless at the camping site, where Grandmère had just dished up the delicious supper she had prepared in his absence. She was wearing her pearls.

'We can do two things,' she said gravely, when he had finished his story. 'We can get into the car and go straight to the police station, or we can eat our supper and wait for the morning.'

'And catch the trout rise,' said Robert hopefully.

'Exactly,' said the Grandmère.

If the police did not discover them that evening nor the next morning it was because Mr Williams insisted that they should wait. So perhaps he was the only one not wholly astonished when shortly before 3 p.m. on the next afternoon Grandmère arrived in her little car, dressed in her most beautiful dress and pearls, crowned by her Fête-Opening-Hat, with Robert by her side, well-groomed and immaculately tidy, to open the garden fête. If both of them smelt faintly of wood smoke nobody said anything about it.

Grandmère was particularly charming to the Sergeant of police.

'We have been camping,' she explained. 'Yes, camping. In a tent.'

The Williams family welcomed Robert like a long lost brother.

Mrs Williams hugged him like a son. 'It was so clever of you to go off and find Grandmère all by yourself,' she said to him. 'But, oh dear! I was so anxious! Just until she telephoned to say you were there.'

He did not know how to explain to her so he went off and bought her an ice cream. Jenny and Sarah invited him to have tea in the gymkhana riders' tent with them, where they introduced him to most of their friends and all of the ponies. David, they said, was very nearly well again and Robert would be able to come home.

After tea he left the garden fête secretly with the Grandmère, joining her in the hidden place where she had put her car.

'We will finish the week-end out,' she told Robert as they drove at top speed towards their camping ground. 'And then we'll go back to the house and have baths and dress for dinner. And we'll go to the pictures every night until David is out of quarantine.'

'David is the only thing left to worry about,' sighed Robert. 'I am nervous about David.'

'David,' said Grandmère, 'is the nicest boy I have ever met except yourself, and you are both going to have a wonderful time when he goes back with you to France.'

'Perhaps,' said Robert, cheering up and looking more hopeful, 'we will be able to go camping.'

THOMAS LOVE PEACOCK

From

MAID MARIAN

Oh! this life
Is nobler than attending for a check,
Richer than doing nothing for a bribe,
Prouder than rustling in unpaid-for silk.

—Cymbeline.

So Robin and Marian dwelt and reigned in the forest, ranging the glades and the greenwoods from the matins of the lark to the vespers of the nightingale, and administering natural justice according to Robin's ideas of rectifying the inequalities of the human condition: raising genial dews from the bags of the rich and idle, and returning them in fertilising showers on the poor and industrious: an operation which more enlightened statesmen have happily reversed, to the unspeakable benefit of the community at large. The light footsteps of Marian were impressed on the morning dew beside the firmer step of her lover, and they shook its large drops about them as they cleared themselves a passage through the thick tall fern, without any fear of catching cold, which was not much in fashion in the twelfth century. Robin was as hospitable as Cathmor; for seven men stood on seven paths to call the stranger to his feast. It is true, he superadded the small improvement of making the stranger pay for it: than which what could be more generous? For Cathmor was himself the prime giver of his feast, whereas Robin was only the agent to a series of strangers, who provided in turn for the entertainment of their successors; which is carrying the disinterestedness of hospitality to its acme. Marian often killed the deer,

> Which Scarlet dressed, and Friar Tuck blessed,
> While Little John wandered in search of a guest.

Robin was very devout, though there was great unity in his religion: it was exclusively given to our Lady the Virgin, and he never set forth in a morning till he had said three prayers, and had heard the sweet voice of his Marian singing a hymn to their mutual patroness. Each of his men had, as usual, a patron saint according to his name or taste. The friar chose a saint for himself, and fixed on Saint Botolph, whom he euphonised into Saint Bottle, and maintained that he was that very Panomphic Pantagruelian saint, well known in ancient France as a female divinity, by the name of La Dive Bouteille whose oracular monosyllable 'Trincq,' is celebrated and understood by all nations, and is expounded by the learned doctor Alcofribas, who has treated at large on the subject, to signify 'drink.' Saint Bottle, then, was the saint of Friar Tuck, who did not yield even to Robin and Marian in the assiduity of his devotions to his chosen patron. Such was their summer life, and in their winter caves they had sufficient furniture, ample provender, store of old wine, and assuredly no lack of fuel, with joyous music and pleasant discourse to charm away the season of darkness and storms.

Many moons had waxed and waned, when on the afternoon of a lovely summer day a lusty broad-boned knight was riding through the forest of Sherwood. The sun shone brilliantly on the full green foliage and afforded the knight a fine opportunity of observing picturesque effects, of which it is to be feared he did not avail himself. But he had not proceeded far, before he had an opportunity of observing something much more interesting, namely, a fine young outlaw leaning, in the true Sherwood fashion, with his back against a tree. The knight was preparing to ask the stranger a question the answer to which, if correctly given, would have relieved him from a doubt that pressed heavily on his mind, as to whether he was in the right road or the wrong, when the youth prevented the inquiry by saying: 'In God's name, sir knight, you are late to your meals. My master has tarried dinner for you these three hours.'

'I doubt,' said the knight, 'I am not he you wot of. I am no where bidden today, and I know none in this vicinage.'

'We feared,' said the youth, 'your memory would be treacherous: therefore am I stationed here to refresh it.'

'Who is your master?' said the knight; 'and where does he abide?'

'My master,' said the youth, 'is called Robin Hood, and he abides hard by.'

'And what knows he of me?' said the knight.

'He knows you,' answered the youth, 'as he does every way-faring knight and friar, by instinct.'

'Gramercy,' said the knight; 'then I understand his bidding but how if I say I will not come?'

'I am enjoined to bring you,' said the youth. 'If persuasion avail not, I must use other argument.'

'Say'st thou so?' said the knight; 'I doubt if thy stripling rhetoric would convince me.'

'That,' said the young forester, 'we will see.'

'We are not equally matched, boy,' said the knight. 'I should get less honour by thy conquest, than grief by thy injury.'

'Perhaps,' said the youth, 'my strength is more than my seeming, and my cunning more than my strength. Therefore let it please your knighthood to dismount.'

'It shall please my knighthood to chastise thy presumption,' said the knight, springing from his saddle.

Hereupon, which in those days was usually the result of a meeting between any two persons anywhere, they proceeded to fight.

The knight had in an uncommon degree both strength and skill: the forester had less strength, but not less skill than the knight, and showed such a mastery of his weapon as reduced the latter to great admiration.

They had not fought many minutes by the forest clock, the sun; and had as yet done each other no worse injury than that the knight had wounded the forester's jerkin, and the forester had disabled the knight's plume; when they were interrupted by a voice from a thicket, exclaiming, 'Well fought, girl: well fought. Mass, that had nigh been a shrewd hit. Thou owest him for that, lass. Marry, stand by, I'll pay him for thee.'

The knight turning to the voice, beheld a tall friar issuing from the thicket, brandishing a ponderous cudgel.

'Who art thou?' said the knight.

'I am the church militant of Sherwood,' answered the friar. 'Why art thou in arms against our lady queen?'

'What meanest thou?' said the knight.

'Truly, this,' said the friar, 'is our liege lady of the forest, against whom I do apprehend thee in overt act of treason. What sayest thou for thyself?'

'I say,' answered the knight, 'that if this be indeed a lady, man never yet held me so long.'

'Spoken,' said the friar, 'like one who hath done execution. Hast thou thy stomach full of steel? Wilt thou diversify thy repast with a taste of my oak-graff? Or wilt thou incline thine heart to our venison, which truly is cooling? Wilt thou fight? or wilt thou dine? or wilt thou fight and dine? or wilt thou dine and fight? I am for thee, choose as thou mayest.'

'I will dine,' said the knight; 'for with lady I never fought before, and with friar I never fought yet, and with neither will I ever fight knowingly: and if this be the queen of the forest, I will not, being in her own dominions, be backward to do her homage.'

So saying, he kissed the hand of Marian, who was pleased most graciously to express her approbation.

'Gramercy, sir knight,' said the friar, 'I laud thee for thy courtesy, which I deem to be no less than thy valour. Now do thou follow me, while I follow my nose, which scents the pleasant odour of roast from the depth of the forest recesses. I will lead thy horse, and do thou lead my lady.'

The knight took Marian's hand, and followed the friar, who walked before them, singing:

> When the wind blows, when the wind blows
> From where under buck the dry log glows,
>   What guide can you follow,
>   O'er brake and o'er hollow,
> So true as a ghostly, ghostly nose?

. . .

Robin and Richard were two pretty men.
Mother Goose's Melody.

They proceeded, following their infallible guide, first along a light elastic greensward under the shade of lofty and wide-spreading trees that skirted a sunny opening of the forest, then along labyrinthine paths, which the deer, the outlaw, or the woodman had made, through the close shoots of the young coppices, through the thick undergrowth of the ancient woods, through beds of gigantic fern that filled the narrow glades and waved their green feathery heads above the plume of the knight. Along these sylvan alleys they walked in single file; the friar singing and pioneering in the van, the horse plunging and floundering behind the friar, the lady following 'in maiden meditation fancy-free,' and the knight bringing up the rear, much marvelling at the strange company into which his stars had thrown him. Their path had expanded sufficiently to allow the knight to take Marian's hand again, when they arrived in the august presence of Robin Hood and his court.

Robin's table was spread under a high overarching canopy of living boughs, on the edge of a natural lawn of verdure starred with flowers, through which a swift transparent rivulet ran sparkling in the sun. The board was covered with abundance of choice food and excellent liquor, not without the comeliness of snow-white linen and the splendour of costly plate, which the sheriff of Nottingham had unwilling-ly contributed to supply, at the same time with an excellent cook, whom Little John's art had spirited away to the forest with the contents of his master's silver scullery.

An hundred foresters were here assembled over-ready for the dinner, some seated at the table and some lying in groups under the trees.

Robin bade courteous welcome to the knight, who took his seat between Robin and Marian at the festal board; at which was already placed one strange guest in the person of a portly monk, sitting between Little John and Scarlet, with his rotund physiognomy elongated into an unnatural oval by the conjoint influence of sorrow and fear: sorrow for the departed contents of his travelling treasury, a good-looking valise which was hanging empty on a bough; and fear for his personal safety, of which all the flasks and pasties before him could not give him assurance. The appearance of the knight, however, cheered him up with a semblance of protection, and gave him just sufficient courage to demolish a cygnet and a numble-pie, which he diluted with the contents of two flasks of canary sack.

But wine, which sometimes creates and often increases joy, doth also, upon occasion, heighten sorrow: and so it fared now with our portly monk, who had no sooner explained away his portions of provender, than he began to weep and bewail himself bitterly.

'Why dost thou weep, man!' said Robin Hood. 'Thou hast done thine embassy justly, and shalt have thy Lady's grace.'

'Alack! alack!' said the monk: 'no embassy had I, luckless sinner, as well thou wottest, but to take to my abbey in safety the treasure whereof thou hast despoiled me.'

'Propound me his case,' said Friar Tuck, 'and I will give him ghostly counsel.'

'You well remember,' said Robin Hood, 'the sorrowful knight who dined with us here twelve months and a day gone by.'

'Well do I,' said Friar Tuck. 'His lands were in jeopardy with a certain abbot, who would allow him no longer day for their redemption. Whereupon you lent to him the four hundred pounds which he needed, and which he was to repay this day, though he had no better security to give than our Lady the Virgin.'

'I never desired better,' said Robin, 'for she never yet failed to send me my pay; and here is one of her own flock, this faithful and well-favoured monk of St. Mary's, hath brought it me duly, principal and interest to a penny, as Little John can testify, who told it forth. To be sure, he denied having it, but that was to prove our faith. We sought and found it.'

'I know nothing of your knight,' said the monk: 'and the money was our own, as the Virgin shall bless me.'

'She shall bless thee,' said Friar Tuck, 'for a faithful messenger.'

The monk resumed his wailing. Little John brought him his horse. Robin gave him leave to depart. He sprang with singular nimbleness into the saddle, and vanished without saying, God give you good day.

The stranger knight laughed heartily as the monk rode off.

'They say, sir knight,' said Friar Tuck, 'they should laugh who win: but thou laughest who art likely to lose.'

'I have won,' said the knight, 'a good dinner, some mirth, and some knowledge: and I cannot lose by paying for them.'

'Bravely said,' answered Robin. 'Still it becomes thee to pay: for it is not meet that a poor forester should treat a rich knight. How much money hast thou with thee?'

'Troth, I know not,' said the knight. 'Sometimes much, sometimes little, sometimes none. But search, and what thou findest, keep: and for the sake of thy kind heart and open hand, be it what it may, I shall wish it were more.'

'Then, since thou sayest so,' said Robin, 'not a penny will I touch. Many a false churl comes hither, and disburses against his will: and till there is lack of these, I prey not on true men.'

'Thou art thyself a true man, right well I judge, Robin,' said the stranger knight, 'and seemest more like one bred in court than to thy present outlaw life.'

'Our life,' said the friar, 'is a craft, an art, and a mystery. How much of it, think you, could be learned at court?'

'Indeed, I cannot say,' said the stranger knight: 'but I should apprehend very little.'

'And so should I,' said the friar: 'for we should find very little of our bold open practice, but should hear abundance of praise of our principles. To live in seeming fellowship and secret rivalry; to have a hand for all, and a heart for none; to be everybody's acquaintance, and nobody's friend; to meditate the ruin of all on whom we smile, and to dread the secret stratagems of all who smile on us; to pilfer honours and despoil fortunes, not by fighting in daylight, but by sapping in darkness: these are arts which the court can teach but which we, by Our Lady, have not learned. But let your court-minstrel tune up his throat to the praise of your court-hero, then come our principles into play: then is our practice extolled: not by the same name, for their Richard is a hero, and our Robin is a thief: marry, your hero guts an exchequer, while your thief disembowels a portmanteau; your hero sacks a city, while your thief sacks a cellar: your hero marauds on a larger scale, and that is all the difference, for the principle and the virtue are one: but two of a trade cannot agree: therefore your hero makes laws to get rid of your thief, and gives him an ill name that he may hang him: for might is right, and the strong make laws for the weak, and they that make laws to serve their own turn do also make morals to give colour to their laws.'

'Your comparison, friar,' said the stranger, 'falls in this: that your thief fights for profit, and your hero for honour. I have fought under the banners of Richard, and if, as you phrase it, he guts exchequers, and sacks cities, it is not to win treasure for himself, but to furnish forth the means of his greater and more glorious aim.'

'Misconceive me not, sir knight,' said the friar. 'We all love and honour King Richard, and here is a deep draught to his health: but I would show you, that we foresters are miscalled by opprobrious names, and that our virtues, though they follow at humble distance, are yet truly akin to those of Cœur-de-Lion. I say not that Richard is a thief, but I say that Robin is a hero: and for honour, did ever yet man, miscalled thief, win greater honour than Robin! Do not all men grace him with some honourable epithet? The most gentle thief, the most courteous thief, the most bountiful thief, yes, and the most honest thief? Richard is courteous, bountiful, honest, and valiant: but so also is Robin: it is the false word that makes the unjust distinction. They are twin-spirits, and should be friends, but that fortune hath differently cast their lot: but their names shall descend together to the latest days, as the flower of their age and of England: for in the pure principles of freebootery have they excelled all men; and to the principles of freebootery, diversely developed, belong all the qualities to which song and story concede renown.'

'And you may add, friar,' said Marian, 'that Robin, no less than Richard, is king in his own dominion; and that if his subjects be fewer, yet are they more uniformly loyal.'

'I would, fair lady,' said the stranger, 'that thy latter observation were not so true. But I nothing doubt, Robin, that if Richard could hear your friar, and see you and your lady, as I now do, there is not a man in England whom he would take by the hand more cordially than yourself.'

'Gramercy, sir knight,' said Robin – But his speech was cut short by Little John calling, 'Hark!'

All listened. A distant trampling of horses was heard. The sounds approached rapidly, and at length a group of horsemen glittering in holyday dresses was visible among the trees.

'God's my life!' said Robin, 'what means this? To arms, my merrymen all.'

'No arms, Robin,' said the foremost horseman, riding

up and springing from his saddle: 'have you forgotten Sir William of the Lee?'

'No, by my fay,' said Robin; 'and right welcome again to Sherwood.'

Little John bustled to re-array the disorganised economy of the table, and replace the dilapidations of the provender.

'I come late, Robin,' said Sir William, 'but I came by a wrestling, where I found a good yeoman wrongfully beset by a crowd of sturdy varlets, and I staid to do him right.'

'I thank thee for that, in God's name,' said Robin, 'as if thy good service had been to myself.'

'And here,' said the knight, 'is thy four hundred pound; and my men have brought thee an hundred bows and as many well furnished quivers; which I beseech thee to receive and to use as a poor token of my grateful kindness to thee; for me and my wife and children didst thou redeem from beggary.'

'Thy bows and arrows,' said Robin, 'will I joyfully receive, but of thy money, not a penny. It is paid already. My lady, who was thy security, hath sent it me for thee.'

Sir William pressed, but Robin was inflexible.

'It is paid,' said Robin, 'as this good knight can testify, who saw my Lady's messenger depart but now.'

Sir William looked round to the stranger knight, and instantly fell on his knee, saying, 'God save King Richard.'

The foresters, friar and all, dropped on their knees together, and repeated in chorus: 'God save King Richard.'

'Rise, rise,' said Richard, smiling: 'Robin is king here, as his lady hath shown. I have heard much of thee, Robin, both of thy present and thy former state. And this, thy fair forest-queen, is, if tales say true, the lady Matilda Fitzwater.'

Marian signed acknowledgment.

'Your father,' said the king, 'has approved his fidelity to

331

me, by the loss of his lands, which the newness of my return, and many public cares, have not yet given me time to restore: but this justice shall be done to him, and to thee also, Robin, if thou wilt leave thy forest-life and resume thy earldom, and be a peer of Cœur-de-Lion: for braver heart and juster hand I never yet found.'

Robin looked round on his men.

'Your followers,' said the king, 'shall have full pardon, and such of them as thou wilt part with shall have maintenance from me; and if ever I confess to priest, it shall be to thy friar.'

'Gramercy to your majesty,' said the friar; 'and my inflictions shall be flasks of canary; and if the number be (as in grave cases I may, peradventure, make it) too great for one frail mortality, I will relieve you by vicarious penance, and pour down my own throat the redundancy of the burden.'

Robin and his followers embraced the king's proposal. A joyful meeting soon followed with the baron and Sir Guy of Gamwell: and Richard himself honoured with his own presence a formal solemnisation of the nuptials of our lovers, whom he constantly distinguished with his peculiar regard.

The friar could not say, Farewell to the forest, without something of a heavy heart: and he sang as he turned his back upon its bounds, occasionally reverting his head:

> Ye woods, that oft at sultry noon
>> Have o'er me spread your massy shade:
> Ye gushing streams, whose murmured tune
>> Has in my ear sweet music made,
> While, where the dancing pebbles show
>> Deep in the restless fountain-pool
> The gelid water's upward flow,
>> My second flask was laid to cool:

Ye pleasant sights of leaf and flower:
Ye pleasant sounds of bird and bee:
Ye sports of deer in sylvan bower:
Ye feasts beneath the greenwood tree:
Ye baskings in the vernal sun:
Ye slumbers in the summer dell:
Ye trophies that this arm has won:
And must ye hear your friar's farewell?

But the friar's farewell was not destined to be eternal. He was domiciled as the family confessor of the earl and countess of Huntingdon, who led a discreet and courtly life, and kept up old hospitality in all its munificence, till the death of King Richard and the usurpation of John, by placing their enemy in power, compelled them to return to their greenwood sovereignty; which, it is probable they would have before done from choice, if their love of sylvan liberty had not been counteracted by their desire to retain the friendship of Cœur-de-Lion. Their old and tried adherents, the friar among the foremost, flocked again round their forest-banner; and in merry Sherwood they long lived together, the lady still retaining her former name of Maid Marian, though the appellation was then as much a misnomer as that of Little John.

JACOB AND WILHELM GRIMM

IRON HANS

Translated by Edgar Taylor and Marian Edwardes

THERE WAS ONCE upon a time a king who had a great forest near his palace, full of all kinds of wild animals. One day he sent out a huntsman to shoot him a roe, but he did not come back. 'Perhaps some accident has befallen him,' said the king, and the next day he sent out two more huntsmen who were to search for him, but they too stayed away. Then on the third day, he sent for all his huntsmen, and said: 'Scour the whole forest through, and do not give up until you have found all three.' But of these also, none came home again, and of the pack of hounds which they had taken with them, none were seen again. From that time forth, no one would any longer venture into the forest, and it lay there in deep stillness and solitude, and nothing was seen of it, but sometimes an eagle or a hawk flying over it. This lasted for many years, when an unknown huntsman announced himself to the king as seeking a situation, and offered to go into the dangerous forest. The king, however, would not give his consent, and said: 'It is not safe in there; I fear it would fare with you no better than with the others, and you would never come out again.' The huntsman replied: 'Lord, I will venture it at my own risk, of fear I know nothing.'

The huntsman therefore betook himself with his dog to the forest. It was not long before the dog fell in with some game on the way, and wanted to pursue it; but hardly had the dog run two steps when it stood before a deep pool, could go no farther, and a naked arm stretched itself out of the water, seized it, and drew it under. When the huntsman saw that, he went back and fetched three men to come with buckets and bale out the water. When they could see to the bottom there lay a wild man whose body was brown like rusty iron, and whose hair hung over his face down to his knees. They bound him with cords, and led him away to the castle. There was great astonishment over the wild man; the king, however, had him put in an iron cage in his courtyard, and forbade the door to be opened on pain of death, and the queen herself was to take the key into her keeping. And from this time forth everyone could again go into the forest with safety.

The king had a son of eight years, who was once playing in the courtyard, and while he was playing, his golden ball fell into the cage. The boy ran thither and said: 'Give me my ball out.' 'Not till you have opened the door for me,' answered the man. 'No', said the boy, 'I will not do that; the king has forbidden it', and ran away. The next day he again went and asked for his ball; the wild man said: 'Open my door', but the boy would not. On the third day the king had ridden out hunting, and the boy went once more and said: 'I cannot open the door even if I wished, for I have not the key.' Then the wild man said: 'It lies under your mother's pillow, you can get it there.' The boy, who wanted to have his ball back, cast all thought to the winds, and brought the key. The door opened with difficulty, and the boy pinched his fingers. When it was open the wild man stepped out, gave him the golden ball, and hurried away. The boy had become afraid; he called and cried after him: 'Oh, wild man, do not go away, or I shall be beaten!' The wild man turned back, took him up, set him on his shoulder, and went with hasty steps into the forest. When the king came home, he observed the empty cage, and asked the queen how that had happened.

She knew nothing about it, and sought the key, but it was gone. She called the boy, but no one answered. The king sent out people to seek for him in the fields, but they did not find him. Then he could easily guess what had happened, and much grief reigned in the royal court.

When the wild man had once more reached the dark forest, he took the boy down from his shoulder, and said to him: 'You will never see your father and mother again, but I will keep you with me, for you have set me free, and I have compassion on you. If you do all I bid you, you shall fare well. Of treasure and gold have I enough, and more than anyone in the world.' He made a bed of moss for the boy on which he slept, and the next morning the man took him to a well, and said: 'Behold, the gold well is as bright and clear as crystal, you shall sit beside it, and take care that nothing falls into it, or it will be polluted. I will come every evening to see if you have obeyed my order.' The boy placed himself by the brink of the well, and often saw a golden fish or a golden snake show itself therein, and took care that nothing fell in. As he was thus sitting, his finger hurt him so violently that he involuntarily put it in the water. He drew it quickly out again, but saw that it was quite gilded, and whatsoever pains he took to wash the gold off again, all was to no purpose. In the evening Iron Hans came back, looked at the boy, and said: 'What has happened to the well?' 'Nothing, nothing,' he answered, and held his finger behind his back, that the man might not see it. But he said: 'You have dipped your finger into the water, this time it may pass, but take care you do not again let anything go in.' By daybreak the boy was already sitting by the well and watching it. His finger hurt him again and he passed it over his head, and then unhappily a hair fell down into the well. He took it quickly out, but it was already quite gilded. Iron Hans came, and already knew what had happened. 'You have let a hair fall into the well,' said he. 'I will allow you to watch by it once more, but if this happens for the third time then the well is polluted and you can no longer remain with me.'

On the third day, the boy sat by the well, and did not stir his finger, however much it hurt him. But the time was long to him, and he looked at the reflection of his face on the surface of the water. And as he still bent down more and more while he was doing so, and trying to look straight into the eyes, his long hair fell down from his shoulders into the water. He raised himself up quickly, but the whole of the hair of his head was already golden and shone like the sun. You can imagine how terrified the poor boy was! He took his pocket-handkerchief and tied it round his head, in order that the man might not see it. When he came he already knew everything, and said: 'Take the handkerchief off.' Then the golden hair streamed forth, and let the boy excuse himself as he might, it was of no use. 'You have not stood the trial and can stay here no longer. Go forth into the world, there you will learn what poverty is. But as you have not a bad heart, and as I mean well by you, there is one thing I will grant you; if you fall into any difficulty, come to the forest and cry: "Iron Hans", and then I will come and help you. My power is great, greater than you think, and I have gold and silver in abundance.'

Then the king's son left the forest, and walked by beaten and unbeaten paths ever onwards until at length he reached a great city. There he looked for work, but could find none, and he had learnt nothing by which he could help himself. At length he went to the palace, and asked if they would take him in. The people about court did not at all know what use they could make of him, but they liked him, and told him to stay. At length the cook took him into his service, and said he might carry wood and water, and rake the cinders together. Once when it so happened that no one else was at hand, the cook ordered him to carry the food to the royal table, but as he did not like to let his golden hair be seen, he kept his little cap on. Such a thing as that had never yet come under the king's notice, and he said: 'When you come to the royal table you must take your hat off.' He answered: 'Ah, Lord, I cannot; I have a bad sore place on my head.' Then the king had the cook called before him and scolded him, and asked how he could take such a boy as that into his service; and that he was to send him away at once. The cook, however, had pity on him, and exchanged him for the gardener's boy.

And now the boy had to plant and water the garden, hoe and dig, and bear the wind and bad weather. Once in summer when he was working alone in the garden, the day was so warm he took his little cap off that the air might cool him. As the sun shone on his hair it glittered and flashed so that the rays fell into the bedroom of the king's daughter, and up she sprang to see what that could be. Then she saw the boy, and cried to him: 'Boy, bring me a wreath of flowers.' He put his cap on with all haste, and gathered wild field-flowers and bound them together. When he was ascending the stairs with them, the gardener met him, and said: 'How can you take the king's daughter a garland of such common flowers? Go quickly, and get another, and seek out the prettiest and rarest.' 'Oh, no,' replied the boy, 'the wild ones have more scent, and will please her better.' When he got into the room, the king's daughter said: 'Take your cap off, it is not seemly to keep it on in my presence.' He again said: 'I may not, I have a sore head.' She, however, caught at his cap and pulled it off, and then his golden hair rolled down on his shoulders, and it was splendid to behold. He wanted to run out, but she held him by the arm, and gave him a handful of ducats. With these he departed, but he cared nothing for the gold pieces. He took them to the gardener, and said: 'I present them to your children, they can play with them.' The following day the king's daughter again called to him that he was to bring her a wreath of field-flowers, and then he went in with it, she instantly snatched at his cap, and wanted to take it away from him, but he held it fast with both hands. She again gave him a handful of ducats, but he would not keep them, and gave them to the gardener for playthings for his children. On the third day things went just the same; she could not get his cap away from him, and he would not have her money.

Not long afterwards, the country was overrun by war. The king gathered together his people, and did not know whether or not he could offer any opposition to the enemy, who was superior in strength and had a mighty army. Then said the gardener's boy: 'I am grown up, and will go to the wars also, only give me a horse.' The others laughed, and said: 'Seek one for yourself when we are gone, we will leave one behind us in the stable for you.' When they had gone forth, he went into the stable, and led the horse out; it was lame of one foot, and limped hobblety jig, hobblety jig; nevertherless he mounted it, and rode away to the dark forest. When he came to the outskirts, he called 'Iron Hans' three times so loudly that it echoed through the trees. Thereupon the wild man appeared immediately, and said: 'What do you desire?' 'I want a strong steed, for I am going to the wars.' 'That you shall have, and still more than you ask for.' Then the wild man went back into the forest, and it was not long before a stable-boy came out of it, who led a horse that snorted with its nostrils, and could hardly be restrained, and behind them followed a great troop of warriors entirely equipped in iron, and their swords flashed in the sun. The youth made over his three-legged horse to the stable-boy, mounted the other, and rode at the head of the soldiers. When he got near the battle-field a great part of the king's men had already fallen, and little was wanting to make the rest give way. Then the youth galloped thither with his iron soldiers, broke like a hurricane over the enemy, and beat down all who opposed him. They began to flee, but the youth pursued, and never stopped, until there was not a single man left. Instead of returning to the king, however, he conducted his troop by byways back to the forest, and called forth Iron Hans. 'What do you desire?' asked the wild man. 'Take back your horse and your troops, and give me my three-legged horse again.' All that he asked was done, and soon he was riding on his three-legged horse. When the king returned to his palace, his daughter went to meet him, and wished him joy of his victory. 'I am not the one who carried away the victory,' said he, 'but a strange knight who came to my assistance with his soldiers.' The daughter wanted to hear who the strange knight was, but the king did not know, and said: 'He followed the enemy, and I did not see him again.' She inquired of the gardener where his boy was, but he smiled, and said: 'He has just come home on his three-legged horse, and the others have been mocking him, and crying: "Here comes our hobblety jig back again!" They asked, too: "Under what hedge have you been lying sleeping all the time?" So he said: "I did the best of all, and it would have gone badly without me." And then he was still more ridiculed.'

The king said to his daughter: 'I will proclaim a great feast that shall last for three days, and you shall throw a golden apple. Perhaps the unknown man will show himself.' When the feast was announced, the youth went out to the forest, and called Iron Hans. 'What do you desire?' asked he. 'That I may catch the king's daughter's golden apple.' 'It is as safe as if you had it already,' said Iron Hans. 'You shall likewise have

343

a suit of red armour for the occasion, and ride on a spirited chestnut-horse.' When the day came, the youth galloped to the spot, took his place amongst the knights, and was recognized by no one. The king's daughter came forward, and threw a golden apple to the knights, but none of them caught it but he, only as soon as he had it he galloped away.

On the second day Iron Hans equipped him as a white knight, and gave him a white horse. Again he was the only one who caught the apple, and he did not linger an instant, but galloped off with it. The king grew angry, and said: 'That is not allowed; he must appear before me and tell his name.' He gave the order that if the knight who caught the apple should go away again, they should pursue him, and if he would not come back willingly, they were to cut him down and stab him.

On the third day, he received from Iron Hans a suit of black armour and a black horse, and again he caught the apple. But when he was riding off with it, the king's attendants pursued him, and one of them got so near him that he wounded the youth's leg with the point of his sword. The youth nevertheless escaped from them, but his horse leapt so violently that the helmet fell from the youth's head, and they could see that he had golden hair. They rode back and announced this to the king.

The following day the king's daughter asked the gardener about his boy. 'He is at work in the garden; the queer creature has been at the festival too, and only came home yesterday evening; he has likewise shown my children three golden apples which he has won.'

The king had him summoned into his presence, and he came and again had his little cap on his head. But the king's daughter went up to him and took it off, and then his golden hair fell down over his shoulders, and he was so handsome that all were amazed. 'Are you the knight who came every day to the festival, always in different colours, and who caught the three golden apples?' asked the king. 'Yes,' answered he, 'and here the apples are', and he took them out of his pocket, and returned them to the king. 'If you desire further proof, you may see the wound which your people gave me when they followed me. But I am likewise the knight who helped you to your victory over your enemies.' 'If you can perform such deeds as that, you are no gardener's boy; tell me, who is your father?' 'My father is a mighty king, and gold have I in plenty as great as I require.' 'I well see,' said the king, 'that I owe thanks to you; can I do anything to please you?' 'Yes,' answered he, 'that indeed you can. Give me your daughter to wife.' The maiden laughed, and said: 'He does not stand much on ceremony, but I have already seen by his golden hair that he was no gardener's boy', and then she went and kissed him. His father and mother came to the wedding, and were in great delight, for they had given up all hope of ever seeing their dear son again. And as they were sitting at the marriage-feast, the music suddenly stopped, the doors opened, and a stately king came in with a great retinue. He went up to the youth, embraced him and said: 'I am Iron Hans, and was by enchantment a wild man, but you have set me free; all the treasures which I possess, shall be your property.'

ANGELA CARTER

THE COMPANY OF
WOLVES

ONE BEAST AND only one howls in the woods by night.

The wolf is carnivore incarnate and he's as cunning as he is ferocious; once he's had a taste of flesh then nothing else will do.

At night, the eyes of wolves shine like candle flames, yellowish, reddish, but that is because the pupils of their eyes fatten on darkness and catch the light from your lantern to flash it back to you – red for danger; if a wolf's eyes reflect only moonlight, then they gleam a cold and unnatural green, a mineral, a piercing colour. If the benighted traveller spies those luminous, terrible sequins stitched suddenly on the black thickets, then he knows he must run, if fear has not struck him stock-still.

But those eyes are all you will be able to glimpse of the forest assassins as they cluster invisibly round your smell of meat as you go through the wood unwisely late. They will be like shadows, they will be like wraiths, grey members of a congregation of nightmare; hark! his long, wavering howl . . . an aria of fear made audible.

The wolfsong is the sound of the rending you will suffer, in itself a murdering.

It is winter and cold weather. In this region of mountain and forest, there is now nothing for the wolves to eat. Goats and sheep are locked up in the byre, the deer departed for the remaining pasturage on the southern slopes – wolves grow lean and famished. There is so little flesh on them that you could count the starveling ribs through their pelts, if they gave you time before they pounced. Those slavering jaws; the lolling tongue; the rime of saliva on the grizzled chops – of all the teeming perils of the night and the forest, ghosts, hobgoblins, ogres that grill babies upon gridirons, witches that fatten their captives in cages for cannibal tables, the wolf is worst for he cannot listen to reason.

You are always in danger in the forest, where no people are. Step between the portals of the great pines where the shaggy branches tangle about you, trapping the unwary traveller in nets as if the vegetation itself were in a plot with the wolves who live there, as though the wicked trees go fishing on behalf of their friends – step between the gateposts of the forest with the greatest trepidation and infinite precautions, for if you stray from the path for one instant, the wolves will eat you. They are grey as famine, they are as unkind as plague.

The grave-eyed children of the sparse villages always carry knives with them when they go out to tend the little flocks of goats that provide the homesteads with acrid milk and rank, maggoty cheeses. Their knives are half as big as they are, the blades are sharpened daily.

But the wolves have ways of arriving at your own hearthside. We try and try but sometimes we cannot keep them out. There is no winter's night the cottager does not fear to see a lean, grey, famished snout questing under the door, and there was a woman once bitten in her own kitchen as she was straining the macaroni.

Fear and flee the wolf; for, worst of all, the wolf may be more than he seems.

There was a hunter once, near here, that trapped a wolf in a pit. This wolf had massacred the sheep and goats; eaten up a mad old man who used to live by himself in a hut halfway up the mountain and sing to Jesus all day; pounced on a girl looking after the sheep, but she made such a commotion that men came with rifles and scared him away and tried to track him into the forest but he was cunning and easily gave them the slip. So this hunter dug a pit and put a duck in it, for bait, all alive-oh; and he covered the pit with straw smeared with wolf dung. Quack, quack! went the duck and a wolf came slinking out of the forest, a big one, a heavy one, he weighed as much as a grown man and the straw gave way beneath him – into the pit he tumbled. The hunter jumped down after him, slit his throat, cut off all his paws for a trophy.

And then no wolf at all lay in front of the hunter but the bloody trunk of a man, headless, footless, dying, dead.

A witch from up the valley once turned an entire wedding party into wolves because the groom had settled on another girl. She used to order them to visit her, at night, from spite, and they would sit and howl around her cottage for her, serenading her with their misery.

Not so very long ago, a young woman in our village married a man who vanished clean away on her wedding night. The bed was made with new sheets and the bride lay down in it; the groom said, he was going out to relieve himself, insisted on it, for the sake of decency, and she drew the coverlet up to her chin and she lay there. And she waited and she waited and then she waited again – surely he's been gone a long time? Until she jumps up in bed and shrieks to hear a howling, coming on the wind from the forest.

That long-drawn, wavering howl has, for all its fearful resonance, some inherent sadness in it, as if the beasts would love to be less beastly if only they knew how and never cease to mourn their own condition. There is a vast melancholy in the canticles of the wolves, melancholy infinite as the forest, endless as these long nights of winter and yet that ghastly sadness, that mourning for their own, irremediable appetites, can never move the heart for not one phrase in it hints at the possibility of redemption; grace could not come to the wolf from its own despair, only through some external mediator, so that, sometimes, the beast will look as if he half welcomes the knife that despatches him.

The young woman's brothers searched the outhouses and the hay-stacks but never found any remains so the sensible girl dried her eyes and found herself another husband not too shy to piss into a pot who spent the nights indoors. She gave him a pair of bonny babies and all went right as a trivet until, one freezing night, the night of the solstice, the hinge of the year when things do not fit together as well as they should, the longest night, her first good man came home again.

A great thump on the door announced him as she was stirring the soup for the father of her children and she knew him the moment she lifted the latch to him although it was years since she'd worn black for him and now he was in rags and his hair hung down his back and never saw a comb, alive with lice.

'Here I am again, missus,' he said. 'Get me my bowl of cabbage and be quick about it.'

Then her second husband came in with wood for the fire and when the first one saw she'd slept with another man and, worse, clapped his red eyes on her little children who'd crept into the kitchen to see what all the din was about, he shouted: 'I wish I were a wolf again, to teach this whore a lesson!' So a wolf he instantly became and tore off the eldest boy's left foot before he was chopped up with the hatchet they used for chopping logs. But when the wolf lay bleeding and gasping its last, the pelt peeled off again and he was just as he had been, years ago, when he ran away from his marriage bed, so that she wept and her second husband beat her.

They say there's an ointment the Devil gives you that turns you into a wolf the minute you rub it on. Or, that he was born feet first and had a wolf for his father and his torso is a man's but his legs and genitals are a wolf's. And he has a wolf's heart.

Seven years is a werewolf's natural span but if you burn his human clothing you condemn him to wolfishness for the rest of his life, so old wives hereabouts think it some protection to throw a hat or an apron at the werewolf, as if clothes made the man. Yet by the eyes, those phosphorescent eyes, you know him in all his shapes; the eyes alone unchanged by metamorphosis.

Before he can become a wolf, the lycanthrope strips stark naked. If you spy a naked man among the pines, you must run as if the Devil were after you.

It is midwinter and the robin, the friend of man, sits on the handle of the gardener's spade and sings. It is the worst time in all the year for wolves but this strong-minded child insists she will go off through the wood. She is quite sure the wild beasts cannot harm her although, well-warned, she lays a carving knife in the basket her mother has packed with cheeses. There is a bottle of harsh liquor distilled from brambles; a batch of flat oatcakes baked on the hearthstone; a pot or two of jam. The flaxen-haired girl will take these delicious gifts to a reclusive grandmother so old the burden of her years is crushing her to death. Granny lives two hours' trudge through the winter woods; the child wraps herself up in her thick shawl, draws it over her head. She steps into her stout wooden shoes; she is dressed and ready and it is

353

Christmas Eve. The malign door of the solstice still swings upon its hinges but she has been too much loved ever to feel scared.

Children do not stay young for long in this savage country. There are no toys for them to play with so they work hard and grow wise but this one, so pretty and the youngest of her family, a little late-comer, had been indulged by her mother and the grandmother who'd knitted her the red shawl that, today, has the ominous if brilliant look of blood on snow. Her breasts have just begun to swell; her hair is like lint, so fair it hardly makes a shadow on her pale forehead; her cheeks are an emblematic scarlet and white and she has just started her woman's bleeding, the clock inside her that will strike, henceforward, once a month.

She stands and moves within the invisible pentacle of her own virginity. She is an unbroken egg; she is a sealed vessel; she has inside her a magic space the entrance to which is shut tight with a plug of membrane; she is a closed system; she does not know how to shiver. She has her knife and she is afraid of nothing.

Her father might forbid her, if he were home, but he is away in the forest, gathering wood, and her mother cannot deny her.

The forest closed upon her like a pair of jaws.

There is always something to look at in the forest, even in the middle of winter – the huddled mounds of birds, succumbed to the lethargy of the season, heaped on the creaking boughs and too forlorn to sing; the bright frills of the winter fungi on the blotched trunks of the trees; the cuneiform slots of rabbits and deer, the herringbone tracks of the birds, a hare as lean as a rasher of bacon streaking across the path where the thin sunlight dapples the russet brakes of last year's bracken.

When she heard the freezing howl of a distant wolf, her practised hand sprang to the handle of her knife, but she saw no sign of a wolf at all, nor of a naked man, neither, but then she heard a clattering among the brushwood and there sprang on to the path a fully clothed one, a very handsome young one, in the green coat and wideawake hat of a hunter, laden with carcasses of game birds. She had her hand on her knife at the first rustle of twigs but he laughed with a flash of white teeth when he saw her and made her a comic yet flattering little bow; she'd never seen such a fine fellow before, not among the rustic clowns of her native village. So on they went together, through the thickening light of the afternoon.

Soon they were laughing and joking like old friends. When he offered to carry her basket, she gave it to him although her knife was in it because he told her his rifle would protect them. As the day darkened, it began to snow again; she felt the first flakes settle on her eyelashes but now there was only half a mile to go and there would be a fire, and hot tea, and a welcome, a warm one, surely, for the dashing huntsman as well as for herself.

This young man had a remarkable object in his pocket. It was a compass. She looked at the little round glass face in the palm of his hand and watched the wavering needle with a vague wonder. He assured her this compass had taken him safely through the wood on his hunting trip because the needle always told him with perfect accuracy where the north was. She did not believe it; she knew she should never leave the path on the way through the wood or else she would be lost instantly. He laughed at her again; gleaming trails of spittle clung to his teeth. He said, if he plunged off the path into the forest that surrounded them, he could guarantee to arrive at her grandmother's house a good quarter of an hour before she did, plotting his way through the undergrowth with his compass, while she trudged the long way, along the winding path.

I don't believe you. Besides, aren't you afraid of the wolves?

He only tapped the gleaming butt of his rifle and grinned.

Is it a bet? he asked her. Shall we make a game of it? What will you give me if I get to your grandmother's house before you?

What would you like? she asked disingenuously.

A kiss.

Commonplaces of a rustic seduction; she lowered her eyes and blushed.

He went through the undergrowth and took her basket with him but she forgot to be afraid of the beasts, although now the moon was rising, for she wanted to dawdle on her way to make sure the handsome gentleman would win his wager.

Grandmother's house stood by itself a little way out of the village. The freshly falling snow blew in eddies about the kitchen garden and the young man stepped delicately up the snowy path to the door as if he were reluctant to get his feet wet, swinging his bundle of game and the girl's basket and humming a little tune to himself.

There is a faint trace of blood on his chin; he has been snacking on his catch.

He rapped upon the panels with his knuckles.

Aged and frail, granny is three-quarters succumbed to the mortality the ache in her bones promises her and almost ready to give in entirely. A boy came out from the village to build up her hearth for the night an hour ago and the kitchen crackles with busy firelight. She has her Bible for company, she is a pious old woman. She is propped up on several pillows in the bed set into the wall peasant-fashion, wrapped up in the patchwork quilt she made before she was married, more years ago than she cares to remember. Two china spaniels with liver-coloured blotches on their coats and black noses sit on either side of the fireplace. There is a bright rug of woven rags on the pantiles. The grandfather clock ticks away her eroding time.

We keep the wolves outside by living well.

He rapped upon the panels with his hairy knuckles.

It is your granddaughter, he mimicked in a high soprano.

Lift up the latch and walk in, my darling.

You can tell them by their eyes, eyes of a beast of prey, nocturnal, devastating eyes as red as a wound; you can hurl your Bible at him and your apron after, granny, you thought that was a sure prophylactic against these infernal vermin . . . now call on Christ and his mother and all the angels in heaven to protect you but it won't do you any good.

His feral muzzle is sharp as a knife; he drops his golden burden of gnawed pheasant on the table and puts down your dear girl's basket, too. Oh, my God, what have you done with her?

Off with his disguise, that coat of forest-coloured cloth, the hat with the feather tucked into the ribbon; his matted hair streams down his white shirt and she can see the lice moving in it. The sticks in the hearth shift and hiss; night and the forest has come into the kitchen with darkness tangled in its hair.

He strips off his shirt. His skin is the colour and texture of vellum. A crisp stripe of hair runs down his belly, his nipples are ripe and dark as poison fruit but he's so thin you could count the ribs under his skin if only he gave you the time. He strips off his trousers and she can see how hairy his legs are. His genitals, huge. Ah! huge.

The last thing the old lady saw in all this world was a young man, eyes like cinders, naked as a stone, approaching her bed.

The wolf is carnivore incarnate.

When he had finished with her, he licked his chops and quickly dressed himself again, until he was just as he had been when he came through her door. He burned the inedible hair in the fireplace and wrapped the bones up in a napkin that he hid away under the bed in the wooden chest in which he found a clean pair of sheets. These he carefully put on the bed instead of the tell-tale stained ones he stowed away in the laundry basket. He plumped up the pillows and shook out the patchwork quilt, he picked up the Bible from the floor, closed it and laid it on the table. All was as it had been before except that grandmother was gone. The sticks twitched in the grate, the clock ticked and the young man sat patiently, deceitfully beside the bed in granny's nightcap.

Rat-a-tap-tap.

Who's there, he quavers in granny's antique falsetto.

Only your granddaughter.

So she came in, bringing with her a flurry of snow that melted in tears on the tiles, and perhaps she was a little disappointed to see only her grandmother sitting beside the fire. But then he flung off the blanket and sprang to the door, pressing his back against it so that she could not get out again.

The girl looked round the room and saw there was not even the indentation of a head on the smooth cheek of the pillow and how, for the first time she'd seen it so, the Bible lay closed on the table. The tick of the clock cracked like a whip. She wanted her knife from her basket but she did not dare reach for it because his eyes were fixed upon her –

358

huge eyes that now seemed to shine with a unique, interior light, eyes the size of saucers, saucers full of Greek fire, diabolic phosphorescence.

What big eyes you have.

All the better to see you with.

No trace at all of the old woman except for a tuft of white hair that had caught in the bark of an unburned log. When the girl saw that, she knew she was in danger of death.

Where is my grandmother?

There's nobody here but we two, my darling.

Now a great howling rose up all around them, near, very near, as close as the kitchen garden, the howling of a multitude of wolves; she knew the worst wolves are hairy on the inside and she shivered, in spite of the scarlet shawl she pulled more closely round herself as if it could protect her although it was as red as the blood she must spill.

Who has come to sing us carols, she said.

Those are the voices of my brothers, darling; I love the company of wolves. Look out of the window and you'll see them.

Snow half-caked the lattice and she opened it to look into the garden. It was a white night of moon and snow; the blizzard whirled round the gaunt, grey beasts who squatted on their haunches among the rows of winter cabbage, pointing their sharp snouts to the moon and howling as if their hearts would break. Ten wolves; twenty wolves – so many wolves she could not count them, howling in concert as if demented or deranged. Their eyes reflected the light from the kitchen and shone like a hundred candles.

It is very cold, poor things, she said; no wonder they howl so.

She closed the window on the wolves' threnody and took off her scarlet shawl, the colour of poppies, the colour of sacrifices, the colour of her menses, and, since her fear did her no good, she ceased to be afraid.

What shall I do with my shawl?

Throw it on the fire, dear one. You won't need it again.

She bundled up her shawl and threw it on the blaze, which instantly consumed it. Then she drew her blouse over her head; her small breasts gleamed as if the snow had invaded the room.

What shall I do with my blouse?

Into the fire with it, too, my pet.

The thin muslin went flaring up the chimney like a magic bird and now off came her skirt, her woollen stockings, her shoes, and on to the fire they went, too, and were gone for good. The firelight shone through the edges of her skin; now she was clothed only in her untouched integument of flesh. This dazzling, naked she combed out her hair with her fingers; her hair looked white as the snow outside. Then went directly to the man with red eyes in whose unkempt mane the lice moved; she stood up on tiptoe and unbuttoned the collar of his shirt.

What big arms you have.

All the better to hug you with.

Every wolf in the world now howled a prothalamion outside the window as she freely gave the kiss she owed him.

What big teeth you have!

She saw how his jaw began to slaver and the room was full of the clamour of the forest's Liebestod but the wise child never flinched, even when he answered:

All the better to eat you with.

The girl burst out laughing; she knew she was nobody's meat. She laughed at him full in the face, she ripped off his shirt for him and flung it into the fire, in the fiery wake of her own discarded clothing. The flames danced like dead souls

360

on Walpurgisnacht and the old bones under the bed set up a terrible clattering but she did not pay them any heed.

Carnivore incarnate, only immaculate flesh appeases him.

She will lay his fearful head on her lap and she will pick out the lice from his pelt and perhaps she will put the lice into her mouth and eat them, as he will bid her, as she would do in a savage marriage ceremony.

The blizzard will die down.

The blizzard died down, leaving the mountains as randomly covered with snow as if a blind woman had thrown a sheet over them, the upper branches of the forest pines limed, creaking, swollen with the fall.

Snowlight, moonlight, a confusion of paw-prints.

All silent, all still.

Midnight; and the clock strikes. It is Christmas Day, the werewolves' birthday, the door of the solstice stands wide open; let them all sink through.

See! sweet and sound she sleeps in granny's bed, between the paws of the tender wolf.

ANDREW LANG

THE GOLD OF FAIRNILEE

CHAPTER I
The Old House

YOU MAY STILL see the old Scots house where Randal was born, so long ago. Nobody lives there now. Most of the roof has fallen in, there is no glass in the windows, and all the doors are open. They were open in the days of Randal's father – nearly five hundred years have passed since then – and everyone who came was welcome to his share of beef and broth and ale. But now the doors are not only open, they are quite gone, and there is nobody within to give you a welcome.

So there is nothing but emptiness in the old house where Randal lived with Jean, four hundred and sixty years or so before you were born. It is a high old house, and wide, with the broken slates still on the roof. At the corner there are little round towers, like pepperboxes, with sharp peaks. The stems of the ivy that covers the walls are as thick as trees. There are many trees crowding all around, and there are hills around it too; and far below you hear the Tweed whispering all day. The house is called Fairnilee, which means 'the Fairies' Field'; for people believed in fairies, as you shall hear, when Randal was a boy, and even when my father was a boy.

Randal was all alone in the house when he was a little fellow – alone with his mother, and Nancy the old nurse, and Simon Grieve the butler, who wore a black velvet coat and a big silver chain. Then there were the maids, and the grooms, and the farm folk, who were all friends of Randal's.

He was not lonely, and he did not feel unhappy, even before Jean came, as you shall be told. But the grown-up people were sad and silent at Fairnilee. Randal had no father; his mother, Lady Ker, was a widow. She was still quite young, and Randal thought her the most beautiful person in the world. Children think these things about their mothers, and Randal had seen no ladies but his mother only. She had brown hair and brown eyes and red lips, and a grave kind face, which looked serious under her great white widow's cap with the black hood over it. Randal never saw his mother cry; but when he was a very little child indeed, he had heard her crying in the night: this was after his father went away.

CHAPTER II
How Randal's Father Came Home

RANDAL REMEMBERED HIS father going to fight the English, and how he came back again. It was a windy August evening when he went away: the rain had fallen since morning. Randal had watched the white mists driven by the gale down through the black pine wood that covers the hill opposite Fairnilee. The mist looked like armies of ghosts, he thought, marching, marching through the pines, with their white flags flying and streaming. Then the sun came out red at evening, and Randal's father rode away with all his men. He had a helmet on his head, and a great axe hanging from his neck by a chain, and a spear in his hand. He was riding his big horse, Sir Hugh, and he caught Randal up to the saddle and kissed him many times before he clattered out of the courtyard. All the tenants and men about the farm rode with him, all with spears and a flag embroidered with a crest in gold. His mother watched them from the tower till they were out of sight. And Randal saw them ride away, not on hard, smooth roads like ours, but along a green grassy track, the water splashing up to their stirrups where they crossed the marshes.

Then the sky turned as red as blood, in the sunset, and next it grew brown, like the rust on a sword; and the Tweed below, when they rode the ford, was all red and gold and brown.

Then time went on; that seemed a long time to Randal. Only the women were left in the house, and Randal played with the shepherd's children. They sailed boats in the mill-pond, and they went down to the boat-pool and watched to see the big copper-coloured salmon splashing in the still water. One evening Randal looked up suddenly from his play. It was growing dark. He had been building a house with the round stones and wet sand by the river. He looked up, and there was his own father! He was riding all alone, and his horse, Sir Hugh, was very lean and lame, and scarred with the spurs. The spear in his father's hand was broken, and he had no sword; and he looked neither to right nor to left. His eyes were wide open, but he seemed to see nothing.

Randal cried out to him, 'Father! Father!' but he never glanced at Randal. He did not look as if he heard him; or knew he was there, and suddenly he seemed to go away, Randal did not know how or where.

Randal was frightened.

He ran into the house, and went to his mother.

'Oh, mother,' he said, 'I have seen father! He was riding all alone, and he would not look at me. Sir Hugh was lame!'

'Where has he gone?' said Lady Ker, in a strange voice.

'He went away out of sight,' said Randal. 'I could not see where he went.'

Then his mother told him it could not be, that his father

would not have come back alone. He would not leave his men behind him in the war.

But Randal was so sure, that she did not scold him. She knew he believed what he said.

He saw that she was not happy.

All that night, which was the fourth of September, in the year 1513, the day of Flodden fight, Randal's mother did not go to bed. She kept moving about the house. Now she would look from the tower window up Tweed; and now she would go along the gallery and look down Tweed from the other tower. She had lights burning in all the windows. All next day she was never still. She climbed, with two of her maids, to the top of the hill above Yair, on the other side of the river, and she watched the roads down Ettrick and Yarrow. Next night she slept little, and rose early. About noon, Randal saw three or four men riding wearily, with tired horses. They could scarcely cross the ford of Tweed, the horses were so tired. The men were Simon Grieve the butler, and some of the tenants. They looked very pale; some of them had their heads tied up, and there was blood on their faces. Lady Ker and Randal ran to meet them.

Simon Grieve lighted from his horse, and whispered to Randal's mother.

Randal did not hear what he said, but his mother cried, 'I knew it! I knew it!' and turned quite white.

'Where is he?' she said.

Simon pointed across the hill. 'They are bringing the corp,' he said. Randal knew 'the corp' meant the dead body.

He began to cry. 'Where is my father?' he said. 'Where is my father?'

His mother led him into the house. She gave him to the old nurse, who cried over him, and kissed him, and offered him cakes, and made him a whistle with a branch of plane

368

tree. So in a short while Randal only felt puzzled. Then he forgot, and began to play. He was a very little boy.

Lady Ker shut herself up in her own room – her 'bower', the servants called it.

Soon Randal heard heavy steps on the stairs, and whispering. He wanted to run out, and his nurse caught hold of him, and would not have let him go, but he slipped out of her hand, and looked over the staircase.

They were bringing up the body of a man stretched on a shield.

It was Randal's father.

He had been slain at Flodden, fighting for the king. An arrow had gone through his brain, and he had fallen beside James IV, with many another brave knight, all the best of Scotland, the Flowers of the Forest.

What was it Randal had seen, when he thought he met his father in the twilight, three days before?

He never knew. His mother said he must have dreamed it all.

The old nurse used to gossip about it to the maids. 'He's an unco' bairn, oor Randal; I wush he may na be fey.'

She meant that Randal was a strange child, and that strange things would happen to him.

CHAPTER III
How Jean was brought to Fairnilee

THE WINTER WENT by very sadly. At first the people about Fairnilee expected the English to cross the Border and march against them. They drove their cattle out on the wild hills, and into marshes where only they knew the firm paths, and raised walls of earth and stones – *barmkyns*, they called them

369

– around the old house; and made many arrows to shoot out of the narrow windows at the English. Randal used to like to see the arrow-making beside the fire at night. He was not afraid; and said he would show the English what he could do with his little bow. But weeks went on and no enemy came. Spring drew near, the snow melted from the hills. One night Randal was awakened by a great noise of shouting; he looked out of the window, and saw bright torches moving about. He heard the cows 'routing', or bellowing, and the women screaming. He thought the English had come. So they had; not the English army, but some robbers from the other side of the Border. At that time the people on the south side of Scotland and the north side of England used to steal each other's cows time about. When a Scots squire, or 'laird', like Randal's father, had been robbed by the neighbouring English, he would wait his chance and drive away cattle from the English side. This time most of Randal's mother's herds were seized, by a sudden attack in the night, and were driven away through the forest to England. Two or three of Lady Ker's men were hurt by the English, but old Simon Grieve took a prisoner. He did this in a curious way. He shot an arrow after the robbers as they rode off, and the arrow pinned an Englishman's leg to the saddle, and even into his horse. The horse was hurt and frightened, and ran away right back to Fairnilee, where it was caught, with the rider and all, for of course he could not dismount.

They treated him kindly at Fairnilee, though they laughed at him a good deal. They found out from him where the English had come from. He did not mind telling them, for he was really a gypsy from Yetholm, where the gypsies live, and Scot or Southron was all one to him.

When old Simon Grieve knew who the people were that had taken the cows, he was not long in calling the men together, and trying to get back what he had lost. Early one April morning, a grey morning, with snow in the air, he and his spearmen set out, riding down through the forest, and so into Liddesdale. When they came back again, there were great rejoicings at Fairnilee. They drove most of their own cows before them, and a great many other cows that they had not lost; cows of the English farmers. The byres and yards were soon full of cattle, lowing and roaring, very uneasy, and some of them with marks of the spears that had goaded them across many a ford, and up many a rocky pass in the hills.

Randal jumped downstairs to the great hall, where his mother sat. Simon Grieve was telling her all about it.

'Sae we drave oor ain kye hame, my lady,' he said, 'and aiblins some orra anes that was na oor ain. For-bye we raikit a' the plenishing oot o' the ha' o' Hardriding, and a bonny burden o' tapestries, and plaids, and gear we hae, to show for our ride.'*

Then he called to some of his men, who came into the hall, and cast down great piles of all sorts of spoil and booty, silver plate, and silken hangings, and a heap of rugs, and carpets, and plaids, such as Randal had never seen before, for the English were much richer than the Scots.

Randal threw himself on the pile of rugs and began to roll on it.

'Oh, mother,' he cried suddenly, jumping up and looking with wide-open eyes, 'there's something living in the heap! Perhaps it's a doggie, or a rabbit, or a kitten.'

* 'We drove our own cattle home, and perhaps some others that were not ours. And we took all the goods out of the hall at Hardriding, and a pretty load of tapestries, and rugs, and other things we have to show for our ride.'

Then Randal tugged at the cloths, and then they all heard a little shrill cry.

'Why, it's a bairn!' said Lady Ker, who had sat very grave all the time, pleased to have done the English some harm; for they had killed her husband, and were all her deadly foes. 'It's a bairn!' she cried, and pulled out of the great heap of cloaks and rugs a little beautiful child, in its white nightdress, with its yellow curls all tangled over its blue eyes.

Then Lady Ker and the old nurse could not make too much of the pretty English child that had come here in such a wonderful way.

How did it get mixed up with all the spoil? And how had it been carried so far on horseback without being hurt? Nobody ever knew. It came as if the fairies had sent it. English it was, but the best Scot could not hate such a pretty child. Old Nancy Dryden ran up to the old nursery with it, and laid it in a great wooden tub full of hot water, and was giving it warm milk to drink, and dandling it, almost before the men knew what had happened.

'Yon bairn will be a bonny mate for you, Maister Randal,' said old Simon Grieve. 'Deed, I dinna think her kin will come speering after her at Fairnilee. The red cock's crawing ower Hardriding Ha' this day, and when the womenfolk come back frae the wood, they'll hae other things to do forbye looking for bairns.'

When Simon Grieve said that the red cock was crowing over his enemies' home, he meant that he had set it on fire after the people who lived in it had run away.

Lady Ker grew pale when she heard what he said. She hated the English, to be sure, but she was a woman with a kind heart. She thought of the dreadful danger that the little

speering, asking.

English girl had escaped, and she went upstairs and helped the nurse to make the child happy.

CHAPTER IV
Randal and Jean

THE LITTLE GIRL soon made everyone at Fairnilee happy. She was far too young to remember her own home, and presently she was crawling up and down the long hall and making friends with Randal. They found out that her name was Jane Musgrave, though she could hardly say Musgrave; and they called her Jean, with their Scots tongues, or 'Jean o' the Kye', because she came when the cows were driven home again.

Soon the old nurse came to like her near as well as Randal, 'her ain bairn' (her own child), as she called him. In the summer days, Jean, as she grew older, would follow Randal about like a little doggie. They went fishing together, and Randal would pull the trout out of Caddon Burn, or the Burn of Peel; and Jeanie would be very proud of him, and very much alarmed at the big, wide jaws of the yellow trout. And Randal would plait helmets with green rushes for her and him, and make spears of bulrushes, and play at tilts and tournaments. There was peace in the country; or if there was war, it did not come near the quiet valley of the Tweed and the hills that lie around Fairnilee. In summer they were always on the hills and by the burnsides.

You cannot think, if you have not tried, what pleasant company a burn is. It comes out of the deep, black wells in the moss, far away on the tops of the hills, where the sheep feed, and the fox peers from his hole, and the ravens build in the crags. The burn flows down from the lonely places, cutting a way between steep, green banks, tumbling in white waterfalls over rocks, and lying in black, deep pools below the waterfalls. At every turn it does something new and plays a fresh game with its brown waters. The white pebbles in the water look like gold: often Randal would pick one out and think he had found a gold-mine, till he got it into the sunshine, and then it was only a white stone, what he called a 'chucky-stane'; but he kept hoping for better luck next time. In the height of summer, when the streams were very low, he and the shepherd's boys would build dams of stones and turf across a narrow part of the burn, while Jean sat and watched them on a little round knoll. Then, when plenty of water had collected in the pool, they would break the dam and let it all run downhill in a little flood; they called it a 'hurly gush'. And in winter they would slide on the black, smooth ice of the boat-pool, beneath the branches of the alders.

Or they would go out with Yarrow, the shepherd's dog, and follow the track of wild creatures in the snow. The rabbit makes marks like this ∴, and the hare makes marks like this ∶∶; but the fox's track is just as if you had pushed a piece of wood through the snow – a number of cuts in the surface, going straight along. When it was very cold, the grouse and blackcocks would come into the trees near the house, and Randal and Jean would put out porridge for them to eat. And the great white swans floated in from the frozen lochs on the hills, and gathered around open reaches and streams of the Tweed. It was pleasant to be a boy then in the North. And at Hallowe'en they would duck for apples in tubs of water, and burn nuts in the fire, and look for the shadow of the lady Randal was to marry, in the mirror; but he only saw Jean looking over his shoulder.

The days were very short in winter, so far north, and they would soon be driven into the house. Then they sat

374

by the nursery fire; and those were almost the pleasantest hours, for the old nurse would tell them old Scots stories of elves and fairies, and sing them old songs. Jean would crawl close to Randal and hold his hand, for fear the Red Etin, or some other awful bogle, should get her; and in the dancing shadows of the firelight she would think she saw Whuppity Stoorie, the wicked old witch with the spinning-wheel; but it was really nothing but the shadow of the wheel that the old nurse drove with her foot – *birr, birr* – and that whirred and rattled as she span and told her tale. For people span their cloth at home then, instead of buying it from shops; and the old nurse was a great woman for spinning.

She was a great woman for stories, too, and believed in fairies, and 'bogles', as she called them. Had not her own cousin, Andrew Tamson, passed the Cauldshiels Loch one New Year morning? And had he not heard a dreadful roaring, as if all the cattle on Faldonside Hill were routing at once? And then did he not see a great black beast roll down the hillside, like a black ball, and run into the loch, which grew white with foam, and the waves leaped up the banks like a tide rising? What could that be except the kelpie that lives in Cauldshiels Loch, and is just a muckle big water bull? 'And what for should there no be water kye, if there's land kye?'

Randal and Jean thought it was very likely there were 'kye', or cattle, in the water. And some Highland people think so still, and believe they have seen the great kelpie come roaring out of the lake; or Shellycoat, whose skin is all crusted like a rock with shells, sitting beside the sea.

The old nurse had other tales, that nobody believes any longer, about Brownies. A Brownie was a very useful creature

bogle, ghost, spectre.
Whuppity Stoorie, the name of a witch or bad fairy in Border folklore.

to have in a house. He was a kind of fairy-man, and he came out in the dark, when everybody had gone to bed, just as mice pop out at night. He never did anyone any harm, but he sat and warmed himself at the kitchen fire. If any work was unfinished he did it, and made everything tidy that was left out of order. It is a pity there are no such bogles now! If anybody offered the Brownie any payment, even if it was only a silver penny or a new coat, he would take offence and go away.

Other stories the old nurse had, about hidden treasures and buried gold. If you believed her, there was hardly an old stone on the hillside that didn't have gold under it. The very sheep that fed upon the Eildon Hills, which Randal knew well, had yellow teeth because there was so much gold under the grass. Randal had taken two scones, or rolls, in his pocket for dinner, and ridden over to the Eildon Hills. He had seen a rainbow touch one of them, and there he hoped he would find the treasure that always lies at the tail of the rainbow. But he got very soon tired of digging for it with his little dirk, or dagger. It blunted the dagger, and he found nothing. Perhaps he had not marked quite the right place, he thought. But he looked at the teeth of the sheep, and they were yellow; so he had no doubt that there was a gold-mine under the grass, if he could find it.

The old nurse knew that it was very difficult to dig up fairy gold. Generally something happened just when people heard their pickaxes clink on the iron pot that held the treasure. A dreadful storm of thunder and lightning would break out; or the burn would be flooded, and rush down all red and roaring, sweeping away the tools and drowning the digger; or a strange man, that nobody had ever seen before, would come up, waving his arms, and crying out that the Castle was on fire. Then the people would hurry up to the Castle, and find that it was not on fire at all. When they returned, all the earth would be just as it was before they began, and they would give up in despair. Nobody could ever see the man again that gave the alarm.

'Who could he be, nurse?' Randal asked.

'Just one of the good folk, I'm thinking; but it's no weel to be speaking o' *them*.'

Randal knew that the 'good folk' meant the fairies. The old nurse called them the good folk for fear of offending them. She would not speak much about them, except now and then, when the servants had been making merry.

'And is there any treasure hidden near Fairnilee, nursie?' asked little Jean.

'Treasure, my bonny doo! Mair than a' the men about the toon could carry away frae morning till nicht. Do ye no ken the auld rhyme?

> *Atween the wet ground and the dry*
> *The gold of Fairnilee doth lie.*

'And there's the other auld rhyme:

> *Between the Camp o' Rink*
> *And Tweed-water clear,*
> *Lie nine kings' ransoms*
> *For nine hundred year!*'

Randal and Jean were very glad to hear so much gold was near them as would pay nine kings' ransoms. They took their small spades and dug little holes in the Camp of Rink, which is a great old circle of stonework, surrounded by a deep ditch, on the top of a hill above the house. But Jean was not a very good digger, and even Randal grew tired. They thought they would wait till they grew bigger, and *then* find the gold.

CHAPTER V
The Good Folk

'EVERYBODY KNOWS THERE'S fairies,' said the old nurse one night when she was bolder than usual. What she said we will put in English, not Scots as she spoke it. 'But they do not like to be called fairies. So the old rhyme runs:

> *If ye call me imp or elf,*
> *I warn you look well to yourself;*
> *If ye call me fairy,*
> *Ye'll find me quite contrary;*
> *If good neighbour you call me,*
> *Then good neighbour I will be;*
> *But if you call me kindly sprite,*
> *I'll be your friend both day and night.*

'So you must always call them "good neighbours" or "good folk", when you speak of them.'

'Did *you* ever see a fairy, nurse?' asked Randal.

'Not myself, but my mother knew a woman – they called her Tibby Dickson, and her husband was a shepherd, and she had a bairn, as bonny a bairn as ever you saw. And one day she went to the well to draw water, and as she was coming back she heard a loud scream in her house. Then her heart leaped, and fast she ran and flew to the cradle; and there she saw an awful sight – not her own bairn, but a withered imp, with hands like a mole's, and a face like a frog's, and a mouth from ear to ear, and two great staring eyes.'

'What was it?' asked Jeanie, in a trembling voice.

'A fairy's bairn that had not thriven,' said nurse; 'and when their bairns do not thrive, they just steal honest folk's children and carry them away to their own country.'

'And where's that?' asked Randal.

'It's under the ground,' said nurse, 'and there they have gold and silver and diamonds; and there's the Queen of them all, that's as beautiful as the day. She has yellow hair down to her feet, and she has blue eyes, like the sky on a fine day, and her voice like all the mavises singing in the spring. And she is aye dressed in green, and all her court in green; and she rides a white horse with golden bells on the bridle.'

'I would like to go there and see her,' said Randal.

'Oh, never say that, my bairn; you never know who may hear you! And if you go there, how will you come back again? And what will your mother do, and Jean here, and me that's carried you many a time in weary arms when you were a babe?'

'Can't people come back again?' asked Randal.

'Some say "Yes", and some say "No". There was Tam Hislop, that vanished away the day before all the lads and your own father went forth to that weary war at Flodden, and the English, for once, by guile, won the day. Well, Tam Hislop, when the news came that all must arm and mount and ride, he could nowhere be found. It was as if the wind had carried him away. High and low they sought him, but there was his clothes and his armour, and his sword and his spear, but no Tam Hislop. Well, no man heard more of him for seven whole years, not till last year, and then he came back: sore tired he looked, ay, and older than when he was lost. And I met him by the well, and I was frightened; and, "Tam," I said, "where have ye been this weary time?" "I have been with them that I will not speak the name of," says he. "Ye mean the good folk," said I. "Ye have said it," says he. Then I went up to the house, with my heart

mavises, song-thrushes.

379

in my mouth, and I met Simon Grieve. "Simon," I says, "here's Tam Hislop come home from the good folk." "I'll soon send him back to them," says he. And he takes a great stick and lays it about Tam's shoulders, calling him coward loon, that ran away from the fighting. And since then Tam has never been seen about the place. But the Laird's man, of Gala, knows them that say Tam was in Perth the last seven years, and not in Fairyland at all. But it was Fairyland he told me, and he would not lie to his own mother's half-brother's cousin.'

Randal did not care much for the story of Tam Hislop. A fellow who would let old Simon Grieve beat him could not be worthy of the Fairy Queen.

Randal was about thirteen now, a tall boy, with dark eyes, black hair, a brown face with the red on his cheeks. He had grown up in a country where everything was magical and haunted; where fairy knights rode on the leas after dark, and challenged men to battle. Every castle had its tale of Redcap, the sly spirit, or of the woman of the hairy hand. Every old mound was thought to cover hidden gold. And all was so lonely; the green hills rolling between river and river, with no men on them, nothing but sheep, and grouse, and plover. No wonder that Randal lived in a kind of dream. He would lie and watch the long grass until it looked like a forest, and he thought he could see elves dancing between the green grass stems, that were like fairy trees. He kept wishing that he, too, might meet the Fairy Queen, and be taken into that other world where everything was beautiful.

loon, rascal.

CHAPTER VI
The Wishing Well

'JEAN,' SAID RANDAL one midsummer day, 'I am going to the Wishing Well.'

'Oh, Randal,' said Jean, 'it is so far away!'

'I can walk it,' said Randal, 'and you must come, too; I want you to come, Jeanie. It's not so very far.'

'But mother says it is wrong to go to Wishing Wells,' Jean answered.

'Why is it wrong?' said Randal, switching at the tall foxgloves with a stick.

'Oh, she says it is a wicked thing, and forbidden by the Church. People who go to wish there, sacrifice to the spirits of the well; and Father Francis told her that it was very wrong.'

'Father Francis is a shaveling,' said Randal. 'I heard Simon Grieve say so.'

'What's a shaveling, Randal?'

'I don't know: a man that does not fight, I think. I don't care what a shaveling says: so I mean just to go and wish, and I won't sacrifice anything. There can't be any harm in that!'

'But, oh, Randal, you've got your green doublet on!'

'Well! Why not?'

'Do you not know it angers the fair– I mean the good folk – that anyone should wear green on the hill but themselves?'

'I cannot help it,' said Randal. 'If I go in and change my doublet, they will ask what I do that for. I'll chance it, green or grey, and wish my wish for all that.'

'And what are you going to wish?'

'I'm going to wish to meet the Fairy Queen! Just think how beautiful she must be, dressed all in green, with gold bells on her bridle, and riding a white horse shod with gold! I think I see her galloping through the woods and out across the hill, over the heather.'

'But you will go away with her, and never see me any more,' said Jean.

'No, I won't; or if I do, I'll come back, with such a horse, and a sword with a gold handle. I'm going to the Wishing Well. Come on!'

Jean did not like to say 'No', so off they went.

Randal and Jean started without taking anything with them to eat. They were afraid to go back to the house for food. Randal said they would be sure to find something somewhere. The Wishing Well was on the top of a hill between Yarrow and Tweed. So they took off their shoes, and waded the Tweed at the shallowest part, and then they walked up the green grassy bank on the other side, until they came to the Burn of Peel. Here they passed the old square tower of Peel, and the shepherd dogs came out and barked at them. Randal threw a stone at them, and they ran away with their tails between their legs.

'Don't you think we had better go into Peel, and get some bannocks to eat on the way, Randal?' said Jean.

But Randal said he was not hungry; and, besides, the people at Peel would tell the Fairnilee people where they had gone.

'We'll *wish* for things to eat when we get to the Wishing Well,' said Randal. 'All sorts of good things – cold venison pasty, and everything you like.'

So they began climbing the hill, and they followed the Peel Burn. It ran in and out, winding this way and that, and when they did get to the top of the hill, Jean was very tired

bannocks, oatcakes.

and very hungry. And she was very disappointed. For she expected to see some wonderful new country at her feet, and there was only a low strip of sunburnt grass and heather, and then another hill-top! So Jean sat down, and the hot sun blazed on her, and the flies buzzed about her and tormented her.

'Come on, Jean,' said Randal; 'it must be over the next hill!'

So poor Jean got up and followed him, but he walked far too fast for her. When she reached the crest of the next hill, she found a great cairn, or pile of grey stones; and beneath her lay, far, far below, a deep valley covered with woods, and a stream running through it that she had never seen before.

That stream was the Yarrow.

Randal was nowhere in sight, and she did not know where to look for the Wishing Well. If she had walked straight forward through the trees she would have come to it; but she was so tired, and so hungry, and so hot, that she sat down at the foot of the cairn and cried as if her heart would break.

Then she fell asleep.

When Jean woke, it was as dark as it ever is on a mid-summer night in Scotland.

It was a soft, cloudy night; not a clear night with a silver sky.

Jeanie heard a loud roaring close to her, and the red light of a great fire was in her sleepy eyes.

In the firelight she saw strange black beasts, with horns, plunging and leaping and bellowing, and dark figures rushing about the flames. It was the beasts that made the roaring. They were bounding about close to the fire, and sometimes in it, and were all mixed in the smoke.

Jeanie was dreadfully frightened, too frightened to scream.

Presently she heard the voices of men shouting on the hill

below her. The shouts and the barking of dogs came nearer and nearer.

Then a dog ran up to her, and licked her face, and jumped about her.

It was her own sheep-dog, Yarrow.

He ran back to the men who were following him, and came again with one of them.

It was old Simon Grieve, very tired, and so much out of breath that he could scarcely speak.

Jean was very glad to see him, and not frightened any longer.

'Oh, Jeanie, my doo,' said Simon, 'where hae ye been? A muckle gliff ye hae gien us, and a weary spiel up the weary braes.'

Jean told him all about it: how she had come with Randal to see the Wishing Well, and how she had lost him, and fallen asleep.

'And sic a nicht for you bairns to wander on the hill,' said Simon. 'It's the nicht o' St John, when the guid folk hae power. And there's a' the lads burning the Bel fires, and driving the nowt through them: nae less will serve them. Sic a nicht!'

This was the cause of the fire Jean saw, and of the noise of the cattle. On Midsummer Night the country people used to light these fires, and drive the cattle through them. It was an old, old custom come down from heathen times.

Now the other men from Fairnilee had gathered around Jean. Lady Ker had sent them out to look for Randal and her on the hills. They had heard from the good wife at Peel that the children had gone up the burn, and Yarrow had tracked them until Jean was found.

gliff, fright.   *spiel*, shout.   *nowt*, cattle.

384

CHAPTER VII
Where is Randal?

JEAN WAS FOUND, but where was Randal? She told the men who had come out to look for her, that Randal had gone on to look for the Wishing Well. So they rolled her up in a big shepherd's plaid, and two of them carried Jean home in the plaid, while all the rest, with lighted torches in their hands, went to look for Randal through the wood.

Jean was so tired that she fell asleep again in her plaid before they reached Fairnilee. She was wakened by the men shouting as they drew near the house, to show that they were coming home. Lady Ker was waiting at the gate, and the old nurse ran down the grassy path to meet them.

'Where's my bairn?' she cried as soon as she was within call.

The men said, 'Here's Mistress Jean, and Randal will be here soon; they have gone to look for him.'

'Where are they looking?' cried nurse.

'Just about the Wishing Well.'

The nurse gave a scream, and hobbled back to Lady Ker.

'Ma bairn's tint!' she cried. 'Ma bairn's tint! They'll find him never. The good folk have stolen him away from that weary Wishing Well!'

'Hush, nurse,' said Lady Ker, 'do not frighten Jean.'

She spoke to the men, who had no doubt that Randal would soon be found and brought home.

So Jean was put to bed, where she forgot all her troubles; and Lady Ker waited, waited, all night, until the grey light began to come in, about two in the morning.

tint, lost.

Lady Ker kept very still and quiet, telling her beads, and praying. But the old nurse would never be still, but was always wandering out, down to the river's edge, listening for the shouts of the shepherds coming home. Then she would come back again, and moan and wring her hands, crying for her 'bairn'.

About six o'clock, when it was broad daylight and all the birds were singing, the men returned from the hill.

But Randal did not come with them.

Then the old nurse set up a great cry, as the country people do over the bed of someone who has just died.

Lady Ker sent her away, and called Simon Grieve to her own room.

'You have not found the boy yet?' she said, very stately and pale. 'He must have wandered over into Yarrow; perhaps he has gone as far as Newark, and passed the night at the castle, or with the shepherd at Foulshiels.'

'No, my Lady,' said Simon Grieve, 'some o' the men went over to Newark, and some to Foulshiels, and other some down to Sir John Murray's at Philiphaugh; but there's never a word o' Randal in a' the countryside.'

'Did you find no trace of him?' said Lady Ker, sitting down suddenly in the great armchair.

'We went first through the wood, my Lady, by the path to the Wishing Well. And he had been there, for the whip he carried in his hand was lying on the grass. And we found *this.*'

He put his hand in his pouch, and brought out a little silver crucifix, that Randal used always to wear around his neck on a chain.

'This was lying on the grass beside the Wishing Well, my Lady –'

Then he stopped, for Lady Ker had swooned away. She

was worn out with watching and with anxiety about Randal.

Simon went and called the maids, and they brought water and wine, and soon Lady Ker came back to herself, with the little silver crucifix in her hand.

The old nurse was crying, and making a great noise.

'The good folk have taken ma bairn,' she said, 'this nicht o' a' the nichts in the year, when the fairy folk – preserve us frae them! – have power. But they could nae take the blessed rood o' grace; it was beyond their strength. If gypsies, or robber folk frae the Debatable Land, had carried away the bairn, they would hae taken him, cross and a'. But the guid folk have gotten him, and Randal Ker will never, never mair come hame to bonny Fairnilee.'

What the old nurse said was what everybody thought. Even Simon Grieve shook his head, and did not like it.

But Lady Ker did not give up hope. She sent horsemen through all the countryside: up Tweed to the Crook, and to Talla; up Yarrow, past Catslack Tower, and on to the Loch of St Mary; up Ettrick to Thirlestane and Buccleuch, and over to Gala, and to Branxholme in Teviotdale; and even to Hermitage Castle, far away by Liddel water.

They rode far and rode fast, and at every cottage and every tower they asked, 'Has anyone seen a boy in green?' But nobody had seen Randal through all the countryside. Only a shepherd lad, on Foulshiels Hill, had heard bells ringing in the night, and a sound of laughter go past him, like a breeze of wind over the heather.

Days went by, and all the country was out to look for Randal. Down in Yetholm they sought him, among the gypsies; and across the Eden in merry Carlisle; and through

Debatable Land, a no-man's land at the head of the Solway Firth, between England and Scotland.

the Land Debatable, where the robber Armstrongs and Grahames lived; and far down Tweed, past Melrose, and up Jed water, far into the Cheviot Hills.

But there never came any word of Randal. He had vanished as if the earth had opened and swallowed him. Father Francis came from Melrose Abbey, and prayed with Lady Ker, and gave her all the comfort he could. He shook his head when he heard of the Wishing Well, but he said that no spirit of earth or air could have power for ever over a Christian soul. But, even when he spoke, he remembered that, once in seven years, the fairy folk have to pay a dreadful tax, one of themselves, to the King of a terrible country of Darkness; and what if they had stolen Randal, to pay the tax with him!

This was what troubled good Father Francis, though, like a wise man, he said nothing about it, and even put the thought away out of his own mind.

But you may be sure that the old nurse had thought of this tax on the fairies too, and that *she* did not hold her peace about it but spoke to everyone that would listen to her, and would have spoken to the mistress if she had been allowed. But when she tried to begin, Lady Ker told her that she had put her own trust in Heaven, and in the saints. And she gave the nurse such a look when she said that, 'if ever Jean hears of this, I will send you away from Fairnilee, out of the country,' that the old woman was afraid, and was quiet.

As for poor Jean, she was perhaps the most unhappy of them all. She thought to herself, if she had refused to go with Randal to the Wishing Well, and had run in and told Lady Ker, then Randal would never have gone to find the Wishing Well.

And she put herself in great danger, as she fancied, to find him. She wandered alone on the hills, seeking all the places that were believed to be haunted by fairies. At every Fairy Knowe, as the country people called the little round green knolls in the midst of the heather, Jean would stoop her ear to the ground, trying to hear the voices of the fairies within. For it was believed that you might hear the sound of their speech, and the trampling of their horses, and the shouts of the fairy children. But no sound came, except the song of the burn flowing by, and the hum of gnats in the air, and the *gock*, *gock*, the cry of the grouse, when you frighten them in the heather.

Then Jeanie would try another way of meeting the fairies, and finding Randal. She would walk nine times around a Fairy Knowe, beginning from the left side, because then it was fancied that the hillside would open, like a door, and show a path into Fairyland. But the hillside never opened, and she never saw a single fairy; not even old Whuppity Stoorie sitting with her spinning-wheel in a green glen, spinning grass into gold, and singing her fairy song:

> *'I once was young and fair,*
> *My eyes were bright and blue,*
> *As if the sun shone through,*
> *And golden was my hair.*
>
> *Down to my feet it rolled*
> *Ruddy and ripe like corn,*
> *Upon an autumn morn,*
> *In heavy waves of gold.*
>
> *Now am I grey and old,*
> *And so I sit and spin,*
> *With trembling hand and thin,*
> *This metal bright and cold.*

I would give all the gain,
These heaps of wealth untold
Of hard and glittering gold,
Could I be young again!'

CHAPTER VIII
The Ill Years

SO AUTUMN CAME, and all the hillsides were golden with
the heather; and the red coral berries of the rowan trees
hung from the boughs, and were wet with the spray of the
waterfalls in the burns. And days grew shorter, and winter
came with snow, but Randal never came back to Fairnilee.
Season after season passed, and year after year Lady Ker's
hair grew white like snow, and her face thin and pale – for
she fasted often, as was the rule of her Church; all this
was before the Reformation. And she slept little, praying
half the night for Randal's sake. And she went on pilgrim-
ages to many shrines of the saints: to St Boswells and St
Rules, hard by the great Cathedral of St Andrews on the
sea. Nay, she went across the Border as far as the Abbey of
St Albans, and even to St Thomas's shrine of Canterbury,
taking Jean with her. Many a weary mile they rode over
hill and dale, and many an adventure they had, and ran
many dangers from robbers, and soldiers disbanded from
the wars.

But at last they had to come back to Fairnilee; and a sad
place it was, and silent without the sound of Randal's voice
in the hall and the noise of his hunting-horn in the woods.
None of the people wore mourning for him, though they
mourned in their hearts. For to put on black would look as
if they had given up all hope. Perhaps most of them thought

they would never see him again, but Jeanie was not one who despaired.

The years that had turned Lady Ker's hair white, had made Jean a tall, slim lass – 'very bonny', everyone said; and the country people called her the Flower of Tweed. The Yarrow folk had their Flower of Yarrow, and why not the folk of Tweedside? It was now six years since Randal had been lost, and Jeanie was grown a young woman, about seventeen years old. She had always kept a hope that if Randal was with the Fairy Queen he would return perhaps in the seventh year. People said in the countryside that many a man and woman had escaped out of Fairyland after seven years' imprisonment there.

Now the sixth year since Randal's disappearance began very badly, and got worse as it went on. Just when spring should have been beginning, in the end of February, there came the most dreadful snowstorm. It blew and snowed, and blew again, and the snow was as fine as the dust on a road in summer. The strongest shepherds could not hold their own against the tempest, and were 'smoored' in the waste. The flocks moved down from the hillsides, down and down, until all the sheep on a farm would be gathered together in a crowd, under the shelter of a wood in some deep dip of the hills. The storm seemed as if it would never cease; for thirteen days the snow drifted and the wind blew. There was nothing for the sheep to eat, and if there had been hay enough, it would have been impossible to carry it to them. The poor beasts bit at the wool on each other's backs, and so many of them died that the shepherds built walls with the dead bodies to keep the wind and snow away from those that were left alive.

smoored, smothered.

There could be little work done on the farm that spring; and summer came in so cold and wet that the corn could not ripen, but was levelled to the ground. Then autumn was rainy, and the green sheaves lay out in the fields, and sprouted and rotted; so that little corn was reaped, and little flour could be made that year. Then in winter, and as spring came on, the people began to starve. They had no grain, and there were no potatoes in those days, and no rice; nor could corn be brought in from foreign countries. So men and women and children might be seen in the fields, with white pinched faces, gathering nettles to make soup, and digging for roots that were often little better than poison. They ground the bark of the fir trees, and mixed it with the little flour they could get; and they ate such beasts as never are eaten except in time of famine.

It is said that one very poor woman and her daughter always looked healthy and plump in these dreadful times, until people began to suspect them of being witches. And they were taken, and charged before the Sheriff with living by witchcraft, and very likely they would have been burned. So they confessed that they had fed ever since the famine began – on snails! But there were not snails enough for all the countryside; even if people had cared to eat them. So many men and women died, and more were very weak and ill.

Lady Ker spent all her money in buying food for her people. Jean and she lived on as little as they could, and were as careful as they could be. They sold all the beautiful silver plate, except the cup that Randal's father used to drink out of long ago. But almost everything else was sold to buy corn.

So the weary year went on, and Midsummer Night came round – the seventh since the night when Randal was lost.

Then Jean did what she had always meant to do. In the afternoon she slipped out of the house of Fairnilee, taking a little bread in a basket, and saying that she would go to see the farmer's wife at Peel, which was on the other side of Tweed. But her mind was to go to the Wishing Well. There she would wish for Randal back again, to help his mother in the evil times. And if she, too, passed away as he had passed out of sight and hearing, then at least she might meet him in that land where he had been carried. How strange it seemed to Jean to be doing everything over again that she had done seven years before! Then she had been a little girl, and it had been hard work for her to climb up the side of the Peel Burn. Now she walked lightly and quickly for she was tall and well grown. Soon she reached the crest of the first hill, and remembered how she had sat down there and cried, when she was a child, and how the flies had tormented her. They were buzzing and teasing still; for good times or bad make no difference to them, as long as the sun shines. Then she reached the cairn at the top of the next hill, and far below her lay the forest, and deep within it ran the Yarrow, glittering like silver.

Jean paused a few moments, and then struck into a green path which led through the wood. The path wound beneath dark pines; their topmost branches were red in the evening light, but the shade was black beneath them. Soon the path reached a little grassy glade, and there among cold, wet grasses was the Wishing Well. It was almost hidden by the grass, and looked very black, and cool, and deep. A tiny trickle of water flowed out of it and flowed down to join the Yarrow. The trees about it had scraps of rags and other things pinned to them, offerings made by the country people to the spirit of the well.

CHAPTER IX
The White Roses

JEANIE SAT DOWN beside the well. She wished her three wishes: to see Randal, to win him back from Fairyland, and to help the people in the famine. Then she knelt on the grass, and looked down into the well-water. At first she saw nothing but the smooth black water, with little waves trembling in it. Then the water began to grow bright within, as if the sun was shining far, far below. Then it grew as clear as crystal, and she saw through it like a glass, into a new country – a beautiful country with a wide green plain, and in the midst of the plain a great castle, with golden flags floating from the tops of all the towers. Then she heard a curious whispering noise that thrilled and murmured, as if the music of all the trees that the wind blows through the world were in her ears, as if the noise of all the waves of every sea, and the rustling of heather-bells on every hill, and the singing of all birds were sounding, low and sweet, far, far away. Then she saw a great company of knights and ladies, dressed in green, ride up to the castle; and one knight rode apart from the rest, on a milk-white steed. They all went into the castle gates; but this knight rode slowly and sadly behind the others, with his head bowed on his breast.

Then the musical sounds were still, and the castle and the plain seemed to waver in the water. Next they quite vanished, and the well grew dim, and then grew dark and black and smooth as it had been before. Still she looked, and the little well bubbled up with sparkling foam, and so became still again, like a mirror, until Jeanie could see her own face in it, and beside her face came the reflection of another face, a young man's, dark, and sad, and beautiful. The lips smiled

394

at her, and then Jeanie knew it was Randal. She thought he must be looking over her shoulder, and she leaped up with a cry, and glanced around.

But she was all alone, and the wood about her was empty and silent. The light had gone out of the sky, which was pale like silver, and overhead she saw the evening star.

Then Jeanie thought all was over. She had seen Randal as if it had been in a glass, and she hardly knew him: he was so much older, and his face was so sad. She sighed, and turned to go away over the hills, back to Fairnilee.

But her feet did not seem to carry her the way she wanted to go. It seemed as if something within her were moving her in a kind of dream. She felt herself going on through the forest, she did not know where. Deeper into the wood she went, and now it grew so dark that she saw scarcely anything; only she felt the fragrance of brier-roses, and it seemed to her that she was guided towards these roses. Then she knew there was a hand in her hand, though she saw nobody, and the hand seemed to lead her on. And she came to an open place in the forest, and there the silver light fell clear from the sky, and she saw a great shadowy rose tree, covered with white wild roses.

The hand was still in her hand, and Jeanie began to wish for nothing so much in the world as to gather some of these roses. She put out her hand and she plucked one, and there before her stood a strange creature – a dwarf, dressed in yellow and red, with a very angry face.

'Who are you,' he cried, 'that pluck my roses without my will!'

'And who are *you*?' said Jeanie, trembling, 'and what right have you on the hills of this world?'

Then she made the holy sign of the cross, and the face of the elf grew black, and the light went out of the sky.

She only saw the faint glimmer of the white flowers, and a kind of shadow standing where the dwarf stood.

'I bid you tell me,' said Jeanie, 'whether you are a Christian man, or a spirit that dreads the holy sign,' and she crossed him again.

Now all grew dark as the darkest winter's night. The air was warm and deadly still, and heavy with the scent of the fairy flowers.

In the blackness and the silence, Jeanie made the sacred sign for the third time. Then a clear fresh wind blew on her face, and the forest boughs were shaken, and the silver light grew and gained on the darkness, and she began to see a shape standing where the dwarf had stood. It was far taller than the dwarf, and the light grew and grew, and a star looked down out of the night, and Jean saw Randal standing by her. And she kissed him, and he kissed her, and he put his hand in hers, and they went out of the wood together. They came to the crest of the hill and the cairn. Far below them they saw the Tweed shining through an opening among the trees, and the lights in the farm of Peel, and they heard the night-birds crying, and the bells of the sheep ringing musically as they wandered through the fragrant heather on the hills.

CHAPTER X
Out of Fairyland

YOU MAY FANCY, if you can, what joy there was in Fairnilee when Randal came home. They quite forgot the hunger and the hard times, and the old nurse laughed and cried over her bairn that had grown into a tall, strong young man. And to Lady Ker it was all one as if her husband had come again, as he was when first she knew him long ago; for Randal had his face, and his eyes, and the very sound of his voice. They could hardly believe he was not a spirit, and they clasped his hands, and hung on his neck, and could not keep their eyes off him. This was the end of all their sorrow, and it was as if Randal had come back from the dead; so that no people in the world were ever so happy as they were next day, when the sun shone down on the Tweed and the green trees that rustle in the wind around Fairnilee. But in the evening, when the old nurse was out of the way, Randal sat between his mother and Jean, and they each held his hands, as if they could not let him go, for fear he should vanish away from them again. And they would turn round anxiously if anything stirred, for fear it should be the two white deer that sometimes were said to come for people escaped from Fairyland, and then these people must rise and follow them, and never return any more. But the white deer never came for Randal.

So he told them all his adventures, and all that had happened to him since that Midsummer Night, seven long years ago.

It had been with him as it was with Jean. He had gone to the Wishing Well, and wished to see the Fairy Queen and Fairyland. And he had seen the beautiful castle in the well, and a beautiful woman's face had floated up to meet his on the water. Then he had gathered the white roses, and then he heard a great sound of horses' feet, and of bells jingling, and a lady rode up, the very lady he had seen in the well. She had a white horse, and she was dressed in green, and she beckoned to Randal to mount on her horse, with her before him on the pillion. And the bells on the bridle rang, and the horse flew faster than the wind.

So they rode and rode through the summer night, and they came to a desert place, and living lands were left far behind. Then the Fairy Queen showed him three paths, one steep and narrow, and beset with briers and thorns: that was the road to goodness and happiness, but it was little trodden or marked with the feet of people that had come and gone.

And there was a wide smooth road that went through fields of lilies, and that was the path of easy living and pleasure.

The third path wound about the wild hillside, through ferns and heather, and that was the way to Elfland, and that way they rode. And still they rode through a country of dark night, and they crossed great black rivers, and they saw neither sun nor moon, but they heard the roaring of the sea. From that country they came into the light, and into the beautiful garden that lies around the castle of the Fairy Queen. There they lived in a noble company of gallant knights and fair ladies. All seemed very mirthful, and they rode, and hunted and danced; and it was never dark night, nor broad daylight, but like early summer dawn before the sun has risen.

There Randal said that he had quite forgotten his mother and Jean, and the world where he was born, and Fairnilee.

But one day he happened to see a beautiful golden bottle of a strange shape, all set with diamonds, and he opened it. There was in it a sweet-smelling water, as clear as crystal, and he poured it into his hand, and passed his hand over his eyes. Now this water had the power to destroy the 'glamour' in Fairyland, and make people see it as it really was. And when Randal touched his eyes with it, lo, everything was changed in a moment. He saw that nothing was what it had seemed. The gold vanished from the embroidered curtains, the light grew dim and wretched like a misty winter day. The Fairy Queen, that had seemed so happy and beautiful in her bright dress, was a weary, pale woman in black, with a melancholy face and melancholy eyes. She looked as if she had been there for thousands of years, always longing for the sunlight and the earth, and the wind and rain. There were sleepy poppies twisted in her hair, instead of a golden crown. And the knights and ladies were changed. They looked but half alive; and some, in place of their bright green robes, were dressed in rusty mail, pierced with spears and stained with blood. And some were in burial robes of white, and some in dresses torn or dripping with water, or marked with the burning of fire. All were dressed strangely in some ancient fashion; their weapons were old-fashioned, too, unlike any that Randal had ever seen on earth. And their banquets were not of dainty meats, but of cold, tasteless flesh, and of beans, and pulses, and such things as the old heathens, before the coming of the Gospel, used to offer to the dead. It was dreadful to see them at such feasts, and dancing and riding, and pretending to be merry with hollow faces and unhappy eyes.

And Randal wearied of Fairyland, which now that he saw it clearly looked like a great unending stretch of sand and barren grassy country, beside a grey sea where there was no tide. All the woods were of black cypress trees and poplar, and a wind from the sea drove a sea-mist through them, white and cold, and it blew through the open courts of the fairy castle.

So Randal longed more and more for the old earth he had left, and the changes of summer and autumn, and the streams of Tweed, and the hills, and his friends. Then the voice of Jeanie had come down to him, sounding from far away. And he was sent up by the Fairy Queen in a fairy form, as a hideous dwarf, to frighten her away from the white roses in the enchanted forest.

But her goodness and her courage had saved him, for he was a christened knight, and not a man of the fairy world.

pulses, lentils.

And he had taken his own form again beneath her hand, when she signed him with the Cross, and here he was, safe and happy, at home at Fairnilee.

CHAPTER XI
The Fairy Bottle

WE SOON GROW used to the greatest changes, and almost forget the things that we were accustomed to before. In a day or two, Randal had nearly forgotten what a dull life he had lived in Fairyland, after he had touched his eyes with the strange water in the fairy bottle. He remembered the long, grey sands, and the cold mist, and the white faces of the strange people, and the gloomy queen, no more than you remember the dream you dreamed a week ago. But he did notice that Fairnilee was not the happy place it had been before he went away. Here, too, the faces were pinched and white, and the people looked hungry. And he missed many things that he remembered: the silver cups, and plates, and tankards. And the dinners were not like they had been, but only a little thin soup, and some oatmeal cakes, and trout taken from the Tweed. The beef and ale of old times were not to be found, even in the houses of the richer people.

Very soon Randal heard all about the famine; you may be sure the old nurse was ready to tell him all the saddest stories.

> *Full many a place in evil case*
> *Where joy was wont afore, oh!*
> *Wi' Humes that dwell in Leader braes,*
> *And Scotts that dwell in Yarrow!*

And the old woman would croon her old prophecies, and tell them how Thomas the Rymer, that lived in Ercildoune, had foretold all this. And she would wish they could find these hidden treasures that the rhymes were full of, and that maybe were lying – who knew – quite near them on their own lands.

'Where is the gold of Fairnilee?' she would cry; and, 'Oh, Randal! can you no dig for it, and find it, and buy corn out of England for the poor folk that are dying at your doors?

> *Atween the wet ground and the dry*
> *The gold of Fairnilee doth lie!*

'There it is, with the sun never glinting on it; there it may bide, till the Judgment Day, and no man the better for it.

> *Between the Camp o' Rink*
> *And Tweed-water clear,*
> *Lie nine kings' ransoms*
> *For nine hundred year!'*

'I doubt it's fairy gold, nurse,' said Randal. 'It would all turn black when it saw the sun. It would just be like this bottle, the only thing I brought with me out of Fairyland.'

Then Randal put his hand in his velvet pouch, and brought out a curious small bottle. It was made of something that none of them had ever seen before. It was black, and you could see the light through it, and there were green and yellow spots and streaks on it. In bottles like this, the old Romans once kept their tears for their dead friends.

'That ugly bottle looked like gold and diamonds when I found it in Fairyland,' said Randal, 'and the water in it smelled as sweet as roses. But when I touched my eyes with it, a drop that ran into my mouth was as salt as the sea, and immediately everything changed: the gold bottle became this glass thing, and the fairies became like folk dead, and the sky grew grey, and all turned waste and ugly. That's the way with fairy gold, nurse; and even if you found it, it would all be dry leaves and black bits of coal before the sun set.'

'Maybe so, and maybe no,' said the old nurse. 'The gold o' Fairnilee may no be fairy gold, but just wealth o' this world that folk buried here lang syne. But noo, Randal, ma bairn, I maun gang out and see ma sister's son's dochter, that's lying sair sick o' the kin-cough at Rink, and take her some of the medicine that I gae you and Jean when you were bairns.'

So the old nurse went out, and Randal and Jean began to be sorry for the child she was going to visit. For they remembered the taste of the medicine that the old nurse made by boiling the bark of elder-tree branches; and I remember it too, for it was the very nastiest thing that ever was tasted, and did nobody any good after all.

Then Randal and Jean walked out, strolling along without much noticing where they went, and talking about the pleasant days when they were children.

CHAPTER XII
At the Catrail

THEY HAD CLIMBED up the slope of a hill, and they came to a broad old ditch, beneath the shade of a wood of pine trees. Below them was a wide marsh, all yellow with marsh flowers, and above them was a steep slope made of stones. Now the dry ditch, where they sat down on the grass, looking towards the Tweed, with their backs to the hill, was called the Catrail. It ran all through that country, and must have been made by men very long ago. Nobody knows who made

kin-cough, whooping cough.

it, nor why. They did not know in Randal's time, and they do not know now. They do not even know what the name Catrail means, but that is what it has always been called. The steep slope of stone above them was named the Camp of Rink; it is a round place, like a ring, and no doubt it was built by the old Britons, when they fought against the Romans, many hundreds of years ago. The stones of which it is built are so large that we cannot tell how men moved them. But it is a very pleasant, happy place on a warm summer day, like the day when Randal and Jean sat there, with the daisies at their feet, and the wild doves cooing above their heads, and the rabbits running in and out among the ferns.

Jean and Randal talked about this and that, chiefly of how some money could be got to buy corn and cattle for the people. Randal was in favour of crossing the Border at night, and driving away cattle from the English side, according to the usual custom.

'Every day I expect to see a pair of spurs in a dish for all our dinner,' said Randal.

That was the sign the lady of the house in the forest used to give her men, when all the beef was done, and more had to be got by fighting.

But Jeanie would not hear of Randal taking spear and jack, and putting himself in danger by fighting the English. They were her own people after all, though she could not remember them and the days before she was carried out of England by Simon Grieve.

'Then,' said Randal, 'am I to go back to Fairyland, and fetch more gold like this ugly thing?' and he felt in his pocket for the fairy bottle.

But it was not in his pocket.

'What have I done with my fairy treasure?' cried Randal, jumping up. Then he stood still quite suddenly, as if he

403

saw something strange. He touched Jean on the shoulder, making a sign to her not to speak.

Jean rose quietly, and looked where Randal pointed, and this was what she saw.

She looked over a corner of the old grassy ditch, just where the marsh and the yellow flowers came nearest to it.

Here there stood three tall grey stones, each about as high as a man. Between them, with her back to the single stone, and between the two others facing Randal and Jean, the old nurse was kneeling.

If she had looked up, she could hardly have seen Randal and Jean, for they were within the ditch, and only their eyes were on the level of the rampart.

Besides, she did not look up; she was groping in the breast of her dress for something, and her eyes were on the ground.

'What can the old woman be doing?' whispered Randal. 'Why, she has got my fairy bottle in her hand!'

Then he remembered how he had shown her the bottle, and how she had gone out without giving it back to him.

Jean and he watched, and kept very quiet.

They saw the old nurse, still kneeling, take the stopper out of the black strange bottle, and turn the open mouth gently on her hand. Then she carefully put in the stopper, and rubbed her eyes with the palm of her hand. Then she crawled along in their direction, very slowly, as if she were looking for something in the grass.

Then she stopped, still looking very closely at the grass.

Next she jumped to her feet with a shrill cry, clapping her hands; and then she turned, and was actually *running* along the edge of the marsh, towards Fairnilee.

'Nurse!' shouted Randal, and she stopped suddenly, in a fright, and let the fairy bottle fall.

It struck on a stone, and broke to pieces with a jingling

sound, and the few drops of strange water in it ran away into the grass.

'Oh, ma bairns, ma bairns, what have you made me do?' cried the old nurse pitifully. 'The fairy gift is broken, and maybe the gold of Fairnilee, that my eyes have looked on, will ne'er be seen again.'

CHAPTER XIII
The Gold of Fairnilee

RANDAL AND JEAN went to the old woman and comforted her, though they could not understand what she meant. She cried and sobbed, and threw her arms about; but, by degrees, they found out all the story.

When Randal had told her how all he saw in Fairyland was changed after he had touched his eyes with the water from the bottle, the old woman remembered many tales that she had heard about some charm known to the fairies, which helped them to find things hidden, and to see through walls and stones. Then she had got the bottle from Randal, and had stolen out, meaning to touch her eyes with the water, and try whether *that* was the charm and whether she could find the treasure spoken of in the old rhymes. She went

> *Between the Camp o' Rink*
> *And Tweed-water clear,*

and to the place which lay

> *Atween the wet ground and the dry,*

that is, between the marsh and the Catrail.

Here she had noticed the three great stones, which made a kind of chamber on the hillside, and here she had anointed her eyes with the salt water of the bottle of tears.

Then she had seen through the grass, she declared, and through the upper soil, and she had beheld great quantities of gold. And she was running with the bottle to tell Randal, and to touch his eyes with the water that he might see it also. But, out of Fairyland, the strange water only had its magical power while it was still wet on the eyelashes. This the old nurse soon found; for she went back to the three standing stones, and looked and saw nothing, only grass and daisies. And the fairy bottle was broken, and all the water spilt.

This was her story, and Randal did not know what to believe. But so many strange things had happened to him, that one more did not seem impossible. So he and Jean took the old nurse home, and made her comfortable in her room, and Jean put her to bed, and got her a little wine and an oatcake.

Then Randal very quietly locked the door outside, and put the key in his pocket. It would have been of no use to tell the old nurse to be quiet about what she thought she had seen.

By this time it was late and growing dark. But that night there would be a moon.

After supper, of which there was very little, Lady Ker went to bed. But Randal and Jean slipped out into the moonlight. They took a sack with them, and Randal carried a pickaxe and a spade. They walked quickly to the three great stones, and waited for a while to hear if all was quiet. Then Jean threw a white cloak around her, and stole about the edges of the camp and the wood. She knew that if any wandering man came by, he would not stay long where such a figure was walking. The night was cool, the dew lay on the deep fern; there was a sweet smell from the grass and from the pine-wood.

In the mean time, Randal was digging a long trench with his pickaxe, above the place where the old woman had knelt, as far as he could remember it.

He worked very hard, and when he was in the trench up to his knees, his pickaxe struck against a stone. He dug around it with the spade, and came to a layer of black burnt ashes of bones. Beneath these, which he scraped away, was the large flat stone on which his pick had struck. It was a wide slab of red sandstone, and Randal soon saw that it was the lid of a great stone coffin, such as the ploughshare sometimes strikes against when men are ploughing the fields in the Border country.

Randal had seen these before, when he was a boy, and he knew that there was never much in them, except ashes and one or two rough pots of burnt clay.

He was much disappointed.

It had seemed as if he was really coming to something, and, behold, it was only an old stone coffin!

However, he worked on until he had cleared the whole of the stone coffin-lid. It was a very large stone chest, and must have been made, Randal thought, for the body of a very big man.

With the point of his pickaxe he raised the lid.

In the moonlight he saw something of a strange shape.

He put down his hand, and pulled it out.

It was an image, in metal, about a foot high, and represented a beautiful woman, with wings on her shoulders, sitting on a wheel.

Randal had never seen an image like this; but in an old book, which belonged to the monks of Melrose, he had seen, when he was a boy, a picture of such a woman.

The monks had told him that she was Dame Fortune, with her swift wings that carry her from one person to another, as luck changes, and with her wheel that she turns with the turning of chance in the world.

The image was very heavy. Randal rubbed some of the dirt and red clay off, and found that the metal was yellow. He cut it with his knife; it was soft. He cleaned a piece, which shone bright and unrusted in the moonlight, and touched it with his tongue. Then he had no doubt any more. The image was *gold*!

Randal now knew that the old nurse had not been mistaken. With the help of the fairy water she had seen *the gold of Fairnilee*. He called very softly to Jeanie, who came glimmering in her white robes through the wood, looking herself like a fairy. He put the image in her hand, and set his finger on his lips to show that she must not speak.

Then he went back to the great stone coffin, and began to grope in it with his hands. There was much earth in it that had slowly sifted through during the many years that it had been buried. But there was also a great round bowl of metal and a square box.

Randal got out the bowl first. It was covered with a green rust, and had a lid; in short, it was a large ancient kettle, such as soldiers use in camp. Randal got the lid off, and, behold, it was all full of very ancient gold coins, not Greek, nor Roman, but like those used in Britain before Julius Caesar came.

The square box was of iron, and was rusted red. On the lid, in the moonlight, Jeanie could read the letters SPQR, but she did not know what they meant. The box had been locked, and chained, and clamped with iron bars. But all was so rusty that the bars were easily broken, and the lid torn off.

Then the moon shone on bars of gold, and on great plates and dishes of gold and silver, marked with letters, and with what Randal thought were crests. Many of the cups were studded with red and green and blue stones. And there were beautiful plates and dishes, purple, gold, and green; and one of these fell, and broke into a thousand pieces, for it was of some strange kind of glass. There were three gold sword-hilts, carved wonderfully into the figures of strange beasts with wings, and heads like lions.

Randal and Jean looked at it and marvelled, and Jean sang in a low, sweet voice:

> 'Between the Camp o' Rink
> And Tweed-water clear,
> Lie nine kings' ransoms
> For nine hundred year!'

Nobody ever saw so much treasure in all broad Scotland.

Jean and Randal passed the rest of the night in hiding what they had found. Part they hid in the secret chamber of Fairnilee, of which only Jean and Lady Ker and Randal knew. The rest they stowed away in various places. Then Randal filled the earth into the trench, and cast wood on the place, and set fire to the wood, so that next day there was nothing there but ashes and charred earth.

You will not need to be told what Randal did, now that he had treasure in plenty. Some he sold in France, to the king, Henry II, and some in Rome, to the Pope; and with the money which they gave him he bought corn and cattle in England, enough to feed all his neighbours, and stock the farms, and sow the fields for next year. And Fairnilee became a very rich and fortunate house, for Randal married Jean, and soon their children were playing on the banks of the Tweed, and rolling down the grassy slope to the river, to bathe on hot days. And the old nurse lived long and happy among her new bairns, and often she told them how it was *she* who really found the gold of Fairnilee.

You may wonder what the gold was, and how it came there? Probably Father Francis, the good Melrose monk, was right. He said that the iron box and the gold image of Fortune, and the kettle full of coins, had belonged to some regiment of the Roman army: the kettle and the coins they must have taken from the Britons; the box and all the plate were their own, and brought from Italy. Then they, in their turn, must have been defeated by some of the fierce tribes beyond the Roman wall, and must have lost all their treasure. That must have been buried by the victorious enemy; and *they*, again, must have been driven from their strong camp at Rink, either by some foes from the north, or by a new Roman army from the south. So all the gold lay at Fairnilee for many hundred years, never quite forgotten, as the old rhyme showed, but never found until it was discovered, in their sore need, by the old nurse and Randal and Jean.

As for Randal and Jean, they lived to be old, and died on one day, and they are buried at Dryburgh in one tomb, and a green tree grows over them; and the Tweed goes murmuring past their grave, and past the grave of Sir Walter Scott.

MARY DE MORGAN

THE POOL AND THE TREE

ONCE THERE WAS a tree standing in the middle of a vast wilderness, and beneath the shade of its branches was a little pool, over which they bent. The pool looked up at the tree and the tree looked down at the pool, and the two loved each other better than anything else on earth. And neither of them thought of anything else but each other, or cared who came and went in the world around them.

'But for you and the shade you give me I should have been dried up by the sun long ago,' said the pool.

'And if it were not for you and your shining face, I should never have seen myself, or have known what my boughs and blossoms were like,' answered the tree.

Every year when the leaves and flowers had died away from the branches of the tree, and the cold winter came, the little pool froze over and remained hard and silent till the spring; but directly the sun's rays thawed it, it again sparkled and danced as the wind blew upon it, and it began to watch its beloved friend, to see the buds and leaves reappear, and together they counted the leaves and blossoms as they came forth.

One day there rode over the moorland a couple of travellers in search of rare plants and flowers. At first they did not look at the tree, but as they were hot and tired they got off their horses, and sat under the shade of the boughs, and talked of what they had been doing. 'We have not found

413

much,' said one gloomily; 'it seemed scarcely worth while to come so far for so little.'

'One may hunt for many years before one finds anything very rare,' answered the elder traveller. 'Well, we have not done, and who knows but what we may yet have some luck?' As he spoke he picked up one of the fallen leaves of the tree which lay beside him, and at once he sprang to his feet, and pulled down one of the branches to examine it. Then he called to his comrade to get up, and he also closely examined the leaves and blossoms, and they talked together eagerly, and at length declared that this was the best thing they had found in all their travels. But neither the pool nor the tree heeded them, for the pool lay looking lovingly up to the tree, and the tree gazed down at the clear water of the pool, and they wanted nothing more, and by and by the travellers mounted their horses and rode away.

The summer passed and the cold winds of autumn blew.

'Soon your leaves will drop and you will fall asleep for the winter, and we must bid each other good-bye,' said the pool.

'And you too when the frost comes will be numbed to ice,' answered the tree; 'but never mind, the spring will follow, and the sun will wake us both.'

But long before the winter had set in, ere yet the last leaf had fallen, there came across the prairie a number of men riding on horses and mules, bringing with them a long waggon. They rode straight to the tree, and foremost among them were the two travellers who had been there before.

'Why do they come? What do they want?' cried the pool uneasily; but the tree feared nothing. The men had spades and pickaxes, and began to dig a deep ditch all round the tree's roots, and then they dug beneath them, and at last both the pool and the tree saw that they were going to dig it up.

'What are you doing? Why are you trying to wrench up my roots and to move me?' cried the tree; 'don't you know that I shall die if you drag me from my pool which has fed and loved me all my life?' And the pool said, 'Oh, what can they want? Why do they take you? The sun will come and dry me up without your shade, and I never, never shall see you again.' But the men heard nothing, and continued to dig at the root of the tree till they had loosened all the earth round it, and then they lifted it and wrapped big cloths round it and put it on their waggon and drove away with it.

Then for the first time the pool looked straight up at the sky without seeing the delicate tracery made by the leaves and twigs against the blue, and it called out to all things near it: 'My tree, my tree, where have they taken my tree? When the hot sun comes it will dry me up, if it shines down on me without the shade of my tree.' And so loudly it mourned and lamented that the birds flying past heard it, and at last a swallow paused on the wing, and hovering near its surface, asked why it grieved so bitterly. 'They have taken my tree,' cried the pool, 'and I don't know where it is; I cannot move or look to right or left, so I shall never see it again.'

'Ask the moon,' said the swallow. 'The moon sees everywhere, and she will tell you. I am flying away to warmer countries, for the winter will soon be here. Good-bye, poor pool.'

At night, when the moon rose, and the pool looked up and saw its beautiful white face, it remembered the swallow's words, and called out to ask its aid.

'Find me my tree,' it prayed; 'you shone through its branches and know it well, and you can see all over the world; look for my tree, and tell me where they have taken it. Perhaps they have torn it in pieces or burnt it up.'

'Nay,' cried the moon, 'they have done neither, for I saw

415

it a few hours ago when I shone near it. They have taken it many miles away and it is planted in a big garden, but it has not taken root in the earth, and its foliage is fading. The men who took it prize it heartily, and strangers come from far and near to look at it, because they say it is so rare, and there are only one or two like it in the world.'

On hearing this the pool felt itself swell with pride that the tree should be so much admired; but then it cried in anguish, 'And I shall never see it again, for I can never move from here.'

'That is nonsense,' cried a little cloud that was sailing near; 'I was once in the earth like you. To-morrow, if the sun shines brightly, he will draw you up into the sky, and you can sail along till you find your tree.'

'Is that true?' cried the pool, and all that night it rested in peace waiting for the sun to rise. Next day there were no clouds, and when the pool saw the sun shining it cried, 'Draw me up into the sky, dear Sun, that I may be a little cloud and sail all the world over, till I can find my beloved tree.'

When the sun heard it, he threw down hundreds of tiny golden threads which dropped over the pool, and slowly and gradually it began to change and grow thinner and lighter, and to rise through the air, till at last it had quite left the earth, and where it had lain before, there was nothing but a dry hole, but the pool itself was transformed into a tiny cloud, and was sailing above in the blue sky in the sunshine. There were many other little clouds in the sky, but our little cloud kept apart from them all. It could see far and near over a great space of country, but nowhere could it espy the tree, and again it turned to the sun for help. 'Can you see?' it cried. 'You who see everywhere, where is my tree?'

'You can't see it yet,' answered the sun, 'for it is away on the other side of the world, but presently the wind will begin to blow and it will blow you till you find it.'

Then the wind arose, and the cloud sailed along swiftly, looking everywhere as it went for the tree. It could have had a merry time if it had not longed so for its friend. Everywhere was the golden sunlight shining through the bright blue sky, and the other clouds tumbled and danced in the wind and laughed for joy.

'Why do you not come and dance with us?' they cried; 'why do you sail on so rapidly?'

'I cannot stay, I am seeking a lost friend,' answered the cloud, and it scudded past them, leaving them to roll over and over, and tumble about, and change their shapes, and divide and separate, and play a thousand pranks.

For many hundred miles the wind blew the little cloud, then it said, 'Now I am tired and shall take you no further, but soon the west wind will come and it will take you on; good-bye.' And at once the wind stopped blowing and dropped to rest on the earth; and the cloud stood still in the sky and looked all around.

'I shall never find it,' it sighed. 'It will be dead before I come.'

Presently the sun went down and the moon rose, then the west wind began to blow gently and moved the cloud slowly along.

'Which way should I go, where is it?' entreated the cloud.

'I know; I will take you straight to it,' said the west wind. 'The north wind has told me. I blew by the tree to-day; it was drooping, but when I told it that you had risen to the sky and were seeking it, it revived and tried to lift its branches. They have planted it in a great garden, and there are railings round it and no one may touch it; and there is one gardener who has nothing to do but to attend to it, and people come

417

from far and near to look at it because it is so rare, and they have only found one or two others like it, but it longs to be back in the desert, stooping over you and seeing its face in your water.'

'Make haste, then,' cried the cloud, 'lest before I reach it I fall to pieces with joy at the thought of seeing it.'

'How foolish you are!' said the wind. 'Why should you give yourself up for a tree? You might dance about in the sky for long yet, and then you might drop into the sea and mix with the waves and rise again with them to the sky, but if you fall about the tree you will go straight into the dark earth, and perhaps you will always remain there, for at the roots of the tree they have made a deep hole and the sun cannot draw you up through the earth under the branches.'

'Then that will be what I long for,' cried the cloud. 'For then I can lie in the dark where no one may see me, but I shall be close to my tree, and I can touch its roots and feed them, and when the raindrops fall from its branches they will run down to me and tell me how they look.'

'You are foolish,' said the wind again; 'but you shall have what you want.'

The wind blew the cloud low down near the earth till it found itself over a big garden, in which there were all sorts of trees and shrubs, and such soft green grass as the cloud had never seen before. And there in the middle of the grass, in a bed of earth to itself, with a railing round it so that no one could injure it, was the tree which the cloud had come so far to seek. Its leaves were falling off, its branches were drooping, and its buds dropped before they opened, and the poor tree looked as if it were dying.

'There is my tree, my tree!' called the cloud.

'Blow me down, dear wind, so that I may fall upon it.'

The wind blew the cloud lower and lower, till it almost

touched the top branches of the tree. Then it broke and fell in a shower, and crept down through the earth to its roots, and when it felt its drops the tree lifted up its leaves and rejoiced, for it knew that the pool it had loved so had followed it.

'Have you come at last?' it cried. 'Then we need never be parted again.'

In the morning when the gardeners came they found the tree looking quite fresh and well, and its leaves quite green and crisp. 'The cool wind last night revived it,' they said, 'and it looks as if it had rained too in the night, for round here the earth is quite damp.' But they did not know that under the earth at the tree's roots lay the pool, and that that was what had saved the tree.

And there it lies to this day, hidden away in the darkness where no one can see it, but the tree feels it with its roots, and blooms in splendour, and people come from far and near to admire it.

JEAN GIONO

THE MAN WHO
PLANTED TREES

FOR A HUMAN character to reveal truly exceptional qualities, one must have the good fortune to be able to observe its performance over many years. If this performance is devoid of all egoism, if its guiding motive is unparalleled generosity, if it is absolutely certain that there is no thought of recompense and that, in addition, it has left its visible mark upon the earth, then there can be no mistake.

About forty years ago I was taking a long trip on foot over mountain heights quite unknown to tourists, in that ancient region where the Alps thrust down into Provence. All this, at the time I embarked upon my long walk through these deserted regions, was barren and colorless land. Nothing grew there but wild lavender.

I was crossing the area at its widest point, and after three days' walking, found myself in the midst of unparalleled desolation. I camped near the vestiges of an abandoned village. I had run out of water the day before, and had to find some. These clustered houses, although in ruins, like an old wasps' nest, suggested that there must once have been a spring or well here. There was indeed a spring, but it was dry. The five or six houses, roofless, gnawed by wind and rain, the tiny chapel with its crumbling steeple, stood about like the houses and chapels in living villages, but all life had vanished.

It was a fine June day, brilliant with sunlight, but over this unsheltered land, high in the sky, the wind blew with unendurable ferocity. It growled over the carcasses of the houses like a lion disturbed at its meal. I had to move my camp.

After five hours' walking I had still not found water and there was nothing to give me any hope of finding any. All about me was the same dryness, the same coarse grasses. I thought I glimpsed in the distance a small black silhouette, upright, and took it for the trunk of a solitary tree. In any case I started toward it. It was a shepherd. Thirty sheep were lying about him on the baking earth.

He gave me a drink from his water-gourd and, a little later, took me to his cottage in a fold of the plain. He drew his water – excellent water – from a very deep natural well above which he had constructed a primitive winch.

The man spoke little. This is the way of those who live alone, but one felt that he was sure of himself, and confident in his assurance. That was unexpected in this barren country. He lived, not in a cabin, but in a real house built of stone that bore plain evidence of how his own efforts had reclaimed the ruin he had found there on his arrival. His roof was strong and sound. The wind on its tiles made the sound of the sea upon its shore.

The place was in order, the dishes washed, the floor swept, his rifle oiled; his soup was boiling over the fire. I noticed then that he was cleanly shaved, that all his buttons were firmly sewed on, that his clothing had been mended with the meticulous care that makes the mending invisible. He shared his soup with me and afterwards, when I offered my tobacco pouch, he told me that he did not smoke. His dog, as silent as himself, was friendly without being servile.

It was understood from the first that I should spend the night there; the nearest village was still more than a day and a half away. And besides I was perfectly familiar with the nature of the rare villages in that region. There were four or five of them scattered well apart from each other on these mountain slopes, among white oak thickets, at the extreme end of the wagon roads. They were inhabited by charcoalburners, and the living was bad. Families, crowded together in a climate that is excessively harsh both in winter and in summer, found no escape from the unceasing conflict of personalities. Irrational ambition reached inordinate proportions in the continual desire for escape. The men took their wagonloads of charcoal to the town, then returned. The soundest characters broke under the perpetual grind. The women nursed their grievances. There was rivalry in everything, over the price of charcoal as over a pew in the church, over warring virtues as over warring vices as well as over the ceaseless combat between virtue and vice. And over all there was the wind, also ceaseless, to rasp upon the nerves. There were epidemics of suicide and frequent cases of insanity, usually homicidal.

The shepherd went to fetch a small sack and poured out a heap of acorns on the table. He began to inspect them, one by one, with great concentration, separating the good from the bad. I smoked my pipe. I did offer to help him. He told me that it was his job. And in fact, seeing the care he devoted to the task, I did not insist. That was the whole of our conversation. When he had set aside a large enough pile of good acorns he counted them out by tens, meanwhile eliminating the small ones or those which were slightly cracked, for now he examined them more closely. When he had thus selected one hundred perfect acorns he stopped and we went to bed.

There was peace in being with this man. The next day I asked if I might rest here for a day. He found it quite natural – or, to be more exact, he gave me the impression that nothing could startle him. The rest was not absolutely necessary, but I was interested and wished to know more about him. He opened the pen and led his flock to pasture. Before leaving, he plunged his sack of carefully selected and counted acorns into a pail of water.

I noticed that he carried for a stick an iron rod as thick as my thumb and about a yard and a half long. Resting myself by walking, I followed a path parallel to his. His pasture was in a valley. He left the dog in charge of the little flock and climbed toward where I stood. I was afraid that he was about to rebuke me for my indiscretion, but it was not that at all: this was the way he was going, and he invited me to go along if I had nothing better to do. He climbed to the top of the ridge, about a hundred yards away.

There he began thrusting his iron rod into the earth, making a hole in which he planted an acorn; then he refilled the hole. He was planting oak trees. I asked him if the land belonged to him. He answered no. Did he know whose it was? He did not. He supposed it was community property, or perhaps belonged to people who cared nothing about it. He was not interested in finding out whose it was. He planted his hundred acorns with the greatest care.

After the midday meal he resumed his planting. I suppose I must have been fairly insistent in my questioning, for he answered me. For three years he had been planting trees in this wilderness. He had planted one hundred thousand. Of the hundred thousand, twenty thousand had sprouted. Of the twenty thousand he still expected to lose about half, to rodents or to the unpredictable designs of Providence. There remained ten thousand oak trees to grow where nothing had grown before.

That was when I began to wonder about the age of this man. He was obviously over fifty. Fifty-five, he told me. His name was Elzéard Bouffier. He had once had a farm in the lowlands. There he had had his life. He had lost his only son, then his wife. He had withdrawn into this solitude where his pleasure was to live leisurely with his lambs and his dog. It was his opinion that this land was dying for want of trees. He added that, having no very pressing business of his own, he had resolved to remedy this state of affairs.

Since I was at that time, in spite of my youth, leading a solitary life, I understood how to deal gently with solitary spirits. But my very youth forced me to consider the future in relation to myself and to a certain quest for happiness. I told him that in thirty years his ten thousand oaks would be magnificent. He answered quite simply that if God granted him life, in thirty years he would have planted so many more that these ten thousand would be like a drop of water in the ocean.

Besides, he was now studying the reproduction of beech trees and had a nursery of seedlings grown from beechnuts near his cottage. The seedlings, which he had protected from his sheep with a wire fence, were very beautiful. He was also considering birches for the valleys where, he told me, there was a certain amount of moisture a few yards below the surface of the soil.

The next day, we parted.

The following year came the War of 1914, in which I was involved for the next five years. An infantryman hardly had time for reflecting upon trees. To tell the truth, the thing itself had made no impression upon me; I had considered it as a hobby, a stamp collection, and forgotten it.

The war over, I found myself possessed of a tiny demobilization bonus and a huge desire to breathe fresh air for a while. It was with no other objective that I again took the road to the barren lands.

The countryside had not changed. However, beyond the deserted village I glimpsed in the distance a sort of greyish mist that covered the mountaintops like a carpet. Since the day before, I had begun to think again of the shepherd tree-planter. 'Ten thousand oaks,' I reflected, 'really take up quite a bit of space.'

I had seen too many men die during those five years not to imagine easily that Elzéard Bouffier was dead, especially since, at twenty, one regards men of fifty as old men with nothing left to do but die. He was not dead. As a matter of fact, he was extremely spry. He had changed jobs. Now he had only four sheep but, instead, a hundred beehives. He had got rid of the sheep because they threatened his young trees. For, he told me (and I saw for myself), the war had disturbed him not at all. He had imperturbably continued to plant.

The oaks of 1910 were then ten years old and taller than either of us. It was an impressive spectacle. I was literally speechless and, as he did not talk, we spent the whole day walking in silence through his forest. In three sections, it measured eleven kilometers in length and three kilometers at its greatest width. When you remembered that all this had sprung from the hands and the soul of this one man, without technical resources, you understood that men could be as effectual as God in other realms than that of destruction.

He had pursued his plan, and beech trees as high as my shoulder, spreading out as far as the eye could reach, con-firmed it. He showed me handsome clumps of birch planted five years before – that is, in 1915, when I had been fighting at Verdun. He had set them out in all the valleys where he had guessed – and rightly – that there was moisture almost at the surface of the ground. They were as delicate as young girls, and very well established.

Creation seemed to come about in a sort of chain reaction. He did not worry about it; he was determinedly pursuing his task in all its simplicity; but as we went back toward the village I saw water flowing in brooks that had been dry since the memory of man. This was the most impressive result of chain reaction that I had seen. These dry streams had once, long ago, run with water. Some of the dreary villages I mentioned before had been built on the sites of ancient Roman settlements, traces of which still remained; and archaeologists, exploring there, had found fishhooks where, in the twentieth century, cisterns were needed to assure a small supply of water.

The wind, too, scattered seeds. As the water reappeared, so there reappeared willows, rushes, meadows, gardens, flowers, and a certain purpose in being alive. But the transformation took place so gradually that it became part of the pattern without causing any astonishment. Hunters, climbing into the wilderness in pursuit of hares or wild boar, had of course noticed the sudden growth of little trees, but had attributed it to some natural caprice of the earth. That is why no one meddled with Elzéard Bouffier's work. If he had been detected he would have had opposition. He was undetectable. Who in the villages or in the administration could have dreamed of such perseverance in a magnificent generosity?

To have anything like a precise idea of this exceptional character one must not forget that he worked in total solitude: so total that, toward the end of his life, he lost the habit of speech. Or perhaps it was that he saw no need for it.

In 1933 he received a visit from a forest ranger who notified him of an order against lighting fires out of doors for fear of endangering the growth of this *natural* forest. It was the first time, the man told him naively, that he had ever heard of a forest growing of its own accord. At that time Bouffier was about to plant beeches at a spot some twelve kilometers from his cottage. In order to avoid travelling back and forth – for he was then seventy-five – he planned to build a stone cabin right at the plantation. The next year he did so.

In 1935 a whole delegation came from the Government to examine the 'natural forest.' There was a high official from the Forest Service, a deputy, technicians. There was a great deal of ineffectual talk. It was decided that something must be done and, fortunately, nothing was done except the only helpful thing: the whole forest was placed under the protection of the State, and charcoal burning prohibited. For it was impossible not to be captivated by the beauty of those young trees in the fulness of health, and they cast their spell over the deputy himself.

A friend of mine was among the forestry officers of the delegation. To him I explained the mystery. One day the following week we went together to see Elzéard Bouffier. We found him hard at work, some ten kilometers from the spot where the inspection had taken place.

This forester was not my friend for nothing. He was aware of values. He knew how to keep silent. I delivered the eggs I had brought as a present. We shared our lunch among the three of us and spent several hours in wordless contemplation of the countryside.

In the direction from which we had come the slopes were covered with trees twenty to twenty-five feet tall. I remembered how the land had looked in 1913: a desert. . . . Peaceful, regular toil, the vigorous mountain air, frugality and, above all, serenity of spirit had endowed this old man with awe-inspiring health. He was one of God's athletes. I wondered how many more acres he was going to cover with trees.

Before leaving, my friend simply made a brief suggestion about certain species of trees that the soil here seemed particularly suited for. He did not force the point. 'For the very good reason,' he told me later, 'that Bouffier knows more about it than I do.' At the end of an hour's walking – having turned it over in his mind – he added, 'He knows a lot more about it than anybody. He's discovered a wonderful way to be happy!'

It was thanks to this officer that not only the forest but also the happiness of the man was protected. He delegated three rangers to the task, and so terrorized them that they remained proof against all the bottles of wine the charcoal-burners could offer.

The only serious danger to the work occurred during the war of 1939. As cars were being run on gazogenes (wood-burning generators), there was never enough wood. Cutting was started among the oaks of 1910, but the area was so far from any railroads that the enterprise turned out to be financially unsound. It was abandoned. The shepherd had seen nothing of it. He was thirty kilometers away, peacefully continuing his work, ignoring the war of '39 as he had ignored that of '14.

I saw Elzéard Bouffier for the last time in June of 1945. He was then eighty-seven. I had started back along the route through the wastelands; but now, in spite of the disorder in which the war had left the country, there was a bus running between the Durance Valley and the mountain. I attributed the fact that I no longer recognized the scenes of my earlier journeys to this relatively speedy transportation. It seemed to me, too, that the route took me through new territory. It took the name of a village to convince me that I was actually in that region that had been all ruins and desolation.

The bus put me down at Vergons. In 1913 this hamlet of ten or twelve houses had three inhabitants. They had been savage creatures, hating one another, living by trapping game, little removed, both physically and morally, from the conditions of prehistoric man. All about them nettles were feeding upon the remains of abandoned houses. Their condition had been beyond hope. For them, nothing but to await death – a situation which rarely predisposes to virtue.

Everything was changed. Even the air. Instead of the harsh dry winds that used to attack me, a gentle breeze was blowing, laden with scents. A sound like water came from the mountains: it was the wind in the forest. Most amazing of all, I heard the actual sound of water falling into a pool. I saw that a fountain had been built, that it flowed freely and – what touched me most – that someone had planted a linden beside it, a linden that must have been four years old, already in full leaf, the incontestable symbol of resurrection.

Besides, Vergons bore evidence of labor at the sort of undertaking for which hope is required. Hope, then, had returned. Ruins had been cleared away, dilapidated walls torn down and five houses restored. Now there were twenty-eight inhabitants, four of them young married couples. The new houses, freshly plastered, were surrounded by gardens where vegetables and flowers grew in orderly confusion, cabbages and roses, leeks and snapdragons, celery and anemones. It was now a village where one would like to live.

From that point on I went on foot. The war just finished had not yet allowed the full blooming of life, but Lazarus was out of the tomb. On the lower slopes of the mountain I saw little fields of barley and of rye; deep in the narrow valleys the meadows were turning green.

It has taken only the eight years since then for the whole countryside to glow with health and prosperity. On the site of ruins I had seen in 1913 now stand neat farms, cleanly plastered, testifying to a happy and comfortable life. The old streams, fed by the rains and snows that the forest conserves, are flowing again. Their waters have been channeled. On each farm, in groves of maples, fountain pools overflow on to carpets of fresh mint. Little by little the villages have been rebuilt. People from the plains, where land is costly, have settled here, bringing youth, motion, the spirit of adventure. Along the roads you meet hearty men and women, boys and girls who understand laughter and have recovered a taste for picnics. Counting the former population, unrecognizable now that they live in comfort, more than ten thousand people owe their happiness to Elzéard Bouffier.

When I reflect that one man, armed only with his own physical and moral resources, was able to cause this land of Canaan to spring from the wasteland, I am convinced that in spite of everything, humanity is admirable. But when I compute the unfailing greatness of spirit and the tenacity of benevolence that it must have taken to achieve this result, I am taken with an immense respect for that old and unlearned peasant who was able to complete a work worthy of God.

Elzéard Bouffier died peacefully in 1947 at the hospice in Banon.

GABRIEL HEMERY

THE MAN WHO HARVESTED TREES (AND GIFTED LIFE)

YOUTH & MAJESTY
2002

A GREAT RUSTLING wave swept over them, stirring a sea of russet beneath their feet and shaking a fresh precipitation of weary leaves from the canopy. The noisy static of a thousand fractured petioles faded away, revealing the high-pitched whistle of a treecreeper feeding somewhere overhead.

Sylvain watched an oak leaf settle gently in his great niece's hair, where it lingered unchallenged as an elegant barrette. The sudden hush only accentuated the awkward moment they'd reached in their conversation. 'They say the best time to plant a tree was 20 years ago.'

He paused, noticing the little girl's moistening eyes but tight lips. With some relief he used the opportunity to lean against the corky ridges of the great oak's stem. Those who knew him might compare his weathered face to the bark of an ancient oak, the verdigris sheen of its mossy nooks matching his eyes.

'And this tree's a gift, handed down by an ancestor,' he said finally.

Tears began to trickle down her flushing cheeks. 'But why are you . . .?' she started, her words fading to a whisper.

Sylvain waited, watching her wipe her eyes with a trembling hand.

'Why are you killing it?' asked Alona finally.

Sylvain bent down stiffly, placing the heavy long-bar chainsaw by his side. 'This is a magical place. You may not believe me, but of all the trees in this great forest, I love this one most of all. Many years ago, I played here with my friends, especially during the long summer evenings. We made dens among the woodland ferns. Sometimes I only had the company of my faithful Korthals Griffon, and we'd play tug-of-war with branches. I would've been about your age and the tree was grand, even then.'

Alona looked down, stirring the leaf litter with her toes in frustration.

Sylvain gazed upwards, spotting the treecreeper as it began a spiralling climb. 'I remember your mother and I standing exactly here, sheltering from a summer cloudburst under the tree's great canopy, when she first told me about you growing inside her.' He placed an expansive arm round Alona's tiny frame and caught a teetering tear with his rough fingers, smearing her cheeks with earthy face paint. Many years later, Alona would recognise this as her baptism as a kindred spirit of the forest, but at that moment she only felt deep sorrow. 'Do you remember two years ago,' continued Sylvain, 'we were near here collecting acorns and picking ceps when—?'

Alona stifled a heart-breaking sob. 'Please don't cut it down!' Her tears spotted the dry leaf litter between her feet.

The old forester held her more tightly and waited patiently. A roe deer barked, and birdsong filled the air between the rustling gusts. Her chest spasmed but the little girl remained silent. Sylvain's thoughts soon became lost in a charm of memories. A great expanse of oaks surrounded them, their canopies dancing in the wind, revealing glimpses of tenacious pines on the high slopes beyond. In the fertile valley nearby stood a tumbling ruin, once a humble house or perhaps a shepherd's shelter. In the cold hearth stood a contorted rowan, its flame-red berries and orange-green foliage flickering in the dying breaths of the unseasonal mistral.

Finally, Alona's gaze drifted hesitantly from the leaf litter to her great uncle's huge chainsaw, taking in his steel toe-capped boots, and moving upwards to his lichen-stained knees. They settled, finally, on the fine motes of sawdust suspended on the silver-grey hairs of his forearm.

Sylvain hiked up his heavy salopettes and eased himself down against the sturdy oak bole to sit snugly between two of its giant buttresses. 'Come on,' he said softly, pointing to a cosy gap between him and the curving arms of the tree. 'I'll tell you the story of this great oak.'

Alona shuffled over to nestle between the old forester and the tree.

'Once upon a time, this was our ancestors' tree, and now it's ours. One day, the forest will nurture your children's children.'

REAP & SOW
2002

It was a long time ago, and I was only 10 years old, yet I can still remember tiny details from that memorable day.

The incense of leaf mould and wood smoke always pervaded Sylvain's home and infused his work clothes. That day he also wore the unfamiliar perfume of sweat. The work would have been impossible for most people his age, but for his consummate skills gained during a lifetime working as a forester in the great forest.

I was small for my age and he seemed like a giant to me. His legs were huge like the birch stems all around, dressed in sawdust-coated salopettes and shod in heavy chainsaw boots, and when he stood next to me his head was high among the great canopies. I felt as insignificant as a wood mouse. Yet there we sat, huddled together in the embrace of the great oak, the three of us connected to one another, and to the Earth.

Sylvain's story was thrilling. He gifted me a glimpse of Earth's mysteries and wonders, and I think for the first time in my young life I sensed my true self in the wider world. From our cosy pew in the natural forest choir, we gazed through great columns of trees, holding aloft their vaulted canopies of living green. In the distance lay a sunlit tree-clad firmament. I listened in wonder as he told me that all we now looked across had not so long ago been a desert of dry grass. Then, we would have sat alone on a bare and stony soil, scorched by the sun, and flailed by the mistral. Flocks of hardy Tunis sheep and drifts of wild lavender would have been among the few signs of life on the barren slopes.

It was almost one century ago, in 1910, when a solitary shepherd had turned paysagiste and ecowarrior. Every evening the shepherd carefully selected 100 acorns and stored them in a hessian sack ready for the next day's mission. Setting out before dawn, he explored the arid slopes with his flock. Once satisfied by a place, he'd drill into the dusty earth with an iron rod and tenderly sow each acorn. Every day, without fail, he planted another 100 acorns. The guerrilla forester didn't know who owned the land, nor did he care.

So became his life's work and growing legacy. He had no ego, no greater motive than simple generosity, yet through his quiet campaign he began to leave his mark on Earth. Little-by-little, year-by-year, seedlings appeared, then saplings flourished. Those trees spared by the ever-advancing sheep soon provided modest protection for their younger tree brethren. Within decades the soils began to enjoy relief from the baking sun, and received nourishment from the fallen leaves. When the heavy winter downpours came, the precious life-giving soils were protected for the first time in living memory.

In the beginning, the shepherd planted only acorns, but before too long he also gathered beech mast to sow on steeper slopes, and birch seed to scatter in the valley bottoms. Later, he learned to germinate hardy pine seedlings suited to the craggy ridge tops, and shade-bearing silver firs to prosper beneath the maturing oaks. Isolated pockets of young forest matured and merged, forming a green mirage among the once barren hills.

At first, few people noticed the subtle creation, and only then those most closely connected to the land. The hunters switched their quarries, from the game of the steppe to the forest, like the leaping roe deer and crepuscular woodcock. Eventually, some said a great 'natural' forest had miraculously appeared.

Elzéard Bouffier – for that was the shepherd's name – eventually sold his flock of ewes as he came to realise that they were detrimental to forest growth. He became a beekeeper, so rich was the young forest with wildflowers, yet still he never considered himself a forester. He planted lime and sweet chestnut trees so that their pollen would soon nourish his bees in early spring, knowing that one day he could sell tree-flower honey at the local market.

The flourishing forest conceived its own clouds, and streams flowed over the once scorched land. Government officials were drawn to visit the miraculous young forest, eventually deciding after many committee meetings that it was so precious it must be protected. Elzéard retreated deep into the forest, building himself a modest stone shelter among the trees, but every day he would walk ever further to reach its green fringes and sow his 100 tree seeds.

* * *

Listening to the Old Forester's story, held in close embrace between man and tree, a dormant seed germinated in my soul. I became conscious of new life-forces; the wood-sedge spikes brushing against my sandaled toes, the tiny seedlings emerging from the soil, the weight of the huge branches arching over my head. The tinny buzz of a hoverfly near my ear was answered by the glissando mew of a honey buzzard flying high above the tree canopy. This forest was growing tenaciously on Earth, just like the moss carpeting my embracing root buttresses, or the fungi sucking on the nearby rotting stump. I could not have expressed this then, but I felt how the great oak tree linked Heaven and Earth; yin and yang, giving and taking, circulating vitality for Mother Earth. And there was me, my tiny self, living my life as part of a vast natural system.

With the wisdom of years, I came to realise this thriving man-made forest was proof of Gaia herself. But then, with my young impressionable mind, I was dazzled by how so much power could be wielded by a single man; by a humble and elderly shepherd.

It was a spellbinding rendition of the shepherd's creation. Sylvain then confessed to me that he'd once been the shepherd's disciple. With proud reverence the Old Forester told me the story of his life-changing summer with Elzéard Bouffier, when he himself was also 10 years old.

It was 1947 when Sylvain's schoolmaster decided to integrate his students with the town's older generation. When Sylvain first visited Elzéard Bouffier in the hospice he'd found the shepherd sitting alone by an upstairs window, gazing out across the tree-clad hills. Visitors were infrequent, the orderly had informed him, and Bouffier was evidently content in his own industrious company. In front of him on the table lay a pile of acorns and a small hessian sack half-filled with carefully-selected tree mast.

Sylvain had been encouraged, like all boys in his class, to visit the hospice once every week during the long summer break. Yet after his first visit he couldn't resist stopping-by every day that his mother allowed. The two would sit across from one another, a pile of tree seed lying between them ready to be sorted. Quiet-spoken and mild-mannered, Bouffier's stories of ewes and bees, steppe and forest, were other-worldly. While he listened, the boy learned to separate the good seeds from the bad. From their elevated pew, gazing out across the treescape, the scenes in his tales seemed almost extra-terrestrial. When he talked, carers and fellow incumbents alike would linger with bended ear, a task suspended or unread book in hand.

Each day, their industry complete and stories shared, the young Sylvain carried a hessian sack filled with 100 tree seeds away from the hospice. He sowed these on his way home, following the method imparted by his new shepherd friend. He sought out forest clearings ripe for replanting, or naked road boundaries. Sometimes, clandestinely, he selected languishing field corners where the plough could not reach. At first the boy found the 100 seeds to be far too many. His back would ache from the toil, while the skin on his hands, unused to working in the gritty soil, cracked and blistered. But day-by-day his stamina grew, and his resolve deepened. As he worked, he imagined how his trees, like those of the shepherd, would one day tower high above.

Towards the end of that eventful summer they sat together as usual sorting seed, talking occasionally. Outside the tired and sun-beaten forest shimmered in a heat haze. It was Sylvain's last visit of the summer, the school term due to

443

begin the next day. The shepherd was quieter than usual, appearing a little frail. He suddenly leaned across the cluttered table, scattering seed to the floor, and wrapped the young boy's soft hands within his callused fingers. 'If you love the forest, you must harvest its trees. You know this, don't you Sylvain? A forest is bountiful for man, as well as for nature.'

It was the last time the two were ever together. Later that year, Elzéard Bouffier, Shepherd and Creator, died aged 89.

During the lengthy storytelling the Old Forester and I devoured our cheese and hedge-pickle sandwiches. We remained nestled together in the folds of the great oak. My tears had evaporated and with them most of my sorrow. I understood a little and I knew now what must be done. The gift of a tree, let alone an entire forest, was made not for it to be preserved, but to be conserved and to give life to all. The shepherd had bestowed this great oak tree and the other trees round us as gifts to us all.

'You can be my mark over here,' Sylvain urged as we finally left the embrace of the great tree, heading away from her haven towards a small clearing to the north. 'If she falls in this gap here we can make sure she won't damage her younger siblings.'

We stood together looking back towards the tree, now far enough away for us to see its highest branch. Holding out his fist with thumb raised, he counted how many times it was taller. 'She must be 30 metres tall,' he mumbled, chewing on the hazel twig clenched between his teeth.

I followed in his leaf wake as he returned to stand with his back against its bole, and then attempted to match his giant strides as he paced two-times the tree's height across the forest floor. We reached the safe spot where he said I would act as his target. I was instructed to stand on the spot, as still as if I were rooted to the forest soil. 'It'll take some time Alona, so be patient. First I'll remove her buttresses so she falls gracefully,' Sylvain explained. 'Next, I'll take a wedge away from her bole on the side facing you and then make the felling cut from the back. You must not move!'

I remained nervously fixed to my lonely spot not fully comprehending how Sylvain would fell the tree, as he began his long walk back to her. I remember a tingling blend of fear and anticipation as I watched his now diminutive figure circle round her great girth once more. He looked repeatedly up to her crow's nest, and then to me as his target. He was planning her scuttling meticulously.

It became eerily quiet. The wind had died away and the forest itself seemed gripped by the doldrums. Soon the roar of the chainsaw deadened my thoughts as I watched Sylvain work. Waves of fresh sawdust washed over his legs and arms as he toiled, first in front of the tree, and then as he continued his labours, around her back. Eventually his movements seemed to slow as though he'd reached a critical moment. When he reappeared from behind the bole he was moving slowly, the chainsaw spewing a meagre trickle of sawdust. He stopped abruptly and straightened, withdrawing the limp saw. In the brief following silence, Sylvain raised his arm. I thought at first that he was signalling to me, but without pausing he leaned gently forward against her massive bole, then turned his back on the tree and on me, and stepped away. A snapping crack ricocheted between the trees. The whole forest seemed to be falling towards me. I screamed as the world started to spin.

445

FOUND & LOST
2009

Every year, as autumn ignited, Mum and I returned to the forest. We always looked forward to our holidays in the glowing sylvan spectacle, and relished our reunion with Sylvain. The Old Forester was simply 'family' to me.

I was 17 years old when life took an unexpected turn. We undertook a reluctant pilgrimage in early summer rather than autumn, returning to a verdant forest bursting with life. Sylvain had died peacefully in his sleep.

Every soul from the little town of Vergons paid their respects, lining the town's narrow winding streets before his funeral. Afterwards, according to his wishes, family and friends journeyed to the heart of the forest. 'Don't waste any good timber on a coffin for me!' he'd once chuckled, talking of his passing with casual abandon, as though death was of no consequence. We had been instructed to scatter his meagre ashes to fertilise an oak tree he'd grown from seed and planted as a young boy 62 years before. Fulfilling his final wishes, we were to commit his soul to the forest.

I led the sad procession from the church and through the forest to his final resting place. I held him in a small oak casket clutched tightly against my chest. I remembered our momentous day together when we'd felled the great oak, my weakness in fainting, and how Sylvain had carried me in his strong arms all the way home to my mother. Now it was me who carried him home to his final resting place.

The year was also memorable because I met Dara for the first time. I'd known of him by name only as Sylvain had talked about working with a young apprentice my age. Seeing each other for the first time at Sylvain's funeral, we exchanged tear-glazed glances, and walked awkwardly side-by-side during the forest procession. I realised later we were both instantly attracted to one another. He wore his dark hair tied back in a ponytail which framed an outdoor-weathered face with intelligent eyes. His bearing suggested an inner strength and finely-tuned physique honed by nature's gym.

The two of us met again later in the autumn when Mum and I returned for our usual family holiday. Dara came to our rental cottage and invited me to join him on a fungus foray. While he seemed a little uneasy in the company of a young woman, the forest was evidently his natural home. He recognised the calls of every woodland bird, pointing out the high-pitched calls of mixed flocks of long-tailed tit, treecreeper, and goldcrest moving high in the treetops. The screaming alarm calls of jays preceded us as we explored the forest ever deeper. Dara knew exactly where to search under oak canopies for ceps and among the glossy beech litter for morels. Later that evening, Mum pan-fried the fungi in sizzling salted butter, seasoned with freshly-ground black pepper. The three of us savoured nature's greatest gourmet gift, washed down with a luscious Folle Noire.

Dara called for me every day and we soon became inseparable. We walked together for miles, chatting all the way, comparing our different experiences of growing up in a town and the forest. Before long, I admit our conversations were interrupted by kissing, and that slowed us more than a little.

'The oldest trees in the forest are 99 years old this year,' he told me one day, as we embraced under a majestic sweet chestnut, its twisting helter-skelter bark disappearing into a green-gold crown of toothy leaves.

Dara talked about how the Old Forester had upheld the philosophy of Elzéard Bouffier, nurturing the forest in tune with nature while ensuring it sustained life for all. 'Sylvain worried about the short-sighted attitude of some who were supposed to be caring for the forest,' he explained. The forest had become moribund without active care, while some people thought that nature could be conquered and ordered to please its master. People had forgotten that the land had once been a dry grassland of little value. In some areas still without trees, the government actually paid the farmers to graze their sheep.

'You'd think conservationists, of all people,' huffed Dara, 'would grasp the concept of sustainability!' He paused, looking up to the canopy for solace. 'I guess people find it difficult to think beyond their own lifetimes. Areas of the forest have been abandoned in the interests of nature, yet some people don't realise that wildlife depends on the work of the forester; whether it's coppicing to bring light to the forest floor, or their vision in providing new trees and fresh genes to thrive in future.'

I nodded silently, absorbing his words. Dara spoke with a passion and knowledge I'd never witnessed before.

'It's bigger than all these things though, isn't it? Forests are essential to our survival. We can't continue to live as we do for much longer.'

Dara was a forester and ecowarrior, and his resonating words only drew me closer to him. He'd helped me to see how the forest was now under the care of our generation, until we passed it on to the next. I would soon be an adult, and I questioned for the first time what I might contribute myself as an Earth citizen.

On the penultimate day of the vacation and during another long walk, I had an epiphany. Dara and I had crested a high ridge, pausing to recover our breaths after a steep climb. The

448

view had ensnared us, so we perched together on the low branch of a contorted pine, gazing across the fading wooded valleys unfolding before us.

It was a magical place and I found myself unearthing the tale of my momentous day in the forest as a young girl. I told Dara how I'd sobbed at the impending demise of the great oak tree, of Sylvain's spell-binding account of the forest creation, and how he'd revealed his own relationship with the shepherd.

Dara showed a great deal of interest. He asked about the great oak we'd felled, and the young trees we'd planted afterwards. I was unsure exactly where we'd been in the vast forest, but I told him there was one feature I remembered well; an old stone ruin.

Next morning, he returned to collect me from the cottage. It would be our last day together and I was in a sullen mood. I felt miserable at the thought of us being apart and was dreading the return to school for my final exam-laden year. He fidgeted at the front door in evident excitement, with bleeding scratches and reddening welts across his bare arms. Before I could question him he rushed past me. 'Let's get going, I've got something to show you!' he shouted, heading for the kitchen. 'We'll need some food and drink. We've a long walk ahead.'

Dara hadn't exaggerated. We walked further that day than ever before, eventually reaching an area I was sure I'd never even been to. I sensed it was the very heart of the forest and furthest away from any habitation. The great oaks and towering Douglas-firs were the grandest I'd seen.

We came to a dense thicket of young oaks. The trees were about three times our height and growing among them was a tangled mass of sapling birch and vicious bramble. We started weaving our way through the thicket, following a narrow path which appeared freshly beaten. 'Close your eyes,' he said with mischievous excitement. I waited for a kiss that never came. Instead, he held my shoulders firmly and encouraged me forward: 'Careful now, up a step . . . Alona, open your eyes.'

We were stood in the centre of the thicket. Next to me, Dara seemed unable to contain himself. I couldn't see why he was so excited, and I looked at him quizzically.

'Look down!' he exclaimed.

I was standing on a large tree stump, cut long-ago, judging by the giant brackets of fungus growing from its fluted rim. The outline section of two great buttress roots reached out towards Dara. My heart skipped a beat. *Could this be . . ? Was this the stump of the great oak tree that Sylvain had felled with me?*

All round us, I realised, were the oaks I'd helped to plant seven years before. There would be at least 200 of them.

I questioned him about how he knew this was the place so indelibly marked in my memory. The great stump would have been invisible from outside the thicket of young trees.

'It was the ruin you mentioned,' he explained. 'Come on, this way!'

We weaved our way once more through the thicket following another path he'd cleared. Soon we reached the tumbling stone ruin which looked the same as it had all those years before.

'You realise this was the home of the shepherd?' quizzed Dara.

My mind reeled. Everything dropped into place. This had been the epicentre for the creation, and the home of the shepherd-cum-beekeeper. The Old Forester had brought me here that day with a clear purpose. Watching the felling of the tree made me witness the affinity between people and trees.

Dara and I spent the day clearing brambles away from the young oak trees. Many were growing vigorously, although beeches had regenerated naturally where some oaks had failed. *These are my trees – I planted these!* I experienced a deep emotion, not unlike the day we'd felled the great oak. This time I was proud of what I'd achieved, what I'd gifted to the forest and to other people. I asked Dara why he thought Sylvain and I had planted so many young trees after we felled the great oak.

'At first the trees compete for light, which is good as they grow straighter and with fewer branches,' he explained. 'Then it's like growing mustard and cress. Over time you pinch out what you need, and the remaining trees will have more space and a greater share of light and sustenance.'

I thought about how foresters inherited the forest of another and left a legacy of their own to a future generation, like a baton passed between athletes in the slowest of relays.

We shared the final sandwich, sitting side-by-side next to the ruin's ancient fireplace, basking in the evening warmth of the sun's dying embers. Before leaving I picked two pocketfuls of small red fruits from the gnarled tree growing from its hearth. Mum always made a fine rowan-berry jelly.

We started for home as twilight descended, the eerie scream of a vixen heralding our departure. Lesser horseshoe bats circled rapidly in the canopy overhead, feeding on midges clouding the still evening air. My mind was overcome with conflicting emotions and memories. I was so proud of the trees I'd planted as a young girl, especially now that I could see how they promised a forest of the future. My thoughts returned to the day of the tree felling with the Old

451

Forester, and I sensed again his love and kindness enfolding me. Yet thinking of Dara and our imminent separation I was overwhelmed with sadness. We struggled on in silence under a moon-less night sky, our way occasionally lit by the magical blue-green glow of foxfire.

We halted in sight of the cottage sitting in a cage of shadowed tree boles, its windows beaming jagged fingers of light towards us. I embraced Dara, serenaded by a crescendo of cicadas. Once again, I watered the forest floor with my tears.

LOST & FOUND
2010–2052

During the busy year of exams which followed, I lost touch with Dara. In the autumn of 2010, I'd just started reading bioengineering at the regional university, when my mother fell seriously ill. She passed away just months later. After, I welcomed any distraction, concentrating on my studies and assembling a close circle of friends at university. Quite unexpectedly I started a relationship with a new boyfriend which quickly became serious.

Time advanced rapidly during an exciting and busy period of my life. Within five years, I'd gained my degree, embarked on an academic career, married my university sweetheart, and become pregnant with my first child. I was happy and fulfilled.

The forest always held a place in my soul, while my work at the university ensured a direct and professional connection with trees. We created our family home on the outskirts of the forest and every day our children played among the trees. When I saw a forester at work, I sometimes caught myself wondering about Dara. Was he still working in the forest, did he have his own family, how might he look? Yet I dared not search for him and, if I'm honest, I deliberately avoided close encounters with forest workers. I was fearful of the emotions that a chance meeting might unearth.

I was appointed Professor of Cellulosics in 2036 while I was in my early forties. Soon afterwards my research group engineered a new stable form of bioscaffold providing a breakthrough for *in vitro* organ culture. We discovered that hardwood derivatives, especially from oak, provided superior nanoscale fibrillated cellulose. I led the research division of the university spin-out company which was soon busy fulfilling global orders. My share of the company ensured our family was comfortably affluent. It was gratifying that the quality of life had improved for so many people thanks to these medical advances. Sometimes I wondered whether a random passerby in the street, or stranger at a party, might be living with a kidney, lung, or heart, made by our company and born of the forest.

At that time a multitude of materials were beginning to be derived from plant and bacteria nano-engineered cellulose, although it was still a relatively nascent technology. I remember being amazed by new triple-cell windowpanes installed at home made from the latest transparent nano-crystalline cellulose. Meanwhile our 3D-printer, using lignin-based material, provided for many of our everyday needs. When my teenage son broke his arm while hoverboarding, he was one of the first to be fitted with a biocomposite cast, made from breathable non-absorbent foam next to the skin and a ballistic-tough outer shell. Of course, like all these products it was completely biodegradable. By the mid-40s, most non-moving parts of vehicles were constructed from nano-engineered cellulose and running on biofuels. The carbon-neutral bioeconomy had truly come of age.

My husband's successful architectural practice specialised in town planning with ecobuild principles. He won a major contract to design and build a new Garden City as part of the UN's Asile Plan to assist with accommodating climate refugees. The 16,000-home development was sited on a former industrial zone bordering the forest, ensuring zero impact on food production targets. Every building was constructed using 'massive timber' and met Passivhaus standards. The 43-storey residential tower blocks were state-of-art in their use of cross-laminated timber, and at the time were among the tallest constructed entirely from wood. Ultimately, the development proved to be more Forest City than Garden City, due to the integration of trees in the built environment. Per inhabitant the seasonal energy efficiency ratio was world-leading, thanks to the heating and cooling benefits provided by the trees. It proved to be the origin of our Forest Cities which prevail around the world today.

Naturally, I was immensely proud of my husband's professional achievements. We were both so busy with our careers that I admit, at times, we may not have been very close, but we provided a secure and loving home for our two children. When he was killed during the food riots and civil unrest which swept across Europe in 2049 our family was torn apart, like so many others. Compared to some people though, my children and I were relatively lucky. Our home in the outer suburbs was undamaged and when shortages were at their peak, we were able to forage for food and firewood in the forest.

The world had tilted. Many, many tough years followed before society adjusted to a new social norm, ultimately emerging stronger and greener, laying the foundations for the world we know today.

* * *

I find the New Year is always a moment for reflection. I was thinking of the opportunities and, no doubt, challenges that 2052 might bring, when I realised the trees that I'd planted with Sylvain would be 50 years old. I felt compelled, now in my 60th year, to see them again. My last visit had been with Dara when we were both 17 years old. It felt like a lifetime ago. I wondered if I could even find the trees again.

I recalled that the trees were at the centre of the forest, among the tallest growing anywhere, and of course near the old shepherd's ruin. Accessing 3D Topoview on my VR headset, it didn't take me long to navigate my way there virtually. The stand of old-growth Douglas-firs looked very prominent, and I marvelled at the bryophytes crowding the giant sweeping branches of their upper crowns. In one particularly proud tree, a great tangle of branches betrayed an eyrie abandoned for the winter and I enjoyed swooping round it, my imagination flying freely just like the eagles would when they returned in spring.

Then I noticed a clearing below and at its heart the ancient shepherd's home. There appeared to be construction work underway with two half-completed wooden extensions next to the stone building. Evidently a roof was also in the process of being erected on the main building which was being transformed from the ruin I remembered. This piqued my interest and I decided that I just had to visit in person. Given that the drone data was derived from a recent flypast, the building work was sure to be underway for some time yet. Perhaps I could arrange for my grandchildren to stay for a long weekend and we could enjoy the excursion together.

It was early spring before my two grandchildren came to visit, but by then I'd organised everything for my return trip to the heart of the forest. It would take a whole day to walk there and back so I prepared a substantial picnic with plenty of snacks and water to sustain the young ones.

The three of us set out before sunrise, confident we could navigate the metalled roads in the predawn glow. We sang, snacked and chatted while we walked. The children wanted to hear again all about my experiences in the forest as a young girl. They loved the story of the shepherd-cum-beekeeper, their inquisitive minds generating so many questions. We were carried along by the dawn chorus.

The veil of darkness lifted as we reached the forest gate and the rays of the sun rising behind the tree stems soon dazzled us as we headed eastwards into the forest. We paused to cut three stout robinia stems for walking sticks, whittling off their vicious thorns. We walked for more hours still, savouring the subtle changes in the forest and the myriad of tree species; from proud and towering sugi thriving in the valleys, to the twisted souls of maritime pine clinging to life on the limestone crags. Signs of felling and replanting welcomed us at every turn, the tracks lined with colossal timber stacks.

The distant sounds of construction betrayed our destination, well before we could hope to glimpse the building site between the crowded trees. On reaching the old-growth firs I knew we were drawing close, yet we became distracted from our mission by the Douglas-fir trees. They were awe-inspiring. Holding our hands together the three of us couldn't close our ring around the base of one enormous bole, even with our cheeks pressed tight against its rough furrowed bark.

As we set off again, my youngest grandchild picked up fir cones from the needle-rich litter. I told them the Native American story from the tree's homeland, and both were spellbound, listening to how the Douglas-fir had provided shelter to little creatures during a forest fire. They counted the tails and hind legs of the surviving 'mice' hiding below the cone's rough scales.

Eventually we rounded the final bend in the track and were confronted by an extraordinary scene. The shepherd's old stone building was a hive of activity, with workers busy on every surface. Two extensions constructed with cross-laminated timbers had been completed, although evidently work was still underway inside, given the whistling and banter floating from its open windows. Around the building, between drifts of newly-planted rowan trees, landscapers were laying a sinuous path. On the roof of the original stone building an elderly man, his grey hair tied back in a ponytail, was nailing-fast a final row of cedar shingles.

There was something about the way he moved and carried himself which caught my eye.

EPILOGUE: MAJESTY & GAIA
2110

'I'm 118 years old you know. Young man, you must allow me a little time to catch my breath!'

'No problem professor,' replied the journalist.

'If it wasn't for my bioscaffold heart, I wouldn't be here at all,' she chuckled. 'Call me Alona, please.'

'Okay, Alona. I'll set the scene first, then introduce you,' he said, preening his shirt collar and jacket lapel. He looked again at the woman before him. Despite her considerable age she possessed a remarkable spirit and a fearsome life-force shone from her eyes. She'd lived through a tumultuous century and would have some amazing stories to share. He was going to enjoy this interview. 'And please don't worry, this is a recorded interview rather than a live stream. Are we ready?' He cleared his throat, more from habit than necessity.

'Good morning and thanks for joining us. I'm Silas Rackham, reporting today from the Bouffier Memorial Centre in south-eastern France. A celebration is shortly to begin, marking the 200th anniversary of the creation in 1910 of the great Haute-Provence forest by Elzéard Bouffier. The humble shelter, his home while he planted its first trees, was converted in 2052 to the visitor centre behind me. It now attracts tens of thousands of pilgrims every year.

'I'm joined by a woman who has dedicated her long life to this forest. Following a highly successful scientific career in cellulosics, she invested her personal fortune in a wide range of cultural initiatives and health programmes centred on the forest. Her second husband Dara, himself a descendant of the forest's creator, spent the best part of his career as a practising forester here, leading the third silvicultural revival. He was the driving force behind the creation of this memorial centre more than 50 years ago.

'I am delighted to speak with you, Professor Bouffier. Can you tell me a little more about the trees we're surrounded by here?'

'Of course, I'm too young to have known Elzéard Bouffier myself, but many of his trees still stand today like these 200-year-old oaks and Douglas-firs. Other stands of trees have been felled and replanted up to three times since then.'

'I believe you knew his apprentice Sylvain very well. He was a relative?'

'Yes, like his mentor, my great uncle planted trees right across the forest. Some of them were felled for their timber many decades ago, while others are now 160 years old. I first came here as a young girl, so the trees I planted are more than one century old, and you can see them there on the other side of the centre.'

'I understand it was the impact of these trees on your own life which inspired you to lobby successfully for the Bouffier Act; for every schoolchild to plant one tree for every year that they're in education?'

'Yes, that's right. In fact, it's my single proudest achievement.'

'I can understand why. So, what's your earliest memory of the forest?'

'My first impression of the forest is a sad one: I remember getting terribly upset when a great oak tree was to be felled.'

The reporter looked genuinely surprised. 'With what I know about you, I find that hard to believe. Tell us a little more!'

'It will take a little time.' Alona smiled. 'Come with me and we'll sit together under this oak tree I planted all those years ago.'

The two started to walk towards the giant tree which stood proudly on the far side of the glade. 'Do you know, my granddaughter's going to fell it later today? It's a very special day for me. She's Head Forester here now, and I'm very proud of her.'

OVID

BAUCIS AND PHILEMON

From

METAMORPHOSES
(BOOK VIII)

Translated by Mary M. Innes

'IN THE HILL-COUNTRY of Phrygia there is an oak, growing close beside a linden tree, and a low wall surrounds them both. I have seen the spot myself, for Pittheus sent me on a mission to that land, where his father Pelops once was king. Not far off is a stagnant pool: once it was habitable country, but now it has become a stretch of water, haunted by marsh birds, divers and coots. Jupiter visited this place, disguised as a mortal, and Mercury, the god who carries the magic wand, laid aside his wings and accompanied his father. The two gods went to a thousand homes, looking for somewhere to rest, and found a thousand homes bolted and barred against them. However, one house took them in: it was, indeed, a humble dwelling roofed with thatch and reeds from the marsh, but a good-hearted old woman, Baucis by name, and her husband Philemon, who was the same age as his wife, had been married in that cottage in their youth, and had grown grey in it together. By confessing their poverty and accepting it contentedly, they had eased the hardship of their lot. It made no difference in that house whether you asked for master or servant – the two of them were the entire household: the same people gave the orders and carried them out. So, when the heaven-dwellers reached this humble home and, stooping down, entered its low doorway, the old man set chairs for them, and invited them to rest their weary limbs; Baucis bustled up anxiously to throw a rough piece of cloth over the chairs, and stirred up the warm ashes on the hearth, fanning the remains of yesterday's fire, feeding it with leaves and chips of dried bark, and blowing on it till it burst into flames. Then the old woman took down finely split sticks and dry twigs which were hanging from the roof, broke them into small pieces, and pushed them under her little pot. Her husband had brought in some vegetables from his carefully-watered garden, and these she stripped of their outer leaves. Philemon took a two-pronged fork and lifted down a side of smoked bacon that was hanging from the blackened rafters; then he cut off a small piece of their long-cherished meat, and boiled it till it was tender in the bubbling water. Meanwhile the old couple chattered on, to pass the time, and kept their guests from noticing the delay. There was a beech-wood bowl there, hanging from a nail by its curved handle, which was filled with warm water, and the visitors washed in this, to refresh themselves. On a couch with frame and legs of willow-wood lay a mattress, stuffed with soft sedge grass. Baucis and Philemon covered this with the cloths which they used to put out only on solemn holidays – even so, the stuff was old and cheap, a good match for the willow couch. Then the gods took their places for the meal. Old Baucis tucked up her dress and, with shaky hands, set the table down in front of them. One of its three legs was shorter than the others, but she pushed a tile in below, to make it the same height. When she had inserted this, and so levelled the sloping surface, she wiped over the table with some stalks of fresh mint. Then she placed upon the board the mottled berry which honest Minerva loves, wild cherries picked in the autumn and preserved in lees of wine, endives and radishes and a piece of cheese, and eggs lightly roasted in ashes not too hot; all these were set out in clay dishes and, after they had been served, a flagon with a raised pattern, just as much silver as their dinner service, was set on the table, and beech-wood cups, lined inside with yellow wax. After a short while, the hearth provided them with food piping hot and the wine, which was of no great age, was sent round again. Then it was set aside for a little, to make way for dessert, which consisted of nuts, a mixture of figs and wrinkled dates, plums and fragrant apples in shallow baskets, and black grapes, just gathered. A shining honeycomb was set in the midst of these good things and, above all, there was cheerful company, and bustling hospitality, far beyond their means.

'As the dinner went on, the old man and woman saw that the flagon, as often as it was emptied, refilled itself of its own accord, and that the wine was automatically replenished. At the sight of this miracle, Baucis and Philemon were awed and afraid. Timidly stretching out their hands in prayer, they begged the gods' indulgence for a poor meal, without any elaborate preparations. They had a single goose, which acted as guardian of their little croft: in honour of their divine visitors, they were making ready to kill the bird, but with the help of its swift wings it eluded its owners for a long time, and tired them out, for age made them slow. At last it seemed to take refuge with the gods themselves, who declared that it should not be killed. "We are gods," they said, "and this wicked neighbourhood is going to be punished as it richly deserves; but you will be allowed to escape this disaster. All you have to do is to leave your home, and climb up the steep mountainside with us." The two old people both did as they were told and, leaning on their sticks, struggled up the long slope.

'When they were a bowshot distant from the top, they looked round and saw all the rest of their country drowned in marshy waters, only their own home left standing. As they gazed in astonishment, and wept for the fate of their people, their old cottage, which had been small, even for two, was changed into a temple: marble columns took the place of its wooden supports, the thatch grew yellow, till the roof seemed to be made of gold, the doors appeared magnificently adorned with carvings, and marble paved the earthen floor. Then Saturn's son spoke in majestic tones: "Tell me, my good old man, and you, who are a worthy wife for your good husband, what would you like from me?" Philemon and Baucis consulted together for a little, and then the old man told the gods what they both wished. "We ask to be your priests, to serve your shrine; and since we have lived in happy companionship all our lives, we pray that death may carry us off together at the same instant, so that I may never see my wife's funeral, and she may never have to bury me." Their prayer was granted. They looked after the temple as long as they lived.

'Then, one day, bowed down with their weight of years, they were standing before the sacred steps, talking of all that had happened there, when Baucis saw Philemon beginning to put forth leaves, and old Philemon saw Baucis growing leafy too. When the tree-tops were already growing over their two faces, they exchanged their last words while they could, and cried simultaneously: "Good-bye, my dear one!" As they spoke, the bark grew over and concealed their lips. The Bithynian peasant still points out the trees growing there side by side, trees that were once two bodies. This tale was told me by responsible old men, who had nothing to gain by deceiving me. Indeed, I myself have seen the wreaths hanging on the branches, and have hung up fresh ones, saying: "Whom the gods love are gods themselves, and those who have worshipped should be worshipped too." '

R. K. NARAYAN

UNDER THE BANYAN TREE

THE VILLAGE SOMAL, nestling away in the forest tracts of Mempi, had a population of less than three hundred. It was in every way a village to make the heart of a rural reformer sink. Its tank, a small expanse of water, right in the middle of the village, served for drinking, bathing, and washing the cattle, and it bred malaria, typhoid, and heaven knew what else. The cottages sprawled anyhow and the lanes twisted and wriggled up and down and strangled each other. The population used the highway as the refuse ground and in the backyard of every house drain water stagnated in green puddles.

Such was the village. It is likely that the people of the village were insensitive: but it is more than likely that they never noticed their surroundings because they lived in a kind of perpetual enchantment. The enchanter was Nambi the story-teller. He was a man of about sixty or seventy. Or was he eighty or one hundred and eighty? Who could say? In a place so much cut off as Somal (the nearest bus-stop was ten miles away), reckoning could hardly be in the familiar measures of time. If anyone asked Nambi what his age was he referred to an ancient famine or an invasion or the building of a bridge and indicated how high he had stood from the ground at the time.

He was illiterate, in the sense that the written word was a mystery to him; but he could make up a story, in his head, at the rate of one a month; each story took nearly ten days to narrate.

His home was the little temple which was at the very end of the village. No one could say how he had come to regard himself as the owner of the temple. The temple was a very small structure with red-striped walls, with a stone image of the Goddess Shakti in the sanctum. The front portion of the temple was Nambi's home. For aught it mattered any place might be his home; for he was without possessions. All that he possessed was a broom with which he swept the temple; and he had also a couple of dhoties and upper cloth. He spent most of the day in the shade of the banyan which spread out its branches in front of the temple. When he felt hungry he walked into any house that caught his fancy and joined the family at dinner. When he needed new clothes they were brought to him by the villagers. He hardly ever had to go out in search of company; for the banyan shade served as a clubhouse for the village folk. All through the day people came seeking Nambi's company and squatted under the tree. If he was in a mood for it he listened to their talk and entertained them with his own observations and anecdotes. When he was in no mood he looked at the visitors sourly and asked, 'What do you think I am? Don't blame me if you get no story at the next moon. Unless I meditate how can the Goddess give me a story? Do you think stories float in the air?' And he moved out to the edge of the forest and squatted there, contemplating the trees.

On Friday evenings the village turned up at the temple for worship, when Nambi lit a score of mud lamps and arranged them around the threshold of the sanctuary. He decorated the image with flowers, which grew wildly in the backyard of the temple. He acted as the priest and offered to the Goddess fruits and flowers brought in by the villagers.

On the nights he had a story to tell he lit a small lamp and placed it in a niche in the trunk of the banyan tree. Villagers as they returned home in the evening saw this, went home, and said to their wives, 'Now, now, hurry up with the dinner, the story-teller is calling us.' As the moon crept up behind the hillock, men, women, and children gathered under the banyan tree. The story-teller would not appear yet. He would be sitting in the sanctum, before the Goddess, with his eyes shut, in deep meditation. He sat thus as long as he liked and when he came out, with his forehead ablaze with ash and vermilion, he took his seat on a stone platform in front of the temple. He opened the story with a question. Jerking his finger towards a vague, far-away destination, he asked, 'A thousand years ago, a stone's throw in that direction, what do you think there was? It was not the weed-covered waste it is now, for donkeys to roll in. It was not the ash-pit it is now. It was the capital of the king. . . .' The king would be Dasaratha, Vikramaditya, Asoka, or anyone that came into the old man's head; the capital was called Kapila, Kridapura, or anything. Opening thus, the old man went on without a pause for three hours. By then brick by brick the palace of the king was raised. The old man described the dazzling durbar hall where sat a hundred vassal kings, ministers, and subjects; in another part of the palace all the musicians in the world assembled and sang; and most of the songs were sung over again by Nambi to his audience; and he described in detail the pictures and trophies that hung on the walls of the palace. . . .

It was story-building on an epic scale. The first day barely conveyed the setting of the tale, and Nambi's audience as yet had no idea who were coming into the story. As the moon slipped behind the trees of Mempi Forest Nambi said, 'Now friends, Mother says this will do for the day.' He abruptly rose, went in, lay down, and fell asleep long before the babble of the crowd ceased.

The light in the niche would again be seen two or three days later, and again and again throughout the bright half of the month. Kings and heroes, villains and fairy-like women, gods in human form, saints and assassins, jostled each other in that world which was created under the banyan tree. Nambi's voice rose and fell in an exquisite rhythm, and the moonlight and the hour completed the magic. The villagers laughed with Nambi, they wept with him, they adored the heroes, cursed the villains, groaned when the conspirator had his initial success, and they sent up to the gods a heart-felt prayer for a happy ending. . . .

On the day when the story ended, the whole gathering went into the sanctum and prostrated before the Goddess. . . .

By the time the next moon peeped over the hillock Nambi was ready with another story. He never repeated the same kind of story or brought in the same set of persons, and the village folk considered Nambi a sort of miracle, quoted his words of wisdom, and lived on the whole in an exalted plane of their own, though their life in all other respects was hard and drab.

And yet it had gone on for years and years. One moon he lit the lamp in the tree. The audience came. The old man took his seat and began the story. '. . . When King Vikramaditya lived, his minister was . . .' He paused. He could not get beyond it. He made a fresh beginning. 'There was the king . . .' he said, repeated it, and then his words trailed off into a vague mumbling. 'What has come over me?' he asked pathetically. 'Oh, Mother, great Mother, why do I stumble and falter? I know the story. I had the whole of it a moment ago. What was it about? I can't understand what has happened.' He faltered and looked so miserable that his audience said, 'Take your own time. You are perhaps tired.'

'Shut up!' he cried. 'Am I tired? Wait a moment; I will

tell you the story presently.' Following this there was utter silence. Eager faces looked up at him. 'Don't look at me!' he flared up. Somebody gave him a tumbler of milk. The audience waited patiently. This was a new experience. Some persons expressed their sympathy aloud. Some persons began to talk among themselves. Those who sat in the outer edge of the crowd silently slipped away. Gradually, as it neared midnight, others followed this example. Nambi sat staring at the ground, his head bowed in thought. For the first time he realized that he was old. He felt he would never more be able to control his thoughts or express them cogently. He looked up. Everyone had gone except his friend Mari the blacksmith. 'Mari, why aren't you also gone?'

Mari apologized for the rest: 'They didn't want to tire you; so they have gone away.'

Nambi got up. 'You are right. Tomorrow I will make it up. Age, age. What is my age? It has come on suddenly.' He pointed at his head and said, 'This says, "Old fool, don't think I shall be your servant any more. You will be my servant hereafter." It is disobedient and treacherous.'

He lit the lamp in the niche next day. The crowd assembled under the banyan faithfully. Nambi had spent the whole day in meditation. He had been fervently praying to the Goddess not to desert him. He began the story. He went on for an hour without a stop. He felt greatly relieved, so much so that he interrupted his narration to remark, 'Oh, friends. The Mother is always kind. I was seized with a foolish fear . . .' and continued the story. In a few minutes he felt dried up. He struggled hard: 'And then . . . and then . . . what happened?' He stammered. There followed a pause lasting an hour. The audience rose without a word and went home. The old man sat on the stone brooding till the cock crew. 'I can't blame them for it,' he muttered to himself.

'Can they sit down here and mope all night?' Two days later he gave another instalment of the story, and that, too, lasted only a few minutes. The gathering dwindled. Fewer persons began to take notice of the lamp in the niche. Even these came only out of a sense of duty. Nambi realized that there was no use in prolonging the struggle. He brought the story to a speedy and premature end.

He knew what was happening. He was harrowed by the thoughts of his failure. I should have been happier if I had dropped dead years ago, he said to himself. Mother, why have you struck me dumb . . . ? He shut himself up in the sanctum, hardly ate any food, and spent the greater part of the day sitting motionless in meditation.

The next moon peeped over the hillock, Nambi lit the lamp in the niche. The villagers as they returned home saw the lamp, but only a handful turned up at night. 'Where are the others?' the old man asked. 'Let us wait.' He waited. The moon came up. His handful of audience waited patiently. And then the old man said, 'I won't tell the story today, nor tomorrow unless the whole village comes here. I insist upon it. It is a mighty story. Everyone must hear it.' Next day he went up and down the village street shouting, 'I have a most wonderful tale to tell tonight. Come one and all; don't miss it. . . .' This personal appeal had a great effect. At night a large crowd gathered under the banyan. They were happy that the story-teller had regained his powers. Nambi came out of the temple when everyone had settled and said: 'It is the Mother who gives the gifts; and it is she who takes away the gifts. Nambi is a dotard. He speaks when the Mother has anything to say. He is struck dumb when she has nothing to say. But what is the use of the jasmine when it has lost its scent? What is the lamp for when all the oil is gone? Goddess be thanked. . . . These are my last words on this earth; and

474

this is my greatest story.' He rose and went into the sanctum. His audience hardly understood what he meant. They sat there till they became weary. And then some of them got up and stepped into the sanctum. There the story-teller sat with eyes shut. 'Aren't you going to tell us a story?' they asked. He opened his eyes, looked at them, and shook his head. He indicated by gesture that he had spoken his last words.

When he felt hungry he walked into any cottage and silently sat down for food, and walked away the moment he had eaten. Beyond this he had hardly anything to demand of his fellow beings. The rest of his life (he lived for a few more years) was one great consummate silence.

ACKNOWLEDGMENTS

DOROTHY BAKER: 'Summer' from *Penguin New Writing*, 21, ed. John Lehmann (Harmondsworth: Penguin 1944). Papers of Dorothy and Howard Baker are held by the Department of Special Collections and University Archives, Stanford University Libraries, Stanford, California.

JOHN LORNE CAMPBELL: 'Why Everyone Should Be Able to Tell a Story' in *Stories from South Uist*, Routledge & Kegan Paul, 1961. Copyright © the Estate of John Lorne Campbell.

ANGELA CARTER: 'The Company of Wolves' from *The Bloody Chamber and Other Stories* by Angela Carter. Published by Vintage Classics. Copyright © The Estate of Angela Carter. Reproduced by permission of the Estate c/o Rogers, Coleridge & White Ltd., 20 Powis Mews, London W11 1JN.

DAPHNE DU MAURIER: 'The Apple Tree'. Copyright © 1952 by Daphne Du Maurier, renewed. Reprinted by permission of Curtis Brown, Ltd, and by permission of Curtis Brown UK.

RODERICK FINLAYSON: 'The Totara Tree' was originally published in *Brown Man's Burden*, Unicorn/Griffin Press, Auckland, New Zealand, 1938. It was reprinted in *Brown Man's Burden and Later Stories*, ed. Bill Pearson, Auckland University Press/Oxford University Press, Auckland, 1973. It is included in *A Roderick Finlayson Reader*, Cold Hub Press, Lyttelton, 2020. The Estate of Roderick Finlayson.

DAMON GALGUT: 'Shadows' from *Small Circle of Beings*